THE
2

by

E. Thornton Goode, Jr.

WORKBOOK PRESS LLC
187 E Warm Springs Rd,
Suite B285, Las Vegas, NV 89119, USA

Website: https://workbookpress.com/
Hotline: 1-888-818-4856
Email: admin@workbookpress.com

Ordering Information:
Quantity sales. Special discounts are available on quantity purchases by corporations, associations, and others.
For details, contact the publisher at the address above.

Library of Congress Control Number:

ISBN-13:   000-0-000000-00-0 (Paperback Version)
                000-0-000000-00-0 (Digital Version)

REV. DATE: 08/07/2022

IN DEDICATION

This book is, first of all, dedicated to Randall Guynes. His personality, his friendship of almost 40 years and our many late night conversations gave me the character of Warren Glass. Knowing him has made this story possible.

This story is also dedicated to my younger brother, Henry, who I consider the adventurer of the family. He bought a boat to sail around the world. What can I say? If that doesn't take brass, nothing does. I doubt his wife and children will let him do it though, especially with the pirates in Somalia. But it's alright. I'm sure he will think of something just as daring to do.

IN APPRECIATION

I want to thank my Algerian friend, Hakim Benachour, who was extremely helpful in the editing of this work. My high school English teacher, Mrs. Brakebill, would be proud of him with his knowledge of English grammar. He speaks four languages fluently and teaches English at the university in Bejaia, Algeria. Hakim and I met through social networking on the computer. One day, I hope we will meet in person so I may properly thank him.

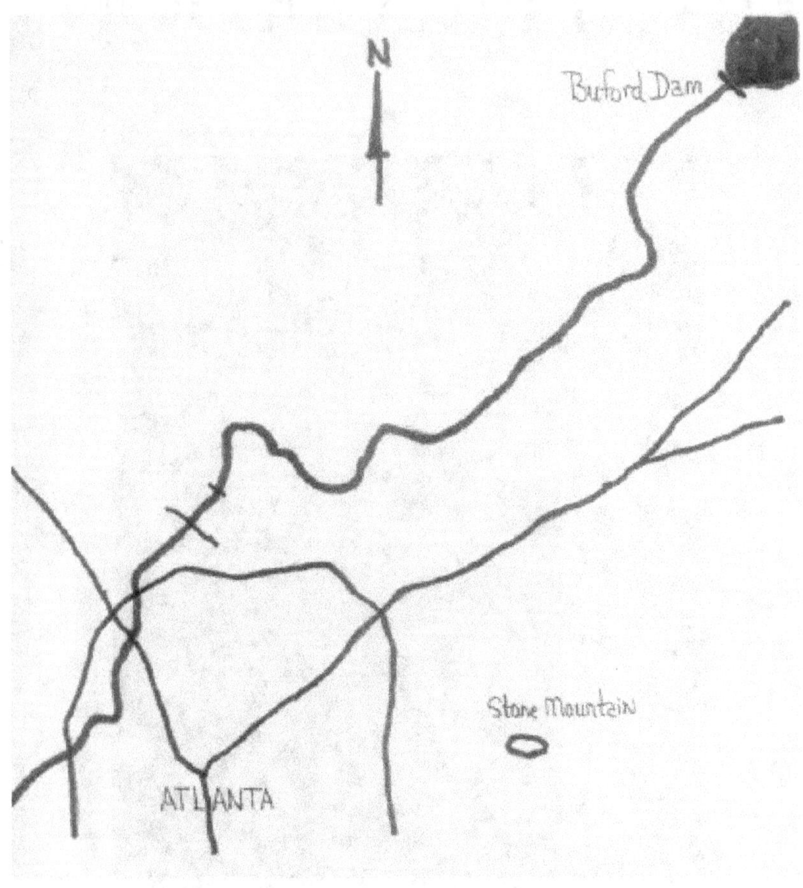

This is a basic map of the Atlanta area. It will help you in the understanding of locations mentioned in the story. The following more detailed map will also help

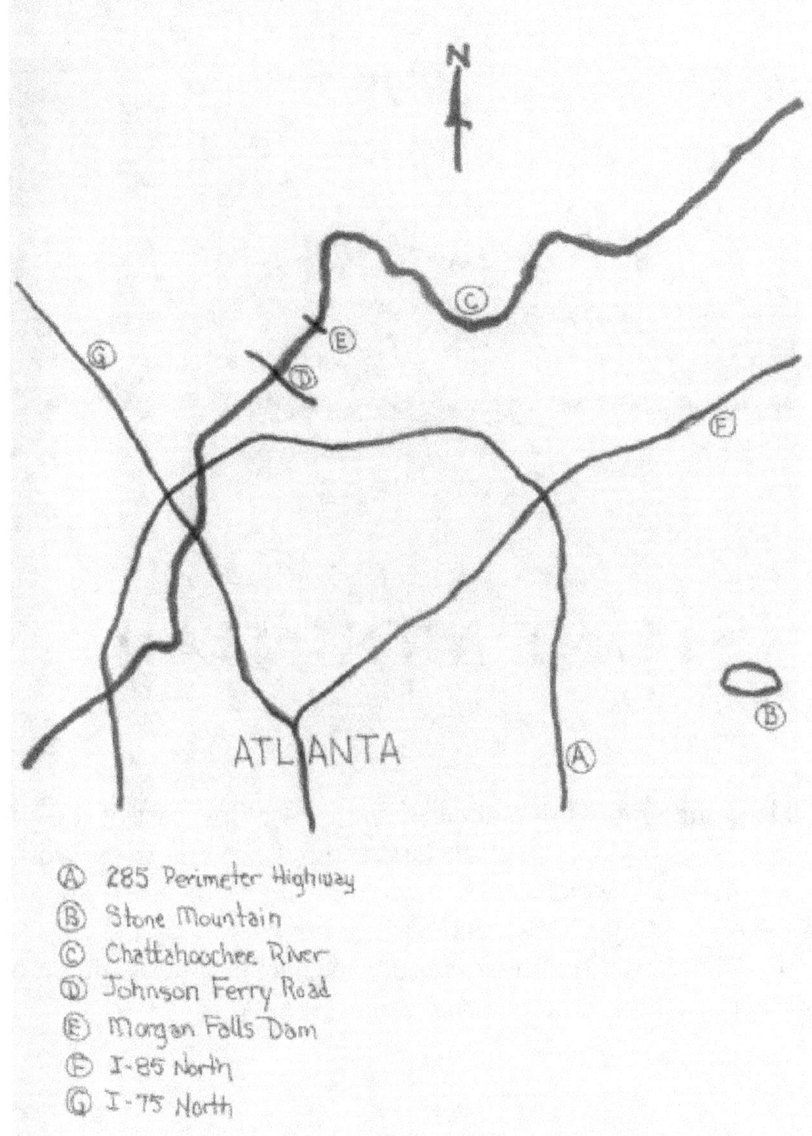

This is a more detailed map of the area. Specific locations are marked on the map.

Stone Mountain

This granite monolith is located some 14 miles, east of the city of Atlanta, Georgia. One of the largest relief carvings in the world, the Confederate Memorial, is located on its north face. The top can be reached by taking a cable lift or by walking up the western slope. The view from there is quite spectacular. It should be on your list of things to do when you visit Atlanta.

This is the Confederate Memorial carving on the north face of Stone Mountain.

PROLOGUE

What is a friend? Everyone has at lest one: special friend, old friend, new friend, good friend, best friend. But what does that mean? The group, Queen, sang, *You're My Best Friend* and there was Harry Nilsson with *Best Friend*. And who cannot remember the great song written by Carole King and sung by James Taylor: *You've Got A Friend*? In life and in fiction, there have been names that just cannot be said without the other: Stanley and Livingston, Lewis and Clarke, Huntley and Brinkley, Abbot and Costello, Holmes and Watson, Cisco and Poncho are just a few. Their relationships as friends most likely vary as to importance, but still, the names are forever connected.

Webster's defines a friend as 'a person whom one knows, likes and trusts'. But I believe that friendship can be deeper than described in the definition. And how far will we go for a friend? Sometimes we place our very lives in the judgment and hands of a friend. Do you have such a friend?

This story deals with a friendship that goes beyond all expectations. They will have to do things they could never have foreseen and rely on knowledge they thought they would never use.

One of my best friends, Tris Coffin, once told me: 'Thornton, let me tell you. Lovers come and go, but friends are forever.' And as I have lived my life, I have found that to be very true. I have been extremely blessed to have some longstanding, unbelievably great friends in my life. I would wish such friends for others. A true, reliable and trusted friend is worth more than his weight in gold.

Do you have a friend like that? A friend that is…FOREVER?

CHAPTER I

Well, everybody, hello. My name's Phillip Martin and I'm a freelance reporter. I also write a column in the major Atlanta newspaper regarding the strange, unusual, weird and stories of adventure. I swear. If I weren't seeing it with my own two eyes, I'd never have believed it. Here is the whole group, in this enormous room. How could anyone have ever known the damn room was here? I stand here, contemplating the situation. And who'd have ever thought that I would get the chance to be covering this story? It's just totally unbelievable.

I start to speak into the small microphone of the tape recorder I have hanging around my neck. "Yeah. We're all standing here looking around the room in utter amazement. Even though the discovery was made almost two months ago, it took this long to gather specific members of several important organizations together. Actually, I guess you could consider it a real feat to get all these experts, reporters, camera crews, archaeologists, and representatives from National Geographic Society and the Smithsonian Institution here so quickly. But when they heard of the potential magnitude of the find, they all took the quickest of action to get here. Seems no one wanted to be left out when they realized the enormity of it. They did have to limit the number of people who could be here, being unsure of the safety of the location and the narrowness of the entrance and halls. But right now, I'm glad to have been one of the 'chosen few'. What can I say? Somebody pinch me 'cause I don't believe it. I just don't believe it."

The huge room is filled with the mixture of all the hushed voices expressing their commentary and astonishment of the space and its decor. Suddenly, an unseen light begins to fill the entire space. The electric lights being used earlier are no longer necessary. Then, from where no one can discern, comes a clear, quiet voice.

"Ladies and gentlemen, please stand clear of the three-tiered dais."

Everyone is startled by the voice, especially to be in English, and all heads turn to peer at the three layered stone platform. Acknowledging the request, everyone moves back, but their eyes continue to stare at the platform. Momentarily, a beautifully carved chair with thick red cushions materializes near the center of the raised area. A figure appears, standing at the edge of the top tier. And although he is some kind of illusion, he looks to be virtually real in every sense. It is the figure of a slender built man. He looks to be in his sixties and dressed in a fine white linen robe. Heavy embroidery of golden thread, accented with many faceted and polished colored stones, embellishes the neckline of the robe, the bottom hem and the ends of the long sleeves. On his feet are sandals of gold, partially hidden by the garment's many folds. His position on the platform makes him appear taller than he really is and everyone has to look slightly upward to look into his face. A band of gold, set with one large, faceted, green stone, encircles his head. His wavy, salt and pepper hair is parted on the left and periodically interrupts sight of the band.

The old man looks out across the spacious room with dark brown eyes that seem to sparkle with glee. His skin seems ageless and a smile comes to his kind face.

"You know. The way he looks out at us all, you would think he could really see everyone that's here. He's so damn real looking; it's hard to believe he's only a holographic projection." I whisper to myself.

As the old man smiles, the gleam in his eyes begins to grow, and he stretches out his arms. "Ladies and gentlemen, I greet you with friendship and love. I bring many gifts, with the hope they will benefit Mankind." He gestures with his right hand, pointing in the direction of two doors, one on the north side and one on the south side of the room.

I have never been surprised at the power of suggestion. It's kind of funny how everybody looks in the indicated direction, as if the request had come from a real person. But I'm just as guilty. I look, too.

"But I'll get to those later." The old man pauses a moment, then continues. "Some of you may be wondering who I am and what I'm doing here, but that, too, will come later. First, I must tell you the story. It's the story of Warren and Jim. You have to know them and what happened to them before any of this will make sense."

The figure looks upward with a laughing face, as if no one would ever believe or understand. Then he looks back again, scanning the room.

"Before I begin, I want you all to get comfortable. Have a seat on the floor, and adjust your cameras and recorders." He chuckles quietly, tilting his head back. "Bet you'll never guess how I know you have cameras and recorders. But don't worry. You'll understand, once the story's told. It'll all be perfectly clear. I'll give you a few seconds, as I have to get comfortable myself." He walks to the chair and sits, fluffing the cushions around himself. "I just happen to be thinking that maybe technology has made cameras and recorders obsolete. Has something else taken their place?" He smiles. "Well, whatever you have, I know you are recording this event with something."

I've got my small camcorder and tripod. Glad I have several video packs. Everyone else is hustling to get everything set and in place. I turn off my tape recorder and start the camcorder.

All with cameras and recording equipment had been scurrying to start and adjust the equipment, not wanting to lose a moment of the event. Only their quiet commands and technical terms break the silence. Finally, everyone is settled and all eyes are fixed on the striking holograph, which now seems to glow with an inner light, similar to the qualities of a Rembrandt painting. A few moments pass.

The old man smiles and his face reflects a peaceful quality. "I hope everyone's ready. If so, I'll begin. First of all, I must tell you, this is really the story of a great friendship, the love of human beings for one another. And it all began a long time ago. But maybe not so long ago." He lifts his left hand and moves his thin fingers over his closely trimmed, salt and pepper beard and mustache. A confused expression comes to his face. It's an expression of one having a great amount of important information to explain, but not knowing quite where to begin.

"Yes, it was in October. But then, I guess I should explain about Warren and Jim first, Warren Glass and James Stone. After all, it's really about them. Two men thrown into an extraordinary situation. They were so different and yet..." He pauses and stares into space. Laughingly, he starts again. "So different, different as day and night, different backgrounds, different interests."

He stops for a moment and looks out across the group. "By the way, for those of you who'd like to smoke, please feel free to light up. You still have cigarettes, don't you? Or has smoking finally been eliminated?" He laughs out loud. "I doubt it! Cigarettes are forever, just like death and taxes!" He slaps his knee and leans back in a loud laugh.

I'm amazed at the suggestion. If I pull out my smokes now, and light up, I'll be assassinated. Regardless of how bad we all want one, you'd be an idiot to even consider doing such a thing. Everyone knows there are two places one dare not smoke. One is a museum. The other's a major archaeological find. Then again, there are the public buildings, stores, not to mention the city transit. But I guess it's for the best. I've been trying to quit and it hasn't been easy. Now, here, the old guy keeps suggesting we smoke. Yeah. I'm not the only one who's suffering. By the expressions on their faces, I see several others sharing my sentiments.

After a moment, the old man returns from a rather reminiscent state. "Oh! Sorry about that. Now, where was I? Oh yes, Warren and Jim!"

"Warren Glass grew up in the Dallas, Texas area. He was always interested in sports and the outdoors. Baseball and football were high school favorites. While in high school, his father passed away, forcing him to take a job in his free time. He pumped gas and worked on cars, when he wasn't in school or active with sports. In his senior year, he became captain of the football squad and was chosen 'Best Player of the Year'. He considered it a real feather in his cap, as he wasn't the biggest player on the team, five foot ten and one hundred and sixty-five pounds."

"Warren also had all the qualities of a leader. But even though he was head of his class and very outgoing, Warren was a very closed person. Hardly anyone knew him well. He preferred to be a loner."

"Receiving several scholarships, he went on to college. His areas of study included Political Science, Economics, and Statistical Analysis. During his sophomore year, he married his high school sweetheart, Linda Rogers. His post-graduate work was done in Kansas. The completion of his Masters Thesis required a trip to Guatemala for economic studies."

"James Stone, on the other hand, was raised and educated in Virginia, and was from one of Virginia's old established families. He was five foot six and one hundred and twenty-five pounds. His interests included music, cooking, and the arts. College studies included Architectural Engineering, Ceramic Engineering, as well as Urban and Regional Planning. The architecture of the Classical Period as well as the ornate Seventeenth and Eighteenth Centuries were his favorite."

"He was never outgoing, until he went to college. Only a few people became close friends and knew him well. They tolerated, yet enjoyed his outrageousness. His penchant for interjecting French phrases into his conversation would drive them up the wall. No one knew why he did it, just part of his insane personality. His musical abilities made him a prize at parties. Give him a piano, guitar, saxophone and he became a one man band."

"His art and music reflected his flights of fantasy and melancholia. And he loved old movies, too. Many times when he'd be telling the story line of one of the old tearjerkers, he'd start to cry. Like *The Enchanted Cottage*." The old man smiles, pausing for a moment, as if recalling some long lost memory. "Everyone loves that story." There was another pause before continuing. "And horror movies! Especially the really bad ones." He laughs out loud.

"After college, he moved to Atlanta, started his own catering business, and bought a house. Remodeling gave him the chance to try out all the things he'd learned in his architecture classes. His love of ornamentation was reflected in the process."

"Atlanta's where the two met. Warren, his wife Linda and their two sons moved in next door, about two years after Jim bought his house. In no time, they had become great friends."

"Jim, with his unending persistence, finally broke through the invisible wall surrounding Warren. Warren was Jim's confidant, because he knew how to listen, always had good suggestions, and never lied to him."

"Warren was always amazed as to where Jim obtained so much knowledge. He was chockfull of strange and little known facts. He also saw Jim rather like a child. Jim's mother referred to him as 'her child that never grew up'. But Warren didn't care. In Jim, there was the childhood craziness he'd never been able to have. Warren had no problem discussing personal things with Jim. He knew their talks would remain theirs. When they were together,

Warren always felt free as a bird. He could be as crazy as he wanted, *sans souci*…without care."

"So, now you know a little about them." The old man turns, crosses his legs, and then adjusts his garments. He stares out, looking over everyone's head. The confused expression returns to his face, as he starts to organize his thoughts. "Let me see." His head turns, as if looking down at everyone seated around him. He smiles. "Yes. Yes. That's right! It was in October when it all started."

CHAPTER II

"For Christ's sake!" Warren balked. "You and your 'sixteen trunks packed by Victorine'. It's a damn good thing we're taking two rafts. What in hell did you bring anyway?" Warren knew the reference to the luggage packed by the Ryerson's maid, for the voyage aboard the ill-fated Titanic, would catch Jim's attention. Jim had this 'thing' about that ship. He'd even had dreams about being on board as a passenger. If any reference would catch his attention, the Titanic would. But Jim said nothing, so Warren went on with his survey of the back of the station wagon and what was going into it.

"We're only going for a week, not two months!" Warren grunted as he lifted the last of the five questionable boxes, marked 'DO NOT OPEN', into the wagon. Knowing Jim rather well, he had some idea as to their content, but nothing more was said. It would do no good. He lifted the large ice cooler. This would help keep the perishable foods cool during the trip. If it became necessary, they could put food in plastic bags and put them in the water to keep it cool at night. The temperature of the water in the Chattahoochee this time of the year was quite cool. Then back in the cooler during the day.

He turned and brushed back the wavy brown hair obstructing his left eye. He stared at Jim, hoping for some reply.

Jim just stood there with a big grin on his face, and after perusing the back of the wagon asked the obvious question. "Have we got everything?" He looked directly at Warren and grinned again.

"I think we have EVERYTHING!" Warren spoke loudly, then began to mumble the things packed in the car to confirm his mental list. "Tent, cooking utensils, sleeping bags, rafts, guns, ammo, machete..." After a few moments, he paused, looked at the five boxes, then turned to Jim. "What's in the boxes anyway?"

Jim moved quickly to the passenger door, ignoring the question. "Make sure we've got the life jackets, field glasses, and cigarettes. The camera is already in the front seat. In that last bag you put in the wagon, there are several rolls of toilet paper. I just can't see using autumn leaves to wipe my ass. You might want to keep several lengths of it in your coat pocket so you'll have it when you need it." He gave another big grin.

Warren shut the back of the wagon then got into the driver's seat. He fastened his seat belt and stared the ignition. 'BUZZZZZ', the rasping noise came from the dashboard. He looked over at Jim.

"I know! I know! I always forget. *Je regrette.* MY car doesn't do that." Jim hurriedly buckled his belt.

Warren pulled out his pocket watch. "Not bad. We're right on time. It's still early. If all goes well, we will be on the river before noon. Traffic on a Saturday shouldn't be bad." He returned the watch to his left pants pocket then reached into his flannel shirt pocket and pulled out the half empty pack of cigarettes and lighter. The lighter in the dash of the car did not work. Handing them to Jim, he put the car in gear and the wagon pulled away from the curb. "We've got two cartons in the back and a few packs in the glove compartment. That should hold us for the week."

"You must have been reading my mind." Jim pulled two cigarettes from the pack and tamped them on the large college ring he wore on his left hand. He put them in his mouth, lighted the ends, and gave a draw. As he did, a scene from the movie, *Now Voyager,* passed through his mind. He gave a slight chuckle and handed one of the cigarettes to Warren. His whole thought pattern changed as he spoke. "This should really be an experience. I'm so excited." This would be something different, as he'd never been camping before in his life.

Warren had also been looking forward to the outing. He needed the break to get away from the everyday rat race. He knew Jim was excited, but wondered how he would hold up, a week in the outdoors. It would be interesting to see his reaction, over the week, to cooking on a fire rather than on his adjustable gas stove. The entire concept of the 'uncivilized' would give Jim a greater appreciation for the finer things in life and modern conveniences. He laughed to himself.

They had nearly finished their cigarettes when Jim broke the silence. "Looks like a pretty long trip from start to finish. Sure we can do it in the time we are going to be out?" Then he was silent.

"Buford Dam to Charlie Brown. Yeah. We can do it."

Jim went into the glove box of the wagon and pulled out the map he had to record the trip, unfolded it and started looking at the area from the starting point to the end point.

They would be pushing off from the base of Buford Dam, north east of Atlanta. Then, Linda would be picking them up on Monday afternoon at the Charlie Brown Airport, located west of the city. This gave them just over a week to have their outing.

Warren was taking a sabbatical of several weeks from his collegiate teaching position. His motivation was to complete a book on a local economic factor. The last year was spent gathering facts and getting his basic outline ready. This outing would be a good diversion to mull through a lot of the information and to discuss it with Jim, but mainly just to chill out.

Warren saw Jim as a paradox. He couldn't imagine how anyone would know so much, and never read a book. Jim told him he would listen intently to a subject of interest. 'Don't make me read it. Tell me about it or show me.' This seemed to be his motto. Warren enjoyed discussing things with him, because he was a good sounding board. Sometimes he'd give a completely different perspective. It was a great way to hash out his thoughts.

*   *   *   *   *

It was late morning as they drove over the earthen dam. A side road took them to one of the parking areas below the dam, on the north bank of the river. Warren drove the car as close to the riverbank as he could.

Jim could not get over the size of the earthwork dam. It looked so much bigger than the one hundred and ninety-two feet of its actual height. The water from Lake Lanier would pour through the sluices on the north end, through a channel between the dam and the riverbank, and then into the original river. His mind started imagining all the disaster movies where the dams broke, and all that water came flooding down. He grabbed his camera and took a few pictures.

"This trip will make another nice slide show!" He laughed as he remembered the moans and groans over his eight hundred slides of Europe everyone had endured. He heard a groan from Warren's direction, a fitting gesture of anguish in anticipation of the future show.

Warren started unpacking and moving things toward the river when he heard Jim yell. "Hold it right there!" Jim's camera clicked. "Okay! Got it!"

This was just the pause necessary for Warren to realize what was happening. Jim was doing it again. It was incredible. He had the great knack of avoidance. When there were others, THEY ended up doing the work while he supervised, directed, commented, or watched.

"Get your fucking ass over here and help get this stuff moving!" Warren laughingly yelled out. "Most of it's yours anyway!" He referred to the five cardboard boxes.

Jim immediately jumped, grabbing things from the back of the station wagon. He finally came to the first raft and grabbed it up in both arms, carrying it to the river's edge. He unrolled it and began to blow it up with the bicycle pump.

Warren put the second raft under his right arm, the oars under his left, and started down to the river. He knew they would basically use the oars as a periodic steering implement in their leisurely drift down stream. "When that one's done, blow this one up!" He returned to the wagon and sat on the open gate.

Looking down to the river, he watched Jim pumping up the raft. He hung his head, shaking it in disbelief. He gave a slight chuckle. It was Jim's unorthodox ways. He was pumping away, using his whole body: up, down, up, down, bending at the waist, instead of just using his arms. He looked like one of those toy feather-headed birds that dunks into a glass of water. He continued to laugh to himself and shake his head. He spoke quietly to himself. "What's a mother to do?" It was just one of the little idiosyncrasies that made Jim a rare kind.

Warren began to reflect on the five boxes. He was quite curious as to their contents, but knew it didn't matter. Regardless of how unnecessary or frivolous, they were there. Yes, it would be an interesting trip. Thank God the two rafts were larger than the ones typically used for rafting on the river. Otherwise, everything would never have fit. He smiled in his thoughts.

He got out the cigarettes, lighting two. "Want a cigarette?" He yelled.

In the time it took Jim to reach the car, Warren had returned to his contemplation. He was looking over his right shoulder down river. Smoke drifted from his mouth. His blue eyes seemed to stare into infinity.

Jim took a puff and sat on the open tailgate of the wagon, next to Warren. In the moment of silence, he reflected on his friendship with Warren. Warren had helped him with many projects as well as some of his personal problems and troubles. His company was never dull, but Jim knew Warren was someone you could never figure out. There were times when he wondered what Warren was thinking, but knew better than to ask. If Warren wanted to discuss it, he would. If he didn't, he wouldn't.

Warren had been a significant help in the remodeling of his house over the past years. This was reciprocated when Jim would help Warren and Linda with their remodeling. His background in architecture was a great boon.

Warren turned, crushing out his cigarette, and looked at the second raft. It was still deflated. He stood up and headed for the rafts. "Now! I'll show you how it's really done."

In no time at all, the second raft was in the river, ready for loading. Warren placed most of the supplies and equipment in the bottom of the raft. Jim was amazed at how Warren packed everything so compactly.

Then there were the five boxes. Warren was just about to load the first one when he heard Jim yelling from the wagon.

"Wait! Not yet! I have to put them in these." He held up several plastic trash bags, waving them in the air. He ran to the rafts. "The bags will keep them dry."

"I don't believe this!" Warren shook his head, laughing.

"That's alright. My 'sixteen trunks packed by Victorine' will be just fine when we set sail." Jim joked sarcastically.

"Should we call the rafts 'Titanic One' and 'Titanic Two'?" Warren laughed. He completed the loading, placed the machete, rifle and shotgun on top of everything, then covered the second raft with the tarpaulins.

Jim noticed Warren's guitar next to his recorder, as the tarps went down. "Your guitar! I thought you might want it with us. I'm sure we could use it…as a paddle." Jim laughed and jumped back, expecting a reprisal from Warren for his sarcasm. "Ohhhhhhh! That was Uuuuggglllyyyy!" He added.

"Fuck you, too, asshole! That's alright. You'll get yours when you're least expecting it. Maybe I'll take your recorder and shove it up your ass! Here." He handed Jim a six pack of beer. "Put the beer up there!" He pointed to the front of the first raft. "I'll hang it over the side to keep it cold. The pistol goes there, too, just in case we happen to see a snake."

Jim cringed at the word. Snakes were one of his greatest fears. It was likely there would be no contact with snakes due to the time of the year and the cooler weather. He took the pistol, ammo, the map of the river, and the red marking pen, putting them in another plastic bag.

Warren would be showing him how to use the pistol during the trip. The last time Jim fired one was in college. His roommate, Jan, had one and let him shoot it a couple of times at some bottles and cans.

All in readiness to leave, Warren parked the wagon. Linda was coming up that afternoon to pick up the wagon, as she had other things to do that morning and couldn't ride up with them. He made one last check to make sure they had everything, then slipped the keys into his pants pocket and headed for the rafts. "Oh God! The patches!" He ran back and reached under the front seat, retrieving the tin containing the patches and glue to repair the rafts and air mattresses, if they got a leak. He also remembered the extra packs of cigarettes in the glove compartment. Finally satisfied he'd forgotten nothing; he turned and yelled to Jim. "That's it! Let's get moving!" He walked to the rafts.

Warren had his life jacket on in a flash and threw the other one to Jim, who of course, fumbled. Why did I know he was going to miss it? He just shook his head. Warren knew Jim too well.

Jim struggled to get the jacket on then commented sarcastically. "Maiden voyage and I get caught in 'Day Glow Orange'. How *déclassé*."

"Shut up and get your damn ass in the raft! And get up front. I'll stay in the back and steer." Warren handed Jim the cigarettes and lighter after Jim got settled. "Try not to burn a hole in the raft. I'd hate for this to be a disaster before we even get started." He laughed and positioned himself at the rear.

Jim lit two and handed one to Warren. "I don't believe it! We're actually on our way! Hope we didn't forget anything."

"If we did, we'll just have to do without it. But with all this shit, I don't see how we could have left anything behind." Warren jabbed again with his reference to the five boxes.

Warren pulled at the oars, directing the first raft out into the current. The second raft was close behind, in tow.

The rafts inched down the Chattahoochee River. The only sounds were those of the water and the cool breeze through the early autumn leaves.

CHAPTER III

Warren pulled out his pocket watch. The gold filigree glinted in the sunlight. He recalled how Jim always considered the ticking exceptionally loud. The black ornate hands indicated eleven fifteen on the raised black Roman Numerals over the white porcelain face. Warren was quite fond of the watch, as it had been a gift from one of his top students.

The river slowly pulled the rafts along. The leaves were just beginning to take on their fall color. Some of the bright colored leaves fell from the overhanging trees and dotted the dark water with many undulating patterns. A few large rocks, jutting from the surface, created ripples and currents causing the patterns to constantly change. To Jim, it was like a living splatter painting. Bright sun, shadows, and color made every movement a new artwork. Of course, he had not resisted capturing it on film. He sat in the front of the raft, clicking away.

"What time is it?" Jim saw Warren returning the watch to his pants pocket.

"Eleven fifteen." Warren paused for a moment. "How far down do you think we are?" They had been on the river just under an hour.

Jim immediately retrieved the map from the plastic bag. With the red pen held in his mouth, he unfolded the map with both hands, then began to garble through his teeth. "Well, let's see. From my estimation, we should be about…here." He placed his finger on the map and turned it in Warren's direction. Quickly pulling the map back, he placed a red dot on it, labeling it 'eleven fifteen', then returned it and the pen back into the bag.

Jim had pulled the map away so quickly, Warren had no time to see, but it really didn't make any difference. The movement down stream was dependent on the flowing water. After all, this was a leisure outing, not a trip to break a speed record for going down the Chattahoochee. There was plenty of time. There were several parks along the river with places to picnic. They would choose those so they could build a fire. Though there were not places to camp, they would have to be careful not to get caught.

He saw Jim pick up his camera again and noticed a glint of humor in his eyes. Warren immediately realized the source of his glee. He could almost hear Jim saying the words. 'Another epic tale, accompanied by umpteen-jillion slides.' He thought he would be sarcastic. "Did you bring enough film?" He braced for the inevitable reply.

"I'm sure ten rolls, thirty-six exposures each, will be enough." Jim continued looking at the riverbank, as he answered, knowing full well Warren had asked the question to goad him. Immediately, he broke into the Paul Simon song. "'Kodachrome. Gives us those nice bright colors. Gives us the greens of summer.'" Then he could not restrain his laughter. When he turned, Warren began to laugh, too. The sound of their laughter filled the air.

"When's it cigarette time?" Jim yelled.

Warren reached into his flannel shirt. "It's the last of this pack. Here. Light them up." He handed the pack and the lighter to Jim. He didn't dare toss them, as they'd surely end up in the river.

Jim removed the last two cigarettes from the pack, folded the empty, and put it in the bottom of the raft. As he tamped them on the large blue zircon in his ring, his eyes passed over the slightly damaged area in the gold on the ring's side. The memory of how it happened passed through his mind. It was an unexpected accident. While throwing rice, at the wedding of one of his college buds, not only did the rice leave his hand, but so did the ring. It just missed the bride's head. Everyone heard it as it bounced down the sidewalk: 'ping', 'ping', 'ping'. The edge of one numeral and the top of the waving American flag sustained minor damage. Thank God it hadn't hit Florence on the head. He thought of it weighing the same as twenty-three pennies. The rings of Virginia Tech were noted for their weight and gold content. He would have hated to be the cause of a postponement in Florence and Mel's honeymoon. His mind popped back to reality as he lit up.

"Thanks." Warren took the cigarette Jim extended in his direction. "From the park maps of the river that I've checked, there should be one about two hours down river that has a place where we can build a fire. That'll give us some time to get settled before nightfall. We'll stay there two nights, then move on." He took a draw on his cigarette. "Would you grab me one of the beers?"

Jim reached into the water along side the raft and pulled one of the cans free from the six pack. He turned to Warren, a sinister look on his face. "What would happen if I accidentally dropped them in the water, and they sank?"

Warren gave a Cheshire grin as he took the beer from Jim. "How would you like to die?"

'Pussssh' went the can, as he pulled the tab. He dropped the tab into the opening of the can. After a few swigs, he handed the beer to Jim, who took a small sip and gave it back.

"What are we going to do first when we get to camp?" Jim thought out loud. His dark brown eyes continued to peruse the riverbanks trying to absorb as much of the surrounding beauty as he could.

"Just wait'll we get there." Warren replied.

Soon they came to a bend in the river. There, some fifteen feet from the shore, was a flat bar about twelve feet wide and a foot higher than the water level. Jim thought it too bad they couldn't camp there; it was so nice and level. But it was absurd. Any rise in the water would prove to be a disaster. He imagined the dam breaking and a wall of water coming down upon some unsuspecting person on the bar.

Then there were the regular water releases from the dam that would raise the water level at those times. These flows of water could be extremely dangerous, if one was out in the river, as the river could become a raging torrent. They had to watch for these rises and quickly move to the bank. When the river returned to normal, they could move onward.

Jim's thought was broken by the sound of Warren's voice. "I have to take a leak. Don't unbalance the raft." Warren braced himself against the side of the raft and unzipped his pants.

Jim immediately positioned his camera over his right eye and organized a picture through the lens. He gave a slight laugh at the sight and the thought of the resulting slide.

"What's so funny?" Warren was still splashing the water when he heard the telltale 'click'. His head turned quickly. "Why you son-of-a-bitch! Will they print that?"

Jim started laughing out loud. "Sure they will."

Warren finished, zipped up his pants and repositioned himself back in place. "You wait! Just wait!" He commented in a vengeful tone, pointing and shaking a finger at Jim.

Warren knew there was a park at Abbots Bridge that they could use and they would be there by late afternoon.

Finally, Warren saw the location and directed the rafts to the left bank. Jim jumped from the raft, as it hit the bank, then ran up to the clearing to look around. Warren remained behind to secure the rafts.

"We will set up the tent in a secluded place near the picnic area where we can build a fire and cook. But we want the tent to be kinda hidden so no one calls and reports us."

Warren began to remove the tarpaulins from the second raft and roll them up. "Here. Take the guns and machete up to the camp area." He handed the rifle and shotgun to Jim, then began to remove the supplies and equipment when he saw the five boxes. "Is there any need to unload 'Victorine's trunks'?" He yelled out in slight jest.

"No! Not yet! They're for the end of the trip." Jim's voice resounded from the clearing. "The spot's clean. Come see!"

Warren grabbed the folded tent, holding it under his right arm, the cooking utensils under his left, and headed to a place that Jim thought was good for the tent. "Looks good." He set everything down and headed back to the rafts. "Why don't you scout out for some fire wood? I'll get everything we need up here, then start the fire."

Within the next hour and a half, Warren moved the necessities from the rafts to the site and had the tent completely set up. The remaining items left in the second raft, he covered with the tarps.

Jim had collected several small piles of wood from branches and sticks found in the nearby forest. Warren told Jim to take the small shovel and dig a shallow trench around the tent. This would prevent any excess water from getting into the tent, should it rain. There was no forecast of rain for the entire week, but one never knew when it might happen. The trench was just a precaution.

In just over two hours, the basic camp was established and Warren had started the fire. He got his fishing gear and headed for the river. Jim placed some rocks around the fire and leveled the rectangular metal grill he'd brought from his barbecue at home. Soon the fire was ready for cooking. Jim decided to gather a little more wood, before he started dinner. He wanted to make sure it was dry so as not to create the smoke that wet wood would have a tendency to do.

It was almost six thirty when Jim went down to the river where Warren was casting. Warren reached in his pocket and handed Jim the cigarettes and lighter. "Wondered how long it was going to take you to come for them."

"Thanks." Jim took the cigarettes from Warren's hand and pulled one from the pack. "Want one?"

"Nah. Finished one not too long ago."

"How many so far?" Jim questioned.

"A couple." Warren answered; figuring out the question referred to the number of fish he'd caught.

Jim looked up into the sky. "Well, snap it up. The sun will be gone in about an hour and it will be almost dark."

At that moment, a fish struck the lure. "Want to reel this one in?"

"I just lit my cigarette. You go ahead." Jim watched as Warren pulled in the fish. He hit his left palm against his forehead. "Damn! I don't have my camera."

"That's okay. There'll be plenty of shots like this in the next few days." Warren laughed.

Jim finished his cigarette and walked back up to the campsite. Warren was planning to clean the fish, a sight he had no desire to watch. There was no problem in cutting or cooking the fish, but there was no way he wanted to see it cleaned. He was curious as to the fillet process Warren was going to use. Maybe he knew some tricks not shown in the gourmet books he'd read. But as Warren indicated, there would be another time to watch.

The setting sun in the west created various shadows and glints of light through the leaves in the many tall trees. Sparks of light danced across the slow moving water. There was a slight breeze, visible in the moving leaves at the tops of the trees. Occasionally, several would break loose and fall like pieces of color from above.

The scene was one of total peace and relaxation.

Jim picked up the coffeepot, then went down to the river to fill it with water. "Should have a pot of coffee in about thirty minutes." He alerted Warren before returning to the fire. He placed the pot on the grill and squatted by the fire to watch. After a few minutes, he went through the supplies and pulled out one can of corn and one of peas. He opened them, leaving the lids still on top. The cans would act as their own cooking container. He placed them on the grill to heat. The fish fillets Warren had prepared would not be started until they were just about ready to eat, since fish cooks so quickly.

In the meantime, Warren got his guitar from the tent. He sat by the fire strumming familiar chords.

Jim was quite impressed how far Warren had come with his learning. Only two years earlier, he'd started with chords and strumming techniques from a book. Now it was virtually automatic for him to switch chords and maintain the beat. Both chimed in to sing *Puff the Magic Dragon*; *Wonder Where I'm Bound*; and *Take Me Home, Country Road*.

Soon it was time to start the fish. Jim heated some slices of bacon in the light metal pan, along with some lemon juice. It seemed strange how good the fish smelled when it began to fry. The aroma of the food filled the air, but the open fire made it different.

Darkness ushered in the night sounds of crickets and frogs. The only influence of civilization was the sound of an occasional passenger jet, passing high overhead, leaving or going to the Atlanta airport. Warren placed a kerosene lantern in the tent and another near the fire area. Jim was surprised how much light they produced.

The meal was ready. "It's not a Julia Child Special, but it'll be filling." Jim placed portions of food on the metal plates. Then it crossed his mind what he planned near the end of the trip. He gave a little chuckle, but dismissed it. He didn't want to wish it away. He handed a plate to Warren. "Watch out for bones."

Warren tasted the fish. "Not bad. Not bad at all."

While they ate, their conversation drifted to the information Warren had gathered for his book and the relationship of the data to its objective.

"Another cup?" Jim reached for the coffeepot. Warren extended his metal cup. After a few sips, Jim started gathering the metal pieces. "Thought I'd get the dishes washed. Well, the eating pans or whatever they're called, before we go to bed."

Warren picked up the large flashlight from inside the tent, as the natural light of day was gone. "I'll hold this and the pistol in case there's a snake." He knew this was very unlikely, but wanted to rattle Jim's cage a little.

"You just had to say that, didn't you?" Jim did not need to hear that, his phobia coming through again. He picked everything up and headed for the river. Warren was right behind. He washed the utensils in the water as Warren moved the beam of light around the area. Jim could hardly look at each dish; his eyes were constantly on the move.

"There really shouldn't be any snakes, it being mid October, but you never can tell." Warren spoke with a touch of laughter in his voice.

Jim's fear of snakes reached the point of the absurd. He could watch a program on TV that had snakes in it and he'd be afraid to put his feet on the floor. He realized this was ridiculous, but he sometimes couldn't understand his own mind.

The time of the dishwashing passed, without incident, and they returned to the fireside for another cup of coffee. Warren pulled out the cigarettes, put one in his mouth, lit it, and handed it to Jim. He then lit himself one.

"It's so different. Almost scary." Jim looked in all directions into the darkness.

"Yeah. But it's so peaceful. There's nothing like being in the wild." Warren blew a puff of smoke into the air. He pulled out his watch. "Ten twenty-three! I don't believe it's that late."

Jim had the map out and was making notes on it. "Ten twenty-three? You're kidding!" He quickly made a few additional marks and folded the map again.

Warren stood up, stretching with a slight yawn. "Okay. Let's call it." He pulled out a cigarette handing it to Jim. "For later if you want." He headed for the tent.

"Thanks. And I promise I'll be quiet when I come to bed."

The air was cooling off. To Jim, the temperature felt to be in the mid-fifties. He always hated the cold. He could never get warm. Cooling off was no problem, but keeping warm was impossible. If he had his way, it would be eternal summer.

"Okay. See you tomorrow."

Jim knew there was no problem about waking Warren. Linda always said that when he fell asleep, it almost required an 'Act of God' to wake him. The fire was almost out. This was good as they didn't need anyone seeing the glow of a fire and report it. He sat down on a nearby rock, looking out through the night. He turned off the lantern. The cool air against his face made him give a slight shudder. He tried to absorb the sounds of the night. It was so peaceful he couldn't believe they were not that far away from the Capital City of the South. Really beautiful, he thought. There was the sound of the leaves as they brushed one another in the light breeze.

He began to reflect on the outing so far and how much fun the day had been. It was funny. He knew he'd never have done an outing like this on his own, but his trust in Warren had removed every anxiety. For him, this was all new. For Warren, it was old hat. "Guess it's like anything. You always trust those you think are competent." A comparison came to mind involving someone driving a car. If he trusted the driver, he had no problem sleeping while the car was in motion. Otherwise, he found himself wide awake and constantly pressing an invisible brake pedal or reaching forward to stop himself from hitting the dashboard.

Then his mind began to look inward as he lit the cigarette with a twig from the fire. He began to think of himself and his relationship to those around him. After getting on his own, he began to really look at people and what they were all about. It finally sank in that people accept you for what you are, regardless of your shortcomings, or they do not call you friend. One of the things that always bothered him was his height. Maybe a few days on the rack would make me taller. He thought with humor. But then there were his assets. His love of music had brought him to learn to play the saxophone, recorder, guitar, and the piano. Painting and sculpture had brought some minor public recognition, as had some of his culinary arts.

His tastes were for the elaborate. The more detailed and ornate, the more he liked it. The Louis XV and XVI styles were his favorite furnishings. He laughed to himself. Warren and Linda were completely the opposite. Their taste in furniture went to the modern, Danish, teakwood, chrome and glass. Warren and he were so different. Warren was to Walter Gropius' Bauhaus and Frank Lloyd Wright's Taliesin West, as he was to the Greek Revival's Windsor Plantation, and the Eighteenth Century's Palace of Versailles. He could only attribute their friendship to their diverse interests, backgrounds, and areas of knowledge. They had absolutely nothing in common.

He took the last puff of his cigarette, put it out, then took one more look around. The only light was that of the lantern in the tent, as the fire had died down. He hated to sleep, but knew he had to.

He went into the tent, zipped the flap shut, removed his clothes, and jumped into the sleeping bag. The lining of the bag was cool against his naked body, but he didn't mind. He could endure this better than wearing underwear or pajamas. They were too uncomfortable. He reached over and turned off the lantern. Darkness enveloped the entire scene. He could hear Warren's low breathing in the other sleeping bag. He lay there staring into the blackness. He wasn't sure how long it was, but he finally fell asleep.

CHAPTER IV

Warren woke up, reached over and pulled his watch from his rolled up shirt. It was ten thirty-four in the morning. How could he have slept so long? But it didn't matter, he felt great. He probably needed the sleep. He looked over at the lump in the adjacent sleeping bag. Jim was still asleep. He quickly put on his clothes. He felt the air was rather brisk. When he got outside, there was a slight breeze that blew through his hair. It was time to get the fire going again. There was no telling how much longer 'sleeping beauty' would be in the sack. A few twigs and sticks to start and the flames were back. He took the coffeepot down to the river for water. It was like ice. Walking back, his hands were still wet and the breeze made them feel the cold more acutely.

All of a sudden, a great idea crossed his mind. Laughing to himself, he quietly walked into the tent and over to Jim's sleeping bag. He pushed his right hand into the bag, pressing the open palm against Jim's sleeping body.

"AHHHHHHH! You FUCKING SHIT! Asshole! Son-of-a-bitch!" The screams yelled out as the sleeping bag came alive like some writhing worm in agony.

Warren laughed out loud as he moved his hand around, touching Jim again and again. Still laughing, he ran from the tent. "He's awake now." He laughed. He went to the fire, preparing the pot for coffee.

"Just wait! JUST WAIT! You'll get yours!" The yells continued from the tent. After a few moments, Jim emerged, fully clothed, but pushing his shirt into his pants. He came to the fire. He was laughing as he spoke. "You wait! I'll think of something real

UGLY to get you back."

"I have to admit, that was a dirty trick." Warren was still laughing. In a minute, they both settled down and the subject changed. "Want anything for breakfast?"

"Just coffee." Jim sat next to the fire, his hands stretched out over the heat. "Slept like a log." He yawned and reached for the cups. "Been up long?"

"Just a while."

"What time is it?"

"A little before eleven." Warren answered.

"God! Did we sleep that long? Can't believe YOU slept that long. You're usually up at the crack." Jim rubbed his hands together.

"Think I'm going to have to shave today." He ran his right hand over his face.

"Nah. You don't want to do that!" Jim turned and looked at Warren. "After all, it's holiday and you don't have to shave." He paused for a moment, scrutinizing Warren's face. "It might be interesting to see what you look like with a beard and mustache."

"Well, I don't know how you got through the 'itch stage'. I tried once before and thought I was going to go mad."

"But just think how it'll keep your face warm. I love mine." Jim stroked his dark brown beard and mustache with his left hand. "By the end of the week you should be well on the way with it. Don't worry. I'll keep it trimmed for you. And when Linda picks us up on Monday, we'll look like the Bobbsey Twins."

"Well. Okay. But if it starts itching like crazy, I'm going to cut it off. And Linda will probably want it off when we get home. We'll see."

Finally, the coffee was ready. Jim poured. Warren prepared a bowl of cereal, then mixed some powdered milk with water to go over it. This was revolting to Jim. He remembered, as a child, his mother mixing some powdered milk, then whipping it into a foam. It looked so good. He took one of the beaters and began to lick the foam. The first taste almost made him gag. What he had expected was not what was in his mouth. This was a complete insult to his taste buds. From that day forward, the words 'powdered milk' were not in his vocabulary.

He watched Warren spooning in the cereal, wanting to throw up with each bite. "How can you eat that gross shit? I don't think there's anything worse than the taste of that…stuff." He couldn't even say the words.

"It's not so bad, once you get use to eating it." Warren continued spooning.

Soon he had finished, then washed his bowl at the river. When he returned, Jim was getting things ready for the day's outing. He grabbed his camera and camera case, putting a few granola bars in it for a snack later. "Do you want the machete?"

"Yeah. Bring it along and I'll carry the shot gun, just in case we run into a wild animal that could be a problem." Warren put the hunting knife under his belt and they were off.

As they left the campsite, Jim expressed concern for their things and possible theft. Warren reassured him there should be no problem. They continued on their way.

The day was bright and crisp. Jim took many pictures. Their great coupe was the discovery of someone's vegetable garden. They were very careful to be conservative with what they took. Since the garden was so large, what they took would not be missed. Jim still thought they were stealing, and knew when he got back, there would be a trip to the confessional with several 'Hail Marys' said in penitence. It was rather suspenseful though. It made the adrenaline flow. They stuffed the camera case with several tomatoes. Warren used the machete to dig up several potato plants and onions. Several other vegetables were added to their loot. He took off his flannel shirt and used it as a carry all.

Jim began to think of their meal that night. Lettuce and tomatoes for the salad and veggies for some soup. Because of the number of potatoes they had gathered, he was sure they would last for some time. He would save several tomatoes for later meals. Warren saw several opportunities to shoot a few birds, but didn't use the gun. He knew there could be some possible legal problem with firing a gun this close to the city and civilization should they be caught, and he didn't want to draw attention to themselves.

As they arrived back at camp, Warren reflected on the day's events. He was quite surprised at Jim's ability to keep up with him. This was a real feat, especially with the amount of walking and the climbing over rocks and hills they did.

Jim actually enjoyed the trek. It was more exercise than he was accustomed to doing, but he felt it did him good. Maybe this whole outing with its exercise might help him get a little more in shape. A few days of this and he was sure he'd be able to enter the Peachtree Road Race the next year.

When they got back to the camp, Warren went to the tent and got his guitar. While Jim prepared dinner, Warren played several melodies.

"Play the one I like." Jim asked as he stirred the soup.

Warren strummed the introductory chords, then they both joined in the singing of *Mr. Bojangles*.

After they had eaten, they sat with their coffee and cigarettes. Their discussion continued from the night before on the subject of Warren's book. Night brought the sounds of the frogs and crickets, just as it did the previous evening. A lull finally came in their conversation. Jim changed the subject.

"You know, I can't tell you how much I've enjoyed the trip. It's like, well, there's nothing I can compare it to. But it's great. And I want to thank you for letting me come with you."

"Well. What can I say? I'm just a great guy." Warren joked.

"Hey, you're my best friend. Everyone should be so fortunate to have a friend like you. If it hadn't been for your comments and suggestions, well, what can I say?" Jim thought for a second at his candidness and was slightly embarrassed, but then realized he was talking to the best friend he'd ever had, and if he couldn't talk and be honest with him, there was no one with whom he could be.

Warren sensed Jim's embarrassment and set aside his guitar. "Listen. There's no reason for you to feel funny about what you just said. And I want you to know I thank you." He shook his head and smiled. "Let me tell you. Sometimes if it weren't for you and your craziness, I think I'd loose it. You're the only one who's taken the time to get to know me and my quirks, and I wouldn't have it any other way. Thanks for being my friend." He extended his right hand toward Jim.

Jim shook Warren's hand and smiled. "Guess I never figured a football hero would ever have anything to do with some nerdy guy. But it was never my thing to play sports."

"There's a lot of things you know that you never could have learned by running fifty-eight yards for the touch down."

"That's easy for you to say. I'd just like to know how it feels, the crowd cheering and all."

Warren puffed up his body and snickered sarcastically. "Well, that's true. Not everyone can be a football hero, the crowd roaring…" He waved his arms in the air, a huge smile on his face.

"What a shit!" Jim laughed, shaking his head.

"Bands playing, people screaming your name."

"That's alright. I've got a few good points, too!" Jim yelled.

"And we could find them, too, if we get a magnifying glass." Warren positioned his arms, expecting a physical reprisal from Jim.

Jim just sat staring at the dark sky. "Maybe I'll have to rethink my feelings." He turned looking right at Warren. "BITCH!"

They both laughed out loud.

Finally, Warren spoke again. "I have to admit that sometimes you do get a bit emotional about things. Actually, it's a sight to see. And I can always tell when it's happening. Your voice changes pitch and you get louder and louder. I love to get on a subject I know will provoke you, just to watch the transformation."

"Yeah. And most of the time I fall for the trap. Takes me a while, but I finally realize what you're doing. That's when I really have a fit, mainly at myself for falling for it…again."

It was Warren's logical and contriving mind, enabling him to pull these tricks. Jim didn't feel too bad, as Warren had the ability to do this with everyone, and it was all in jest.

Their conversations were never dull and sometimes would last into the wee hours. Jim loved it. The many subjects and ideas made him think.

"Well, before we get into another 'all-nighter', I think we should call it."

Warren was right. They did have to move camp the next day. They finished the last of their cigarettes and headed for the tent.

"Should be interesting tomorrow, new territory. Move over Lewis and Clark." Jim hailed.

The lantern went out and the darkness closed in. Warren thought ahead to prevent a comment from Jim, and wrapped his watch in his shirt, as he had done the night before. This would muffle the ticking Jim hated.

In no time at all, they were both asleep.

CHAPTER V

Warren was the first to wake, as usual. His eyes were staring at the roof of the tent. He reached over and checked his watch. It was not easy to see, as it was coming light out. It was five minutes until seven. He quietly put on his pants and walked out into the cool air. He walked down to the river and put his hand in the water. He was surprised. The water was cold, but not as cold as he had expected. Returning to the tent, he grabbed the bar of soap and a towel, then went back to the river. He removed his clothes and placed them on a nearby rock. Slowly, he started into the water.

The river bottom was covered with large smooth rocks with pockets of smaller stones and sandy dirt. There was no question. The water was cold. It took a moment to mentally prepare his body for the encroaching cold. Each step brought the water higher on his body. He was about eight feet from the river's edge, in water almost waist deep, when it happened. He took the next step and there was nothing. There was no return, as he lost his balance.

"OH SHIT! AAAAAHHHHHHHH!!!!" He yelled, as the water closed over his body. He felt as if he had been thrown into a freezer. When he surfaced, he had no thought of the bar of soap, floating away, some ten feet from him. Finally, he made his body accept the cold and went after the soap. He began to quickly wash; realizing his body could not stand the frigid temperature for long.

Jim was awakened by the sound of Warren's alarming yell and the sound of splashing water. He scrambled from the sleeping bag and ran out of the tent. Because of his sleeping habit, the cold air hit him like an Arctic blast. The echo of Warren's yell in his head, kept him from returning to the tent for his clothes. He was hastily looking around when he heard the splash of water from the river. He ran down to the bank. It was early dawn and the rays of the sun were just beginning to come up over the horizon. He looked out into the river.

Warren was washing his face and had his head half way under the water when Jim arrived. All that flashed through Jim's mind was that Warren was drowning. He quickly moved through the cold water, over the rocks, toward Warren. The temperature was unbearable, but he kept on. Finally, Warren lifted his head, just in time to see Jim slip from the same rock he had, only minutes earlier.

"SHIT! FUUUUCK!!!!!" Jim splashed beneath the surface. His yell was muffled by the water closing over his head.

When he came to the surface, his face had a look of surprise, shock, and anguish. Warren yelled out. "Are you okay!?" He moved quickly toward Jim.

Jim could hardly speak from the shock of cold that pierced his body. Finally, he gathered up enough stamina to form words. "For Christ's sake, I thought you were drowning! What the fuck are you doing in here anyway!?" His teeth chattered like castanets.

Warren looked directly at Jim and began to laugh. "You look cold."

"Why you fucking shit! You asshole! I'm freezing! Fuck if I'll ever save you again."

Warren continued to laugh.

Jim instantly saw the entire situation, pictured in his mind. Seeing the humor of the moment, he, too, began to laugh.

"I swear. I had no intention of this happening. I slipped on that same damn rock, and, well, here I am. Since there was nothing I could do, I thought I'd go ahead and take advantage of the situation and take the bath I really wanted."

"Well, I thought you were drowning. I panicked when I saw your face under the water."

"I was just rinsing the soap off."

"Well it scared the shit out of me. But I guess since I'm here, I might as well wash up, too, before my body turns into an iceberg." Jim reached for the soap, his teeth still chattering.

They quickly soaped up and rinsed off. Warren knew they had to get out before the cold really did affect them. When they got out of the river, the air seemed warm. They ran back to the tent. Warren grabbed his towel on the way. He threw several sticks and twigs on the fire while they dried off.

"I have to admit, I feel much better, and cleaner. But if it hadn't happened that way, I'd never have set foot in the water." Jim commented, briskly rubbing the towel over his chest. He got to his middle. "Now! Just look. My dick was small enough, but now look at it! I think it disappeared!"

They both laughed out loud at how the cold can affect the body.

"I know that's right." Warren looked down at himself and laughed. There was a few minutes pause while he finished drying off. "So you thought I was drowning, and you jumped in to save me. Nice to know you'd go that far for me. And now, just think. You can become a member of the Polar Bear Club!"

"Polar Bear Club my ass. If it happens again, you're going to die! That's all I have to say." Jim quickly put on his clothes and coat. He grabbed the coffeepot, then ran down and filled it in the river.

Warren put on his clothes and coat and set the frying pan by the fire.

Jim returned, prepped the pot and set it over the fire. "It's a shame I didn't get any pictures. No one will believe we did it." He had finally stopped shivering.

With breakfast over, the packing of the rafts began.

"I've got all the trash in a plastic bag." Jim yelled. "We'll empty it when we get home."

Warren was loading the rafts. The deflated air mattresses were rolled up with the sleeping bags. Warren dismantled the tent and folded it neatly. It amazed Jim how such a large tent could be reduced to such a small folded square.

After the rafts were ready to go, Jim wet down the coals of the fire, spread them out, then wet them down again. He wanted to make sure they were completely out. Warren carefully put the vegetables they deviously obtained the day before, into another plastic bag, and placed them in the second raft.

They double checked the area. Warren looked at his watch. It was ten twenty-one. Jim opened the map and scribbled on it with his red pen, put it back in the plastic bag, and got into the raft. Warren pushed them clear of the bank and they were off again.

The entire day was sunny and lazy. Periodically Warren would turn the steering over to Jim so he could fish. By mid-afternoon, Warren had six on his stringer, and it was time for a beer. Jim pulled one from those hanging over the side.

"This must be Georgia Four Hundred up ahead." Jim could see an overpass coming up. "Civilization! Progress!" He yelled. The rafts slipped slowly beneath the structure.

Just south of Roswell Road, they set up camp again in a secluded part of the park. They were staying there for three nights and just chill and relax. They would move camp again on day six of their outing.

The plan was to set up camp again on night six. "We're going to set up just below Morgan Falls Dam. After we carry the rafts and stuff around the dam, we'll set up on the west side of the river."

*   *   *   *   *

They had to row when they reached the waters backed up by the dam, as the natural flow had been reduced by the structure. By early evening on day six, they established their campsite in the park, below Morgan Falls Dam, on the west bank.

Jim went out gathering wood. When he returned, Warren got the fire started, while he prepared to fix the night's meal.

"Cigarette break!" Warren yelled. He sat on a log and looked around. "It sure is beautiful. Hard to believe we're in the city." The ground was littered with the first autumn leaves of yellow, orange, red, and brown. The setting sun created shadow displays on the water.

Jim had taken many photographs during the day. Many of the pictures would be used as inspiration for future paintings.

Warren took the line of fish from the water and cleaned them. He called Jim to watch the way he cut the fillets.

"Have you completely finished the cleaning? I don't want to see any guts." Jim yelled back.

"Yeah. That's all done."

Soon the air was filled with the aroma of frying fish. They both agreed it did smell good, but attributed it to the fact they hadn't eaten since morning.

"I have to admit, you've handled the cooking quite well. I'm really surprised." Warren commented.

"It's not so bad. But I do have to watch it more closely, no gas jets to control the heat. Actually it's been great fun. I've rather surprised myself." Jim paused for a second. "But wait'll you see what I fix on Sunday. I think you're really going to be surprised."

"Of that, I'm sure." Warren asked no further. Sometimes it was not necessary to go further with questions. He was sure that Sunday night's meal would be one to remember.

When they had finished dinner, Warren washed the utensils. They sat around the fire having their cigarettes and coffee, discussing a few items related to the remodeling they were both doing on their houses. Soon it was time to turn in.

*   *   *   *   *

They woke up at mid-morning. It was Friday. It would be another day of relaxation. They both had enjoyed their 'get away'. It was like a new lease on life.

Warren set Jim up to do some fishing. Several hours later, he had only caught a few small ones that had to be thrown back. They also did a little exploring. They didn't have to go far to realize how close to 'civilization' they really were. Several large homes and apartment complexes were located not too far from their campsite. It was late afternoon when they got back.

Later that night, they laughed and joked about some of the things they did during the week. It was hard for Jim to accept the fact the camping trip was nearly at an end. "Seems like the week just flew by. Can't believe it's almost over." He paused and looked at Warren.

"Yeah. But we'll do it again. Maybe this spring."

Jim smiled. He would have another adventure to look forward to in six months.

In the morning, they would move the camp for the last time. They would stay at that site until Monday morning, then drift the final stretch to the airport pick-up point on Monday afternoon.

Warren noticed the air was considerably cooler when they started to turn in. A light wind caused the leaves to tumble down making small scraping noises against the roof and sides of the tent as they fell.

Little did they realize, but the next day would be a most significant day. The wheels of fate were starting to turn.

CHAPTER VI

"JESUS, MARY, AND JOSEPH! What the hell happened to the weather?" The loud muffled burst came from inside Jim's sleeping bag.

Warren had been awake for some thirty minutes, but he lay quietly in his sleeping bag. He was thinking of the day's trip, but was quite aware of the cold. His breath turned to visible vapor in the air. What could have caused such a strange occurrence at this time of the year? His mind tried to figure out the freak cold snap. There was nothing about it in the week's forecast before they left.

"I DON'T BELIEVE THIS!" The yelling continued from Jim's sleeping bag. "OKAY GOD! THIS IS SUPPOSED TO BE OCTOBER, NOT MID-WINTER AT THE NORTH POLE!"

Warren began to smile. He looked at the lump in the middle of Jim's sleeping bag, all scrunched up, trying to keep warm. The smile slowly developed into a low chuckle, then to laughter. He could not help himself.

"What the fuck's so funny! I hear you laughing over there!" The sound came again. "I'm cold as shit and you're over there laughing your ass off!"

Warren continued to laugh. He knew it was beginning to get to Jim. It would be only a few moments before there would some sort of reaction. He proved to be correct.

"Just wait! Remember the other day?" Jim totally ignoring the cold, quickly bolted out of his sleeping bag and jumped over on to Warren, who immediately pulled his bag closed. With great effort, he finally maneuvered his right hand into the bag, pressing it against Warren's back. "Now, isn't that funny? See how nice and warm it is out here!"

"Get your fucking cold hands off me!" Warren tossed and turned trying to avoid Jim's reach. In doing so, he threw Jim back onto his own bedding.

Jim lay there laughing, pleased at his revenge.

Warren stuck his head out, laughing. "Get some damn clothes on before you freeze your fucking balls off."

Jim instantly became aware of the cold again, scrambling for his clothes. "JESUS 'H'! What's with the weather? I can't understand why it's so damn cold."

"Oh it's good for you." Warren joked as he crawled from his bedding.

"The hell you say!" Jim finished buttoning and zipping up his clothes and then put on his coat. He started out of the tent. "I'm going to get the fire started again."

The sky was extremely overcast with heavy gray clouds. They were so low the haze hid the tops of the taller trees. Jim stood for a moment looking up into the dimness of ending night. "Looks like snow clouds out here." He yelled to Warren, still in the tent. "What time is it?"

Warren stepped out as he finished buckling his belt. He checked his watch. "Almost quarter to eight!" He looked up at the clouds. The heavy gray blanket blocked a great deal of the very early morning dawn, but even with the small amount of light, the illumination produced was that of a day during a good snowfall. It would surely rain, if it didn't snow. He thought.

"I just know those are snow clouds." Jim continued placing twigs on the fire.

Soon the fire blazed and Jim got ready to prepare their breakfast.

Warren went to the river, filling the pot for the coffee. When he got back, he put it on the grill. They sat waiting for the coffee before starting the bacon and eggs. Warren lit a cigarette, handed it to Jim, then lit himself one. They continually made comments about the weather.

It was around eight forty-five when breakfast was over and they sipped their coffee. Warren lit two cigarettes, using a twig from the fire. "Maybe there's an ice storm coming." He perused the sky again.

It was time to dismantle the camp. Warren quickly took down the tent, folded it, and packed it in the raft. Jim extinguished the fire. The water hitting the hot coals created a billow of steam that rose in the cold, still air. By now, they had it down pat and the routine was done much faster than the first time they took the camp down. They made their last checks around the site to make sure they'd left nothing behind. Then it was time to start down river. Warren was always adamant about them wearing their life jackets, even though they were somewhat cumbersome over their coats. But he knew they could save their lives if for some reason they ended up in the water. Warren checked his watch as they pushed off. It was nine twenty-eight.

Almost twenty minutes later, they passed under the bridge for Johnson Ferry Road. Jim took a mental note of how long it was from the campsite and would mark it on the map later.

It seemed to be getting colder and the mist appeared to be getting thicker. "Jim, watch ahead so we don't hit anything." He handed him one of the oars to use as a prod to push them away from any approaching object.

"Aye! Aye! Captain!" He saluted and turned to closely watch the waters ahead. He could see some one hundred feet before the gray of the water joined with the gray of the mist, blending into a continuous nothingness. "No icebergs yet!" He joked. Then, all of a sudden he could see a thick dense fog ahead, like a wall getting closer and closer. "Look at that fog! It's thicker than pea soup!"

Warren's concern was obvious in his voice. "Make sure you keep your eyes peeled for anything in the way. If something snags the rafts, it's all over."

Momentarily, they entered the thick cloud. The temperature plummeted and visibility went virtually to zero. Jim could see only about ten to fifteen feet, and that was with intense concentration. "Holy Shit! I can't see a damn thing!"

"Shut up and watch." Warren could not understand the freak cloud. The temperature seemed to drop below freezing.

"Christ on a crutch! Do you see? Do you see?" Jim yelled.

Warren could make out small crystals of ice in the haze. They were collecting on Jim's dark hair, beard, and mustache. It just didn't make any sense. He had no explanation for the strange occurrence. "Make sure you watch closely." He emphasized again. The air was still and there wasn't a sound. The light was very odd, too. The fog seemed to glow with a white inner light.

"Ahhhh!" Jim yelled out.

"What's the matter?" Warren feared the worse. He could imagine the rafts running into some unseen catastrophe.

"Nothing! Nothing! The fog's doing tricks with my eyes."

They were in the cloud for just about fifteen minutes. Then, they pulled away. They turned and watched the white wall slowly recede from the rear of the second raft, as they continued to drift southward. The ice crystals on their hair and clothes began to melt. The temperature was definitely warmer and the visibility returned to what it had been earlier. The banks became visible again, but the heavy gray clouds still hung low from the sky.

"Well what do you make of that?" Jim looked at Warren.

"You've got me."

Jim turned again looking at the riverbanks. He noticed it immediately. "What the hell's going on? Warren, what time is it?"

Warren pulled out his watch. "Ten twenty-six."

Jim got out his map and pen, then started to write. He looked up. "From what I can gather, the next overpass is at I two eighty-five. And look at the trees. I don't get it. We have to do some evaluation here."

Warren looked out across the water at the banks and the trees. There were absolutely no leaves on the deciduous trees. On top of that, there were no leaves on the ground having autumn colors. They were all a dark, dead brown. Something was not right. "You say the next reference point is two eighty-five? Let's do some quick calculations. It seems to me that it was…" He paused to rethink the events of the day. "Our campsite was just north of the Johnson Ferry Road. We went under it about eighteen to twenty minutes before we went into the fog bank."

Jim had been doing some quick measurements and calculations. "Looks to me like with the flow and drift we were in, it would take an hour and a half to go from the campsite to two eighty-five. No more than two hours." For a moment, he watched the shoreline go by. He did some more scribbling on the map. "Yep! At this rate of drift, one and a half to two hours." He folded the map, putting it and the pen back in the plastic bag. "I've got everything marked on the map."

They drifted on for some thirty minutes. Neither said a word. They just kept looking at the banks of the river and trying to figure out what was going on. Finally, Warren's curiosity got the best of him. He directed the rafts to the left bank.

Jim was glad they were going ashore. He had to pee, and there was no way he would try the act Warren pulled on their first day out. He knew he'd probably fall in the river.

Reaching the bank, Warren jumped out and pulled the rafts to the edge. Jim jumped out and ran for the large rock jutting out into the river.

"Where are you going?"

"I have to take a leak." In a moment, he was standing on top of the rock and the stream of water arched down into the river. He imagined the scene from a distance, thinking of the famous 'Manneken Pis' statue. This pose also made him regain his thoughts of the temperature. It was quite cold. Completing his little exhibition, he zipped up his pants, leaped down from his granite pedestal, and ran to the rafts.

Warren was examining the terrain. He reached down and picked up a hand full of leaves, looking at them closely. Their state of decomposition indicated they had been on the ground for some time. This did not make sense to him. He stopped for a second, realizing 'Mother Nature' was calling him, too. He wouldn't be as blatant as Jim, mainly, because there was no other vantage point as perfect as Jim's, from which to perform. As he stood by a tree, he laughed recalling Jim perched atop the rock, pissing in the river. He, too, was aware of the cold when he exposed himself to the air.

When he returned to the rafts, he saw Jim sitting on the side of the first raft. He was obviously waiting for a cigarette as he mimed the motions of smoking. He lit one and handed it to Jim, then went and sat on a nearby rock. Still mulling over the situation, he lit himself a cigarette. "I just don't get it." He blew a puff of smoke into the air and shook his head.

"Maybe we can find something out when we reach the bridge." Jim commented.

Warren knew they had not gone under the overpass in the mist. First of all, there had not been enough time to reach it. Second, he was sure he would have heard traffic noise, if they had. He crushed out his cigarette. "Let's get moving."

He looked at Jim as they pushed off. As usual, Jim still had about a quarter of his cigarette to go. It amazed him how long Jim could make a cigarette last.

They drifted for another half an hour, continually watching the shore. They waited in anticipation of the bridge. Minutes later, the silence was broken by Jim's voice. "Where the hell is it?" He reached for the map to reevaluate his previous analysis. "We should have been there by now."

Warren knew Jim was right. They should have been there. He steered toward the left bank. Looking up, he saw there was still no break in the overcast. "We have to find out what's wrong, real quick." He tied the rafts to a small tree with the rope. "I don't think they're going anywhere."

Jim looked at the several connections between the rafts and the tree. "Not unless there's a tidal wave." He joked.

Warren had to laugh, remembering Jim's deep seated terror of tidal waves. Jim had always thought how stupid the fear was and could not pinpoint its development. Several times they had discussed the problem. Jim would recall, in great detail, his dreams about them. But then, he had his own fears. One was spiders. Some of his 'spider dreams' had made him wake in a cold sweat. Jim had virtually no fear of them at all. On many occasions, he watched Jim pick one up and put it elsewhere so that it would be out of harm's way. Jim hated to see them killed. Everything had its place, he would remind everyone. His mind finally returned to the problem at hand. "We're going back, even if we have to go all the way back to the same place in the river where last night's campsite was located. We're going to get to the bottom of this, one way or another. We can leave the life jackets here till we get back." Warren placed his in the first raft.

Jim took off his life jacket and placed it in the bottom of the first raft, then went to the supplies in the second raft and pulled out two cans of beans and franks. He opened them and handed one to

Warren with a spoon. "Sorry they're cold, but them's the hazards. *Quelle dommage.*"

Finishing their quick lunch, Warren picked up the machete and Jim grabbed his camera. He wasn't sure why, as it was a terrible day for pictures. Somewhere up river there might be an answer to their puzzle.

Jim was excited at the question and the quest for the answer. It was like getting lost and not knowing where you were; yet you should know where you were. It was a real strange dilemma. He noticed Warren had checked the time, prior to leaving. Then it crossed his mind and he blurted out. "What if someone steals our stuff?"

"I doubt it." Warren replied without breaking his stride. "Who the hell is going to be out here near the river in this weather?"

After a while, they became aware the temperature had warmed. They attributed it to their physical activity of walking.

Every once in a while, Warren would pause for a second, visually take a bearing on his surroundings, then continue. Jim did the same trying to find something significant. Suddenly he yelled. "Look!" He pointed across the river. "That tree over there! I remember it." It was a sprawling, bent, yet graceful tree, hanging out over the river. The large bare branches were like giant arms reaching into the grayness.

"I see why you'd remember that one." Warren commented. "Looks like one of those grand live oaks around a plantation house in Louisiana or Mississippi."

They continued on their way. Warren removed the necessary leafless undergrowth with the machete. The river remained to their left and was constantly in sight. Shortly, Warren checked his watch. It was going on one o'clock in the afternoon. He stopped and began to reanalyze their problem. "Let's go over it again."

"Well, it was virtually nine thirty when we left this morning, around an hour and a half on the river before our fifteen minute pee break, then, another half hour on the river. That's a total of two hours on the water."

"That's what I thought, too." Warren agreed. "And at the rate we're going, we should be back at last night's campsite in less than another hour and a half. We'll have to watch the far bank to see it." He pulled out the cigarettes and lighter. As he leaned against a large oak-like tree, right foot against the trunk, knee up, the lighter accidentally fell to the ground.

Jim reached down and picked it up. In the process, he was slightly amazed at what he saw. "Warren. Look at this."

Warren moved to a crouched position beside Jim to see what he was talking about.

"I don't get it. This is impossible." Jim was fingering a small bunch of flowers. Each blossom had five waxy petals, blue-green in color, with centers of pale yellow. He continued to examine the ground around himself. There was another small vine growing beneath the nearby leaves. The oval leaves of the vine were fresh and a deep green. He pulled a nearby branch towards himself. "Look at this." The leaf buds on the ends of the stems of the bush were turning green. "I can't explain this either. Looks like these buds are about to open. What happened here? This is really weird." He continued to analyze the buds.

They both stood up and looked closely at the entire area. "Maybe this spot's protected from the cold." Jim thought out loud. "Maybe this place doesn't know winter's on its way. It's the water keeping a constant temperature, the hot house theory." He paused for a moment. "Nah! The water's moving. That blows that thought."

"Let's go." Warren interrupted. "Maybe something will give us a clue."

Ten minutes later, Jim yelled out. "There's my rock!"

Warren pulled out his watch. It was one eighteen. "Yeah, I remember."

The tall massive trees stretched their branches high into the haze. The banks were still covered with leafless underbrush and periodic stands of bamboo. The river wandered like a gray band to the south. The land to their right was rather flat, but sloped up quickly, after about thirty feet. Large outcroppings of rocks rose above the undergrowth.

After some time, Warren checked his watch again. He scanned the area very intently. "Two thirty. Just a bit further."

Jim ran ahead, as if some great rationalization would be in front of them, engraved across a rock in large letters. "Come on! Let's hurry."

Warren finally caught up with him. He was leaning on a rock, puffing and slightly out of breath. "Ready for a cigarette?" He already knew the answer and got them out.

Jim jumped onto the rock, wrapping his arms around his knees, pulling them tight against his chest. Warren looked at him and began to chuckle. "You look like some kind of gargoyle. Some wings and horns would make it complete."

Jim drew a puff on his cigarette and blew smoke rings into the air. Then he made an ugly face. He moved his arms back to imitate wings.

They both laughed.

As the laughter died, they both instantly became aware of it. How could they have missed it? Could it have been so subtle, it never penetrated their hearing? Had their minds been so intently concentrating on the visual, their hearing had been turned off? But there it was. The sound of pouring water. Lots of water. They both looked at one another.

"That's water!" Jim blurted.

"Come on! Let's see!" Warren crushed his cigarette and started moving in the direction of the sound.

Jim was right behind, still puffing the last bit of his cigarette. Finally, they came to the spot.

It did not require close scrutiny for Warren to realize what he was seeing. It was a natural formation.

The river was about one hundred feet wide. A course of rock stretched from one bank to the other, creating a waterfall three feet high. The entire river poured over the spillway.

"Wait a minute." Jim looked at Warren. "I don't understand." He looked closer at the waterfall and could see the natural layers of stone between the banks. It was not a man-made structure. But they had never gone over a waterfall. He quickly looked at Warren hoping for some answer.

"Okay! I give up!" Warren spoke with a touch of humor in his anxiety. He continued to stare at the cascading water. He pulled out his watch. It was two fifty-one. "Jim, what time was it when we left this morning?"

Jim was mesmerized by the pouring water, but Warren's question alerted him again. "If you ask me that question one more time, I'm going to engrave it on your forehead."

"You're right. I don't know why I asked again. It was around nine thirty." He mumbled the rehash of the trip. "Do you think it was this cool when we left camp?"

"COOL! What's this 'cool' shit! It was fucking COLD! That's C...O...L...D. COLD!"

"Okay! Okay! It was cold! But there were leaves on the trees?"

"Right!"

"You know, when we took our break, I checked the leaves on the ground. They were brown and decayed. That's the way the rest of the trip's been so far."

"Yeah. And we've got plants that think it's spring. And a waterfall that shouldn't exist. I can't figure it out either. But what ever happened, happened between here and my rock."

"You're right there. And I think it all happened while we were in the fog."

"Well how the hell do you change everything in just a few minutes?" Jim questioned.

"We'll worry about that in a while. First, we have to find out where we were in the fog. That's the point we're looking for. Let's see. It took us…"

"It was ten twenty-six!" Jim blurted. "I remember! That's when we first noticed the leaves, and that was before the rock and a few minutes after we came out of the fog."

"Christ, you're right! I'd forgotten!" Warren smiled. The first pieces of the puzzle seemed to be within their grasp.

He reached down and picked up a large stick. He turned, throwing it into the river, just upstream from where he and Jim were standing. It landed, as he had hoped, near the middle of the river. With his foot, he quickly marked a spot on the ground and pulled out his watch. As the stick came drifting down, it reached the point that coincided with the mark on the ground. Warren walked along the bank, following the stick and checking his watch. Finally, he stopped and made another mark on the ground. Turning, he started back, stepping off the distance. When he got back to the first mark, he handed the watch to Jim. "Time me for sixty seconds. I'll tell you when to start and when to stop." He ran back to the second mark and passed it. Then he turned and walked at a constant pace. At the mark he yelled. "Now!" He kept walking.

Jim was watching the sweep hand and noted the position when Warren yelled. After the sixty seconds, he alerted Warren. "Stop! Sixty seconds are up."

Warren made a quick mental calculation. "Great! We've been walking a little slower than the flow of the river. I was right. And since that's right, we should be somewhere near last night's campsite. It should be right there across the river."

"Wait a minute!" Jim protested. "If that's so, then where the fuck's the Johnson Ferry Road overpass? We haven't gone under it yet. Could you let me in on the game plan here?"

"I'll explain later. We need to go back to the point where we first noticed the leaves, or should I say, the lack of leaves. Should take us just under an hour."

Jim noticed it was three sixteen, as he handed the watch back to Warren. Immediately they were on their way. Warren got out the cigarettes. After lighting, he handed one back to Jim, who was tagging close behind him.

"Thanks!" Jim said with a smile.

"Try to notice things. Anything that might give us a specific point of reference. We need that real bad." Warren continued at a constant pace.

Virtually forty minutes went by when Jim suddenly stopped. "Keep going! I'll be right with you!" He had been looking out into the river. There it was. He quickly rounded up a few stones and piled them near the river's edge. He did not want to take too long to mark the spot, as Warren had already disappeared somewhere ahead.

Finishing his task, he ran to catch up. He stopped after a few seconds and listened intently. He heard nothing. He kept running. He stopped again, cupping his hands around his ears to gather any sound. Still nothing. Panic took charge. All that went through his mind was the thought that Warren had disappeared from the scene and he was left all alone in this place. His heart began to pound in terror. He ran on and yelled. "Warren! Warren! I'm back here! Don't leave me! I'm coming. Warren!" He tripped on a stone and fell. Tears began to fill his eyes. His panic exploded.

Then in the distance he heard the reassuring sound. "I'm here! I've reached the spot."

Jim's face lighted with glee. He got off the ground and quickly ran in the direction of Warren's voice.

Warren looked up as Jim ran toward him. He could see the anxiety that filled his face. "What's the matter?"

"I thought I'd lost you." Jim was trembling. "And I banged the shit out of my knee."

Warren smiled to calm him. "Don't worry, I won't let you get lost. I promise I will never leave you behind. Remember that. I promise."

"Be careful what you promise. One of these days, you may have to choose regarding that matter." He smiled. He felt so much better and he began to regain his wits.

Warren saw the panic leave Jim's face and he went back to the question at hand. "This should be the spot, or real close to it, where we first saw the leaves this morning." He lit a cigarette and handed it to Jim. This would help calm him further. "What were you yelling about back there?"

Jim took a draw. "I've got another spot back there." He pointed up stream.

"What makes you so sure?"

"It was this morning, in the raft, when I saw it. I didn't see it on the way up because I wasn't looking at it in the right direction. Come on, I'll show you!"

It took only a few minutes to get to the place where Jim had piled the stones. Jim pointed out into the river. There was a large curving log next to a rock, jutting from the water. "It looked like a big snake to me when I saw it this morning in the fog. And it scared the shit out of me. That's when I yelled in the raft."

Warren thought for a moment. "Oh yeah. I remember now."

He paused for a split second, realizing what Jim had just said. "You saw it while we were in the fog." He wanted to reconfirm what he thought he heard.

"Yeah! We were in the fog when I saw the log." Jim replied.

Warren laughed out loud. "Do you know what you just said? You have given us the best thing that you could imagine. You have pinpointed the spot better than the location of the leaves. At this spot, we were still in the fog. What ever happened is related to this area of the river. This is the closest point at which we can tell where we are, versus where we were. And it happened just up river from this point, since the log is here. I'm sure that here's where we may find our answer." He noted the surroundings and that the sky was still heavily overcast "You know, I'm getting hungry."

"*Je regretted, mon ami!*" Jim commented, shrugging his shoulders. "Do you want to go back to the rafts?"

"Hell no! It's more important to get this spot firmly established. Let's get some more rocks on this pile." As they gathered additional stones for the pile, Warren kept his mental analysis going. He had an uneasy feeling that all was not well, but he just couldn't put his finger on it. At the time of their trip that morning, everything before this location was in an autumn period; everything after seemed to be in very early spring. The waterfall made it worse. They were not on another branch of the river. Maybe there had been a shift in the ground after they had passed that point, an earthquake. What a stupid thought. Then there was the problem of the missing bridge on Johnson Ferry Road. They would have climbed over the ruins of it had there been a quake. It was time to compare notes with Jim. "Jim! Let's have a cigarette."

They sat on the ground some fifteen feet from the pile and lit their cigarettes.

"Well. I've got some good news, and I've got some bad news." Warren tried to be humorous.

"Okay? Have I heard this one?" Jim questioned sarcastically, then gave a slight laugh.

"No, no. This isn't a joke. I'm talking about the situation we're in." He paused for a moment in hopes that what he was about to say would make sense. But he knew it would be useless. How can you make sense out of something that makes no sense? He began to speak. "I know this is going to sound strange, but I think, ah, I think we're…lost."

Jim looked at him and began to laugh. "LOST! Did you say lost?"

"NO! No! Wait a minute. I mean we're just a little disoriented."

"What's the good news?"

Warren hesitated. "The good news? I lied. There isn't any good news." He waited for the inevitable harassment. Sure enough, it came.

"You have to be kidding! We're lost? How the fuck do you get lost when you know where you are? I mean, we're on the Chattahoochee. I could show you on the map, but it's back at the rafts, and we're just northwest of the largest metropolitan area in the state of Georgia or the southeast, for that matter."

"Now just wait! Let me explain." Warren interrupted. "What I'm trying to say is that we have a few puzzle pieces to put together. Now here are a few. Tell me what you think." He paused again.

"First off, we have the waterfall, then we have the change in the leaves, you know, from being on the trees to being off the trees. Then there's the Johnson Ferry Road bridge. Let's talk about the fall first." Here is where Jim was going to come back with both barrels, but he had to explore all avenues. And then again he might have something significant to add to the thought. He started again. "It's possible there was a minor quake causing the falls. We didn't notice it because we were in the wa…"

"MINOR QUAKE MY ASS!" Jim rebelled. "I don't consider a shift of some two to three feet in the earth's crust a minor quake. Yeah. Guess it could have been a shift in the Brevard Fault, but I don't think so. It runs basically from the southwest to the northeast. Not east west. And the noise would have been deafening. I remember. I was still in grad school at Tech. I was in Richmond when a small quake shook the area. Made the chandeliers at Miller and Rhodes swing. It sounded like a jet plane was going through the place."

"Okay! Okay! I'm just throwing out ideas right now and need some feedback. So just shut up for a minute. Now. If there'd been one, it would have shifted the river and washed away the campsite across the river." Warren kept trying to make his words sounding believable, but he realized they really sounded like crap. "Okay! How about the 'leaf thing'? Maybe a cold snap caused them all to fall very quickly." He saw that Jim was forming some ideas of his own. He could tell by the way his face took on a sly look.

"I've got it!" Jim interrupted. His voice mocked the great Rod Serling and the tones of the classic television program. "'De!, de!, de!, de!…De!, de!, de!, de!'…It was an outing to be remembered. Little did James Stone and Warren Glass realize, but they would find themselves somewhere in…the 'Twilight Zone'!… 'De!, de!, de!, de!…De!, de!, de!, de!'" He began to laugh out loud.

Warren had to laugh, too. Jim's short scenario did break the tension. "Have you quite finished? And I thought you were coming up with some great revelation." He shook his head. "But did I get some useful information?"

There was a brief pause as they both looked at one another and said in caustic unison. "NOOOOOOOOOOO!" They laughed at their idiocy. They would discuss this further at some later time. It was obvious nothing of value would be expressed at that moment. They went back to building the pile until it was nearly four and a half feet tall and conical in shape.

It was getting dark as they finished. They quickly gathered a little bit of wood for a fire. The small fire was a welcome sight. Soon, it was the only light in the darkness. Jim knew it would keep wild animals away, or so he thought. The machete seemed a small weapon to ward off a bear or whatever.

"God, am I hungry!" Warren complained, grabbing his stomach.

"Don't think about it." Jim said sympathetically.

Warren lit a cigarette, gave it to Jim, then lit himself one. They sat next to one another and peered into the flames.

"You know. It's really been different going to bed early." Jim said softly. "What a change of pace, and this is the first night you don't have your guitar."

Warren's mind was still on food. He was thinking of ham, chicken, potatoes, beans, and other such things. This train of thought was interrupted.

"Do you have any more thoughts on our dilemma?"

"Not really. But I think we'll have it together soon. Just a little more info. Once we've got all the facts, it'll all fall into place. I do feel this spot's really important, especially if we don't find another that's better."

"To be honest, I don't remember a thing north of here, especially with any relation to the trip this morning." Jim added.

"Guess this is it then." Warren concluded.

"Hey!" Jim joked. "If you can figure this thing out, you can write another book. I think it would be neat for you to write a book called <u>Getting Lost Without Really Trying</u>." He leaned over and poked Warren in the side. "It would be sensational." He laughed.

"Yeah it would." Warren was laughing, too. "If only I could explain how to get 'unlost'."

After a while Warren suggested they try to get some sleep. He brushed the ground with his hands to clear away the small stones and things that would make sleeping uncomfortable. Jim did the same. Warren stretched out on the ground, pulling the machete close to his left side. He lay on his back, staring into the darkness.

Jim was to the right of Warren, lying on his right side, his back to Warren. "Warren?" He said softly. "What do we do if it rains?"

"That's the least of our worries right now." He moved his right arm across Jim's body. He felt Jim's right hand upon his arm. It was comforting to know that Jim was there. It gave him an inner strength.

The still dark night was silent except for the gurgling of the nearby river and the crackle of the coals in the fire. There were no sounds of crickets or frogs. The air was heavy and cold. There wasn't a breeze. The two huddled close to keep warm.

Slowly Warren's inner tension eased when he realized that Jim was asleep. Finally, he, too, was asleep.

CHAPTER VII

Phillip looks around the room, as the holograph tells the story. He cannot believe his eyes. Who the hell would have ever thought this place existed?

The striking figure rises from his chair, pausing in his tale. "Ladies and gentlemen, please feel free to have another cigarette. You might want to send someone out to get some munchies, maybe a beer or two." He laughs with a gleam in his eyes. "I'm going to get something myself. Be right back." The figure moves to the edge of the dais and disappears.

Phillip notices the murmur build as the figure vanishes. Everyone had become so comfortable, thinking the old man was real; all are startled when he just vanishes before their eyes.

After a few seconds, he reappears and walks to the chair. Turning, he holds a large gold tray. There is an ornate goblet on the tray along with beautifully arranged foods, fruits, and flowers. He sits and places the tray in his lap. He looks down at the tray and seems to meticulously choose a few grapes, which he picks and puts in his mouth.

Phillip looks at the food. Suddenly, his mouth begins to water and he realizes how hungry he really is. Observing others in the group, it is obvious they feel the same way. He watches several of the head personnel direct their underlings towards the entrance. Then he remembers the stash he keeps in his coat for times like these. He reaches into the pocket, pulling out a few granola bars. Not looking, he unwraps one of the bars.

Finally, the gentleman smiles and resumes his account. "Doesn't

this look nice? Fixed it myself. Just a few things I threw together."
He picks a few more grapes and puts them into his mouth, then
takes a sip from the goblet. "Ah. *C'est bien.*" He looks out across
the group.

Phillip sits crunching on one of his granola bars. I'd like to
smack that old guy up side the head. If he were so ingenious to
figure all this out, you'd think he'd know we'd be starving and
want something to eat, too. I'll be real surprised if the guys from
National Geo and the Smithsonian don't have their lunch catered.
He chuckles at the thought and the image that came to his mind.

The old man continues his story. "Now let's see. Where was I?
Oh yes! I remember."

CHAPTER VIII

When Jim awoke, he noticed Warren was not next to him. He sat up with a start.

An unseen sunrise began to illuminate the heavy gray sky. Warren was bending over the coals, restarting the fire. He looked around and up through the bare trees, their tops penetrating the low billows of mist. The air was as still as the day before. Maybe Jim was right. Maybe this is the 'Twilight Zone'. He saw Jim sit up. "Come on over and get warm. There's going to be a lot we have to do today."

"Is it very late?" Jim yawned, stretching his arms.

Warren pulled out his watch. "Ten minutes to eight."

Jim scrambled to the fire, holding his hands over the flames. "I can't believe it. I slept like a rock last night. I must have really been tired."

Warren smiled. "What did I tell you!?"

A moment later Jim jumped up and headed for a nearby tree. "'Mother Nature' calls." He was gone only a few minutes. He was thinking of food as he returned to the fireside. He knew Warren was starving. Warren was accustomed to eating three meals a day and they hadn't had a thing since the beans and franks the day before. His eating habits were quite different. He recalled a time Warren had compared him to a snake. 'He eats a meal, then doesn't eat anything for a day or more, but then, watch out! He'll eat you out of house and home.' Jim laughed to himself.

Warren was putting a few more rocks on the pile. It was almost five feet high now. The rocks hit with a 'thump', as he wanted to make sure they were firmly in place. He stood back, looked at the pile, then the river, and then back at the pile again. No high water will wash that pile away. He turned to Jim. "I'm sure the answer's right here, but I just can't put my finger on it."

Jim could see the concern on Warren's face. He knew how annoyed Warren could become when he was not in total control of a situation, or at least have a handle on what was happening. It made him feel as if he'd been thrown in a blender, not knowing which end was up.

"This is probably the best puzzle I've ever had to solve. Better than the crossword puzzles in the Washington Post." He joked. He turned to Jim. "That's enough rocks on the pile. Not much more we can do here. Let's get back to the rafts. I have to eat something."

He reached into his flannel shirt pocket, pulling out the pack of cigarettes. "Only two left." He lit them, handing one to Jim.

"You know, I'm glad we didn't start back last night." Jim commented. "Don't think I'd have made it."

Warren smiled. He knew he had really been pushing Jim, but was pleased to see that he constantly made the effort to keep up. He knew Jim would not give up. He might be small, but he's a fighter. Warren took the last puff, threw the cigarette to the ground, crushing it with his foot. He looked at Jim, still smoking the last quarter of the cigarette. How does he do it? He just shook his head.

Jim finished his smoke, then ran to the river to get a double handful of water to put on the fire. Warren spread out the coals, crushing them with his boots. He ran his hands through the black ashes. There were no hot spots. The fire was out. They could now start their trek down river.

When they finally returned to the rafts, Jim was glad no one had tampered with their things. It was something bothering him in the back of his mind.

Warren picked up a few rocks and placed them in a ring on the ground. "I'll get ready to start the fire, if you'll get some wood."

Jim combed the nearby area collecting limbs and twigs. He found several large pieces of wood that were rather hard to handle, but would be good for a lasting fire. Warren was going to have to cut them with the hatchet.

After igniting leaves under the wood, the fire soon blazed. Jim got the utensils and prepared to start cooking. Warren took the coffeepot and headed for the river.

"Would you put some water in this, too?" He handed another pot to Warren.

As Jim began the cooking, Warren began unloading the rafts. "Think we'll set up camp here until we get this mess straightened out."

"Want me to help?"

"No. I'm starving and want you to get something fixed before I die." Warren joked.

Jim laughed, knowing how hungry Warren was. "Don't forget the cigarettes."

"I'm one step ahead of you." Warren was pulling one of the packs from the raft and unwrapping the cellophane. He'd already taken the necessary things from the raft and placed them near the campsite. Sitting by the fire, he lit a cigarette for them both.

"God, that smells good!" The aroma of the sizzling bacon filled the air. He watched Jim put several of the eggs into the pot of water he'd filled earlier. "You're not going to fry them?"

"They've been in the cooler, but I'm checking to make sure

they're not spoiled." Jim looked at the blank expression on Warren's face. An explanation was needed. "If they seem to want to float, it's possible they're bad. That way, you can take and break them in a separate bowl. Then you smell them to make sure." He held the pot up to Warren so he could see. The eggs were all on the bottom of the pot, no ends sticking up toward the surface.

Warren looked on with approval. "Great. Now get them in the pan!"

Jim laughed as he retrieved one of the eggs, breaking it, and placing it into the hot grease. The other eggs followed. He took the metal plates and placed them against the grill to heat them up, before putting the food in them.

Soon it was time to eat. He handed Warren a potholder so he wouldn't burn his hand. The eggs and bacon sizzled as he placed them into the metal plates. The coffee would be ready by the time they finished eating.

While sipping his cup, Warren reiterated how much they needed to get done that day.

Jim rooted through the supplies for the sugar and powdered cream. "Not until I've finished my coffee, and a *fumar*. Now where in hell did I put that, ah, here it is." He pulled the two items from the supplies and dumped them into his cup. "Now. What's on the agenda for today?"

"I want you to stay here and set up camp. Try to catch something for dinner. I'm going to take a quick walk east to try and find a road or something that'll give us a bearing. When I get back, we'll make a decision on how to proceed." He lit a cigarette for them both. "I'll take the machete to mark the path, and the pistol. No. I better leave that with you. I'll take the rifle."

Jim wanted to go, but realized the camp did need to be set up, and Warren could move much faster without him. He was concerned about them separating. "Do you think it'll be alright to split up?

What if something happens? I'd never know!"

"Don't worry. I don't think it will take long to find something. Atlanta is kinda just over the hill from here, but don't worry if I'm not back by this afternoon."

"Well, if you're not back soon enough, I'm going to come looking for you. So you better mark the trail really well." He took a long draw on the cigarette.

"This is ridiculous! Sounds like I'm going away to war or something. We're in Atlanta. Now what could happen?"

"You could get mugged!" Jim joked. "Guess this does have over tones of a bad soap opera: the two lost souls in the woods. I've got it! 'Hansel and Gretel'! I'll be 'Hansel'."

"Believe it!" Warren laughed.

They finished their coffee as Warren prepared to leave. He did have some concern about being separated, but he could think of nothing else to do to help them with their problem. Going further down river would shed no further light on the situation. He had to go east and find a road. That would help establish where they were. As much as he would like Jim to tag along, it was important to get the camp established.

"I'll set everything up and have dinner ready when you get back. I think you're right. After a long trek, I'd have no desire to cook, and since eating is SOOOOOO essential to some of us." He looked at Warren.

"What are you looking at me for? You're the one who eats like a pig!" Warren countered Jim's sarcastic remark, then quickly returned to the matter at hand. "Just make sure you keep the pistol handy, in case of some animal. And if it's real big, get in the raft and push off into the river, it might be safer there. And don't shoot a hole in the raft!"

"Gee! Thanks for that happy thought! I really needed it!" Jim stated sarcastically. "If it's the *Beast of Hollow Mountain* or *Caltiki, the Immortal Monster*, I'll TRY to get away."

"I'm sure YOU will." Warren laughed. He was not familiar with the creatures, or their significance. He was sure they were from some horror films Jim had seen and had used them to exaggerate the situation. This was not an uncommon thing for Jim to do, but he could sense, even through the sarcasm, that Jim was uneasy over being left alone.

Warren checked his watch. "Twelve thirty-three. Better late than never."

"I'll keep the home fires burning…literally."

Walking east, Warren was quickly consumed by the undergrowth and woods. Jim stood for some time listening, as Warren's footsteps faded into silence. He quickly lay on the ground, his left ear to the dirt. All he heard was the muffled sound of the running water in the river. He laughed out loud, realizing what he had done. Fantasy set in. He jumped up, holding his forearm and palm out in a greeting gesture. "How! Me heap good scout, 'Kemo Sabe'!" He continued to laugh as he returned to reality again.

There was much to be done before Warren got back. He was determined to do a good job getting the camp organized. He quickly cleared the area with the hatchet, and made a spot for the tent. He had watched Warren each time he had set the tent up, but it was those special knots that he hoped he could remember, without making a mess of the tie lines.

It took him almost forty-five minutes, but he did it. He stood back, smiling, as he admired the tent.

He placed the sleeping bags, air mattresses, guitar and his recorder inside. Several times, while Warren played the guitar, he'd play the melody line with the recorder. Most everything he moved up to the tent.

Finally, he came to the five boxes. He opened one of the plastic bags that protected one of the boxes. "Still dry. Great!" He resealed the bag and carried the boxes to the tent. Finally, he had everything piled next to the tent and covered with the tarpaulins. He used rocks to hold the corners down. With the small shovel he dug a shallow trench around the pile and the tent. He continued with further organization.

More firewood was gathered, then he got out the fishing equipment and headed to the river.

The rafts were still tied as Warren had left them. He was glad Warren had rented the extra large rafts, so everything would fit. Small rafts would never have done the job. He thought of the five boxes. He recalled Warren's warning to go out into the river should it become necessary. "Christ, the way those rafts are tied up, it would take me forever to get away." He looked at the knots. "Well, son-of-a-bitch! He used the knot like he used for the tent, no problem." He thought it rather dumb for him to think that Warren would not have used the special knot, the one that with one jerk would come undone, but while tied, they were extremely secure. In time, Warren would show him how to make the knot and would become proficient in making one.

He was soon ready to cast his line when he remembered the gun. He ran to the tent and brought it to the river. He placed it on the tackle box. After a moment, he picked it up again to make sure it was loaded. He felt rather silly having the gun with him, but knew it was the right thing to do. Warren would never have said anything about keeping the gun near, if he had not thought it important.

Daylight was dimming as Jim finished his fishing. He'd caught four that were of good size. He left them on the catch line, so they would be fresh when Warren got there. Actually, it was his lack of desire to clean them. Warren could have those honors. He packed up the fishing gear and brought it back up to the tent. It was time to stoke the fire again.

He began to recall the previous days and how much fun he'd had. He hoped Warren had not found him too incompetent. He felt rather confident though. Warren would have made some sort of comment, if he'd not been happy about how things were going.

The gray sky still hung low, just at the treetops. Maybe it would lift by tomorrow. He wondered why Warren was not back, but was sure it had to be for some good reason. He might show up any minute.

It was Sunday and he knew this would be their last night out and decided to prepare what he'd planned for ages. He went to the five boxes. From the first one he opened, he pulled out a five branch, brass candelabrum. He laughed and thought it too bad he didn't bring the cut glass prisms for it. He then pulled out the small linen tablecloth, and placed it on the ground near the candelabrum. Then there were the two napkin rings and napkins, the box of candles, and the sterling flatware. He left the other assorted goodies in the box. He closed it and started on another.

From the second box, he pulled a silver coffeepot and silver tilt pot with warmer. Packed among the softer things in the box were two china plates, cups and saucers.

He looked at the third box. It was an entire case of Chivas Regal. He opened the box and pulled out one of the bottles.

The fourth box was opened. At the top, wrapped in paper, were two each of wine, water, and liqueur goblets made of silver. There were two bottles of Amaretto. He pulled one bottle out, putting it next to the bottle of scotch.

The boxes re-closed, he stacked them inside the tent. He put three of them end-to-end, then placed the tablecloth on top. Then he placed the candelabrum with the candles in the middle.

He knew he had better hurry, as Warren could return any minute. He wanted to make sure Warren would be surprised. Down went the plates, goblets, napkins, and other items. On the other box he placed the coffeepot and warmer. Then he stood back to see how it looked.

The light of the lantern gave an amber glow to the scene. He quickly removed the candles from their holders, ran them out to the fire and burned the tips. "That's better." He commented out loud. He placed them back into the candelabrum. The scotch and Amaretto bottles he placed on the last box, along with the liqueur goblets. He stood in the doorway and smiled. That's it! He turned off the lantern in the tent.

He took the other lantern and went over to the fire, setting it on a nearby rock. He stirred the coals and placed a few more pieces of wood on them. The air had cooled significantly. He could see his breath. It was time to get his coat.

He sat by the fire and began his vigil for Warren. Dinner would not be started until Warren got back. He knew there would be much to discuss at Warren's return with several laughs, too.

The ground was cool. He placed the pistol at his side on top of the tackle box. He looked to the east into the darkness and waited.

CHAPTER IX

Warren found it fairly easy travel. The heavy gray mist hung like a low blanket. He'd crossed a few creeks. The elevation had risen all afternoon, and the terrain got steeper. By evening, he reached the top of a high ridge. The mist was all around him. There were a great number of fir trees in the area.

He was going to continue further, but the terrain began to slope downward. It would be best to be on high ground if it should rain. It was time to stop for the night. He hoped Jim wouldn't worry.

He was extremely concerned over the fact he'd not come across a highway or a residential area. It just didn't make sense. Had he been walking in circles? Maybe tomorrow would bring something better. He prepared a spot for a fire, gathered a pile of wood and settled down.

The light of the fire beamed through the blackness. Having no one there to talk to, he just watched the flames. Their mesmerizing effect finally put him to sleep.

When he awoke, it was early light. He pulled the watch out. It was eight seventeen. The heavy grayness had lifted and he could see the sky above. He thought of the bacon and eggs back at camp.

I'd better find out where the hell I am. He stood up and stretched his arms. He looked around at the large firs; their large sprawling limbs came right down to the ground. They were like massive Christmas trees, just before being decked with lights and ornaments. The Great Tree at Rich's Department Store crossed his mind and why they had never used one of these trees, instead of bringing one from so far off. These are just as beautiful as the ones they had brought in from who knows where.

He looked for the tallest one, one that could be climbed with not too much effort. He started up.

After a while, he was nearing the top. He was finally about forty feet from the ground. As his head rose higher and higher, the surrounding countryside became clearer. At last, he was higher than most of the surrounding trees.

Then all became alarmingly confused. The instant visual of what he saw was a storm to his brain and its thought processes. All clamored, trying to figure out and analyze what he was seeing.

The tree he was in was on the crest of the highest ridge. He was facing southeast. All he could see was the forest of firs and leafless hardwoods stretching down and away to the east and when he turned right, it was the same to the west. The ridge was in a northeast to southwest direction. He could see for miles to the east, the south and to the west. As the ridge continued to the southwest, it sloped down.

Almost directly west, about five miles away, he could see a small column of smoke rising in the still air. "Jim must have put some wet wood on the fire." He chuckled. The early morning sky was clear blue, with small fluffy clouds. Looking east, some fifteen miles away and a bit south, he could see Stone Mountain.

Two things had become instantly and disturbingly evident. It seemed beyond comprehension. His mind tried to keep up with what he was seeing.

Directly to the southeast, the firs and hardwoods continued for miles. "Okay! The 'City in the Trees' seems to have been swallowed up by the damn trees. Either the trees grew over seven hundred feet tall in the last week, or the damn city has been wiped off the map. Where the fuck's Atlanta?" He yelled out loud. "Where the hell are all the damn buildings?" If he could see Stone Mountain and the smoke from the fire at the camp, he sure as hell would be able to see the major skyscrapers in downtown. For a split second, he remembered how Jim would always refer to one of the buildings as Atlanta's Empire State Building.

Then there was the sun. It was coming up on the western horizon, not the east. Warren checked his watch. It was eight fifty-four. Was there some way he could have slept the entire day away? Wrong. It really was morning.

He was amazed and dumbfounded. He continued to survey the area for miles. He looked at the sky again. He couldn't remember when he'd ever seen it so clear. He looked southwest. The concrete chimney of the power plant was not there. It would definitely be visible from where he was, especially with its flashing strobe lights to prevent an aircraft from hitting it.

And with regards to aircraft, there wasn't a plane in the sky, nor could he hear one.

He stood in the tree for just a little while longer, trying to analyze what was going on. Finally, he became aware of his stomach again. It was time to start back to camp. It would be interesting to see Jim's reaction to this mind blower.

When he reached the ground, he hurriedly put out the fire, grabbed his gun and machete then headed back. The notches on the trees made it easy to return the way he'd come.

Back at camp, Jim woke with a start. He had fallen asleep, sitting near the fire. He couldn't believe the morning sunlight filtering through the bare trees onto the water. The air was crisp and clean. He reached for some wood and placed it on the coals. A few of the pieces were wet and caused a column of white smoke that rose straight and high into the air. "Maybe I could send some smoke signals." He laughed.

Warren had not returned as yet, but Jim was quite sure there would be some good explanation. He hoped everything was okay.

Suddenly, he remembered the lantern. Warren would kill him for letting it burn out. He was sure it was not good for the wick. He put it in the tent next to the other one.

He went and checked the fish he had caught the last afternoon. They were alive and well. Since there was nothing more to do, he decided to do some exploring around in the immediate area.

He was quite surprised at the vegetation. It all looked like it was beginning to bud out. There were several low patches of growth that were blooming. These were in protected areas between rocks and in crevices.

Soon it was time to return to camp. He would hate to be gone when Warren got back.

Reaching the site, he made preparation for breakfast. He wouldn't begin until Warren returned, or he got so hungry he couldn't stand to wait anymore. He did a few more tasks around the site to clear it more. Everything was still in its place from the night before. He left everything as it was. The last night out had come and gone.

He then thought of Warren's wife. Linda was going to be furious that they were not at the pick up spot that afternoon. But Warren would have to deal with that.

It was early afternoon, when he heard a rustle in the woods to the east. He had been putting a few sticks on the fire when he heard the noise. He stopped and looked up.

"Don't shoot! It's only me." The loud voice came from somewhere in the undergrowth. "You got some coffee?"

Jim grabbed the pot sitting at the edge of the grill keeping warm. He poured a cup as Warren emerged from the woods. He was glad to see him. "Okay! What's the news? And what the hell took you so long?"

Warren was shaking his head when he took the cup. "Well. Where do I begin? It's going to sound real strange, I know."

"I sure hope you called Linda and told her we ran into a bit of a problem. She's going to kill you when we get back."

Warren began to laugh, knowing what he did. "First of all, I think you better sit down and have a cup with me."

Jim poured, put his regular dose of sugar and one pack of powdered cream into it, then sat near Warren waiting for the story.

"Once upon a time…" Warren began to laugh.

"Cut the crap." Jim was eager to know where they were and what had gone wrong.

"You're not going to believe this, I just know it! I don't even believe it. And I saw it. Been thinking about it all during the trip back here, trying to figure it out."

Jim's face was filled with question. He knew what Warren was about to tell had to be unusual, or he'd have never made such a big deal out of it.

"Here are the facts, as I know them." Warren paused. "We are about ten miles northwest of downtown Atlanta." He paused for a while longer.

"Yes?" Jim questioned for him to go on, making motions with his hands trying to pull it out of Warren.

"The only problem is…there's no downtown Atlanta."

Jim's face took on a strange questioning look, then he began to laugh. "There's no downtown Atlanta. That's a good one. And what did YOU eat while you were out there in the woods?"

Warren sat silent waiting for Jim to stop his comments. He couldn't blame him, as he would probably be doing the same thing if he had heard what he'd just said.

Finally, Jim stopped his laughter. He looked right at Warren.

"That's right. There's no Atlanta, no town, no nothing. Not even people."

Jim, still thinking it a joke, broke into the refrains of a song. "'Streets full of houses, no one's home. Everyone's gone to the Moon. Everyone's gone to the Moon.'" He stopped short, and looked directly into Warren's eyes. "You're serious! You REALLY are serious!"

"I sure as hell am. And there's more."

Jim was speechless. All he could do now was try and comprehend what Warren was saying.

"I could see all the way to Stone Mountain, and there's absolutely no sign of a living soul. Nothing but trees as far as the eye can see. And to top that, there's the sun."

Jim looked up at the brightness in the sky. "The sun rose in the west this morning." He hurriedly went to the tent and got the compass. He shook it to make sure it was reading properly. The north arrow pointed in an up river direction. He knew that was correct. "Well, north is still north."

Warren looked at the face. "I don't care what the compass indicates. The sun came up over there this morning." He pointed across the river to the west. Warren got an inquisitive look on his face and stroked his new, but still very short beard and mustache, with his right hand. "Maybe Velikovsky was right after all."

Jim was familiar with the author-scientist from the many discussions he and Warren had had concerning his famous and controversial book. It had been the subject of many of their famous all night bull sessions. "You mean about the flip on the axis?"

"Yeah. Maybe the earth hit something and flipped it again. But that wouldn't explain where downtown went." For a moment he stared into space. "From what I can gather, we've been put into one of two situations. Either we're way in the future, sometime after Atlanta has disappeared, or we're somewhere in the past, and it hasn't been built yet."

Jim's brain was whirling trying to accept this story. All he knew is that they had not passed under I-285 yet, there was a waterfall where it should not be, Johnson Ferry Road overpass was not where it should be, and the weather had gone a bit spastic. He had not examined the sun because of the trees, but then, he took note of the rays and their direction. It was now afternoon and the rays were going from the east to the west. He knew this was not correct. They should be going from west to east. He looked at the compass again. He stood in shock and amazement. Slowly, it all began to sink in. "*SACRA MERD!*" He quickly turned to Warren, as if he had all the answers. "How in hell did this happen? What are we going to do? How do we get back?"

"It's not my fault! Don't blame me!" Warren quickly defended himself. "We do have to do something though, and the answer is somewhere back at the pile of stones. Tomorrow we'll go back, set up temporary camp there, and see what we can do."

"Why don't we go now?"

"Mainly because there's not enough time today and also, I'm starving. Tomorrow will be soon enough." He paused then changed the subject. "By the way, where are the cigarettes?"

Jim calmed down, realizing Warren was right. The next day

would be soon enough. "They're in the tent." He began to organize the pans and utensils to cook.

Warren walked to the tent and through the opening. "My God. I don't believe it." His head was shaking in disbelief when he turned from the tent. He saw Jim smiling. "It really looks nice, I have to admit, if I've said it once, I've said it a thousand times, no one is one ups on you." He looked back into the tent. "Son-of-a-bitch! You brought some Chivas with you."

"That's your special treat. Go ahead and open it. And don't worry. There's a whole case of it. It's so when you get home you can say this scotch came all the way down the Chattahoochee."

"You know, no one will believe it."

"Fuck them! You know the truth, and that's all that counts."

Warren went and poured himself some scotch in one of the cordial glasses. In the other, he poured some Amaretto. "Here you go." He handed one of the small goblets to Jim.

Jim lifted the glass to his lips, but before he could sip, the smell hit his nose. "Wrong!" He handed the goblet back to Warren. "This is your scotch."

"Sorry about that." Warren corrected his mistake.

Jim took a sip. "That's better."

Warren sat by the fire with Jim and they began to discuss their dilemma further. "We have to try and get back. That's the first thing. But I don't know if we can get back."

"Well, if we got here, we should be able to get back." Jim sounded quite sure of himself. "And just think what people are going to say when we show them. We'll be the ones who found the hole. I can hardly wait! Scientists will be able to come here to study and explore. It's a fantastic opportunity."

"Tomorrow will tell the tale. We'll try then. We better cover all the things we can, related to the pile of rocks." Warren continued.

"What do you mean? We know everything about the spot. It's the only location I can remember that has some significance to the time we got here."

"Are there any other significant things you remember?" Warren questioned. "Anything, regardless of how it might sound."

"Well. One thing I really remember is, that it was fucking cold."

"True." Warren agreed. "It was unusually cooler."

"It was colder than a brass bra on a witch's tit in December." Jim yelled.

"Okay! Okay! And when we got onto the river, we ran into the fog. The cloud with the ice crystals in it."

"Yeah. That's where I saw my snake log."

"The snake log seems to be the only thing we can first put our fingers on related to this time. Everything before the fog was in the autumn. Everything after the fog is here. It is quite clear that what ever happened to us occurred in the fog, and at that point in the river. Somewhere just north of the rock pile, we should be able to get back through."

"What if?" Jim paused for a moment. "I remember this movie where the hole closed up and they couldn't get back through again. They were caught in another place and couldn't get back. What if we're stuck here, all by ourselves, no body else, no nothing?" His face began to fill more and more with concern.

Warren could see the panic building. It had to be stopped. "Don't worry! Tomorrow we'll find the way back, and we'll be just fine." He wasn't sure how true his words were, but he had to do something to calm the brewing storm. He carefully watched Jim's expression to see if additional reassurance might be needed.

He hated to lie, but this was one of those situations where a lie was needed to keep the sanity and their survival could depend on it, should it come to the worse. His comments had worked. There was going to be no panic. Then his own mind began to whirl and he wondered what they would do if they couldn't get back. That would be one hell of a note, he thought.

"So you think there'll be no problem?"

"Don't worry about it right now. We'll get it all straight tomorrow." Warren emphasized.

Jim put the back of his left hand against his forehead, tilting his head back, then in a slow, high pitched mimic, he spoke. "'That's all right. I can't think about it right now. I'll think about it tomorrow, at Tara! After all, tomorrow is another day.'"

Warren laughed, shaking his head. He had given Jim a perfect opening for his antics. But he really didn't mind. It proved Jim was calm and not overly worried.

Jim had completely forgotten about preparing dinner, he was so taken by their predicament.

Warren raised his goblet. "Before I get bombed, when do we eat?"

"Oh! Sorry about that. Do you want something quick or something nice?" Jim held the frying pan up. "Now, I caught some fish that are down in the river."

"You get everything ready, and I'll go clean them up." Warren set the silver liqueur goblet down and headed for the edge of the river.

"You know, I was going to fix something really special, but maybe we better wait until we get this thing worked out." Jim yelled to Warren. "Bet Linda's having a shit fit, us not being at the airport this afternoon. She'll probably have the cops out combing the banks."

"Well there's nothing we can do about that until we get back." Warren quickly finished with the fish and walked back to the fire.

Jim had two open cans of vegetables, warming on the grill. "I'll start the fish when the veggies heat up."

"I'm going to get a little more wood while everything's cooking. Call when it's about time." Warren went into the woods to bring some additional fire wood back for the night.

Warren went to light the lanterns. "Who let this lantern burn out?" He looked at them closely. "No major damage this time. Do it again, and I'll have to kill you." He retrieved the gallon container of lantern fuel and filled the reservoirs of each lantern.

Dinner was finally ready. Jim put the empty cans into the plastic trash bag he'd been using during the entire trip. They ate on the tin plates and not the china ones. They decided they wouldn't celebrate until they solved their problem and knew their way out of it. Warren helped Jim put everything back in their boxes.

Warren got his guitar and Jim got his recorder. The still night air carried the melodic strums and flute tones into the darkness. After several cups of coffee, a few glasses of drink and a few songs, it was time to get ready to sleep. They both knew the next day was going to be very interesting.

Warren leaned over from his sleeping bag and turned the lantern off. "Good night Jim. See you in the morning."

"Night Warren."

There were a few moments of silence. Suddenly, the darkness was pierced as Jim yelled out. "'Good night, John Boy!'"

They both laughed.

CHAPTER X

Neither slept well, each pondering their predicament. It was three after eight, as Warren checked his watch. Soon, they were both up and quickly ate breakfast.

"When we find the hole, we'll come back and get everything. For now, we'll bring just the essentials. I thought about it all last night. And I think the hole is out in the river, so we'll need a raft. That's probably why we couldn't get through while we were on the bank. Raft, oars, air pump and life jackets, that's it!"

They were on their way by nine o'clock. Warren carried the deflated and rolled raft on his left shoulder, the shot gun on his right. Jim carried the oars, life jackets and air pump.

It was late morning when they arrived at the rock pile. They had not stopped for a cigarette during the entire walk. When they had everything prepped, they stood by the stone marker and Warren lit a cigarette for each of them. They seemed to savor each puff.

The cigarettes finished, they got into the raft and pushed off.

"Now here's the plan." Warren directed. "We're going to row up stream and come down like we did before. You sit in front just like you did when we passed this way, and tell me when you see the snake log. You have to imagine the fog the way it was, too. I'll be back here and steer. When we reach the right spot, we're both going to row against the current in the opposite direction from which we came. That should retrace our path back up river and we should be able to go back through the hole. But we have to be in the right spot."

Warren kept the raft near the edge of the river until they were far enough up river to be in position. This kept it out of the main current, making it easier to maneuver. Then he rowed out to the middle. Slowly the raft began to drift. Jim kept a watch on the log, and tried to guide Warren so they would approach it just as they had when they were in the fog. In a few minutes, the position was right. "NOW!" Jim yelled.

They both paddled against the slow current. For nearly ten minutes, they rowed. Warren stopped and looked around. Nothing had changed.

"Everything looks the same." Jim panted.

"Okay. Let's try it again. Maybe we missed the spot."

The drift gave them some minutes to rest before it was time to row again. Jim watched carefully. "NOW!" He yelled.

After another ten minutes, Warren looked around. "SHIT! Nothing yet." His annoyance was clear. "We'll do it again."

Several more tries proved futile. Both were exhausted as they returned to shore.

"I don't know what the fuck we're doing wrong!" Warren said in exasperation. "We've covered every damn inch of that river. We couldn't have missed it."

"We'll rest a bit and try it again." Jim suggested.

"It's somewhere out there. That hole has to be there. And it has to be in that stretch we covered." Warren looked up river from where they sat by the stone pile.

They tried numerous times that afternoon, without success. As they came ashore the last time, nothing was said. They just sat in the raft exhausted. Some twenty minutes passed. Warren spoke. "Maybe it's the time of day. Maybe we have to go through at the same time we did the first time."

"Ten twenty-six." Jim uttered. "Well. Just before ten twenty-six. We were in the fog for about fifteen minutes before you checked your watch…at ten twenty-six."

"Right. But just before ten twenty-six. We'll stay here tonight and rest. Then we'll be ready and on the river bright and early tomorrow. We'll be in position by ten o'clock."

They pulled the raft up on the bank. They stayed on the same spot where they had stayed a few nights earlier. They gathered wood for the fire.

As they sat by the fire, Jim surprised Warren when he pulled two apples from his pocket, handing one to Warren. "I just knew we'd be here tonight. Sorry it's not more, but as Grandma Kempka use to say, 'Beggars can't be choosers'."

Warren was still hungry when the apple was gone. He decided to try his luck looking for something in the woods. He was gone for almost an hour, and when he returned, he had some small, four footed animal he had cleaned before coming back to camp so Jim wouldn't see the process.

Jim took the sticks Warren had cut with his hunting knife, and fixed a spit over the fire. He wasn't sure what the animal was, but it didn't matter. It was late by the time it was ready.

"It's a bit tough." Jim commented, as he took a bite of the roasted meat. "But it is food."

"Sure wish we had our pot of coffee." Warren thought out loud.

When they finished, it was time to rest. They slept in the raft this time, instead of on the ground.

The air was cool and the stars were bright in the sky above.

CHAPTER XI

As morning broke, Warren got up and put some wood on the warm coals to take off the chill. They had three hours before they would make their attempt to go down river again. 'Mother Nature' was calling. He was glad Jim had been giving out lengths of toilet paper to save in their pockets. When he returned, Jim was still asleep. He was using the life jacket as a pillow. His body was all curled up.

"Come warm up by the fire." Warren called out.

"Sounds like a good idea." Jim stretched and yawned. "What time is it?"

"We've got time. It's only seven thirty. The sun should be up soon."

They both were rather quiet as they squatted by the fire. Warren went for his cigarettes. "Want one?" He pitched the pack in Jim's direction.

Jim lit one and reached across the fire, handing the pack back. "Warren, what if we can't get back? I mean, what if we can't find the right spot? What are we going to do?"

"Don't worry. Whatever happens, we'll do okay."

They finished their cigarettes in silence.

Jim picked up a nearby stick and began to poke in the fire. Nothing was said, but Warren could sense Jim's anxiety. Several times he thought of the consequences of not making it back and it absolutely terrified him, too. He knew Jim would be like the proverbial fish out of water in this environment. Would he be able to survive? Would he hold it together? Jim was almost too 'civilized' and his need for people was so overwhelming.

Back when Warren had only known Jim a short time, it became perfectly clear that he was in a constant search of approval from his friends, trying to justify his existence. If only he would come to the realization that it wasn't necessary.

Then he began to think of his own possibilities of survival. He was much more prepared to cope with this situation, but even for him it would not be easy. He was accustomed to physical activity. Jim, on the other hand, was not. For Jim, strenuous activity was playing through the three movements of a sonata on the piano. His small frame was not oriented to heavy work and long periods of exhaustive labor. Alone, Jim would perish. But together, they just might make it.

Some time later, Warren checked his watch. "Well I guess it's time to give it that old college try."

They got into the raft and started up stream.

"We'll get in position and I'll watch the time to make sure we try at the right time. Since we were out of the fog just before ten twenty-six, we were in the fog from just after ten. So the way I figure it, we start rowing back up stream at around eight after ten. We will be in the same area at the same time we were the other day."

They maneuvered the raft near the serpent-like log, paddling when needed to hold the raft in place. At the designated time they would row up stream. Hopefully, they would make it through the rip in time.

"Everything look okay?" Warren questioned while checking their position.

"Looks okay here. Seems to be the right spot." Jim readied for the moment when they would make their attempt.

"Just a few more minutes." Warren held the timepiece in the palm of his right hand. He kept staring at it. "Almost!"

Jim grabbed his oar in anticipation.

"Get ready! Ten, nine, eight, seven, six, five, four, three, two, one, NOW!

They paddled against the current for the next five minutes. Both kept looking to see some dramatic change, but it was still the same. "Let's keep rowing for a few more minutes." Still there was no change. "Let it drift back and we'll try it again." Warren continued to watch the banks.

The raft drifted down and into the position near the log again. "NOW!" Yelled Jim.

They rowed again for nearly ten minutes. There was still no change. Warren looked at his watch, now on the bottom of the raft where he placed it prior to their first rowing attempt. "One more time, Jim."

The raft drifted again, as it had the time before, until it reached the place near the log. "NOW!" Jim yelled.

Again the effort proved fruitless. Nothing had changed. They were still where they had been. Warren knew it was too late. It was almost eleven o'clock. All the factors he had taken into consideration were acted upon, but there had been no difference. He looked at the banks with disgust. "Let's go back to the marker."

When the raft hit the bank, Warren just sat there, staring at the bottom. "Damn it! I just don't know what's wrong. We did it all right. Everything's been taken into account. Everything!"

"Maybe it's gone, like in the movie. The door closed and we can't get back." Even though Jim was negative with his comment, he wanted to hear something positive from Warren.

Warren did not want to think of it, but he knew Jim was right. The door must have closed and there was no way back. This was hard to accept. Worse of all, it would be impossible to tell Jim this grim reality. His mind began to spin trying to think of a way to break it to him. "Jim, go put out the fire, and make sure it's out real good. We're going back to camp."

Jim went without question to extinguish the fire. After a while he returned. He spoke softly. "Fire's out!"

Warren lit them both a cigarette. Before putting the pack back into his pocket, he tilted the pack, looking inside. There were eight left. He placed the pack very carefully into the pocket of his flannel shirt, then tapped the pocket with his right hand.

Jim watched. It seemed Warren was putting something treasured, away for safekeeping. The expression on Warren's face was one of extreme concern.

"We have to take stock. We'll row down river to camp and take stock of what we've got on hand. There's a lot to do."

Jim watched for obstructions in the water. Nothing had been said for some time until Jim got up enough courage to speak. "Doesn't look good, does it?" He didn't turn around.

Several seconds of silence passed before Warren responded. "No it doesn't. I think we're really in a big mess, and I don't know where to find the answer."

"So you think we're going to be here a while?" Jim tried not to sound depressed.

"Yeah. I think we are." Warren said calmly.

Neither looked at the other for the next hour as they privately pondered their plight.

Jim spoke softly. "Warren? Are we going to die? Winter's coming…and the snow. I don't want to die out here in the snow."

"We're going to be okay!" Warren answered in a commanding voice. "We've got a lot to do, but we're going to be just fine. Everything's going to be just fine."

It was mid-afternoon when they pulled into camp. Jim went to get more firewood. Warren started taking an inventory of their food supplies and ammunition for the guns.

"Why don't you fix us a nice pot of coffee." Warren tried to sound cheerful. He continued with the inventory. "We'll decide on something to eat when I get finished."

After about twenty minutes, the coffee was ready. Jim went into the tent, into one of the boxes, and brought out the two china cups and saucers. He came back to the fire and poured the coffee into them, then handed one to Warren. He looked right into Warren's eyes. "We may be lost in oblivion, but we still can be civilized." He smiled.

Warren smiled as he took the cup and saucer from Jim.

The remainder of the afternoon was spent going over the things they had and their importance. Warren was glad they had thrown nothing away. The trash they kept could become useful. Finally, he made a decision. "Since the bacon and eggs won't keep, you might as well go ahead and fix them to eat.

Jim placed the bacon in the frying pan and placed it on the grill. He watched every piece as it cooked. "Well. We better enjoy this, as I don't know the next time we might be going by the grocery store for more." He tried to display some humor.

Warren drew in a deep breath. He knew Jim was right. He picked up his cup and sipped his coffee. This, too, would soon be gone. He knew of nothing that would replace it. "There's enough for about three more pots. I'm sure going to miss the coffee."

"I know what you mean. We tend to take so much for granted. Soon another slice of civilized Americana will slip away into history." He paused in his commentary and looked directly at Warren. "We are NOT going to turn into animals! We ARE going to remember everything we know, even the things we thought weren't important. We WILL stay civil." He looked up river. "Maybe we'll wake up tomorrow and all this will have been some crazy dream."

"If this is a dream, I want to know whose it is. I wish they'd hurry up and wake up." Warren joked. Soon he was serious again. "We have several decisions to make."

"WE?" Jim questioned.

"Yes, WE!" Warren answered emphatically. "I may know more about what's going on out here, but your input will be extremely helpful."

Jim looked surprised. "ME? Helpful!? Out here?"

"You know more than you think you do. One of these days you're going to wake up and realize it. Maybe today's the day."

It gave Jim a good feeling to know Warren wanted his opinion. He realized Warren would have the final say, but his comments would be heard. "What about a permanent campsite. I know we can't stay here. A major rainfall and we'd wash away."

"Correct! We really need a clear place to set up, one that's better for our protection. A place where we can see something as it approaches, that'll give us some time to prepare."

Jim was not too pleased at the prospects of 'things' being out there. "The *Beast of Hollow Mountain*?" He spoke unconsciously.

Warren gave him a strange look. "No, I doubt it. But there are probably things such as bear, wildcat, and the like that we have to be aware of. And who knows, maybe there are people out there."

"People? But I thought you said…"

"I did. But who knows. One quick scan of the country side is not positive proof there aren't any."

Jim looked up with a glimmer of hope on his face. "That's true. There really could be people out there. And it should be interesting to try and find out what happened and where the hell we are."

"We need to think about the permanent campsite." Warren interrupted.

Jim was still pondering their dilemma. "If we're stuck here, we might as well make the best of it. We'll make it an adventure."

"Jim, the campsite. You know…the campsite. We really need to talk about it."

"I have no idea where to set up a camp. Did you have a place in mind?"

"I've thought a little about it and came up with a place that might be just right." Warren answered. "How about Stone Mountain? It's only some nineteen or twenty miles to the east. And there are a lot of advantages to living over there."

Jim started to laugh. He looked up and raised his hands into the air. "God! You just can't get some people to leave the suburbs, can you?!" He looked right at Warren, still laughing. "You sound like some damn real estate commercial."

Warren thought for a moment. "You know, you're right! I can't believe I sounded like that."

"It's the TV conditioning. You're forgiven. Actually, I was thinking more in the line of somewhere in downtown, well, where downtown use to be."

"But there are no vantage points there."

"Sure there are!" Jim quickly defended his selection. "Just think, should they ever decide to rebuild Atlanta again, that property will be worth a fortune. We'll be millionaires. No. Billionaires!"

"Would you get serious!"

"Okay. Okay. Just couldn't help myself. But why Stone Mountain? As you said, it is twenty miles away."

"We can use it to periodically scout the countryside. You can see for miles from the top. It would be a place we could never loose sight of, should we ever be out and can't find the camp. As last resort, climb a very tall tree and look around. Maybe it will point you in the way to go to get home."

"Good point! Good point! But how are we going to get all this stuff there? You sure in hell can't hail a cab?"

"We'd have to make a few trips and carry everything."

"A FEW TRIPS!" Jim yelled. "I could only carry one box at a time. It'll take forever!"

"Wrong." Warren calmed Jim down. "I'll make two drag litters to carry stuff. You know, like the Indians did, and the horses pulled them."

"Oh yeah. The two sticks in the 'V' shape, with a bunch across them to hold the stuff."

"You're thinking now. See. I told you, you knew more than you thought you did."

"How long do you think it'll take to get there?"

"Well." He thought for a moment. "We can probably go, about a mile a day."

"TWENTY DAYS! A MONTH! Shit! I sure hope we can carry a lot in the first load. How about if we move half the stuff for a while, then come get the rest of the stuff and move it to the spot where we left off, etcetera, etcetera."

"Oh! I see what you're trying to say. You want us to move a little at a time over short distances."

"Yeah! That's what I meant."

"I'm afraid it'll take too long to do it that way."

"That's true." Jim agreed. "Especially with winter coming on. There wouldn't be enough time to build a shelter and do all the other things we need to do to get ready for winter." He paused for a moment thinking of the cold to come. "Let's get our asses in gear and get this stuff moving."

"We'll start out early tomorrow morning, but tonight we'll get everything packed and ready to go."

Warren got the hatchet and went looking for materials to construct the litters. He finally came across a stand of bamboo. Cutting four pieces, about two inches in diameter, he made them into eight foot lengths. Some smaller pieces he used to make the cross members and yokes.

He took one of the fifty foot lengths of nylon rope and tied the members of one litter together. He ran the rope continuously to prevent cutting it. He did the same with the other litter. He knew the two lengths of rope were too valuable to cut.

Jim tried one of the litters out, by getting into the small end, then holding it around his waist.

"Okay, now for the real test!" Warren picked up several items and put them on the litter Jim was holding. "How's that?"

Jim leaned forward and pulled. "Not too bad. I think I can carry more. Put a little more on."

Warren added a few more items.

"Some more!" Jim instructed.

Warren put more on the litter. He was afraid Jim would be unable to pull the load or would tire quickly.

Jim leaned forward and pulled. "I think that's about it. We do have some hills to go over."

Warren was surprised Jim could move what he had put on the litter. If Jim could carry that load, he would be able to carry nearly all the rest. They would only have to leave a few items behind. These could be picked up at a later date. "Well, we won't be able to get all of it, and we'll have to leave some stuff here, until next time." He knew Jim would have to realize that much of the things he brought would have to stay behind.

"I know we have to take the essentials, so I guess we'll have to leave most of my stuff here." He said it, not wanting to, but knowing he had to. "I'll repack and put it all in plastic bags to keep dry."

Warren walked over and put his left hand on Jim's right shoulder and patted him a few times. He could sense Jim's sadness in his face, at the thought of leaving his silver and china behind. "Don't worry." He said softly. "I promise, we'll come back for it real soon. But for now, we'll move it to high ground and cover it with one of the deflated rafts. That'll help protect it from the weather."

Jim smiled. "Thanks Warren."

Warren deflated the rafts, rolled the first one tightly, then put it on his litter. Jim repacked the silver, china, candelabrum, and other items from his notorious five boxes. He placed all the items back into the cardboard boxes and plastic bags. He also wrapped his class ring in a napkin and placed it in the box with the china. It would prevent him from losing it. Little did he realize, but it would not be back on his finger again for a very long time. He and Warren moved the boxes to a higher location, and covered them with the deflated second raft. They used several large rocks to hold the raft tight against the ground.

Jim stood for a few moments looking at the covered boxes. It was like someone standing at a gravesite.

"I promise we'll be back real soon." Warren reassured.

They returned and began to load the other items on the litters. All foodstuffs, cooler, shotgun, liquor, ammo, air pump and the like, Warren put on his litter and covered it with the first tarp. He was going to carry the rifle and machete. The folded tent, the deflated raft and air mattresses, sleeping bags and the rest of their clothes, he placed on Jim's and covered it with the second tarp. Finally, all was secure. This would protect everything in case of bad weather. From this time until they arrived at Stone Mountain, they would sleep in their sleeping bags without a tent. There would be no time to set it up every night.

As night arrived, it was time to turn in. Jim fixed the last of the bacon and eggs for dinner. As they sat and drank their coffee, they puffed on a cigarette.

"Only one carton left. We'll have to make them last. When they're gone, there's no more." Jim puffed the last few draws and crushed out the butt.

As they got into their sleeping bags, they both lay thinking of their situation and prospects for the future.

Jim thought of possible difficulties ahead and how different life was going to be. Warren thought of this wife and family. An inner sad feeling told him he would never see them again. One comforting thought came to his mind. He knew that with the large insurance policy he had taken out on himself, Linda and his children would be set financially.

Silence and darkness surrounded the camp. They were finally asleep.

CHAPTER XII

When the sun came up, it was another clear but crisp day. Jim fixed another pot of coffee. This time it was not a full pot, and not as much coffee. Maybe he could stretch out the last of it. He even reused the previous night's grounds. They munched a few granola bars and an apple. After the fire was out, it was time to start. Jim put the grill and the coffeepot under the tarp of his litter and made sure all was secure. Warren grabbed the machete and slung his rifle over his shoulder. He would lead the way. Jim took one last look at the pile covered with the second raft. Then they were off.

Checking the compass, they started due east. They would turn further south; after they crossed the high ridge Warren saw when he first traveled to the east. As Jim pulled along behind, he thought of how nice it would be to have a set of wheels on the litter.

After an hour, they stopped to rest. Warren continually looked for the easiest route through the woods. As they got away from the river, the forest grew high above them and the undergrowth was sparse. This made it somewhat easier to maneuver. Warren tried to avoid large outcroppings of rock, for fear they might make the travel more difficult. It would be hard enough ahead. They would have to cross several creeks and streams, as well as the high ridge between them and Stone Mountain. The ridge was not far away. Warren was rather glad it would be crossed early in the trip. This would put a difficult obstacle behind them early.

They'd been traveling for some time when Warren stopped. "Is it doing okay?" He turned to Jim.

"You sort of get used to it after a while. 'My kingdom! My kingdom for a horse!'" Jim yelled.

"You and me both!" Warren laughed and pulled out the cigarettes. He continued to survey the surroundings. It was still strange to him that the trees and bushes looked as though they were beginning to bud out. Also, small patches of low growing vine plants had evidence of small flowers. It was very confusing and didn't make sense.

After their short break to smoke their cigarette, they mustered up to start again.

"Warren, let's keep going as long as we can this time."

"Okay! But we have to rest and be alert. We can't tire too much in case of an emergency." Warren was pleased the going had not been as hard as he had imagined. They were making good progress, even if it seemed to be slow.

Jim was aware of the sounds of birds high in the trees. They had been there all the time. He realized he had just taken their sound for granted. It was expected to hear birds in the wild and they should be there. But now, he actually listened to the sound.

Warren periodically checked the compass to make sure they were heading in the right direction. He knew that as afternoon approached, they could practically follow the setting sun, if they could see it through the trees. "Be sure you observe the surroundings. We're going to have to be familiar with it for the future. It'll give us some relation as to where we are versus where we want to go."

Easy enough for Warren to say, but Jim thought of the old saying: 'You can't see the forest for the trees'. It was true. Every tree looked similar. Of course, he could see the difference in the deciduous and the evergreens. The rock outcroppings were not much help. There were no significant and distinct oddities that would make you necessarily remember them.

As they continued on, the terrain rose and fell with each hill and valley. The hills seemed to get higher and the valleys, shallower.

They were heading for the ridgeline.

As late afternoon arrived, Warren decided it was time to make camp. He wanted to do a bit of hunting before dark and catch them something to eat. He put the rifle on his litter and picked up the shotgun. Jim would stay, start the fire and prepare a spot for the night.

"Here's some toilet paper in case you might need some more." He handed Warren some neatly folded sheets. "Be very frugal. We can't run down to the nearest Publix and get more."

Warren headed directly east to investigate the terrain ahead. He was gone about and hour and a half, when he came to the top of the ridge. He was surprised they had come so far that day. He had been marking trees along the route for them to follow the next day. Now, at the top of the ridge, he thought he might investigate their location. He found a tall evergreen and began to climb. After a while, his head poked above the treetops and he could see all around. Stone Mountain was to the southeast. They were right on track. He looked in all directions to see if he saw any signs of other inhabitants. There appeared to be nothing except for the sign of smoke from Jim's fire in the west.

On his way back, he spotted several squirrel-like animals that would make good eating. He hated to use the shells, but he knew he had no choice. In the future, he would build traps and maybe make a bow and arrows.

Jim heard the muffled sound of several shotgun bursts somewhere to the distant east. He smiled. Warren had something for dinner. He had prepared the fire and spread out the sleeping bags nearby.

About an hour later, Warren returned to camp with three dead creatures. Jim was glad to see Warren had already cleaned them. "I found a small creek just ahead and cleaned them there. They should be ready to roast. I have the skins, too. We might be able to use them down the road."

Jim took the three animals and spread them on the grill over the hot coals. He had done some searching himself and found several fungi growing on a nearby rotting log. They were saving the last of the fresh potatoes and tomatoes from the garden they robbed over a week earlier. Hopefully these might be used as seed in the spring. He had also saved the apple cores with the seeds. There was no guarantee they would grow, but they had to try.

The canned goods they were keeping for emergency situations only, during the upcoming winter. These would keep almost indefinitely, as long as they were taken care of.

"Meat and mushrooms! Maybe it'll taste like chicken. Well that's not too bad. Could be worse."

"That's right. It could be nothing!" Jim replied. "So. Let's hear it for the mighty hunter!"

Finally, night closed in on the camp. Tomorrow would be another tough day of travel. They turned in early. As they lay there, they quietly talked over a few points.

"By the way, I only used a few of the toilet paper sheets. The rest are in my coat pocket."

"Good! And how are the *fumars* doing?"

"I smoked four today, and you had only two. That leaves us with nine packs and four cigarettes."

"Not bad. Not bad at all."

They could see the clear night sky through the treetops. The stars were bright. Jim couldn't remember when he had seen them so bright.

CHAPTER XIII

It was fourteen days later and late afternoon, when they arrived near the western base of Stone Mountain. The entire trip had been rather uneventful, except for one major obstacle. They had to cross one stream that had a rocky bottom. It was about four miles to the west of the mountain. It was necessary to unload the litters and put everything in the raft to get across. It took a few trips to do it. They would put some things in the raft and Warren would row it across and unload it, then row back. They reloaded the raft with the rest of the items and Warren repeated the trip. Lastly, he came back to pick up Jim and bring him across. Jim didn't care. It prevented him from having to get in the cold water.

It had finally become evident that in this time and place, winter was not approaching. It was spring. The deciduous trees were beginning to leaf out, and the weather was beginning to warm.

"Well we finally got here! I can hardly believe it." Jim was relieved. "When we establish permanent camp, I want to go back and get the rest of the stuff."

"Don't worry! We will, but we really need to get ourselves set up first. We don't know all that might be out there. Tonight we'll make temporary camp. Tomorrow we'll explore the area around the base of the mountain, and choose a permanent sight."

"I'm exhausted." Jim complained. "I don't even think I could eat."

"Let's just get some rest and tomorrow we'll get an early start." Warren agreed, as he, too, was quite tired.

Jim rolled out the sleeping bags as Warren started the fire. Warren was surprised he wasn't hungry, especially since they hadn't eaten since the previous night. He lay there contemplating their situation, just as he'd done on many of the previous evenings. He still couldn't put the puzzle together. It definitely was obvious they were in the right place, but the time was not easy to establish. They left in early fall and here it was early spring. They left a time when there was a city, to come to a time when it did not exist. This continued the question, whether it was the past or the future. Then there was the question of the sun rising in the west.

Suddenly Warren's mind flashed. "Quick! Get up! Get the binoculars! We've got to hurry before it gets dark! One question will be answered in about thirty minutes."

They both hurriedly put on their clothes and coats. Warren grabbed the shotgun and machete, and started to the northeast. "Grab the flashlight in case it gets dark before we get back."

"Okay!" Jim yelled, as he quickly tied his shoes and grabbed the binoculars and flashlight. He ran to catch Warren.

In about thirty minutes, they had moved northeastward, along the northern side of the large granite mass that formed the mountain. They had come upon several large open areas, where outcroppings of stone slabs prevented the trees from growing. Jim thought these to be great areas to set up a permanent campsite. Soon they came to a large open area, just over a thousand feet from the northern base of the mountain.

"Quick, give me the binoculars!" Warren grabbed them and ran north, to the far side of the open space. Jim watched and wondered what this was all about. He watched Warren quickly spin around and raise the binoculars to his eyes. They quickly moved up and down and sideways. Then Warren pulled them away, moved his head as before, then repeated the process with the binoculars.

"Of course!" Jim yelled. "I understand!" He ran to the north side of the area and turned around to look.

"Nothing." Warren uttered. "Not a single chip is gone."

Jim looked up with Warren, scanning the north face of the monolith before them. It was quite smooth. There wasn't the slightest evidence of the monumental Confederate Memorial carving they expected to see. There wasn't any evidence the sculpture had ever been started.

Warren continued to scrutinize the surface of the rock face. "If the carving had been done and worn away, due to time and weather, the face would still wear unevenly, even after thousands of years."

"You mean, even after a million years, if not longer. It would take eons to wear away something that size." Jim thought of the huge, three thousand year old Colossus of Memnon and the Sphinx. They still stood with their features visible, even after their great span of existence through wind, rain and weather.

"Yeah, but my point is, that the surface across the entire face is in its natural state. That means, they haven't done it yet. We have to be somewhere in the past."

To Jim, it was amazing how they both were elated to have this additional piece of the puzzle in place. They weren't any better off, and it sure didn't change their situation, but he knew Warren was quite pleased. Knowing that Warren was pleased, gave him a sense of reassurance and hope.

As the light began to fade, they started back to camp. Tomorrow they would do some considerable exploring.

Warren continued to ponder the pieces of their puzzle. He still couldn't figure out why they couldn't return to their own time. He knew approximately where the door in time was located, but the key escaped him. Reversing their direction through the opening was the only logical solution to getting back. This they had tried, and could not get through. Maybe, in time, he would be able to figure it out. But for the present, he knew it was paramount to get organized, so they would be able to survive. With that done, he could work more on finding the key.

CHAPTER XIV

Jim woke to a bright sunny day. He sat up in his sleeping bag. His eyes scanned the area, noticing Warren was not there. He's probably out catching something to eat. The air was crisp, but not as cold as it had been. Many of the surrounding trees and bushes were spotted with the bright yellow-green of small new leaves. A lot of the trees and undergrowth in the area were small and stunted. He was sure it was because of the many large areas of surface stone. There just wasn't enough soil to keep them healthy and allow them to grow to a great height.

He got out of the sleeping bag and dressed, then began to look for additional wood for the fire. The hatchet came in handy to cut larger limbs. Soon the fire was crackling and popping.

Jim checked the supply of food. There was nothing but canned goods and the remaining vegetables and apples he had saved. "Well I see the tomatoes have gone to meet Jesus." One of the tomatoes squished in his hand. He hoped the seeds from it would grow. Maybe if I lay them out on a rock to dry. He took the very ripe tomatoes and mashed the seeds out over the surface of one of the nearby rocks. He placed several small twigs and stones around them to keep the birds away, then continued to ponder what they would eat.

Soon Warren returned to camp. He'd caught some small animal, and already dressed it. "Jim! Take the skin and lay it out over a rock somewhere to dry." He then stopped and sniffed the air. "Do I smell coffee?" He glanced at the fire.

"That's the last of it." Jim sighed.

"But you said it was gone over a week ago."

"I lied! So sue me!" Jim laughed. "I saved some and tried to keep it as long as possible. I was afraid it would go bad if we kept it any longer. That would be a waste. By the way, there's a small creek just south of here. I found it when I went to get some wood. Got water for the coffee there. It looked clean enough. I mean. We have taken water out of the Chattahoochee. What can I say?"

Warren looked at Jim and smiled. "Well, if you can hoard, so can I." He reached into his coat pocket. "I wasn't sure how much longer I'd be able to keep them, but this seems as good a time as any, especially with the last pot of coffee." He pulled from his pocket the last pack of cigarettes. There were ten left in it.

Jim's eyes opened wide. "You SHIT! You said they were gone, too!" He yelled. "Give me one or I'll break your leg three times below the knee-cap!"

"Now, that wasn't nice." Warren looked off into space with a questioned look on his face, then began again in a calm voice. "I think I remember a word. You know. The word that has that special meaning." He lowered his head and snapped his fingers, as if trying to remember something of extreme importance. "You know. It's that word…" He began to smile.

Jim's eyes rolled back as if with agony and he gave a huge sigh. There was a long pause, then with deliberation, he uttered in a very pronounced, straightforward manner. "PLEASE. May I have a cigarette?"

"Well I'll be! He does know 'the word' after all." He extended the pack toward Jim and they both laughed loudly.

Jim quickly poured two cups of coffee, then put the cleaned carcass on the grill. They sat and slowly sipped and smoked. Neither uttered a word and they savored the moment.

"That leaves eight cigarettes to go." Warren reminded, and put them back in his pocket.

As Jim finished his coffee, he watched the meat as it sizzled on the grill. Soon it was ready, and they devoured it in no time. He'd forgotten how hungry he was. He set the coffeepot off the grill to prevent it from burning. They would have some coffee for later. "Guess we should get moving and find a spot to call 'square one'."

"You're right." Warren replied. "And time's a wasting."

"Should I take anything?"

"No. I'll carry the gun and machete. That's all we'll really need."

"I think I'll take the camera case, in case we find some nice morsel to bring home to eat."

Soon they were off. They started to the northeast. This would take them around the north side of the mountain. For most of the morning, they walked, then would periodically scout out around an area to check on local conditions.

Jim was quite surprised at the many open areas about the base of the mountain. The large slabs of rock outcroppings had made the growth of vegetation quite minimal.

By mid-afternoon, they were on the southwestern side. Many areas looked to be good spots for a permanent camp. Warren indicated that so far, the best site had been on the southeastern side. This location provided a stream nearby and it would be protected from the north wind. He was still hoping for something better to come up. If they could find a spot on the southwestern side they would get the morning sun, since the sun was now rising in the west, and it should not be so hot in the afternoon during warm weather.

Then it happened. The spot Warren thought would never occur. A large slab of rock jutted out from the base of the mountain.

It was about ten feet high and virtually flat on the top. A lazy stream meandered about the base of the rock. The entire rock was about ten feet from the rising stone wall of the mountain face. The southern end was separated from the high bank, some twelve feet away, by the creek. "I don't believe it! This is the perfect spot! It's high enough from the stream in case of flood, and it's defendable in case of attack."

"Attack! What the fuck do you mean 'attack'?"

"From wild animals, or whatever. See! The stream almost acts like a moat around almost three-quarters of the rock. We really need to get up there and look at it."

"Well SHIT! If you'd really told me what you were looking for, I could have told you this was here."

"What?" Warren looked at Jim.

"Well, this morning when I went to get some wood for the fire, this is the stream where I got the water. Campsite's only some fifteen or twenty minutes that way." Jim pointed in a northwesterly direction.

"Oh well." Warren shook his head. "We at least know what's around the mountain anyway. Come on, let's get up there and look this thing over. I didn't come this way this morning when I was hunting or I'd have seen it myself."

They made their way between the foot of the mountain and the stream to the south. With some difficulty, they finally worked their way to the top of the slab.

Warren was pleased. The surface was almost flat and fairly smooth. He stood and looked over the surface. The top stretched some forty feet to the south, and was about thirty feet wide in the middle. He began to plan and design out loud. "We could put a hut at the north end. The mountain will protect against the north winds, and we'll have the morning sun and southern exposure."

Then he turned to Jim. "Let's get the stuff and get moving. This will be home for a while."

"Home?" Jim uttered in a questioning voice, then continued in a sarcastic manner. "Damn! And I was hoping for something with columns, three bedrooms, and two and a half baths."

"You asshole!"

Jim then walked to the southern edge of the rock and looked down to the stream below. "I could dam up the stream over there." He pointed southeast. "And make a shallow lake around the entire rock. Then we'd really have a moat around our castle."

"Sounds good to me. We'll be able to ice skate in the winter." Warren chuckled.

Within the next few hours, they had pulled the litters to the site. Jim was very careful with the pot of coffee. He carried it as if it was gold. He had collected the seeds that were drying on the rock, along with Warren's animal skin.

With the ropes, Warren hoisted everything to the top of the rock, then piled it in the center. "We'll leave everything up here to keep it safe. We can get it if we need it." He used both tarpaulins to cover everything and put rocks on the corners to hold them in place.

As they finished getting everything to the site, they heard low rumblings way to the west. It sounded like they would get an evening thunderstorm. As time passed, the rumblings grew louder.

Suddenly, a roll of thunder came like the sound of multiple cannon fire. Jim waved his arms in the air and yelled out. "'Miss Scarlet! Miss Scarlet! The Yankees is coming! The Yankees is coming!'"

Warren just looked at Jim and said nothing. He knew it would do no good. Anyway, he thought it was kind of funny, at that moment.

"I think we're in for one tonight." Warren looked to the west and skyward. "Better make sure all is secure. This is going to be our first major storm, and I'm not sure what we're in for. We'll have to set up the tent down there until we can get things more organized up here." He pointed to a spot to the east of the rock slab, between the mountain base and the shallow creek. "Let's hurry up, or we might get drenched."

The light of day finally disappeared in the east, with the coming storm. The mountain concealed the event, as its shadow darkened the area. The rumblings of thunder in the west grew louder. Soon streaks of lightning flashed through the evening sky.

A quick gust of wind blew through the campsite, followed by a calming, gentle rain. Warren thought how glad he was it wasn't a tyrannical storm. The sound of the rain on the canvas tent brought a relaxed atmosphere. The rumblings of thunder were almost a tranquilizing factor. There were no loud bangs or cracks, just the rumbles muffled by the gentle falling rain.

As they lay there in their sleeping bags in the dark, Warren broke nature's display as he turned to Jim. "You okay?"

"Yeah. I'm fine."

There was a long period before Jim spoke again. "Warren? You think we'll ever see home again?"

"I don't know. I really don't know. But don't worry, I'm working on it."

The gentle rain continued, and soon they were asleep.

CHAPTER XV

The rain lasted all night and into the morning. The soothing sound effect made getting up difficult. But then, who really wanted to get out in the rain. The air was still cool. Warren knew he had to go out and hunt something for them to eat. It would be easy to eat what they had saved, but it was imperative they not go into their supplies. "Okay Jim. Get your ass out of bed. You will have to try your hand at fishing today, while I go hunting."

Jim reluctantly got up. He dreaded the thought of getting wet and cold, but after all, this was another time and place. He knew he was going to have to get accustomed to doing things differently. His whole life's routine was going to have to change. Their survival might depend on it.

As they dressed, Jim commented. "Think I'm going to have to wash our clothes in the creek. If they get any dirtier, they'll be able to stand up on their own."

Warren noticed the rain seemed to taper off. By the time they stepped from the tent, it had stopped, but the air was heavy with moisture. To Jim, it felt as if he were standing in a cloud. He could see the mist particles fluttering through the air.

"This reminds me of the morning we got lost." Jim looked into the sky. "You think the fish will bite in weather like this?"

Warren pulled out his watch. "It's eight thirty-three. I'll be back in a few hours." He headed south along the stream with his gun, machete, and hunting knife.

Warren had been gone for about thirty minutes, when Jim caught his first fish. He was surprised at its size, since the stream was not large. How could such a big fish live in such a little creek? He also noticed the stream hadn't flooded during the rain. He recalled the beautiful virgin forest they had passed through, coming to the mountain. His question was answered. Man had not destroyed the natural absorbing power of the forest, making the run off to the creeks and streams a gradual one.

After a short while, he caught another fish. "We shouldn't be greedy." He left the two fish on the catch line in the water, and went back to the tent. The clouds began to lift, so he decided to explore the area.

He got the compass and knife from the tackle box, then started walking in an easterly direction, along the stream. After a while, he saw a rock in the stream and thought he'd cross over. Further south of the stream, he came across several open areas. The edges of the forest, around these areas, were thick with undergrowth, but as he walked further into the forest, the undergrowth became less and less dense.

The forest floor was open, covered with dead leaves and needles from the tree limbs above. The large tree trunks were like huge columns, holding up a roof of cloudy mist. Occasionally, there were outcroppings of stone, as well as clumps of bushes. It was a beautiful sight. No trash or beer cans blemished the view. It was pure, unadulterated, undisturbed nature.

After a while, he started back to camp. On the way, he came across a large amount of fungi, growing and almost covering a large dead log. Stopping, he picked some. This was an edible variety. He broke a piece open to check the interior color and structural make-up. "Looks fine to me." He stuffed his pockets with the gray-white parasite.

As he got nearer the campsite, he was still south of the stream. The bank, on the south side, was about six feet higher than the surface of the water. This was a difference of four feet to the level of the rock. The north bank of the creek was virtually at water level, then gently sloping up toward the base of the mountain. This is where the tent was located. Jim bent down and checked the ground. The thick covering of mulch was rich and workable. It reminded him of the wonderful consistency of the dirt in the P.B.S. TV gardening programs. It always amazed him how workable the dirt was on those programs. It was absolutely disgusting. No lumps, no rocks, just rich, dark soil that was simple as pie to dig in. "Maybe the seeds will grow here." He thought out loud, and looked around. If we cut down a few trees and bushes there would be more sun.

Just then, he saw Warren returning from the east. "Warren! Over here!" He waved his right hand in the air. "I think I've found a spot for the garden. Just need to take out a few trees."

"Sounds good." Warren replied. "You can start immediately. We'll need wood for building as well as for the fire." He stopped and then yelled. "How the hell did you get over there, without getting wet? You had to cross on that rock down stream."

"That's right, sweetie!"

"Well, I've seen several traces of wildlife. I even saw a few that look like deer. Couldn't get one because I didn't have the right shells."

It was still early afternoon and the sky began to clear. Warren waited for Jim to run downstream and cross back over. "If you're going to put a garden over there, we'll need a bridge to get there."

"I thought if we dammed up the river down there." Jim pointed, as he did the previous day. "We'd have our own lake, well, pond, and we could fish off the rock."

"Before we do that, we need to clear your garden spot so you can get your tomato seeds growing, and see if the potatoes will sprout. Make a place for the apple seeds, too. Just in case they do grow. Then we've got to get the rock habitable and accessible. We can use rocks and log pieces to build steps against the face of the mountain and up to the rock surface. I think it would be rather precarious though."

"That might be a good idea. But you're right. It would not be very safe and could crumble." Warren looked up at the ten foot space between the rock and the mountain. He stroked his beard and mustache, now about half an inch long. The dark hair blended with that on his head. "I think we can build a bridge from the rock to the southern bank. That would be much safer and sturdier. About a mile southeast of here, I saw a huge stand of bamboo. We could use a lot of it for building. It would be much easier to cut and carry than wooden logs. We can also use it for protection spikes."

Jim finally questioned the emphasis on protection. "What's this constant reference to protection? Is there something you're not telling me?"

"I've not seen any sign of humans, but there's a segment of the animal population that we have to watch out for. On my hunting trip last week, I saw signs of wild boar, and we can expect a bear or cat from the mountains north of here."

"You mean I was out there meandering through the woods, like 'Little Red Riding Hood', and there are lots of 'Big Bad Wolves' out there?"

"Oh yes. I forgot the wolves. They're out there, too." Warren replied. "I doubt if they would stalk us right now, especially since they've not seen anything like us before. They probably see us as a curiosity and don't know if we're a threat or not. I'm sure there have been lots of eyes beyond our campfires." Warren paused. "Now, do you see why I've not said anything? You'd have been unbearable to live with. Every noise would have been your *Beast of Hollow Mountain* or that…*Caltiki* thing."

"Well, when can we move to the rock?"

"When we get it ready." Warren answered. "And not until. So

keep the fire up. And should it rain, we'll have to protect it. When we build the hut, on the rock, we'll put in a fireplace."

"Will there be room for a crystal chandelier?" Jim laughed.

Warren ignored the comment completely. "Let's get the fire started and we can heat up the last of the coffee and have a cigarette."

By late afternoon, Jim had found enough wood that wasn't too wet, so he could start the fire. Additional wood was added carefully to prevent extinguishing the coals. The last of the coffee was poured, and they both lit a cigarette.

Warren cleaned the fish. Jim powdered them with flour, then put them in the frying pan. He wasn't sure how they would cook without a little oil. No matter, he knew they would be eaten. He also cooked up some of the fungi he'd found that day. "How gross!" He thought out loud. "Will my stomach survive this punishment?" He then thought of the wonderful seven course meal he had eaten years earlier, at that fantastic restaurant in New Orleans. "Oh, to be there again." He sighed.

"What?" Warren questioned.

"I was just thinking about a terrific restaurant I once went to in New Orleans."

"Don't tell me. I don't want to hear it." Warren had also been thinking of their diet and what to do about it. There wasn't much he could do about that problem.

"Tomorrow we'll start clearing the area across the stream for your garden spot. With the hatchet it's going to take a while. Why don't you build a raised bed? You can start your seeds there, then transfer them later to the garden."

"That's a good idea. I'll start preparation tomorrow." Jim felt like he was actually going to be of significant help.

It was just about time to call it. Night was approaching, and the only light was that of the fire.

Warren got out his guitar and Jim, his recorder. They both sang a few songs and played a few tunes before going to sleep.

Tomorrow would be the beginning of their new life at their new home site. They would have to do many things to keep themselves from extinction. Food was one major problem. Their diet had changed significantly from what they were accustomed. Then there was the question of their health. There was no way they could tolerate a major illness. No doctor or drug store was around the corner. It would be an extreme adjustment. Would they be able to cope with such radical changes?

CHAPTER XVI

Over the next two weeks, much was accomplished. Jim made a rectangular area, with small rocks, and filled it with topsoil. He took the ashes from the fire, adding them to the soil for nourishment. He had heard that burned organic matter was supposed to be good for helping things grow. In the foot deep soil, Jim planted the tomato seeds, potato pieces, and the apple seeds. Also, some of the small bulbs of the wild onions he had pulled the week before. It would be interesting to see if any of them would grow.

Warren had been clearing the area south of the creek. He was right. Even with the hatchet and machete, it was slow going. His first step was to find trees that were about a foot in diameter. Larger ones would be almost impossible to move, even when rolled on short log sections. He could see that most of the pine type trees were about the right size, but none were the towering giants they had witnessed during their previous outings. Even the deciduous trees were fewer and smaller.

Then it became obvious. The remains of a few large stumps were sticking a foot or less above the ground. One slash of the hatchet sent pieces of black char into the air. The previous giants had succumbed to the worse enemy of the forest. "I'll bet it was a hot one to have consumed such massive trees." He thought out loud. "Nature can sometimes be so cruel."

He had cut almost twenty trees during the two week period. The pines were almost forty to fifty feet high. Each tree would give them at least three ten foot sections. These would be used for wall construction of the hut. He was sure he could pick some thirty nice logs from the bunch to build the hut. The rest could be used for various projects that might come up.

Jim began to collect rocks, piling them up so they could later be moved to the top of the slab. He had mainly been clearing the area where he knew his lake would develop. He didn't want them cluttering the bottom.

Warren finally found a tree he'd been seeking to make a bow. Jim wasn't sure what kind it was, but Warren had shaved one of the straight sections and had it drying in the sun. He told Jim they had to conserve their ammunition and a bow would be very beneficial. In time, he would make one for Jim and teach him how to use it. He would make some temporary arrows using the bamboo. Jim knew they would be saving feathers from now on, to apply to Warren's arrows.

Jim was rather pleased that he knew how to make stone arrow tips. Being raised in Virginia, he had lived on a farm where there once was an Indian village. He could go out, during tilling time, and find old arrowheads by the box full. It was especially good hunting after a rain. He was familiar with the process the Indians used. He even tried it once, but quit before he ever accomplished a completed tip. It took so long. He did get an appreciation for the Indian's tenacity. How he wished he had a box of those tips now. Yes. He knew he would have to keep an eye out for the right kind of rocks to make the tips. It would be a continuous search from then on.

The weather during the two weeks had been very favorable. Jim had caught fish from the creek for most of their meals. Warren had gone hunting a few times and had killed one small deer, then cut most of the meat into strips and had them drying in the sun. Jim thought there had to be a better way. Warren had the skin and bones drying, too.

It was beginning to look like a graveyard someone dug up. Jim knew it was important to keep everything. It was not a time to throw things away. Even the empty beer and food cans would become useful items somewhere down the road.

The trees had put on a display of early green. Many began to flower. Several of the forest plants began to peek through the ground. Jim had seen early evidence of fern in large clumps around the creek banks. There were great numbers of large flowering bushes. It would not be much longer before they would be in bloom. There were many fir and spruce type trees in the forest. Their graceful limbs came right to the ground: instant living Christmas trees.

Then he thought of snow and the cold. His mind began to panic thinking of no food and that they could starve or freeze to death. I can't think about that now, and anyway, Warren said we'd be just fine. He quickly dismissed the terror from his mind.

They had worked hard and long. Jim had been keeping a count of their days, since he had an idea there was trouble. He'd cut thirty-seven notches on a stick he'd been keeping. On this day they got up early.

"Okay Warren. Today your beard and mustache get trimmed." Jim rooted in one of the boxes and pulled out the small pair of scissors and a comb he'd brought. "You sit right down here." He pointed at one of the piles of rocks he'd made during his collecting.

Warren obeyed; knowing there'd be no end to it if he didn't.

Jim began to clip. "We WILL remain civilized." He stressed emphatically. "I just hope you don't mind trimming mine."

"I'll try, but don't blame me if I botch it."

After some fifteen minutes, he had clipped Warren's dark beard so it was about a quarter of an inch in length. As time went on, Jim would maintain Warren's beard at around three-quarters of an inch long. "The hair's next, but not today." He cut the hair under the chin and on the neck as short as he possibly could. When Jim was done, it was his turn.

Warren began to cut away. He kept making moans with every cut.

"It can't be all that bad." Jim replied.

"Well, a hairstylist I'm not, so don't blame me." After twenty minutes, Warren stood back. "That's not too bad, not great, but not bad!"

Jim took his hand and felt his beard and under his chin. "Feels okay. Thanks." He took the scissors and comb, and returned them to the box.

"Well, today is going to be a rest day." Warren declared. "What do you want to do on this fine morning?"

The air was warmer. Coats had not been needed, during the day, for the last week. During most of the time, Warren had to remove his shirt since he got so warm cutting the trees. Jim, being quite cold natured, had not been so courageous.

"There's been something I've wanted to do since we got here." Jim blurted out. "I'd love to get in the creek and take a bath. These damn washes we've been doing with water heated in the pot, is for the birds."

"Water's still too cold." Warren commented.

"Yeah. I guess you're right. OK. I have another idea. I want to climb to the top of the mountain, and it's such a beautiful day." He paused, stood up, and stretched his left hand into the air, his right on his chest. Warren knew he was in for it. Jim broke into song. "'And on a clear day, you can see forever. On a clear day, you can see forever. On a clear day, you can see, forever, and ever, and ever, and ever, and ever.'" He paused. "I can never remember how many 'evers' there are. Anyway. 'And ever more.'"

"Spare me! We'll climb Stone Mountain." Warren could say no more.

Jim fried up some of Warren's dry deer meat. He couldn't think of eating it uncooked. It was like eating shoe leather, but it was food, and it filled the void.

Warren checked the camp before they left. He carried the machete and rifle. The gun would probably not be needed, but he wanted to be sure they had protection if it became necessary.

They walked to the west face of the mountain. This side was quite gradual in its slope and could be climbed much easier than any of the other sides. Warren made this observation during one of his several hunting trips.

As they made their ascent, they noticed the trees were getting smaller and less frequent. They grew only in the cracks and crevices, where some soil and water could feed the starving root systems. Jim thought how several of them would have made nice bonsais. Finally, Warren broke the silence. "Treat time." He pulled two cigarettes from his pocket along with the lighter.

"Now there's only four left after these." Jim sighed. "But you know, I'm trying not to think about them."

"Yeah, I know. I think I work harder by trying not to think about them."

They both laughed, then lit up. Jim coughed as he inhaled. He even got a bit dizzy. Warren inhaled. He, too, gave a cough, pulled the cigarette from his mouth, and looked at it. "God, I feel a bit dizzy." He puffed again. This time, it was better, but still not the same. "Is this what it's like not smoking for fourteen days? Maybe we need to quit!"

"Whether we want to or not, we'll have no choice soon." Jim commented. "It's funny though, I'm not enjoying it like I used to."

"I hate to admit it, but I feel the same." Warren agreed.

They both took a few more puffs, then crushed out the remains on a rock.

As they walked further, they rose higher in elevation. The horizon was becoming visible through open spaces in the sparse growing trees and underbrush.

"Instead of being the fish in the bowl, we'll be able to stand out of the bowl and look around." Warren commented as he continued onward and upward. "We'll really get a birds-eye view from the top."

"I can hardly wait!" Jim expressed. "You're the only one who's seen everything from tree-top level. Now it's my turn."

"And this will be one hell of a view, significantly above tree-top level." Warren added.

After about an hour and a half, they were halfway up the side. Warren started to stop for a look.

"Don't stop!" Jim yelled out. "We can't look until we get to the top."

"Okay! Okay!" Warren climbed on.

Soon it finally occurred to him that they were following a trail. It actually startled him. A trail they didn't make. He wanted to blurt out loud, but thought he would just calmly bring it to Jim's attention. He stopped short.

"I said we can't look until we get to the top. Now, don't cheat!" Jim yelled his game plan again.

"I'm not." Warren answered in a cool and calm manner. "But there's something I want you to notice, if you haven't already." Warren snickered to himself, knowing Jim hadn't realized the trail.

"Okay, what am I supposed to see?" He looked back from where they had come, to the sides, and then ahead. "I don't see anything."

"Look REAL hard and tell me what you see." Warren insisted.

Jim looked again and started to describe the surroundings. "Well, I see a few trees over there, some over there, some bushes over here, some rocks down there, some bushes by the trail up there, some sky above." He looked at Warren with that 'well, I haven't missed anything' expression.

"Look again, REAL HARD, and tell me what you see."

Jim started again and strained to see some real unusual things, proving he hadn't missed anything. "I see some trees over there. I think they are some sort of pine tree. I see some bushes over here, and they're getting leaves on them, and I see some nice, smooth rocks down over there by those trees, and there are a few bushes ahead by the trail, beginning to lea…" He stopped short and stared ahead. His entire face went through a multitude of expressions, his mind questioning the existence of the six foot wide path ahead. Then softly he began. "That's a path. How could I have missed it? I'm an artist and usually notice things. How could I have missed it?" He looked at Warren. "You didn't cut it either? Did you?" He looked hard at Warren. "You didn't cheat and come up here on one of your hunting trips, and not tell me, did you?"

"No. I swear I didn't."

Jim saw Warren was telling the truth. "Animal trail?"

"A six foot wide path? No. It's too regular and precise to be animal. Someone deliberately put this path here. I don't know how long we've been on the path or where we picked it up. It all of a sudden was just here."

"Let's get moving. I want to see where it goes." Jim began to run ahead.

Warren ran ahead, too. "Get behind me, since I've got the gun. You never know, there could be something ahead."

Both began to move quickly up the slope. Jim could hardly contain his curiosity. He kept trying to see ahead as well as watch the trail to prevent from tripping. Finally, they came to where the trees were non-existent. Only wind-blown shrubs and bushes, standing a few feet high, grew sparsely over the smooth rocky surface.

They still could not see the top, because of the curving slope. But slowly, something was there, coming into view. They would stop for a short moment trying to make out what was becoming visible. Soon, Warren stopped. "I don't believe it!"

Ahead of them was an opening eight feet wide in a stone wall constructed some eight feet high. Each stone in the wall was perfectly cut and placed. The surface was very smooth.

"People!" Jim blurted. "There are people! Maybe they know where we are and how to get back."

They both ran through the portal.

The wall was some three feet thick. The inside was as smooth as the outside. From inside, it was obvious the wall formed a solid ring around the entire top of the mountain. It looked to Jim to be about eighty feet in diameter, maybe a little more. There were strange markings and symbols on the walls. In the center area, there were several geometrically shaped stones and a tower some twenty-five feet high. A three foot wide, stone, stairway spiraled around the tower to the top.

"This can't be for real!" Warren exclaimed. "I'm surprised I couldn't make out this tower when I saw the mountain when I climbed the trees. Maybe I did and just didn't realize what I was seeing."

Jim had run to the spiral stair and started to the top of the tower. Finally, he peered over a stone wall at the top. "This is incredible!" He yelled. "I don't believe it! God! And the view is fantastic. You literally can see forever from up here. Hurry up, Warren! Get up here and look!"

Warren quickly climbed to the top. A four foot high stone wall surrounded the ten foot diameter top of the tower. He, too, was amazed at the view. The day was so clear, no haze, and the sky was a clear blue.

From the top, he looked down into the ring of stone. The floor of the ring was marked with many lines, circles, and shapes. All were very geometrically laid out. He thought they had either religious or astrological meanings, possibly both.

Jim pointed to the geometrical marks. "I'll bet this is someone's observatory. Maybe a sacred temple to the Moon God!"

Warren looked down and studied the markings. "I think you're right. Those look like star and planet positions." He then began to look at the glyphs on the inside of the wall. The symbols were not discernible, as they were much like Egyptian hieroglyphics, but there were many human figures shown in Greek-style togas, or nude. "You know, this really blows the mind. Now, I have no idea as to where we are in time. And all this makes it look like the Greeks discovered America long before Leif Erickson or Columbus. But what are the Greeks doing this far west? Why didn't it show up in history?"

"Maybe it was lost with all the knowledge when the library at Alexandria burned." Jim theorized.

"Maybe. Maybe so!" Warren continued to peruse the walls. "I can hardly believe this. But the big question is, where are they now?"

"Maybe they went back."

"That wouldn't make sense either. Why would someone take all the effort to construct this, observatory, then leave it?"

Jim had started down to the surface again. Warren was right behind him, as he wanted to look closer at the walls.

After an hour, they were still as puzzled as when they first arrived. Warren was now quite sure it was an observatory, but for what exact purpose evaded him.

He was amazed at the accuracy in the laying of the stones in the wall. The seams were virtually invisible.

"You know?" Jim started. "The last time I visited Stone Mountain, I came up here. There was some story about the remains of an ancient stone wall up here, and they had no idea where it came from. They pushed the rest of it off, as the rocks were a possible hazard to climbers and folks below. The stones of this wall must be those rocks. Something must have happened preventing maintenance of this thing and it just deteriorated, to an unrecognizable form."

"It would have taken thousands of years to erase this, if not a million." Warren commented, as he started analyzing Jim's story.

"Well how about a natural or physical catastrophe that would have disturbed the wall, like and earthquake. Let's take the Parthenon, for example. It stood in all its grace and beauty, until the seventeenth century, I think it was sixteen eighty-seven." He looked off into space as if searching for confirmation of his dates. "Can you believe it? From four thirty-two B.C. to sixteen eighty-seven A.D., over two thousand years it stood in prime condition, until the Turks blew it up during some stupid war. One of the greatest art works of mankind, the perfect example of classical Doric architecture, destroyed by war. It makes me sick."

Warren looked at Jim. "I have a funny feeling the Parthenon hasn't even been built yet."

Jim looked strangely at Warren.

"I've been thinking of what you've been saying, and from what I can figure, we are a long way back in time, and probably way before the Classical Greek Period."

"But what about the Greek figures on the wall?"

"I haven't figured that one out yet. It's another anachronism that just doesn't fit into the puzzle. Well, we know we're not over a million years back, because it's too cold. It probably would have been more tropical. The trees here are not typical of the tropics. Pines, firs, oaks and other such trees are of another, much younger time period."

"How about five hundred thousand years ago?" Jim questioned.

"No. I doubt it. From what I've seen of the terrain, and the heights of the local hills, as well as Stone Mountain, we're not too far back in geological time. Maybe twenty to thirty thousand years, if that."

"Well that sure does screw up the Greek period. Thirty thousand years is even before the great Ages of Egypt. And anyway, I doubt if something this sophisticated would erode away in thirty thousand years."

"This brings in your cataclysm theory. Something must have happened that made this a ruin." Warren looked around. "Maybe it WAS an earthquake!"

"It would have been one hell of one to level these walls." Jim said sarcastically. "But, you know. I can't remember exactly where I heard it, but it was about the Bravard Fault, just west of Atlanta." He looked to the west. "Well. Where Atlanta use to be." He chuckled. "But I heard that if that fault ever did a major shift, it would be about forty feet. And if that happened, every building in the city would be on the ground. Now. That kind of quake would really do some damage here. Yeah."

Warren stood up and looked around again. "Maybe we should get back to camp since it's getting late." He looked at his watch. It was eight after four. "There's a lot to think about."

They worked their way back down to the campsite. The confusing puzzle, as to the time period, really annoyed Warren. He knew they were somewhere in the past, but wasn't sure how far back.

Jim began to get ready to cook something for dinner. He was afraid it was going to be fish again. Oh well, it was better than nothing. Maybe tomorrow will be different. He grabbed up the fishing rod and walked to the creek. Warren joined him to keep him company, and in no time, they had four fair-sized fish.

The setting sun cast the shadow of the mountain over the campsite. Warren had cleaned the fish and gave them to Jim. As they cooked, Warren worked on his bow. With his hunting knife, he slowly shaped the wood, gradually tapering it from the middle to the ends. "This should be ready in about another week."

"I should make you a few arrows." Jim looked at Warren. "And if you lose one, I'll break your legs."

They finished their dinner and readied for bed.

"You know, it's really funny." Jim commented. "I remember when I used to stay up for the late shows. Going to bed this early was inconceivable. But I guess, when there's no light except for the fire, you have to go to bed."

"Yes. I know. We only have half a gallon left of the lantern fuel and I think it best we don't use it unless we really have to. So going to bed with the fading light is our only option. We need our rest, as we've got a full day ahead of us tomorrow." Warren replied. "I have to start moving those logs to the rock soon. That's going to take some time to do and I'm definitely going to need your help."

The darkness of night had already closed in and quiet came over the camp. Tomorrow would bring another period of hard work. It would also bring additional contemplation about their discovery on the top of Stone Mountain. Their thirty-seventh day in this strange time was over.

CHAPTER XVII

Jim woke to find Warren gone. He's probably out moving more of those damn logs. After dressing, he went outside the tent. Warren was nowhere in sight. This was of no concern, so he went to check the progress of his small garden.

The sun must have been up for about an hour. Jim thought of the visit three days before, to the mountaintop. It still had him wondering about the construction and the builders. He was sure Warren was contemplating the same thing. Where the hell is he? He looked down at the garden spot. With glee, he noticed the onions were taking hold. The green tops were crisp and new ones were developing. Well at least something's growing.

Suddenly, there was a loud voice from the east. "Happy Thanksgiving!" Jim looked up to see Warren holding a large feathered bird. It looked like a turkey.

"So that's where you've been!"

"Yeah, I got up before dawn to get us something for Thanksgiving."

"I guess it IS about that time." Jim had a look on his face, as if quickly calculating the time period. "All we need now is the sweet potatoes and cranberry sauce." He laughed. "Happy Thanksgiving!"

Spring was really in the air. The trees were putting out their first set of bright green leaves. The drab colors of the previously unseen winter were fading. Small spring flowers were popping out from rock crevices and from beneath the leaf mulch on the forest floor. The ferns were beginning to revive at the edge of the creek. Azalea-like flowers were showing color in their unopened buds.

Jim was glad to see the weather change. He knew it would be easier to face their situation in warmer weather.

Warren took the bird and disappeared down toward the creek. Jim was aware of the cleaning process to take place, and had no desire to observe it. He got the fire ready for the cooking. After a while, Warren returned with his prize. "I cut it up with my hunting knife. We can roast it on the fire."

"We'll wait until the coals get nice and hot." Warren set the cut pieces down on a rock near the fire, then added a few more pieces of wood to the fire, just to make sure. "Maybe if we build the ring of stones a bit higher."

"Oh, for an oven!" Jim moaned. "I'm going to have one, even if I have to build it myself."

"Don't worry, we'll build one for you when we get everything established up on the rock." Warren added.

They both began to add a few more stones around the top of the ring to make it higher. Jim strategically placed smaller stones to level the metal grill.

"In about thirty minutes, I can rearrange the coals." Warren placed a few twigs in the fire.

Jim pondered what they could have with the bird. He knew that the only things special were the canned goods, but he was afraid to open them. These needed to be conserved for the winter, in case of an emergency.

Soon the coals were ready. "What time is it Warren?"

Warren checked his watch. "Twelve fifteen!" He exclaimed, then placed his watch back in his pocket.

"We'll let it cook slow. Maybe dinner around four thirty to five o'clock. How does that sound?" Jim turned to Warren.

Warren shrugged his shoulders and gestured questioningly. "Sounds good to me. You're the cook!"

"Gee, thanks! Guess I know where I stand." Jim laughed. There was some moment's pause, then he continued on a completely different subject. "Do you think it'll take long to build the hut and the rest of the stuff on top of the rock?"

"Oh, maybe a month or so to build the hut, if we work real hard." Warren answered. "We might even have it finished by Christmas."

"Christmas, and you and Linda were going to Texas, and I was going home." Jim stopped with a sad look on his face.

Warren could see Jim's emotional wheels beginning to turn, and knew he had to put a brake on them. "Oh well. Guess we have to change the plans. Don't worry. We'll have a good Christmas. You wait and see!" He reached over and patted Jim on the right shoulder, with his left hand. Then he moved closer and put his left arm around Jim's neck, and with that hand, patted Jim's left shoulder. After a pause, he spoke slowly and deliberately. "We're going to be alright. Just don't you worry."

Jim put his right arm around Warren's back, and leaned a bit towards him. "Happy Thanksgiving, Warren. And I'd like to say, though I wouldn't wish it on anyone, if I had to be stuck out here with someone, I'd rather it be you than anyone." After a few seconds, Jim pulled away and walked towards the tent. "I'll be right back." Soon he emerged with the two tin cups in his hands. He handed one to Warren.

Warren looked in and smelled, then smiled. "Don't you think it's a bit early?"

"I won't tell if you don't." Jim replied, clinking his cup of Amaretto against Warren's cup of scotch.

"Happy Thanksgiving, Jim." Warren smiled.

"Same to you." Jim smiled back.

They spent most of the day doing light jobs, collecting more wood for the fire from the limbs of trees Warren had cut down. Many were rather dry. Jim had pulled the needles off the pines and put them in his garden. This was to keep the weeds from growing and hold the moisture.

After a while, they sat together by the fire, and discussed their game plans for moving the logs to the top of the rock, as well as the priorities in construction. Finally, they began to discuss their discovery atop Stone Mountain.

"Have you had any more thoughts on who might have built the observatory?" Jim asked.

"Hell no! And it's been bugging me for the last couple of days. I just don't know." Warren shook his head.

"I've been trying to place the time period, too." Jim stared at the fire, then threw in a few more twigs. "I think this area of the country was inhabited by the Indians that migrated from the northwest, after crossing the Bering Strait. I think that was some fifteen to twenty thousand years ago." He paused to correct his statement. "I mean, fifteen to twenty thousand years from the Twentieth Century, where we were, and since we've seen no evidence of an Indian culture, negating the top of Stone Mountain, of course, then that's about where we should be. Fifteen to twenty thousand years ago, uh, from where we were."

"Thank you Professor Stone for that eloquent commentary on the origins of the early Georgians." Warren gave a little laugh. "But it does sound reasonable to me. I'm sorry, but I can't let you just gloss over this 'top of Stone Mountain' thing. It sure as hell just didn't get there by magic." Warren threw a couple of twigs into the fire. "If we're fifteen thousand years into the past, that would explain the types of trees in the area. I've noticed a great number of evergreens typical of a more northern climate, than

Twentieth Century Atlanta. The climate here in the Atlanta area would probably have been similar to that of upstate New York, fifteen thousand years ago." He paused. "Yeah, that would make a lot of sense!"

"Upstate New York!" Jim bolted. "Do you know how cold it gets in upstate New York?" He wrapped his arms around himself and gave a shiver. "A hundred feet of snow, and that's on a good day!"

Warren knew he'd better change the subject quickly. He pulled out his watch. "Four fifty-five! When did you say you were going to check the turkey?"

"God, it's almost five o'clock! I better think of something real quick to serve with the turkey." He jumped up and went to the tent to check the supplies he'd put in the ice cooler. There wasn't much of anything, except for some of the canned food and the mushrooms he'd found the day before. He knew Warren didn't want mushrooms again, and actually, neither did he.

He knew he was going to have to find something green to eat out there. There just had to be something. Their fish and meat diet was not enough, and the mushrooms had no food value. There just had to be something. "Tomorrow, I'm going to look and see if there are any things growing out there for us to eat besides mushrooms." He yelled loudly so Warren could hear.

"I'll second that!" Warren answered in a laugh.

"Warren! There's not a thing to eat with the turkey, except the canned goods, and we're not going into those except in an emergency. Sorry about that!" Jim came back out and walked to the fire. He looked down at the meat cooking on the grill. The aroma of roasting bird had been filling the air for almost an hour. "Well, I have to admit. It sure does smell good. Hope it tastes alright."

Warren laughed. "Jim, I've really got to hand it to you! You've done really well with what you've had to work with. No complaints here."

"I can hardly wait until we build an oven." Jim continued. "It would be so nice."

Soon, it was just after five. They removed pieces of the bird from the grill and began to eat.

"The turkey bird is not that bad. Not quite like a 'Butterball' from the grocery store, but not bad." Jim commented, as he ate one of the legs.

When they had finished, Jim gathered the leftovers and placed them in a plastic bag. "We'll store this in the creek to cool it down good. Maybe a rock to hold it down. The water's cold enough, it'll almost be like a refrigerator." He knew they would be able to store much of their supplies in the creek, during the winter season. The water would probably freeze everything.

He then thought of the cold cellar at Monticello, the home of Thomas Jefferson, near Charlottesville, Virginia. There they would cut ice off the nearby pond and stack it down in the cold cellar. It would keep for an incredible length of time, acting like a huge cooler. Maybe they could build one. Not the size of the one at Monticello, but a smaller one. After all, the one at Monticello was used to store food for lots of people. Theirs would only have to hold enough for two.

"What have we got lined up for tomorrow?" Jim's thought pattern had changed.

"I've got to get those logs moved to the rock and leveled, so we can start the walls of the hut. Another thing, we have to do, is set some posts. That should be a lot of fun." Warren commented.

"No problem!" Jim exclaimed. "All we have to do is heat up the stone and hit it with cold water. That'll crack the shit out of it. May take from now until Jesus comes again, but who cares, we've got plenty of time." He paused for a moment and started laughing.

"What's so funny?"

"Well, if we're fifteen thousand years back in time, Jesus hasn't been here the first time, yet."

Warren laughed. "You're right. And as for the heat treatment on the rock, we'll try that and see how it works. Once we've got it started, shouldn't be too bad."

"How many do we have to set?"

"Don't ask!" Warren joked. "It sure would be nice to set a number of them. Then we'd have a good support for the roof members of the shed areas."

"We'll get an assembly line method going. Start one fire, then another, and another, then start at the first with the cold water. We'll clean the coals at that spot, then get another fire going. We'll continue to the next fire, and so on, and so on. Might as well start them all and do it right the first time." Jim was suggesting a method with which he was sure Warren was familiar. But that was alright. He didn't want Warren to think him a total klutz in the outdoors.

"Sounds real good." Warren continued. "I've got the posts ready. Tomorrow, I'll show you where to put them."

"Isn't it wonderful? I might get my columns after all." Jim began to laugh.

"You and your damn columns." Warren just shook his head.

After a while, night arrived.

"I think we should call it for now. We'll try your experiment tomorrow." Before going to the tent, Warren threw some more wood on the fire, to keep it going, so there would be hot coals the next morning. He had taken one of the tarpaulins off the rock and placed it over the firewood. He made sure it was secure.

As they lay in their sleeping bags, they both found it difficult to fall asleep. The temperature was cool, but it was obvious it was not as cool as it had been, when they first arrived in their new world.

"Sure wish I could take a bath." Jim broke the silence. "This shit of heating up water in a pot, really sucks!"

Warren chuckled. "I know what you mean." After a moments pause, he continued. "Like I said before, you could just jump in the creek, like you did when you thought I was drowning." He started to laugh; knowing Jim would not find it quite as amusing this time.

"Fuck you, too!" Jim immediately responded. "Hell if I'm going to get cardiac arrest just for a bath." The memory, still vivid in his mind, made him start to laugh. "You know, my sister, Cathy, won't go into her pool until the water reaches eighty degrees. Cathy hates the cold, too. Thank God they live in south Texas, or she'd NEVER be able to get in." He paused. "Wonder how she's doing? Wonder how Mom and Dad are? Bet they're all upset at us disappearing. Oh well. Everyone will just have to split up all those nice things I've got. Sure am glad I wrote a will and discussed it with everybody to find out what they all wanted."

"For Christ's sake! Shut up and go to sleep!"

"But I'm just not tired!"

"I know, but try anyway."

Silence resumed over the camp. Warren began to reflect on what Jim had said and thought of his own family situation. Then the silence was broken again.

"Warren?"

"Yes?"

"Happy Thanksgiving."

"You, too."

That was all that was said that night. They finally fell asleep.

CHAPTER XVIII

Warren woke early. He didn't wake Jim, as he knew he'd had a restless night. Several times he'd heard Jim mumble something in his sleep. He could tell by the tones, that Jim's dreams were not pleasant. As he got up and dressed, he looked at the stick Jim had been notching. The mark to be made today would denote the forty-first day in their new world.

He walked outside the tent and rekindled the fire. He thought of being home, getting up, and fixing the pot of coffee. God, how I'd love a cup. He sat down on a nearby piece of log, and poked at the fire. The previous day had been their Thanksgiving. Warren was quite thankful they had survived the forty previous days in this new time. He felt they'd been quite lucky. Things had gone rather well. He devised several snare traps and had caught small animals.

He was concerned their diet was consisting of too much meat, but Jim was working very hard, searching for edible plants. Success had not been good, as many of the plants didn't start growing until the last few weeks. Jim had gone several times to the large stand of bamboo to check for young sprouts, and along the creek banks where the cattail-type plants had been growing. He had said something about preparing some oriental dish with these plants. Then Warren reflected on some leafy plant Jim had discovered several days ago. Jim had done his damnedest, but it reminded him of cooked spinach, which he hated. He had eaten it anyway, knowing he had to have some type of greenery in his diet. He remembered Jim thought it might be a relative of the collard plant.

Then he heard the stirring in the tent. Jim was waking up. It was a major change of lifestyle for Jim. A smile came to his face. I'm sure he really hates getting up at these early hours. Then he yelled to the tent. "Sounded like you didn't sleep too well last night?"

"Didn't! Just couldn't get to sleep. As soon as I did, I'd wake up again. Hope I didn't keep you up."

"Well." Warren paused.

"Sorry about that. Just hit me with a club next time."

Jim came from the tent, stretching his arms. He looked up at the clear blue sky, beginning to fill with the light of the western rising sun.

"Looks like a pretty nice day." He yawned. "When we get the fires started on the rock, I've got to find us some veggies. Thought I'd make some turkey soup." He then looked over at Warren. "And I must trim your hair today. All of it. I'll do it while we're watching the fires."

He walked down toward the creek and pulled out the plastic bag containing the leftover turkey. "Damn, this water's like ice."

"Be glad of it." Warren yelled back. "We'd either die of food poisoning, or we'd have a real case of the blows."

"Want a piece of turkey?"

Warren made some questionable sound, as if not knowing whether he did or didn't.

"How about if I heat some up in the frying pan for you? I might even have some, too!"

"That sounds a little better. Cold turkey, this early in the morning, just didn't seem 'the thing', if you know what I mean."

"Yeah. I know."

Jim got out the frying pan and the largest pot from the camping cook set. He went to the creek, partially filling the pot with water, then brought it back and set it on the grill. He placed several pieces of meat in the pan, and put it on the grill next to the pot of water. "When the water gets hot, I'll put in some of the bones and meat. That'll start the broth." He paused a moment, took a spoon, and banged on the side of the large pot. 'Bong!' 'Bong!' 'Bong!' 'Bong!' 'Bong!' The pot resounded. "*Madames et Messueres! Le soup de jour est poullet avec, avec…*" He stroked his beard with his left hand as his mind went searching to no avail. "*Avec* whatever I can find to put in the damn thing!"

Warren could only shake his head. At least Jim hadn't lost it all yet. "You turkey!" He responded, then began to laugh.

"No! That's in the pan!" Jim pointed to the frying pan and began to laugh.

Soon the pieces were sizzling. The aroma of frying bird aroused their taste buds and made them realize their hunger. After a while, Jim placed the hot chunks in the tin plates and they began to eat.

"You know, it's hard to believe we've been here this long. Today makes forty-one."

Warren could see a worried look come over Jim's face.

"Warren?" Jim's face was serious. "Do you think we'll make it? I mean, through the winter?"

"Would you just shut the fuck up about it!" Warren yelled angrily. He slammed his plate down, stood up, and walked toward Jim. "It's coming to warm weather. What the hell are you talking about winter? Just shut the fuck up about the win…" He stood there, his head bent toward the ground, his hands on his hips. After a few moments of silence, he started again, but in a soft tone of voice. "Jim. I'm sorry." He bent over and grabbed Jim's shoulder, pulling him up. "I'm sorry. I know you're concerned, and so am I, but don't worry, we'll be okay. I promise I'll do everything I can to keep us alive. But don't go weird on me. Believe it or not,

I need you just as much as you need me."

Jim looked directly at Warren. Concern left his face and his voice returned to normal. "Really? You really need me? It's just that I don't know if I'm needed. You'd probably be better off if you were by yourself."

"Hell!" Warren laughed. "What the fuck would I do if I didn't have the best cook in Atlanta here to fix everything?"

Jim laughed jokingly. "You mean, the ONLY cook, now, in Atlanta."

They both began to laugh, and Warren lightly punched Jim's left shoulder with his right fist. Then he looked at the ground and in a joking way, tried to maintain his feelings. "But to tell you the truth, I get scared, too. It's you that keeps me together, and we WILL make it, as long as we keep our heads."

Jim began to laugh. "Oh fuck! You're right! We're going to make it. Come hell or high water, we'll make it. We're going to be just fine." He smiled.

Warren returned his smile. "Now let's get busy. We've got a hell of a lot of stuff to do today."

They finished eating and cleaned up the pans and plates. Jim put several pieces of the bird and the bones into the pot of hot water, then covered it with a lid. The coals of the fire were now low. Jim was glad, as this would keep the pot from boiling over. "It should be okay. Let's get those fires started on the rock."

Warren climbed to the top of the flat rock surface and started stepping off measurements. He took smaller stones, placing them on the points where the fires would be built. "Jim! Get your ass up here and see what you think. I need your architectural expertise."

"Be there in a minute." Jim checked the pot once more, then climbed his way to the top of the rock.

He checked the points where Warren planned to set the posts. After making some mental calculations and imagining the structure in place, he commented. "Looks good to me." He looked over the area one more time. "Yeah. Looks good. I'll get some wood and we'll get these things started."

By mid-morning, the fires were underway. Warren suggested they let the fires burn for about two to three hours before they start the water treatment. Jim piled a heap of wood on each fire. There wasn't anything else to do for a while.

"Okay, Warren. Let's see to your hair." Jim started climbing down to the campsite. Warren was right behind. He wasn't real anxious about the hair treatment, but knew he would feel much better when all was said and done.

It took Jim about thirty minutes to trim Warren's dark brown hair, and a few clips on his beard and mustache. He stood back. "Not bad. Looks real good." He scrutinized his handiwork again. He used his left hand to brush the cut hair from Warren's bare shoulders. "Guess it's my turn." He took off his shirt and sat on the log.

Warren cautiously proceeded to cut Jim's hair. He knew he would get better as time went on. As he finished trimming, Jim wanted him to trim a little on his beard and mustache, too. Warren knew how particular Jim was about his facial hair, but he went on anyway. When he finished, he was quite pleased at the results. "Not great, but not too bad. I'll get better as time goes on."

"Pity there's no one to appreciate our handiwork." Jim joked that there was no one to impress except themselves. He changed the subject. "Guess we really should check the fires."

The afternoon was warm. "Think I'll leave my shirt off and get a little sun." Jim looked up at the sky, then started for the top of the rock.

Warren reached the stone slab first. "Maybe another hour." He began to pile on more wood. Jim joined in the process.

"Think I'll get some pots of water." Jim commented. "Then they'll be ready to pour the minute we need them."

"Wait, I'll help." Warren started down after Jim.

By the time they had the pots and cans of water on top of the slab, it was time to begin work at the first fire. Jim brought the hatchet. He would use the blunt end to help chip the stone, after the cold water shock treatment. Warren had the shovel and they went to the first fire. He took the small shovel and pushed the coals from the spot. Jim immediately applied the cold water to the hot surface. The rock popped and cracked, and a large cloud of steam billowed into the air. Jim took the hatchet and pounded the surface. Chips of hot stone flew everywhere. He quickly dumped more water onto the spot. The steam continued to rise into the air. Jim hit the stone again with the hatchet. A hot chip of stone flew into the air, and hit Warren's upper right arm.

"Son-of-a-bitch!" Warren yelled. "Burnt the shit out of me!" He quickly splashed his arm with some of the cold water. "Shirt goes back on until this shit's finished." He climbed down and went to the tent, picked up his and Jim's shirts, then returned to the top of the rock. Jim had cleared most of the rock from the spot. The process had chipped almost an inch into the surface.

Warren handed Jim's shirt over. Then he put on his own shirt. This would prevent any further burns from flying chips of hot stone.

"I've got an idea." Jim put on his shirt. "When we build the next set of fires, we can confine each one with a ring of stones. That'll keep the fire concentrated over one spot and keep the wind from blowing the heat away."

"Good idea." Warren agreed. He brought several stones and placed them around the spot where Jim had chipped the rock away. He then put the coals he had moved with the shovel back into the ring of stones. The water remaining in the cracks and low spots made the coals sizzle. This dried most of the remaining moisture. After a few minutes, Warren removed the ashes from the hole. "Ready for the next one?"

"Let's go for it." Jim replied, and placed the pots and cans of water near the next location.

Using the shovel, Warren moved the red hot coals and placed them inside the stone ring around their first post-hole. Jim continued with the water and hatchet. This would be the continuing process, making it so each new fire would be started by the one from the next spot to be worked.

By late afternoon, they made the first round on each hole and began the second. The second shock treatment to the stone chipped almost another inch away.

Warren wanted Jim to get the soup ready, as he was beginning to get hungry.

Jim had to make a trip to the woods to get several of the items he was going to add to the pot. He laughed. "Isn't it amazing the power of food, and the power of those who fix it." He paused for a moment. "I could probably rule the world, if I were its only cook. Just think, control of the vast masses, all screaming for food." Then he began to chant. "Food! Food! Food! Food!"

"Oh shut the fuck up and go get your stuff. I'll stay here and continue with the fires." Warren laughed.

Jim climbed down from the rock. "I'll be gone just a little while." He checked the pot, still covered, simmering on the grill. He added a bit more water, then headed for the woods. His first stop would be the stand of bamboo.

On the way, he stopped at the place where the cattail type plants were growing and checked for some of the young sprouts. He took Warren's sharp hunting knife and collected several that were still under the surface of the water.

When he reached the bamboo stand, there were a large number of new shoots coming up. He was pleased at this fact, and cut many of them. He thought of the canned ones he used to buy in the grocery store to make quick oriental dishes. He laughed to himself. "Not quite the same."

He saw a few more he wanted to cut, and moved to the spot. As he did, he heard a rustling somewhere deep in the stand. Panic struck. All he had was the hunting knife. The noise became louder and louder. It was obvious that something large was crashing its way through the stand. He wasn't sure what to do. The lines of Rudyard Kipling's poem flashed through his mind. Something about 'keeping your head, while all around you are losing theirs'. His only thought was to make a mad dash back to camp, to get away. Then there was the real mental conflict. He wanted to see what it was. Then he thought, 'heroes die only once while cowards live to fight another day'. It was definitely the time to take the coward's way out.

He quickly placed the hunting knife in the camera case, along with the goodies he'd been collecting, and started running in the direction of the camp. His curiosity still kept nagging his brain. He couldn't help but periodically look back, trying to see what was making the noise, but could see nothing. He could hardly wait to tell Warren.

The noise of the unseen 'thing' slowly vanished behind him. Whatever it was, it was staying somewhere around the bamboo stand, or headed elsewhere. Jim's mind tried to be logical and rational. Don't be ridiculous, he thought. Of course, there are animals out here. Warren goes hunting all the time. He never gets upset over rustling in the bushes. It's to be expected. He just never thought of 'things' being out there. With all the walks he'd ever taken in the woods, never had he run into a situation where he had been confronted with a major wild animal. There were chipmunk like things, and the like, but never anything like a bear or mountain lion. Those things just never were around. I guess I've frequented only the more tamed woods.

He moved as quickly as possible through the underbrush, along the creek. His heart was slowly beginning to return to it's normal beat. He could hardly wait to tell Warren of his experience. Maybe he would know what it was.

Warren was still working with the fires on top of the rock when Jim came running into camp.

"Warren! I've got to tell you what happened!" Jim yelled. "There's something out there at the bamboo place! I heard it! Scared the shit out of me!"

"What was it?" Warren stopped what he was doing and came to the edge of the rock.

"Who the hell knows? I got out of there as quick as I could! Didn't see a thing."

"Sure it wasn't your imagination?"

"My imagination's not that good."

"Tomorrow we'll check it out. I'm sure we'll find footprints." Warren climbed down and joined Jim at the fire. "Did you get anything for the soup?"

"Sure did, but almost lost it when I ran away." Jim changed the subject, as he was prone to do. "How are the holes coming?"

"Oh, pretty good. Better than I thought. A few more days and we should have it done."

Jim rinsed off the items he had collected, then took the knife and cut them up, putting them in the pot. He took some spices from the tent, and added them to the pot. His small supply would be gone after a while, then there would be nothing to enhance the flavor of their food. Maybe there were some wild spices or herbs, but where would he get salt and pepper? "About thirty more minutes." He stirred the soup and replaced the lid. He added a few more sticks to the fire. He watched to make sure the pot wouldn't boil over as the wood ignited.

Warren went to the tent and got the tin bowls and brought them out. He sat down with Jim to wait for the soup. He pulled the pack of cigarettes from his pocket, and extended it toward Jim. "Want one?"

"Oh, why not." Jim pulled one from the pack. He pulled a burning twig from the fire and extended it toward Warren, holding his cigarette in his mouth. Warren pulled a draw on the cigarette. Then he lit his own. He puffed, then coughed. As he held the cigarette away, he noticed Warren doing the same thing. "Why don't we just admit it to ourselves? We've had it with the cigarettes. They taste worse than they did the day we went to the top of the mountain." Jim coughed again.

"Well, we'll save the last two for posterity." Warren agreed.

They put out their unfinished cigarettes and put them back in the near empty pack. "We'll save them for bee stings." Warren commented.

"Another semblance of civilization bites the dust." Jim laughed. "But, maybe it's not so terrible to give up a few things that are supposedly a sign of the civilized."

Soon the soup was ready and they began to eat. "Not bad." Warren commented.

"Hate to say it, but the salt won't last much longer." Jim sipped the hot broth.

When they were finished, they went to the top of the rock, and completed the fires for the day. Jim helped with the chipping. They went through the process with each hole, then set them alight to burn through the night. It was dark as their task ended.

When they returned to the fire, Jim dished up more soup. They were quiet as they sat eating.

Warren began to reflect on several subjects. One was his pocket watch. He thought how they had come to rely on it less and less. The sun had become their timepiece. They got up as the sun rose, and went to bed not long after it went down. He had been winding it everyday, but had not used it much after that. Most days, he'd been leaving it in the tent.

"We really need to eat all of this." Jim broke the silence. "I'm afraid it'll go bad if we don't." He spooned more soup into Warren's bowl and refilled his own. Warren didn't care if they did have to eat it all, as he was quite hungry.

The only light was that of the fire. The warm air of the day was now cool. Jim had put on his coat. Soon they finished the soup and Jim filled the pot with water, to let it soak overnight.

"I don't know about you, but I'm tired." Jim dropped the tin bowls and spoons into the pot. "I can't believe that me, the night owl of the century, is tired a few hours after sundown." He paused for a moment. "But this is another century."

Warren laughed. "You're right about that. Think we should go to bed. We'll check out your 'noise' tomorrow."

"Did you have to mention that right now? I'd sort of repressed it. Now I'll have nightmares or won't be able to go to sleep."

Warren stared at the roof of the tent, not being able to sleep. He was mulling over the events of the day. He thought of the confrontation with Jim that morning, and began to reflect on what he had said. He really did need Jim. The craziness and silly comments kept his spirits up. Jim was also a big help. His companionship made the days go much easier. He was another voice, another mind, another opinion, in the vast time of no one. He was truly glad Jim was there with him. He'd probably do things differently if he were alone. But with Jim there, he felt needed, and it helped him retain his sanity.

He then thought of the times ahead, and winter. They WOULD survive. They must. He wasn't sure how, but they would survive. He would use every bit of knowledge he had to keep them alive. Jim would be his reason. We will make it. As God is my witness, we're going to make it. I'll keep that crazy idiot, that loony tune, that…my friend. His thoughts stopped and he smiled.

He reached over and gently patted the adjacent sleeping bag. Jim was already asleep. He laughed to himself, recalling how Jim would normally be wide awake at this time. He patted a few more times. "Don't worry, Jim." He whispered softly. "I'll take care of you. We're going to be okay."

Soon, Warren was asleep.

CHAPTER XIX

Phillip Martin checks his camcorder. It is almost time to change out to another tape. He shifts around to get his blood moving since his butt hurts and is somewhat numb from sitting on the cool, highly polished, stone floor. The holographic figure is still seated. The tray of food and drink he'd brought in earlier, had been slowly consumed and was now at his feet. He pauses in his tale.

"Ladies and gentlemen." The figure stands. "There will be a pause in the story so those of you that must take care of business, can. I'll begin again in about three hours. So go get something to eat, go to the bathroom, get additional equipment, or whatever. I'll be back." He moves off the podium and disappears.

Phillip is ecstatic. Damn, I'm starving. He checks his watch to make sure the time would be wisely used. One thing he wants to investigate is the names mentioned by the figure. He recalls a strange incident that occurred just a few months earlier, in the spring. I think it was sometime in March. It was one of those missing person type things that had strange attachments. Kind of a 'much a do about nothing' stories, but slightly weird. A little research will shed some light on it, I'm sure.

A quick discussion was held regarding the bringing in of food and drink to this site and it was decided that there didn't seem to be any harm in doing so. The floors would not be damaged should there be a spill.

He follows most of the discovery party, as they leave the room. Several of the minor characters remain behind to watch equipment and continue recording, should the figure return sooner than expected. He passes easily through the corridors and down the staircases, which are well illuminated by lights installed when they first entered.

Finally out into the open, he punches his cell phone. For some reason, the cell phones would not work in the room. There had to be some kind of interference preventing their use. Probably the thick stone all around. "Hello, Maggie? It's me. I'd like you to do a little research for me before I get back. Warren Glass and a James Stone. Also, check on a Linda Rogers. Yeah, Linda Rogers. See if there's anything on her in the files. Would appreciate it. Got to run, no time. Wait until I tell you about this discovery and show you the video. You're not going to believe it. Okay. Thanks. Bye."

He heads for his car to get some fast food and extras to munch on later in the room. Pit stop is a definite yes. He is about to explode, he needs to pee so bad. Also there is a quick stop at a store to pick up a few more 8mm tapes for the camcorder. Then it's back again, returning as fast as possible to the site. Time is passing quickly.

He swiftly walks through the halls and up the stairs. He almost drops his drinks in his haste. What a damn klutz I can be sometimes. I sure would hate to be the first to drop something. When he arrives, he is surprised his spot on the floor is not occupied. Guess everyone's satisfied with his or her previous location. Phillip repositions himself on the floor. His camcorder on the tripod is still in place from where he placed it when he first sat down. He places the extra hamburgers, munchies, and soft drinks by his side, along with several new 8mm tapes. He has taken them out of their wrappers so as not to cause a disturbance later on should he need to put one in the camcorder. Then he checks his watch. The three hours are almost up. There are only a few more minutes left.

Everyone has returned. Most check their watches. There is a low murmur of multiple conversations echoing through the chamber. Anxiety is building in anticipation. Phillip checks his watch again. The time is up. Actually, it's a few minutes past. This sucks. Maybe something's happened preventing the figure from reappearing. Would they all be left with just a fragment of a story? Now that would be a real bitch. There's nothing like knowing only a piece of a good story, especially when it's tied to an archaeological discovery like this one. I see the others are rather concerned over the fact the old man hasn't shown up, too.

Restlessness is evident. Members of the party are constantly looking at their watches. Everyone is wondering what is wrong and why the figure does not reappear. The low murmuring conversations begin to increase in volume, with concern about the 'no show'.

Phillip begins to recall the items he'd asked his secretary to check out. His mind begins to spin trying to remember the incident he'd thought of earlier. He remembers it being a rather odd event and questionably newsworthy. Glass. Stone. His mind searches. The names seem vaguely familiar, but I just can't remember. But he knew it had some weird twist to it. The anxiety of the moment is interrupting his thoughts.

As quickly as he left, the old man reappears on the podium. You can feel the relief of everyone present. The figure turns and addresses everyone. "I must apologize for the delay, but I wanted to make sure you all had a chance to get comfortable. I'm sure the traffic in Atlanta is still no fun. Now, if everyone is ready, I'll continue." The figure sits in the chair and arranges the pillows to get comfortable.

"Let's see." He peers up and to his right. He scratches his left cheek with his left hand. "Oh yes. I was about to tell you about the next day, but I think we'll move on a bit. We don't want this to drag on forever."

CHAPTER XX

The sun was just beginning to light the early morning sky. The air was crisp.

"Fifty-six days!" Jim thought out loud, as he notched the stick with Warren's knife.

"What?" Warren was standing outside the tent.

"Oh, I was just commenting on the number of days."

"How many has it been?"

"Today makes fifty-six!" Jim set his stick calendar aside and joined Warren sitting by the fire. He immediately got up and went to the creek pulling the plastic bag from the water. He removed a piece of deer meat, then replaced the bag beneath the water to keep the contents cool.

After slicing the meat into several slabs, he began to fry it in the pan. Jim knew Warren was hungry. Warren had been working hard to get the site in order and nearing completion. A few days of rain had put several crimps in the schedule. They never took the time to check out the noise in the bamboo stand. Warren indicated the rains had probably obliterated any evidence of footprints.

On two of the rain days, Warren and Jim had worked to complete the bridge from the rock to the south bank. The bridge was constructed of a few logs put together. It was not and easy task as the logs had to be a minimum of fourteen feet long to span the twelve foot distance from the rock to the bank. It was essential to get the bridge done in order to start moving the logs for the hut to the rock.

Warren had cut the logs for the walls of the hut to around ten feet long. This would make the hut some ten feet square with an interior of about eight feet square. He stacked them one on top of the other, log cabin fashion. Warren stopped at seven logs high. It was too difficult to get them any higher without hurting themselves. The south wall was almost six feet tall. The north wall was around five feet. This would allow the roof to slope.

Jim made great progress with the fireplace at the north end of the hut. The creek bed contained a wealth of the clay mud used as filler between the rocks and logs.

Warren planned to use bamboo poles, across the roof, for support. Bundles of reeds from the creek would be placed on top of this for insulation. One of the tarpaulins would go down on the reeds to make the roof waterproof. Warren hoped to complete this construction within the next week or so. The second tarp they would use to cover things to keep them dry.

Once the hut walls were done, smaller logs were placed in the chipped out holes on the rock's surface on the eastern and southern sides of the hut. They were braced with bamboo, then packed at the base with clay mud mixed with small stones. Jim pounded the clay in and around the logs, with a stick to make sure the footings were as tight as possible. Several rocks were placed around the base of each column for added support. These five foot wide shed areas would be used for storage of wood and to keep hanging meat dry.

Jim had been concerned about their shallow depth in the surface, but then realized these were extenuating times and circumstances, no ten-penny nails, and no concrete. They had done the best they could.

As Jim turned the meat in the pan, Warren sat near the fire watching Jim cook. The only sound was that of the birds, the breeze in the leaves, and the clanking of the fork against the pan on the grill.

Warren began to silently reflect. Jim had been a big help in getting the project to its present state in such a short amount of time. He smiled to himself as he watched Jim, seated in a crossed leg fashion, tending the cooking. He's doing real well. For that fact, I'm not doing bad myself. We've not gone crazy yet, and things are progressing at a very good pace. He finally broke the silence. "I'm going to look at your garden for a second."

"Okay!" Jim responded. "I checked it the other day, and things seem to be doing pretty good. Both the potatoes and tomatoes seem to be growing just fine. The wild onions are growing like crazy. Hope they don't take over." He turned the meat in the pan again.

Warren returned from the garden spot, and sat by the fire again. "Things do look good."

Warren had done well at conserving his ammunition for the guns. He had only used the guns when hunting larger game. His traps had worked fine for smaller animals. He pondered for a moment thinking about the time when the ammo would be gone. He hoped by then they both would have bows and arrows and able to hunt. He would do most of the hunting, but he wanted Jim to be capable, should the need arise. He'd not worked on his bow for a while, but he'd cut several reeds for arrows. Jim split several feathers in half, cut thin splits in the shafts with the razor from the safety kit, then carefully slid the feathers into the splits at the back of the arrow. He used some tacky tree sap to hold the feathers in place. Warren had questioned their durability, but he had no better solution. They would just have to wait and see. He'd probably be able to finish the bow within the next week. Some of the nylon fishing line would be used for the string. He braided several lengths together.

"Well, we're almost through the last tube of toothpaste. Guess I'll have to contrive something for us to use in its place. Been thinking of heating some small rocks in the fire, then crushing them down to fine powder." He laughed for a second. "So much for the enamel on our teeth."

"I can hardly wait." Warren spoke in a joking manner.

"I'll tell you, I sure as hell miss my washing machine. Putting one piece at a time in a pot of hot water, wringing it out, and laying it on a rock to dry, has been the pits. YOUR pants have been a real bitch 'cause they don't fit in the small pot. I've had to use the large pot. Won't be long and the dye will be gone." He paused for a moment. "Faded jeans! You're a man before your time. A trendsetter. Do you think it'll catch on?" He laughed, and served a piece of meat to Warren.

"Speaking of wash, I'm testing out the water today, and taking a bath in the creek." Warren commented.

"That water's ice cold. I can tell you that from getting the meat. If I tried that I'd end up with cardiac arrest." Jim joked. "And don't you pull any of those drowning stunts. I'm not coming in after you this time. You can just drown." He paused. "Just kidding. Just kidding."

Warren had a chunk of meat in his mouth but jumped in immediately to prevent Jim from holding the spotlight. "How can I drown, especially when I was number four in the swim meet in high school." He chewed a bit and swallowed.

"Now don't choke on this wonderful entree we're having." Jim smiled and chuckled. "And why weren't you number one?" He didn't dare look directly at Warren.

Warren came back emphatically. "Well. You can't be *numero uno* at everything, and you can see I don't have a swimmer's body. I'm too, too…"

"Fat?" Jim laughed, winced, and leaned away from Warren, expecting to receive a swipe from his fist.

"Fat! Fat! What do you mean fat?" Warren stood up, took off his shirt and stood in the classic muscleman pose. His skin was tan from working in the sun and his muscles were becoming defined with all the physical labor he had been doing.

"You call this fat?"

"Okay. Okay." Jim laughed. "You can put your shirt back on."

"You'll pay for that one. I'll think of something." Warren sat down and continued eating his meat.

Jim continued to chuckle, then got another piece of meat from the pan, and extended it toward Warren. "Here. Have another piece of meat. It'll keep those pounds from falling right off."

He quickly put the meat back in the pan, started to jump up and run. He knew he'd put on the last straw. His continuous laughter made it impossible to get away. He heard Warren's metal plate as it clanged down on a nearby rock.

It was only a matter of time now, as Warren leaped from his seated position. The time was short and further retreat was impossible, as he felt Warren's powerful right hand grab him around the ankle. It was all over now. It was reprisal time. He could hear Warren. "You've done it now!" Jim continued to laugh and fell to the ground. Warren was on top of him, like an eagle on its prey.

"Now what was that?" Warren grabbed Jim's left arm and pulled it around his back. "What was that?"

"Uncle! Uncle!" Jim laughed. "I give up! I take it back. I didn't mean it."

"Anything else you want to say?" Warren put a hold on him.

"No! Nothing. Nothing else." Jim yelled.

"Are you sure?" Warren began to laugh.

"Yeah! Yeah! I'm sure."

Warren helped him get up. Jim brushed the dirt off his clothes, then gave Warren a punch to the left shoulder. Jim jumped back to a fighter's stance, bouncing up and down.

Warren looked at him with his piercing blue eyes. "You don't know when to quit, do you?" He started to laugh and shake his head.

Jim stopped bouncing, laughed, walked over to Warren, and gave him a bear hug. Warren wrapped his arms over Jim's shoulders. Both were laughing.

After eating, Jim took the metal plates and pan to the creek and began to wash them. After a few minutes, he heard Warren coming up behind him. He turned.

There was Warren with only a towel and the bar of soap in his hand. His belt line separated the tan skin of his upper body from the paler skin of his lower body, the result of wearing his long pants.

"Looks like you need to even out that tan of yours." Jim joked. "By the way, the water's cold as shit."

Warren walked to the water's edge, set down the towel, and continued into the water, almost to his waist. The cold water made his entire body tingle. With one dive, he plunged beneath the surface of the shallow creek. It was the deepest part of the small creek. Jim watched with alert. Warren shortly surfaced and stood up. The water was dripping from the dark brown hair hanging over his eyes. He gave a quick shiver then took the bar of soap and began to lather up.

"Hope you freeze your balls off." Jim laughed.

"What do you mean? Come on in. The water's fine!" He gave a big grin and struggled not to look cold.

"Believe it!" Jim smiled as he sat on the bank to watch. "Let me get you a pot. You can get some more of that mud off the bottom. It's getting more difficult to get it from around the edges."

He paused. "On second thought, maybe not. You better get out before you catch double pneumonia."

Warren continued to wash. Soap bubbles foamed through his hair, beard and mustache.

"I'll go put a few sticks on the fire for when you get out."

"Thanks." Warren responded. "It's beginning to get a bit cool."

"Cool! Huh! Yeah! Sure! Believe it!" Jim commented sarcastically, as he went to roust the fire.

After a few minutes, Warren was standing by the fire rubbing his body briskly with the towel. "Damn! I left the soap on a rock by the creek."

"Don't worry. I'll get it after I get you a pair of clean underwear and your pants." Jim went to the tent, retrieving the articles of clothing, as well as a clean shirt. "Sorry, I didn't have any 'Tide' to get out this Georgia Red Clay."

Even though it was still early morning, the sun was warm. The sky was bright, and white puffy clouds filled the blue.

"Looks like it's going to be a good day." Warren put on his underwear. "Maybe we can get those reeds today and start the roof."

"Sounds good to me." Jim paused a moment and changed the subject. "I'd also like to get started on the dam. We'll have a nice pond when it's finished, and with the water not running so quickly, maybe it will warm up faster. Then I'll consider taking a dip."

"Let's get the hut and fireplace done first." Warren commented. "And what about your garden? It'll be flooded if we build the dam."

"I plan to move everything south of the creek, where you've cleared. That area's nice and sunny, and the dirt looks great. We could get tomatoes the size of grapefruits."

Warren finished drying his hair with the towel.

"Looks like an explosion in a mattress factory." Jim laughed at Warren's hair all puffed up, sticking in all direction. "Come over here." He directed Warren to sit on the rock near the fire, then went to the tent. He came out with the comb and scissors. "I think you need a few strands clipped." He ran the comb through Warren's hair, parted it, made a few snips and stood back. "There. That's much better."

"If you say so." Warren stood up, brushed the few cut hairs off his shoulders, and grabbed his shirt.

Jim went into the tent to put the comb and scissors away. He grabbed a pair of Warren's socks. "Here are some clean socks, too." He walked over and handed them to Warren.

"We'll head for the reeds in a few minutes. We'll bring a litter to carry them back. Let me get my boots on."

"Why don't we take the two ropes with us? We can make litters out of the bamboo at the stand. That'll save time having to drag one of the litters with us. We'll use the larger pieces as roof supports."

"That's a good idea." Warren finished putting on his boots. "That way we won't have to carry a litter all the way there and back again. We'll need the machete and hatchet."

Jim had anticipated this and held them in the air.

"A mind reader!" Warren joked. He was pleased Jim was getting a real sense of what was needed and a feel for how to do certain tasks. Of course, Jim had a college education and was not stupid, but sometimes Warren had to realize he was not exactly a 'natural' when it came to the outdoors.

Warren stood up and went into the tent. He came out with the pistol. "You never know. We might need it. And besides, maybe we'll see something really great to have for dinner."

By mid-day, they'd reached the bamboo stand, cut several poles to make the litter, and use for roof bracing. All the while, Jim recalled the day he heard the noise somewhere in the stand. He tried not to show concern, but with every strange noise, he would look quickly all around. Warren could sense his anxiety, but knew there was nothing he could do.

Soon they were off to the reeds. On the way, Warren stopped several times to listen intently.

"What's the matter?" Jim asked.

"Listen!" Warren paused and stared at the ground. "Sounds like it's coming from over there." He turned, pointing to the northwest.

As they approached, the sound became louder. There stood the remains of a large old tree. The limbs were gone, leaving only the huge trunk. Around a smaller opening in the side, there was a swarm of bees.

"Honey!" Jim yelled. "We now have sugar, natural sugar, and wax! Maybe I can make some candles. The ones I brought with us for the trip are still back at the Chattahoochee."

"Not so quick." Warren commented. "We don't want to disturb this right now. We've already got our chore cut out for us today. We'll check this out later."

Jim began to think of all the things honey reminded him of: honey baked ham, honey rolls, in hot tea, mixed with lemon and bourbon for a cold, a glazing for chicken or duck. Images passed through his mind's eye. He thought of the beeswax candles used on the high altar in church, and how nice they smelled when burning.

Warren could see Jim was in a self-induced trance. He had no idea what was running through his mind. It was Jim's glassy stare into nothingness. "Earth to James." Warren interrupted.

Jim broke his statuesque posture. "Huh?"

"Something's really on your mind. What was THAT all about?"

"Oh. Just thinking about the honey and wax." Jim smiled. "It'll be nice to have the honey for cooking and maybe candles. We don't have to sit in the dark."

"Think we can find this spot again?" Warren prompted.

"Bet your sweet ass we can. I've got it engraved on my memory." Jim paused. "Do you know how to get it out? The honey? Without getting stung all to hell and back?"

"Don't worry, we'll manage somehow. We just don't want to destroy the hive or they'll all leave and we'll be shit out of luck." Warren laughed. "Let's get this stuff back to camp. We've got a couple of trips to make to get enough reeds for the roof."

The greenery over the ground and in the trees gave a wonderful feeling of newness to the woods. Warren began to see things they had not realized were there. Berry bushes and brambles, wild grape were growing in thickets, near outcroppings of rocks and hanging in trees.

There were even patches of wild strawberries. Warren remembered the strawberries he'd eaten in the woods during other camping trips. They'd been rather tasteless. He never thought he'd be looking forward to eating them again. Then he began to remember the large sweet strawberries sold in flats at the farmer's market.

Jim was busy remembering the location of everything. "We'll have to fight off the birds, you know." He stopped short. "Do you think we can transplant some to the garden spot? Just think of it, strawberry patch, berry patch, grape arbor. Biltmore House, eat your heart out." He laughed.

"Not a bad idea, but we'll have to wait until late summer so we don't wreck the fruit that's starting to develop." Warren stopped for a second then laughed. "'Mistress Mary, quite contrary, how does your garden grow?'" He continued to laugh.

"Asshole!" Jim made an ugly face and stuck out his tongue. "I'll 'Mistress Mary' you." He began to laugh, too.

As evening arrived, they had put up the bamboo poles across the roof of the hut and the shed areas. He also started the reed covering. Jim continued to place the stones for the fireplace. He wanted to make sure the flue was as small as possible and yet large enough to remove the smoke. He knew the fireplace was one of the least efficient ways of heating, but it was all they could do. A gas furnace would not be around for several thousand years.

Placing the stones was somewhat like building a house of cards. When a rock would not fit, he would chip it with the blunt end of the hatchet. Mud was a big help in keeping it from completely falling apart. He wondered how it would hold up under the heat of the fire. It might all come tumbling down. It would be just my luck. When he finished for the day, the stones were as high as his neck, the result of several days of construction. When it got much higher, Warren would have to help lift the rocks to the top.

Jim stopped and climbed down from the rock. Since he was hungry, he knew Warren was. Warren hadn't said anything, but Jim had to get something started for them to eat. He went down to the creek and got some of the cool meat from the plastic bag. Soup again. Oh well. Out of the other plastic bag he pulled some of the greenery he'd been collecting. From the garden, he pulled a few wild onions. Within minutes the soup was under way. After an hour, the pot was boiling and it was almost ready to eat.

Darkness was closing in on the site. Warren was still placing reeds on top of the roof structure as Jim yelled. "It's soup! Again! Sorry about that." He had to laugh at Warren's reply.

"Guess it's better than nothing!"

They sat silent, consuming the rather bland concoction. The greenery and meat, even with a touch of salt, was uninteresting, but it did fill the stomach, at least for a while.

As Jim finished his bowl, he broke the silence. "We're just about out of everything. Salt, pepper, toothpaste and toilet paper. There's still some flour left, but it'll be gone the next time I fry up some more meat."

"Yeah, I know, and I must go on another hunting trip. There's not much meat either."

"You're right. Maybe two more meals, and I hate to say it, but it's getting a bit funny. We'll end up with the blows. I'm rather surprised we haven't had them yet with this drastic change of diet."

"Well. I didn't want to say anything, but." Warren laughed.

"Really?" Jim looked surprised. "Guess it's my cast iron constitution, and all that dirt we used to eat as kids, on the farm." He paused and began to reminisce. "Yeah, we used to eat the peanuts, fertilizer all over them, before they were planted in the fields. And the field corn. God, it was hard as rock, but we loved it. We could consume almost an entire ear in about twenty minutes." He laughed. "I also remember the year we grew sweet potatoes. We'd dig them right up, brush them off, and eat them on the spot, skins, dirt and all."

"Yeah." Warren laughed. "I know what you mean. I remember a lot of similar things, except living in the city, it was the back yard garden. Not quite as rural."

Jim dished out the last of the soup. Warren's thoughts shifted to things that needed to be done. Jim, too, began to think of things he wanted to complete at the site.

Finishing his soup, Warren set his bowl down and went into the tent. He came out with his guitar, and Jim's recorder. He sat down again in his usual spot by the fire, set the recorder by Jim, and began to strum. "Well, what do you want to hear?" He twisted a few of the keys to adjust the strings and bring the guitar back to tune.

"Oh anything." Jim finished his soup. He picked up his recorder.

The strains of *Puff the Magic Dragon* floated on the air. Warren followed suit and picked up the song. He began to sing the words on the repeat.

A few songs later, Jim thought of the dishes. "I really should do them, but I really hate the thought of going down to the river in the dark."

"Do the damn things tomorrow." Warren replied.

"I have to get up and go hunting anyway. You can do a few more things here at camp."

"I thought I might go hunting myself, for some more goodies that might be growing out there."

"That's a good idea." Warren agreed. "Play it by ear." He set his guitar down. "Guess we really should turn in. Tomorrow will be here soon enough."

Within the next thirty minutes they were in their sleeping bags.

"Wonder what time it is?" Jim said softly.

"Forget it. If you think I'm going out to the fire so there's enough light to look at my watch, you're crazy." Warren grumbled. "But I guess it's somewhere around half past ten or eleven o'clock."

"That late? Holy shit!" Jim paused. "See you tomorrow, Warren."

"You, too."

They drifted off to sleep to the sounds of the night. Morning would bring the beginning of another day, their fifty-seventh.

All was as well as it could be.

CHAPTER XXI

Jim got up and notched his stick calendar. A questioning look came over his face. He went to one of the boxes in the tent and pulled out his wallet. He finally found the plastic calendar card among the credit cards, driver's license and organ donor card. Counting the days, he smiled. "Warren." Warren was somewhere outside the tent. He called again, but louder. "Warren!" There was still no answer. He put the calendar back in his wallet, then placed it in the box. Walking out of the tent, he called again. "Warr…" His call was interrupted as he practically ran Warren over.

"Yes." Warren looked at Jim's excited face.

"Do you know what today is?"

Warren hadn't thought about it, but began to mentally calculate the date. It dawned on him that it was one of two days. It was either the day before or it was the day, Christmas. "Well. Let's see." He feigned a pause, pretending not to know. He could see the anxious look on Jim's face. It was the expression of an excited child just bubbling to tell a special secret. "What is today?" He gave in to the pressure.

"It's Christmas Eve!" Jim laughed excitedly. "It's Christmas Eve! The day before Christmas."

Warren smiled and looked around. "And there's no snow."

Jim looked around at the green trees and plants near the campsite. "Yeah, it sure doesn't feel like Christmas." He paused. "But that's okay! It's still Christmas, or almost Christmas."

"Well, maybe we should call a holiday." Warren smiled. "We'll do something special." He looked up at the early morning rays of the sun, just coming over the trees to the west. "Maybe we can have something special for dinner today." He went into the tent and got his shotgun and a variety of shells. As he emerged from the tent, he concealed the hatchet under his flannel shirt jacket. "I'll be back in a few hours." He walked to the east. "See what you can do to make it a bit like Christmas while I'm gone."

"Okay!" Jim answered gleefully. "See you in a few hours."

Shortly, Warren disappeared into the woods to the east. The dim light of early morning limited his ability to see into the dark areas of the woods. Jim watched Warren head into the undergrowth. It was now his time to do something. He knew just what to do. Running to the tent, he grabbed up the machete and the small knife from the tackle box. Without realizing it, he started whistling a medley of Christmas carols.

Within the first thirty minutes, he had cut enough evergreen boughs to decorate a mansion. He began to arrange them in bunches around the site. Another trip to the woods brought a collection of late spring flowers, and other greenery. He interspersed these into the evergreen boughs. Within three hours, the camp took on the look of some lost florist shop.

As he stood admiring the scene, he realized he needed to consider the meal. There had to be something to serve with whatever Warren might catch. He headed for the woods again. The honey tree came to mind. Along the way, he picked several of the wild strawberries and put them in his camera case. One of the empty vegetable cans was a great help. He would use it to hold the honey.

Finally, he reached the honey tree. He wasn't sure how he would do it without getting stung to death. The old tree was so huge. He took the machete and started to chisel delicately at the trunk, about five feet off the ground. He knew the hatchet would be too noisy and destructive, that's why he didn't consider bringing it. From the sound, the tree was quite hollow. After some thirty minutes, he had carefully chopped a section of wood for an opening, a little more than a foot square. The tree was only about two inches thick.

Breaking through, he hit one of the wax combs. He knew he had to be careful or he'd have the whole colony down on him. The small knife came in quite handy. He cut a section of the comb loose and put it in the can. Honey dripped like syrup. He cut a bit more of the comb. He used his hands to prevent it from falling into the dark cavity of the tree. As he pulled it free, he was stung twice on his left hand. "Shit!" Hurriedly, he put the second piece of comb into the can, put the piece of tree he'd cut, back in place to cover the hole, then ran from the site, before all hell broke loose.

Two large whelps rose on his hand. He sucked them trying to stop the sting. Wish I had a cigarette now. I could wet the tobacco and put it on the sting. Oh well. The taste of the honey interrupted his thoughts. He licked the sticky syrup from his hand.

On his way back to camp, he found several morsels to add to his collection. He was pleased there would be something nice to eat. He was very pleased to find a few mushrooms. He thought of how he would collect a great number of them during late summer and early fall, and dry them to be used later.

Walking through the underbrush into the campsite, he stopped. He was overwhelmed at what he saw. His eyes began to fill with tears. In the middle of the campsite was a six foot fir tree.

Warren was on the ground beneath the tree. He was putting rocks around to brace it in the hole he'd dug. He crawled out, stood up and saw Jim standing at the edge of the woods. He smiled. "Merry Christmas, Jim!" He yelled and raised his left had, still holding the hatchet. He could just make out Jim's face. It was obvious Jim was crying. He watched him slowly walk toward the tree. He said nothing more.

Jim walked up and stood about five feet from the tree, staring at it. Warren walked over, put his right arm over Jim's shoulders and gave a few light tugs.

"I know it's only the tree, but I knew you'd like it. Sorry we've got no ornaments." Warren looked at the tree.

"Oh Warren. It's so thoughtful. It's the best thing I could think of." Jim continued staring at the tree. He wiped his eyes with his left hand, then put it around Warren's back. "It's real thoughtful. And you know, if you concentrate real hard, you CAN see ornaments and tinsel."

"Wait'll you see what else I've got." Warren pulled Jim toward the tent.

"A wild boar!" Jim exclaimed. "Those things are dangerous."

"It's only a small one, but it'll be great for dinner."

"And I've got some honey." Jim opened his camera case and pulled out the can. "We'll baste it with honey. It'll be great."

"Let me go clean it up and rinse it off at the creek. Then we can get it on the grill." Warren picked up the gutted carcass and his large hunting knife. "I'll go way downstream so you won't see what's going on. Don't want to ruin your appetite."

Jim put some wood on the fire and placed the grill high. The dripping fat would have to be contended with, to prevent the meat from burning as well as the honey. He remembered the time he ruined a pork roast by not watching it. The dripping grease caused a raging fire in his grill and burned the roast to a cinder. This would not happen today.

Within the hour, the meat was on the grill and Jim had washed the mushrooms and strawberries in the creek. He sat by the fire, watching to make sure it did not flame up.

Warren went to the rock to work on the chimney. A few more days of work and it would be completed. Jim planned to chink it with extra mud that summer.

The hut was virtually finished. Several more trips to the reeds would provide enough to amply cover the roof and increase the insulation factor. Warren had also put long bamboo poles over the reeds to keep them in place. These would be secured with twisted vines to the main structural members. Then one tarpaulin would be spread over the reeds and tired down with young green vines.

Jim planned to take long leaves and stems of some of the tall grasses that grew near the creek, and braided them into lengths. These would help in anchoring construction. The braided grass was quite strong and flexible while green. They had to work with it before it dried, as it became stiff at that point. Warren would immediately use each length as Jim finished the braiding. Once in place, drying was of no consequence.

They would not move to the hut, as the days were warm and it was not necessary to shut themselves into the darkness of the hut just yet. Winter would be soon enough. He would be able to check for leaks in the roof with a nice summer rain.

When the fireplace was finished, Jim would test it out. When he did, he found that the flue drew rather well. He was quite pleased that his architectural background had been helpful. They would have to be extremely careful when placing wood in the fireplace, as not to create flying sparks. One burning ember would set the roof on fire and the whole hut would go up in smoke.

Warren suggested they store everything elsewhere during the winter months, in case the hut did burn. They could use the second tarp to cover the stuff. They didn't want to loose it all in a fire. Both agreed that a fire in the hut would only be necessary during the cold months. This would limit the hazard.

Shortly, Warren came down from the rock. He sat in his usual place by the fire watching Jim continue the cooking. He'd been turning the pieces of boar for over three hours. This meat definitely had to be well done. Not coming from your local grocery store, there was no telling what they'd catch if it was not cooked completely.

"Well the chimney's just about finished." Warren spoke up. "Just some mud to fill the cracks and it'll be fine. I can see all the spots that need work. When we build the first fire in it, the smoke should show quite clearly where mud chinking will be needed."

After a few moments of silence, Jim turned to Warren. "Warren, thanks so much for the tree. It's so nice." He turned back to the fire, shifting the meat on the grill. "I remember the Christmas trees at Mom and Dad's, sixteen and eighteen feet tall, by the staircase. They were so beautiful. Mom would always put a bird's nest in the tree. A real one she'd found outside. It's good luck, you know. And the ornaments, birds and tinsel. There were over three hundred little twinkle lights." He turned and looked at the tree. "And your tree's beautiful, too. I'll always remember this."

Warren got up and went to the tent, then returned with his guitar. He sat back down in his place by the fire and began to strum softly. "I remember Christmas at home, too. Linda and the kids were always so excited." He paused and smiled. "You know, I was, too, even though I never let it show. I sort of regret that now."

Jim smiled and looked at Warren. "Well, I always knew there was a heart under that hairy chest of yours. You may not want to admit it, but you really are a sucker for sentiment."

"Look who's talking. I don't know anyone who can cry at the drop of a hat like you can, all those tearjerker movies. Wish I had a dime for every tear you've cried over those things. I'd be a multimillionaire." Warren laughed and gave Jim a jab at his right shoulder. "Yeah, there will never be another one like you."

Jim laughed. "Maybe it's probably a good thing. How would the world survive with another ME around? *Je ne c'est pas?*" He laughed while putting the mushrooms and some of the wild onion tops into a pan, setting it on the edge of the grill. A piece of boar fat was added to grease the surface.

Warren continued strumming chords until they slowly fell into the organized pattern of *Silent Night*. Within moments, they were both humming the song. Slowly the words began to form. "'Sleep in heavenly peace. Silent night. Holy night. All is calm. All is bright.'"

They sang several carols before Jim prepared the two metal plates. The smaller pieces of meat were done. Before handing Warren his plate, he poured some of the honey over the meat.

"Watch out." Jim commented. "This meat's hotter than hell. And that hot honey will burn the shit out of your mouth, if you're not careful."

They'd basically been surviving on the one meal a day that Jim prepared. It had not been easy, but it was helping Warren loose his excess weight. Construction around the camp had him using his physical strength. His muscles were beginning to tone up significantly. He had started feeling pretty good about himself. It had been some time since he'd been in such good shape. He also noticed that he was not as tired or winded when he went on his hunting outings.

Warren was starving. A few bites made him aware as to how hungry he really was. Everything tasted so good. "I think I could eat the whole thing."

Jim laughed. "Why do you think I cooked so much? I knew you were really hungry. Take your time, there's plenty." Jim took a few bites. "Not bad at all, if I do say so myself."

After about thirty minutes, they had nearly eaten all the small pieces of meat, as well as the other goodies Jim had fixed. The larger pieces remained on the grill to continue their slow cooking. Jim would watch them for several hours to make sure they were done. Then he'd put them in the plastic bag and submerge them in the creek to keep them cool.

"How about a few strawberries?" Jim dished half into Warren's metal bowl and half into his. "Don't expect much." Before he started cooking, he had put them in a metal pot, poured honey over them, then let them sit. He hoped it might give them some flavor. He tasted one. "Better than I expected."

"Great idea, the honey." Warren added.

"Well I had to do something. These things are normally as tasteless as an old shoe."

It was already night by the time Jim gathered the dishes. "I'll wash them tomorrow, after all…"

The pause was enough for Warren to realize the obvious line Jim was to quote next. In unison they spoke it aloud.

"'Tomorrow is another day.'"

They both laughed.

Warren stretched his arms in the air, then picked up his guitar again. The chords he strummed were random, but not unappealing. He paused for a moment and stared at Jim. "Wouldn't it be nice to have a cup of coffee?" He chuckled slightly at the wishful statement. "I think I remember how it tasted." He went back to his strumming.

Jim had placed a pot of water on the grill earlier. It was almost at a steam. A smile came to his face. "Yeah. I can remember going home for the holidays. Mom would put on a thirty cup urn. By mid-afternoon she'd have to put on another one." He paused for a few moments as he looked in the pot. "I also remember the mornings I'd come over to your house for coffee."

"Yeah. I'd play the bridge game in the news paper and start the crossword puzzle." Warren laughed. "And of course you were no help at all. You can't spell your way out of a paper bag. It amazes me how you got through six years of college. You sure you didn't get your degree from a mail order catalogue?" He continued to laugh. "Guess it's not nice to poke fun on Christmas Eve."

"That's alright. I'll think of something. Just give me a few minutes." He got up from his position by the fire and went to the tent.

Warren could hear him rummaging but paid no attention. He started singing the phrases of *Hark the Harold*. Looking over to the grill, he noticed Jim's pot of water bubbling. With his right hand, he moved it to the flat rock by the fire. Jim always used it as a trivet. "Your water's boiling!" He yelled toward the tent, having no idea why the water was heating.

"Be out in a minute." Jim's voice sounded from the tent. Soon he emerged with the two metal cups in his hand. Warren could not see because of the darkness. The fire was their only light.

Jim had waited for this moment to have the darkness as a cover. He moved toward his spot by the fire, while Warren played on, not taking much notice. He filled the cups with hot water. With a sterling silver teaspoon from his shirt pocket, he stirred the cups. He turned holding his cup in his left hand, and extended the other cup toward Warren with his right. "I know it's not much help, but Merry Christmas to us anyway."

A curl of steam from the cup drifted across Warren's face. "I don't believe it. I forgot you said you had this stuff."

"Yeah. It was going to be part of that special meal I was going to fix on that last Sunday on the river. I'm glad we have it now. Sorry it's not black, but I guess 'Cafe Mocha' with a splash of Amaretto is better than nothing."

"Never thought I'd say it, but let's hear it for General Foods." He looked at Jim and smiled. "Merry Christmas to us."

They raised their cups and clanked them slowly together, then sipped the hot liquid. They were surprised at the flavor. They attributed it to their recent diet. It had become rather bland since the spices ran out. That one cup of coffee lasted for almost twenty minutes. Finally, they sipped the last drops from the cups. "Just one more, Warren. It's Christmas."

Warren could not resist and handed his cup to Jim with a smile.

Momentarily, they had another steaming cup in their hands. Warren took a few sips, placed his cup down and softly strummed his guitar. His mind recalled past Christmases. "I remember the Christmas I got my first electric train set. I think I was nine years old. It was a Lionel passenger train, the cars lighted, and the whistle blew. Took me almost three hours to set it up. The houses, lights and trees made it look real nice. We set it up so it would go around the Christmas tree." Warren stopped his strum and sipped his coffee again. "Guess I'll never forget those times."

"I know what you mean. Thank God for memories. I think we'd go insane if it weren't for memories." Jim took a sip. "I remember my first electric train, too. We set it up on the dining room table. But we had to take it down to eat." Jim was staring off into space and gave a little laugh. "Wonder how everyone's doing this Christmas Eve? Bet they're all getting ready to go to Midnight Mass. I can almost smell the incense, and all the candles on the altar." He smiled.

"You lucky Catholics." Warren joked. "You got your going to church out of the way the night before. We had to get up Christmas morning and go. Maybe that's why I resent Church. I wanted to stay home and open presents. I even think God would have wanted to open presents first."

"You know, I think you're right." Jim agreed.

They laughed.

Jim turned the meat on the grill. "I'll give it another hour." He poked each piece with the fork.

"You know, Jim, I've had a few more thoughts about the top of the mountain. I mean where it came from. I've been relating it to places like Machu Picchu and the lost cities in Central America. These were centers with thousands of people. Then for seemingly no reason, they completely disappeared, and all we know of them is what they left behind. Maybe that's what happened to the folks who built the wall."

Jim interrupted. "*Je suis* confused. If that's the case, we'd have some kind of metropolis around here, and I sure as hell haven't seen a thing. Not even so much as a Doric column."

"If you just wait a minute! Always interrupting before I can finish what I'm saying. Now. What was I saying, before I was so rudely interrupted?"

"So rudely interrupted!" Jim mocked sarcastically, then stuck his tongue out at Warren.

Warren smiled for a moment, then quickly stuck out his tongue, crossed his eyes, put his thumbs in his ears and waved his hands.

Jim was so surprised that he broke out laughing. "I deserved that." He continued to laugh.

Warren began to laugh. After they finally settled down, Warren continued. "As I was saying, the wall was probably built by people that don't or didn't live nearby, or we'd have seen some kind of evidence, as you so stated. Now if these people didn't live here, where would they have lived? And why would they come here?" He paused a few moments in thought.

"Well, if it were me, I'd not live too far away. That's one long damn trek to get to the top of that rock. Why didn't they build that thing where they lived?"

"I was coming to that." He paused again. "There has to be something special about this location. But I've got no idea what it could be. Now. As to where they lived, your guess is as good as mine."

"Buckhead!" Jim exclaimed.

"Buckhead?"

"Yeah, you know. Out on Andrews Drive, West Paces Ferry Road. You know. 'THE' side of town."

"Asshole." Warren shook his head.

"Roswell?" Jim started to laugh. "Dunwoody?"

"Oh, shut the fuck up!"

"I was just making a few suggestions." Jim laughed.

"Suggestions like that, I can do without right now." Warren paused in his contemplation. "I know wherever it is, it's not close by. We'd have been able to see something when we were up there, and all I could see was forest. My hunting trips have turned up no evidence of other human existence either."

"Maybe they lived by the ocean!" Jim popped up.

Warren looked at Jim with surprise. "That's what I thought, too. But that's one hell of a trip to come here."

"Maybe they don't come that often. Maybe it's a pilgrimage, like in the Canterbury Tales, or the pilgrimages to the Religious Shrines in Europe. Maybe it's like the Shroud of Turin. They only bring it out every ten years or so. Hell! I understand when it's on display, you can't get within a hundred miles of the place because of all the people."

"Keep talking. I think you might have something."

"Well. That's really all I have to say."

"Maybe you've hit it! A religious shrine! That would make it important enough to come long distances."

"But the markings don't look real religious. They're more like astronomy signs."

"What do you mean? Someone who studied architecture and art, as well as religion, you're an idiot not to equate astronomy and religion."

"God, you're right! I AM an idiot. All the damn religions are related to the sky in some way or another. Stonehenge, the Egyptians, the Greeks, the Romans, Aztecs, Mayans." Jim recalled many of the ancient cultures.

"Even the great Cathedrals of Europe are oriented to the East and the Rising Sun. The altar's in the east end and the main entrance always faces west. That's why it's called the West Front. You're right! Maybe it is something religious." Jim paused again. "And here it is, Christmas Eve, the Star in the east." He reached over, turning the pieces of meat on the grill. "There. I think they're about finished." He moved the pieces to the edge of the grill.

"Maybe we'll go up there and check it all again."

Jim became excited. He'd been wanting to go up again. "When?"

"When I get back."

"When you get back? From where?"

"Thought I'd go get the rest of the stuff after the first of the year. Everything's been going pretty good and I'd really like to have all our stuff here before winter sets in."

The weather had been so nice Jim had not thought of the cold. Even with this being Christmas Eve, the thought of snow and ice was inconceivable with all the greenery and flowers. Jim didn't want to think about it. "You're going in about a week?"

"Yeah. It's probably the right time. The hut will be basically finished. When I'm gone, I want you just to chill out and watch everything until I get back."

"What if something happens?"

"Like what?"

"Well. Uhh." Jim fidgeted in anxiety. "*The Beast of Hollow Mountain.* Or you get lost. Or I get lost. Or?"

"Just don't worry. Everything will be fine." Warren paused a moment looking directly at Jim. He could see the uneasiness on Jim's face. "I'd take you along, God knows I could use the company, but someone has to stay here and watch things, and keep the fire going. You'll do a good job holding down the fort." He saw Jim smile. He knew that as long as he could keep Jim's spirits up, everything would run smoothly. "While I'm gone, do something different. Surprise me!"

Jim peered into the darkness as a few projects he'd been thinking about ran through his mind. A smile was on his face and his worried expression changed. He felt needed and necessary.

"How about one more cup of your special coffee before we go to bed?"

"Sure!" Jim jumped up, grabbed the cups and ran to the tent. "I'll have to boil a little more water. It'll only take a few minutes." In a moment, he was out of the tent and back at the fire. Warren carried the metal coffeepot down to the creek and filled it with water. Darkness was not a deterrent, as his eyes were accustomed to the dim light.

Jim set the pot on the grill, and removed the pieces of meat to let them cool. Warren got up and went to the tent. He returned to his place by the fire and strummed his guitar again. He had checked his watch. "One hour and seventeen minutes and it'll be Christmas."

It took almost twenty minutes for the water to boil. Warren was getting tired. It had been a long day. By this time, they were normally asleep. But after all, it was Christmas Eve. Jim poured the hot water into the cups, handing one to Warren.

"Merry Christmas again, Warren." Jim raised his cup.

"You, too, Jim." Warren raised his. He reached in his pocket and pulled out his watch. He brought it with him from the tent to keep track of the time. He knew Jim would constantly be asking the time; the closer it got to midnight. He tilted the watch toward the light of the fire. "Four after eleven." He uttered, then sipped his coffee. He watched Jim smile and sip his coffee.

The air had cooled. Warren felt it to be in the lower sixties. He got up and went to the tent. He returned with Jim's coat.

"Thanks Warren. It is getting a bit cool."

He sat down by the fire again, and took another sip. Momentarily, he reached in his pocket. "Eleven seventeen." He said out loud. He sat his cup down and picked up his guitar again. He looked over at Jim crouched in his spot by the fire. Jim was staring into the flames, holding his cup with both hands. "You okay?"

Jim was slightly startled as Warren's voice broke his mind wander. "Oh. Yeah. Just thinking about Christmas."

Warren continued the soft strumming, breaking only for a periodic sip of his coffee. He watched Jim, still staring into the fire, saying nothing. Then he saw it. The glistening of the fire reflected in the tear running down Jim's left cheek. He slowly put down his guitar, stood up, walked over to Jim, and put his right hand on Jim's right shoulder.

Jim looked up at Warren. His lower lip was under his upper teeth trying not to cry. He stood up.

Warren pulled him close in a hug. He could feel Jim's arms reach around him and his whole body shuddered, as he began to cry on Warren's shoulder. The sound was muffled in Warren's plaid flannel shirt. He patted Jim's back, and put his left cheek against Jim's head.

"How did this happen to us?" Jim cried.

"I don't know, Jim." Warren said softly. "Serendipity, I guess. But don't worry. Everything will be alright." He held Jim for a few minutes. "Come on over and sit with me. We'll finish our coffee." He gave Jim a tight hug and patted his back. Warren could feel Jim's hands move up and down over his back and his body began to relax. Jim would be alright now.

They moved to where Warren had been sitting. Warren had his right arm over Jim's shoulders. Jim wiped his eyes on the right sleeve of his jacket. They sat down, Warren in his regular spot and Jim on the ground next to him, crouching on his folded legs and feet. Warren put his left arm over Jim's shoulder and pulled him near. They sipped their coffee.

After a few moments, Jim spoke softly. "I'm sorry, Warren. I know we don't need problems like this. I just slipped and couldn't help myself."

"Don't sweat it." Warren answered softly with a slight laugh in his voice. He patted Jim's shoulder. He set his cup down and pulled the watch from his pocket. "Well, it's sixteen minutes until twelve. Almost that time." He sat the watch on his knee and picked up his cup again. He looked up. "The sky's as clear as a bell, and look at all those stars."

Jim looked up. The night sky was a deep blue-black studded with a vast number of stars. "It really is pretty."

At that moment, a large bright meteor flashed across the sky.

"Did you see that?" Jim said with surprise.

"Really beautiful!" Warren answered. "It's been a while since I've seen one that big."

"Maybe that's our Christmas Star. Do you think we should go

follow it?" Jim laughed.

"Yeah, and by the time we got back, we'd be old and gray." Warren joked.

"Think I'll touch up our coffee one more time. We'll have a nice fresh cup to usher in Christmas." Jim quickly jumped up and took the cups to the tent. When he returned, he removed the pot of water, still hot on the grill, and filled the cups. He stirred them with his silver spoon, handed Warren his cup and returned to the spot next to Warren.

"Thanks, Jim." Warren tipped his watch toward the fire. "Eleven fifty-eight. Two minutes." He took a sip.

They sat in silence as the time passed. Warren held the watch in his left hand, tipping it toward the light. After a few moments, he popped the lid shut and put it in the upper right pocket of the flannel shirt. "Well. Merry Christmas, Jim." With his left arm he pulled Jim close.

Jim put his right arm around Warren's left calf and gave a shake. "Merry Christmas to you, too, Warren." He raised his cup.

Warren clanged his cup against Jim's.

"God bless us. One and all." Jim chuckled.

They slowly finished their coffee, then Jim got up and placed the pieces of meat in the plastic bag. He sat the pot of hot water on the nearby rock. Warren took the bag down to the creek and submerged it with a rock. Everything was ready so they could go to bed. Soon they were in the tent in their sleeping bags.

"Sorry I don't have a present for you." Jim spoke.

"I don't have one for you either."

"Well, we do have our health and we seem to be doing okay. Guess we should be glad of that."

"Yeah, that's true."

They lay silent, until both were asleep.

CHAPTER XXII

The morning events had gone as usual. There was nothing out of the ordinary.

Warren had gone hunting the day before, without success. He'd been using his newly completed bow. The arrows were few in number. Bamboo reeds did not seem to be the best, but they were the only things presently available. In a test, one hit a tree and splintered. Even with some clay stuffed in the lead end, they tended to wander, as the head was not heavy enough to really keep the shaft steady in flight.

To protect the string, Jim placed a thin piece of animal skin where the arrow would be mounted. With additional skin, he made a quiver to hold the arrows. He also wrapped the handle on the bow with some skin. This would allow Warren a good gripping area.

Warren was pleased at the bow's power and flexibility, when he tested it. He was sure his proficiency would return with a little practice. When time permitted, he planned to make a bow for Jim, then teach him how to use it. He knew Jim would grasp the principle of how to shoot very quickly.

Jim was thinking about his oven and its construction. Warren suggested a spot to build it, on the rock, away from the hut, on the southwest edge of the rock. Maybe it could be completed before the end of the summer.

Warren was proud of Jim and his venturesome qualities. Nothing seemed to deter his desire to seek new food sources. If Jim had fears, he seemed to be dealing with it, as he never made major references to it. During his outings, all Jim ever carried was a six foot stick to which Warren had attached his small hunting knife. Warren remembered Jim commenting he felt like some warrior, with his spear. Warren suggested he carry the machete, too. But he rarely did. He was going to have to talk to Jim about his boldness. Too much boldness could lead to danger.

Warren placed a few more pieces of wood on the fire. Jim had been gone all morning. Suddenly, he could discern the distant strains of some classical piece, sung in a 'la, da, da' manner. "Well at least he's in a good mood." He chuckled to himself. "Maybe he's found something worth while."

In a few moments, the strains of the *Eighteenth Variation on the Paganini Theme*, by Rachmaninoff, grew louder from the woods to the southwest. Entering the camp area, the singing figure stopped, pumped his spear into the air with his left arm, and held his camera case aloft. A smile covered his face and his eyes sparkled.

"Happy New Year!" The yell resounded from the south side of the creek.

Warren smiled. He was glad to hear cheer in Jim's voice. "Happy New Year! Sounds like you're in a good mood. What's up?" He yelled while watching Jim cross the bridge to the rock.

Jim passed the hut, and down the steps they had built on the north face. "It's such a beautiful day, and I feel terrific." Finally, he was standing at the fire with Warren. "Look at some of the things I found." He placed his spear on the ground, opened his camera case and popped it toward Warren.

Warren saw all sorts of things in the case: roots, leaves and fungi. The only things he could recognize were the bright red strawberries. "Looks great, but what's the rest of this stuff? I mean besides the strawberries."

Jim laughed, giving Warren a soft punch with his left fist to Warren's right shoulder. "Just wait! You'll love it." He paused. "You know, there's a lot of things out there. All we have to do is find them." He pulled a few hands full of flower petals from his pocket and put them in the small pot. "These are for later." He carried the pot to the tent. Returning, he reached down for the coffeepot and started toward the creek. "How about some tea?"

"Sounds good." Warren sat down. Jim dominated the moment and he didn't want to disturb it. It was important Jim remain in good spirits. Things would go much smoother. Then, for an instant, the thought of winter flashed through his mind. He quickly dismissed this. It was a bridge they would cross soon enough.

Jim returned from the creek, placed the pot on the grill, rummaged through his camera case and pulled out a root. He extended it toward Warren. "Here! Smell this!"

Warren leaned forward, putting his nose close to the root. "Smells like sassafras."

"Give that man a cigar!" He grabbed the root, throwing it into the coffeepot.

Jim was sure the root was not the sassafras he knew back home, but it was possibly an early relative.

"You were gone before I got up this morning. I don't believe it."

"Couldn't sleep. Just couldn't turn off the mind. If I get tired, I'll take a little nap this afternoon."

"What's the problem?"

"Oh nothing. Just thinking about a few projects."

"Oh really? Like what?" Warren's curiosity was peaked.

"Something like…" Jim paused and stared up at the sky, stroking his beard with his left hand. "Maybe a time machine." He turned to Warren, laughing. "Just kidding. Just kidding." He stirred the pot. "I was thinking about the oven, the dam, and moving the garden spot to the other side of the creek. I'll try to get several things underway while you're gone."

Warren smiled. "Fantastic!" He paused for a few moments. "Yeah, thought I might leave in the next day or two. Things seem to be going pretty good." He paused again. "I want you to keep the pistol handy. I'll take the shotgun. Think you'll be able to hold the fort?"

"I think so." Jim laughed. He was momentarily silent as his mind jumped to another area of concern. "Warren, if by some chance you some how get back, I mean, without me..." He laughed a little trying to cover his fear of being left alone. "I mean."

"Hey!" Warren reached over with his right hand and grabbed Jim's left shoulder. Jim looked up at Warren who stared into his eyes. "We're buddies. 'All for one and one for all.' If we get back, it's going to be together. If I find a way, I'll be back for you. You know damn well you'd not last three months here by yourself. You've got too much to learn before you can stand alone out here. In time, you'll do just fine." He was silent for a moment. "I'll start teaching you a few things when I get back from the trip. One thing that's really important is that you start to hunt. And with a bow and arrows." He stopped to make sure everything was sinking in. "Jim, I'd never leave you here alone. I promised you that in the beginning. I will never leave you behind. You're my best friend, and friends are forever. You hear me?"

"Yeah. I hear you." Jim felt rather stupid. He looked at Warren and smiled. He placed his right hand to his left shoulder, rubbing the top of Warren's hand. "Yeah. I hear you."

Finally, the tea was ready. The honey made it something quite pleasant. After having a few cups, the pot was empty.

"Think I'm going to take a short nap. Do you mind?"

"Nah. I'll clean up the guns while you get some rest." Warren commented as Jim headed for the tent.

"Now don't let me sleep too long."

"I won't. You have to fix New Year's Eve dinner." He laughed.

"I know that's right." Jim laughed as he entered the tent. Virtually immediately, he came back out of the tent and yelled to Warren. "By the way. Did you ever turn your watch back? To regular time? You know it switched from Daylight Savings to regular time over a month ago."

"Actually, I didn't. Not that it really matters here. But just to keep everything in line, I will do it right now."

"No. Don't worry about it. You are right. It really doesn't matter anymore. We don't even use the watch. We will stick with the time that's on it now. It is good enough."

"Okay. Sounds good to me. Yeah. An hour either way doesn't really matter. The sun will rise when it rises. Nothing will change that." He began to laugh.

"And that's the truth." Jim joined the laughter. He turned and entered the tent again.

Warren sat cleaning the guns. His mind began to form a scenario as to what would happen if he accidentally found a way back. Would he be able to come back and get Jim? There was no way Jim could survive alone. "Alone." He softly spoke aloud. If ever there was someone who needed others around him, it was Jim. "He'd die of loneliness." Warren stopped oiling the bolt mechanism of the gun. Holding it in his lap, he looked toward the tent and began to put himself in the same situation. But he was totally different. HE was a survivor. HE could survive. Maybe it was the uncivilized animal within himself. He chuckled. "That's it! I was right all along. Jim's too civilized." He shook his head and continued the cleaning. After a while, he began to quietly whistle. He was not really aware of it, but the melody was *Auld Lang Syne*.

As the hours passed, the day slipped away and darkness began to invade the camp. Warren finished the guns and gathered the food items together near the fire, in anticipation of Jim's cooking plans. Shortly, he heard movement in the tent.

"What time is it?" A yawning yell issued from the tent.

"It's night time." Warren laughed.

"Night time? Why didn't you wake me up sooner? I didn't miss it, did I?"

"No. It's not midnight yet. It's only around eight thirty."

"I'll be out in a minute. I know you're starving!" Jim came stumbling from the tent, zipping his pants, still a little groggy.

"You needed it." Warren commented. "That's okay. I've got everything ready and set by the fire."

"Thanks, that was thoughtful of you." Jim smiled and immediately went about starting the meal.

"Think we might be able to have some of the special coffee tonight?" Warren asked.

"Hell yes! It's New Year's Eve. I'll make us some after dinner." He paused. "Would you like some now?" He looked at Warren and saw a Cheshire smile covering his face, his head nodding rapidly in the affirmative. Jim handed the pot to Warren. "Would you mind getting some water?"

"No problem." Warren grabbed the pot, taking it to the creek. He rinsed it then filled it with water. Quickly returning to the fire, he placed it on the grill. Jim shifted it to a spot that wouldn't hinder his cooking.

Soon the frying pan sizzled with the mixture of meat and other items of Jim's choice. The water in the coffeepot finally started steaming. Jim got the two metal cups and went to the tent. When he returned, he poured the water in each and stirred. He handed one to Warren. "Wait!" Jim jumped up, running to the tent. He returned with his camera. Adjusting the lens and aperture setting, he connected the strobe. "I've not thought about this for weeks. I have to get some more pictures of the area, hut, and the top of the mountain."

Warren looked puzzled.

"Well. Who knows? Should we get back, we'll have these developed and make a mint. Who else do you know has photos of the past? This could be a real gold mine. While you're gone, I might zip up to the top of the mountain. I can't believe I've been so stupid not to take pictures for so long. Dumb! Real Dumb!" He propped the camera on a rock, crouched down beside it to look through the lens, then adjusted the focus. "Warren. Stand right there." He made one final adjustment and set the timer. "You ready?"

"Yeah."

He pressed the button and ran to stand next to Warren. Warren quickly handed Jim his cup and put his arm around him. They looked at the camera and smiled.

'ZZZZZZZZZ'. 'Click'. The bright strobe flashed, momentarily blinding them. They laughed and clanged their cups together.

Jim ran to the rock, picked up the camera and ran it back to the tent. Soon he was back at the fire, sipping the special coffee. "We'll eat in a little while." He stirred the concoction in the pan.

When it was done, Jim served. He constantly criticized the food while he ate. Warren could not understand how he could be so unflattering, especially since there wasn't much to work with. He thought it was pretty good, taking all into consideration.

Together they cleaned up the dishes, pots and utensils. That completed, they sat by the fire with a fresh cup of the special coffee. Now they would wait.

Warren checked his watch, as he had done at Christmas. As they sat, Warren thought how strange it was to be celebrating the New Year when the temperature was so warm.

As the time drew near, Jim ran to the tent with the cups. Returning, he had not only the cups, but also a pot full of flower petals. He handed one of the cups to Warren. "It's not coffee."

Warren took a sip of the scotch. "You know, you never lose the taste for the good things."

Jim sipped his Amaretto, after taking his place by the fire again.

The time finally arrived. Warren tipped his watch toward the fire to see the hands. "Get ready! Fifteen, fourteen, thirteen, twelve…" He counted out loud, closed the watch and put it on a nearby rock. They both stood as they counted. Jim quickly put a handful of petals in Warren's hand. "Nine, eight, seven, six, five, four, three, two, one, Happy New Year!" The colored petals flew into the darkness.

Jim looked at Warren. "Happy New Year, Warren." He gave him a big hug.

"Happy New Year, Jim." He replied.

They clinked the cups together and started singing. Warren put his arm around Jim and they swayed back and forth with the rhythm of *Auld Lang Syne*. As the last words ended, they stood there in silence for some time. Neither moved.

Jim finally turned to Warren, holding his cup in the air. "And it will be a good year. I just know it will." He smiled.

"Yes. It will be a good year." Warren smiled and pulled Jim close with a hug. It was quiet again.

After a few moments, Jim broke the silence. "Guess we'll clean up the confetti, streamers, and champagne glasses tomorrow." He laughed out loud.

Warren could only laugh, too. What could he say? He grabbed Jim in a big hug again. "You crazy idiot."

They sipped the last of their drink, then dropped the cups in the hot water in the coffeepot. He would wash them tomorrow.

Warren zipped the flap of the tent closed. The warmer weather would be bringing the insect population into play. He knew they'd be eaten alive if they didn't start taking precautions. He could feel the cool air on his skin when he removed his clothes. It felt to be around sixty to sixty-five degrees. He unzipped his sleeping bag and opened it, so he wouldn't be covered. He lay naked in the dark.

Jim was already in his sleeping bag. He heard the zipper in the dark and wondered what was happening. "What are you doing?"

"I didn't want to bake tonight. I opened my sleeping bag." Warren quietly answered.

"Bake? Did I hear you say bake? I think you're going to freeze your fucking ass off, if you ask me."

All was silent for a while. Warren was comfortable. Jim finally broke the silence.

"Warren?" Jim's voice was clear in the dark.

"Yeah?" Warren replied.

"Happy New Year."

"Happy New Year, Jim."

The night sounds filled the darkness outside the tent. Soon, the two were asleep.

CHAPTER XXIII

Warren did not leave as soon as he had planned. It was over a week before he did.

It took him less than five days to get to the river. He basically followed the same route they'd taken, going to Stone Mountain. Being alone and traveling light cut the time considerably. He set up a quick camp at the old site by the river.

After resting, he went to the stone marker. Nothing gave a hint as to why or what caused the giant leap in time. Everything was as it had been when they were there last, except for the green leaves and other foliage on all the plants.

The sun had just broken through the darkness, when he awoke. He had been at the river only a day. He'd already constructed a litter, using his hunting knife. The remaining items were packed and ready to go. It would be the last day before heading back to Stone Mountain.

He dressed and decided to go north one more time. He walked along the east bank.

It was almost an hour since he started when he heard strange noises coming from the west bank. He walked closer to the edge of the river, looking across the two hundred feet of water in front of him. He couldn't believe his eyes.

There in the shallows of the west bank was a small group of mastodons. Now he knew. He and Jim had gone back a considerable length of time, as they had thought. The lack of people and the existence of mastodons would put them at least fifteen thousand years into the past.

He stood watching the creatures play and wash themselves. He could hardly contain himself, thinking what Jim was going to say about the woolly animals. Another piece of the puzzle was falling into place, but there were still many pieces missing.

He'd seen no evidence of the furry elephants on the east side of the river. Maybe they had no need to migrate to the east bank. Maybe the river was acting like a natural barrier, halting their crossing, at least for the present. They were probably happy where they were and had no reason to venture east. He watched for nearly half an hour, then realized he had to get moving.

The rest of the day was spent doing some exploring of the area, to see what was growing. He was pleased to find several trees that looked like likely candidates for fruit trees. Many of the vines were like grape. Only time would tell if they would bare fruit.

In the late afternoon, he took a quick swim in the river to clean up, even though it was still quite cold. This would also let him relax, something he really needed to do, as the trip back was going to be a long one. He also knew Jim was going to give him a haircut and trim his facial hair when he got back. Of that, he was glad. If he were by himself, it would be real easy to take an 'I don't care' attitude about his appearance. But Jim would keep them as civilized as he could. Probably not a bad thing. His mind chuckled.

He'd caught a fish, using a length of line and a colored lure brought with him. Warren put it on a stick and stuck it in the ground at a forty-five degree angle over the fire. A few stones helped hold it in place. Soon it was done and quickly consumed.

He thought of Jim and what he was probably doing at that moment. He then thought of the mastodons again. It was going to be funny to see his reaction.

Before retiring, he covered his supplies and made ready for the trip the next day. The supply of dried meat, he'd brought, would be his main stay, on the way back.

As he lay looking up at the clear sky, he watched the light of day pass into evening, and the stars began to come out. It had been seven days, and he missed Jim's craziness, his off the wall comments, and his touches of French. But most of all, he missed his companionship. He never thought there would come a day when he would have such feelings for another man. It was rather surprising. But this man was his friend, and he genuinely missed him. He had to laugh to himself.

"Jim's not even a woman." He spoke quietly. He could not deny the sense of loss, with Jim not there. He knew where he was coming from both mentally and sexually, and his attitudes were very normal, as far as he was concerned. Yet, deep inside, there was something he could not put his finger on, gnawing at him. Maybe it was Jim's cooking, conversation, and friendship. Maybe it was the sensitivity and compassion rubbing off. "It's this stupid situation!" He thought out loud. Something of this magnitude would definitely be enough to shake the foundations of one's inner self. Every day was a new experience, and he never knew what was in store.

Maybe it WAS the situation making him feel the way he did. But could it be his attitudes were changing? Could it be he was reaching out into the darkness for anyone, regardless of who it was or its gender?

He thought of a comment he'd made concerning the situation. He had told Jim he would rather be with him more than anyone else, with the predicament. It was undeniable. It was true. "I'm really fond of the son-of-a-bitch. What do you think of that?"

The sky was now a vast blue-black void, scattered with a thousand lights. For one split second, he found himself asking for help to see them through. This was another momentary shock, chipping at his staunch self-reliance. Had some of Jim's Catholicism crept into his psyche?

He smiled and yelled with hesitant jest at the sky. "Okay God! I give up! Now, please let me go to sleep. I've got a long day tomorrow."

Suddenly, his mind thought of the mastodons. Sure hope they stay on their side of the river, at least for a while. It would be necessary to construct additional protection when he got back. Where there are mastodons, there most likely are other major creatures of destruction. We'd be quick snacks. He knew he'd have to instruct Jim at being more cautious on his outings.

Again it became obvious, he had to stop his mind trip and get to sleep. Dawn would be there soon enough. He wanted to get as far as he could the next day. He wanted to get home to Jim. "I hope he's alright."

The sounds of the night things created a constant, entrancing tone. Warren began to listen. It was working. Drowsiness set in and finally the peace of sleep.

CHAPTER XXIV

Jim woke up as dawn was breaking. He lay there in the tent staring straight up. It was still quite dark inside the tent. He thought of Warren. He'd been gone for almost two weeks. Today would mark their ninety-seventh day in 'Never Land'.

Two weeks alone had forced him to work on a few things to keep his mind off being alone and having concern about Warren. He had worked diligently on the oven and it was completed two days earlier. His main project now was the dam. There was almost two feet of rock, mud and reeds built up at the edge of the mountain, then south, toward the creek. The stones were beginning to become scarce in the immediate area. There were larger ones, but these were impossible for him to lift alone, and he had no desire to play 'chain gang'.

He was quite pleased at the way the oven turned out. The creek mud he used to fill the cracks and the grill fit very well in the cooking chamber. The entire design was based on indirect heating of the food. The fire would be burning in an adjacent chamber. The heat and smoke would flow through the cooking chamber, then out the chimney. Such a cooking arrangement would prevent the fire setting any dripping fat ablaze.

He wanted to wait for Warren to return before testing it out. It would also indicate spots where additional mud fill was needed. All in good time, he thought.

The planned trip to the top of the mountain was cancelled. He wanted Warren to be in any pictures taken there. People in photos can be very helpful in giving scale to the viewer. True, he could have used the timer on the camera, but he really wanted Warren to be there.

Still lying there, he wondered what he would do this day. He could continue work on the dam, but the rocks were getting rather heavy. His arms felt like they'd been stretched to the limit.

Exploring would not be very productive, but he might discover some new something of importance. Be my luck I'd get into trouble, too, and with Warren not here, that could be real dangerous.

He couldn't stand it any more. He was going to go exploring anyway.

Getting up and dressed, he notched the stick. "We've been here for three months already. I can hardly believe it." He set the stick down. "Why does it feel like forever?"

He rekindled the fire. The wood was the last of the Christmas tree. Warren cut it up before he'd left. Jim hated to see it go, but it was dead and all the needles had nearly fallen off.

Taking the old ashes from the fire, he carried them to the garden spot. The ashes were being placed around the plants.

The tomatoes, onions and potatoes were growing quite well. They'd been transplanted to the new garden spot, south of the creek. This task had been completed before Warren had gone to the river. It was necessary to prevent damage to the potatoes, before they started forming. Even a few of the apple seeds had sprouted. These would be moved to the far south side of the garden area, so as not to block the sunlight.

Some of the wild plants were there, too. The strawberries were placed to allow them to spread and not get in the way of the other plants. So far, everything seemed to be doing just fine. Periodic rains had been light and made manual watering unnecessary.

Jim filled the coffeepot with water and threw in a root. In a while, the sassafras tea was ready. He used some of the honey from their honey tree, as they now called it, to sweeten it.

His tea finished, he was ready for his venture. Several flat rocks were placed on the grill to shield it, should it rain. That done, he headed south and into the woods.

The machete and spear were his companions. The pistol remained in the tent. His camera case swung from his left shoulder. This would make it easier to carry any unexpected goody he might find.

Most of the territory was all too familiar now. Certain things he knew as well as the back of his hand. But in about three hours, he began to get into unexplored lands. The excitement made his heart began to beat with anticipation of something new and unknown.

Walking further south for some two hours, he'd crossed two unfamiliar creeks. Finally, he came to a clearing of some size. Tall grass, about five feet high, covered the entire area, along with a few small trees. The machete really came in handy at this point. He kept his eyes peeled for snakes.

On the southern edge of the area, he noticed a group of large trees. There was something about them he recognized. As he got closer, it became clear. They were apple trees. There was no explanation as to their origin. He'd always thought the apple tree was an import from Europe. Maybe they were here in the beginning, but somehow got wiped out by some unknown event. Whatever the case, there they were.

When he reached the trees, he saw there were small fruits beginning to develop. He was ecstatic. Apples keep for such a long time and they can be dried for use later. Plus they were healthy. His mind caused his mouth to water in anticipation of a bite. This was truly a major discovery and made the trip totally worthwhile. Now, even if the seeds that had sprouted back at camp didn't make it, they still had these.

The only thing they had to worry about was the birds and insects. They would surely have a field day before the harvest.

There were a few seedlings growing around the area. Maybe it would make sense to transplant a couple to the garden spot. It made sense to try a transplant. "Good project for the fall." At least the fall in this new time. And if the seeds he had planed grew, they could cross-pollinate them and who knows what might develop. But of course, this would take years. "And! We may still be here."

The sky above was a beautiful blue and white fluffy clouds moved slowly from the northwest. The sun was high and a little east. Jim guessed it to be around two o'clock in the afternoon. It was definitely time to start back. It would be evening before he got to camp.

Although there was the path in the grass, he had no desire to retrace his steps. It might be nice to circle in from the west.

All of a sudden, from the woods east of the clearing, there came a loud long roar. Jim's heart went into shock. The *Beast of Hollow Mountain* popped into his mind. "What the fuck was that?" Every monster in every horror movie, rolled into one, filled his mind's eye. He crouched down behind a clump of tall grass. Finally, it dawned on him the greenery would offer zero protection should it be the creature of doom. He had to get moving. The machete and spear would be of little consequence against whatever made that ungodly noise.

Suddenly, the roar filled the air again. Jim leaped from the spot and ran quickly into the western woods. He headed to the northwest with the same speed as that of his beating heart.

Moving as fast as possible for about an hour, he came to a creek. The water was slow, but there was no immediate crossing point. He headed for the northwest, until a section of the creek appeared that was rather wide, but shallow. Wading across, he continued northeast.

His mind constantly replayed the roar. He wished Warren was there. It would give him an inner strength and confidence somehow.

All of a sudden, his field of vision was filled by a mass of vines, hanging from the trees. It was another stroke of luck. They were scuppernong or grape or muscadine vines. Clusters of small, unripened fruit hung in profusion. This, too, would be another source of winter food. They could be dried like the apples and reconstituted with water. Stewed fruit was not only tasty, but it was good for you, too. "And it would definitely keep you regular." He chuckled.

His mind popped back to the situation at hand. Continuing northeast, another creek crossed his path. It was smaller than the other. He noticed a large patch of what looked to be watercress, growing in the water, against the north bank. He gathered up a hand full and rinsed it off in the creek. Some of this would be for dinner and some he'd save for tomorrow. The greenery would be good for the diet. He stuck the large bunch in the camera case and was off.

In no time at all, he recognized one of the regular landmarks. Reaching familiar territory gave him a warm feeling. It felt safer. Why this sense of security was present, he could not answer. What ever was out there could just as easily come walking into camp as it did roaring through the underbrush, out there in the wilds. It was sort of like the blanket, when you were a kid. If you could jump into bed quick enough and cover your head with the blanket, you were safe from all monsters, regardless of how big and ferocious they were.

Back at camp, he refurbished the fire. The meat in the plastic bag, stored in the creek, was gone. There was nothing to eat except the dry meat, now stored under the shed roof, adjacent to the hut on top of the rock. It seemed the best place to keep it to prevent scavengers or what ever from getting it. It would also stay drier there.

Putting some of the meat into the frying pan, he went to the garden spot to get a few of the wild onions.

He ate the food directly from the pan. He placed the crisp leaves from the creek into one of the metal bowls. Suddenly, there was a reverie of a wonderful French dressing he had when in Paris. It was at the restaurant on the second level of the Eiffel Tower. Sure would perk up the greens. And some salt and pepper would possibly enhance the meat dish. But the nearest grocery store was several thousand years way.

When the sun lowered in the east, the shadow of the mountain crept over the campsite. The air got a little cooler.

As it grew darker, the roar in the woods haunted him. His visibility diminished, from the edge of the camp, to a few feet beyond the firelight. For whatever reason, he got the pistol from the tent. There was a need to think safety.

He began to think about Warren. What if something did happen to him? Survival would be impossible. He caught himself. I must stop this. Mental panic is not good or advisable.

Quickly, he cleaned the pan, bowl and utensils. It was time to think about going to bed. There was no reason to stay up. He moved his sleeping bag and everything of import to the hut, on top of the rock. There was no way he was going to spend the night in the tent, down there in the open. The *Beast of Hollow Mountain* would surely get him. At least on the rock, there would be some difficulty in climbing, except for the bridge over to the garden. But that was alright. Anything that made THAT noise would surly be big enough to crush down the bridge, if it tried to cross it. He began to chuckle at his thoughts. The top of the rock seemed safer than anywhere else, at the moment. A log structure was better than a canvas tent. The story of the 'Three Little Pigs' came to mind, but he quickly dismissed it and laughed.

He crawled into his sleeping bag. It felt strange not being in the tent. It would be nice when Warren got back. He could hardly wait to tell him about the apple trees, the scuppernongs…and the unknown roar.

He stared into the darkness. "Good night, Warren, wherever you are." Those were the last words of the day.

CHAPTER XXV

Today would be Warren's ninth day of travel back to camp. He'd crossed the high ridgeline two days earlier. The large trees blocked the early morning light. It was gray and windy.

Before he could get his bedroll packed on the litter, the day turned to night, or so it seemed. The sky let go a major cloudburst. The rain fell in buckets full.

He could not believe it. Never had he seen such a downpour. He tried to keep going, but the rain was just too heavy. He had to find shelter.

Spotting a nearby outcropping of rocks, he headed for its cover. He leaned the litter against the rock and sat under the shallow stone ledge. Even with the canopy of the forest above, the rain was so dense, it would be necessary to wait out the storm.

The ledge kept out most of the weather, but the gusts of wind sometimes blew the downpour into the space where he was crouched. He really couldn't complain about the rain. It would cool the heat of the past few days. After all, it was now summer, even if he knew it was the end of January. The only thing he disliked was the thought of being completely soaked when the torrent was over.

Sitting only gave him the chance to think. The large creek he had to cross would be a real challenge with the rain. He was sure it would be flooded. All this rain had to go somewhere. Maybe he would take another route. But there really wasn't one. Regardless of how he went, it would be necessary to cross the creek at some point. Maybe he'd wait for them to recede. That could take too long.

This was ridiculous. He could only make a final decision when he reached the water. Then and only then would he know what he was going to do. He reached under the defalted raft covering the litter and grabbed a piece of dry meat to chew on.

When Jim got up, he took the knife and notched the stick. "One hundred days. I really need a more permanent way to keep track of this counting." He thought for a moment. Why was he keeping count of the days anyway? It was rather fruitless since the numbers meant nothing. After several years, termites or something would probably eat the pieces of wood. But the marking of the days did help him. The realization of the number of days they had survived would give them the courage to continue. It was a touch of civilization he had to continue. He was afraid that the more they let go, the more they would revert to primitive existence. This was totally disdainful to him.

A loud rumbling outside disturbed his thoughts. It was the sound of distant thunder. "Bet it's those damn Yankees again." He laughed. When he came out of the hut, he could see the sky to the west was getting dark, blotting out the morning sun. A storm was definitely on its way. He hoped Warren was alright. There was another distant clap of thunder.

He went around the camp picking up items needing shelter. He covered the firewood with the tarp, as he had many times in the past, placing rocks on the corners to prevent it from blowing off. He placed a few flat rocks on the grill to protect the fire. But this wasn't of major concern. He had more matches in one of the boxes in the hut. And if worse came to worse, he could try to use the lens from the camera to focus the rays of the sun on something combustible.

The ropes of the tent were secure. It still stood, even though he'd moved into the hut on the day of the strange noise. The thought of it was still lurking in his mind.

With everything battened down, he went back to the top of the rock. The clouds were getting closer and it was getting darker. Thunder grew louder and the wind began to pick up. He could smell the rain coming. The air cooled, becoming clean and moist to his nose. Within about twenty minutes, the first drops started to fall. Five minutes later, it was a downpour.

He looked out the doorway of the hut. Lightning sent bright flashes across the landscape, followed immediately by loud cracks. Some were so loud they made everything vibrate.

He lay on the sleeping bag. There were rivulets of water running down and off the rocks of the chimney opening of the fireplace. He was pleased there were no other significant leaks.

The storm, though severe, was hypnotic. He soon was asleep.

Jim's rest was disturbed by a violent crash. The only light was that of the lightning outside. Between flashes, there was just darkness. He had no idea what time it was. He wasn't sure if it was day or night. The rain poured down.

I wonder how Warren is faring with this gully washer? What about the garden? Was it being washed away? He tried to see out past the doorway, but it was no use. All he could do was return to his sleeping bag.

For Warren, the day had been a total and miserable waste. It had passed slowly. All he'd done was sit, crouching under the rock trying to keep dry.

He'd thought of Linda and the kids. There was a picnic that came to mind when it rained cats and dogs. The shelter they found leaked like a sieve. By the time they all got home, they were soaked to the skin. He laughed remembering Linda's long hair hanging straight, dripping from the ends. Her clothes clung as if glued to her body. Even her bra and panties were evident under her clothes.

His mind popped back to things at hand. The creek was definitely going to be a challenge. He knew it would be a bitch to get across.

He hoped Jim had taken precautions. This was the worse weather they'd seen while here. He imagined the campsite filling with water and everything washing down stream. He thought of Jim trying to retrieve it all. He laughed, as the image in his mind was quite humorous.

There was nothing he could do. He had to trust Jim's judgment and abilities to deal with the crisis.

As the day drew to a close, Warren knew he might as well try and get some rest. It would be difficult, but there was nothing else to do.

The rain lasted all night, but began to let up as dawn arrived. The worse of it seemed to be over.

Jim rose early, notching the hundred and first day. When he stepped from the hut; the result of the storm was evident.

The stream was now a river. The whole area of the campsite was under water. Three feet of water was up on the tent. Needless to say, the fire was gone. The dam he'd been working on had been a stroke of luck. It had prevented a strong current, which could have washed the tent down stream. But something else held the water back. Something further down stream was creating a natural obstruction, turning the whole thing into a large pond.

Am I glad I moved everything to the hut. And just in time, too. Everything happens for a reason. If I hadn't heard the roar in the woods, I could still be down there, along with everything else, drowning in the water. He shook his head. What luck. The only thing he would have to dry out was the tent and the cut firewood. Many pieces floated around in the swirling water. Some had floated beyond the dam construction.

He crossed the bridge to the garden. The sight was rather a surprise. Although the rain had beaten down several things and knocked some of the small tomatoes off the vines, nothing was damaged beyond recovery. The pine needles and leaves had held the soil, eliminating erosion. He collected the tomatoes, bringing them to the hut before the birds could get them.

Curiosity made him want to investigate the down stream blockage. He grabbed his spear and the machete and was off.

Within thirty minutes, the situation was obvious. A section of the earth bank had caved into the creek, right at the place a log lay across it. Several smaller logs and limbs added to the congestion. The combination created a substantial retainer. It was evident; it would take some time for the stream to recede.

Returning to camp, he waded into the new pond. With some effort, he retrieved the tent and the tarp. These were laid over a rock to dry out. The grill was next. He sure as hell didn't want to lose it. The logs were next. This took some time to gather them all and put them under the shed on the rock.

Now it was time to try and get the fire started again. Everything was soaked. There wasn't a dry twig to be found. The fire's importance was beginning to sink in. He had not anticipated a catastrophe so great as all the wood being wet. "Just like the Titanic. They never thought of anything so horrendous as to damage five consecutive watertight compartments. Oh well."

There was a small supply of wood under the shed roof on the rock. This could be used as a starter, then some of the wet wood could be placed carefully on the fire to prevent from putting it out. He made another decision. Now was as good a time as ever to test out the oven, as this could be considered an emergency situation. No way was he going to light a fire in the fireplace of the hut. Should something go wrong there, everything would be gone. The fireplace was a definite 'wait for Warren' project.

The dryer wood was neatly arranged in the fire chamber. What he needed was an ignition source and something that would start the twigs. Something like newspaper. But of course, there was no newspaper, and he wasn't about to rip up any of the boxes. He considered them too valuable. He also didn't want to waste a lot of matches trying to get the wood started. He racked his brain. He could use some of the lantern fuel, but he didn't dare. It was too valuable and he knew it should be used only in a dire emergency. This was not dire enough.

There had to be something out there that would burn. He just had to go and find it.

Warren's new day also started early. By mid-morning, he'd reached the dreaded creek. The water was significantly out of the banks. He had to wade some three hundred yards in water from a few inches deep to almost a foot deep, before actually reaching the true location of the creek. The water at this point was moving more swiftly. It was a good thing the top of his boots was just over a foot tall.

This was the same place he'd crossed on his trip to the river. At that time, the water was quite shallow. He waded across with no problem in three feet of water. Today was a different story. The stream was now some six to seven feet deep. It would be very difficult to cross with all the swirling currents.

He had no desire to wash away with the limbs and other debris presently floating by him. The only thing he could do was to build a raft to carry everything across. The raft on the litter was deflated and he didn't have the pump. But how was he to know? "What an idiot! Why didn't I bring the pump? How stupid of me. I should have taken a major rain into account. DAMN!"

The one thing that was a real bitch is he really wasn't equipped to build a major raft. What he could do with his hunting knife would consume a great deal of time. He would build a small one, just big enough to hold a single box. He would swim along beside it to keep it from turning over in the current. He removed his clothes, even though they were wet from the rain, and placed them on some limbs to try and let them dry out a little.

With all said and done, he finally had everything across by late afternoon. The whole ordeal was exhausting and cold, but not as bad as he thought it would be. He put back on his clothes and repacked the litter, then headed on his way. This would be the last major obstacle between him and camp.

He forced himself to go about one mile before stopping. A good night's rest would do him good. He so wanted to get his still damp clothes off and get into his dry sleeping bag.

Food was not even a concern, nor was a fire. He probably couldn't get one started anyway with everything soaked. He covered his head. Tomorrow would be a time to try and forge ahead and make up the lost day. Shortly, he was asleep.

Jim spent the whole day looking for something to get his fire started. There was absolutely nothing dry. Finally, he gathered up some dead leaves he found in a slightly protected place among some rocks and spread them on the floor of the hut. Hopefully, they would be dry by morning. This taught him a valuable lesson. From then on, he would keep a special supply of kindling in the hut to prevent this from ever happening again.

By the time night fell, he was bored and disgusted about the fire. He didn't even feel like eating.

Turning in early, he lay on his bedroll, thinking of Warren. He could only imagine what was happening to him and where he was. His thoughts moved to the hut and how well it was built. He was glad there were no major leaks. The tarp covering was working well. There were a few drips down the logs of the walls and the stones of the fireplace, but that was it. These could be handled with no problem.

CHAPTER XXVI

His waking early had almost become automatic. Jim was surprised his inner clock had adjusted to this schedule. He was sure it was because there were no late shows to watch on TV, or canvases to paint until the wee hours of the morning or a piano to practice on. The lack of electric lights made it impossible to do anything after dark, except sit in front of the fire and play the guitar or recorder. It sure would be nice to have my piano. But then again, if he did, he'd get absolutely nothing accomplished that really needed to be.

He notched the wood to mark the one hundred and third day, got dressed, and went outside. The light of dawn showed a clear sky. The water in the stream was finally back to normal. The garden was doing alright. Actually, the rain had been good for everything.

The tomato plants were as big as ever, hanging with small fresh green and red-green fruit. The thoughts of the pickled green tomatoes he use to buy at the store came to mind. He smacked his mouth, laughing, trying to remember the flavor. Oh well. That was another time.

The potatoes and onions were quite healthy. He was also pleased the insects hadn't eaten the whole garden up. Thinking about it, he was rather surprised. There weren't many insects to speak of so far. There was no explanation why, but he didn't care. He was rather thankful.

The fire in the oven was still warm. A few logs kept it maintained very well. All the ashes he used around the garden.

He couldn't help but think of Warren and how he was doing.

When would he return? Was he alright? He knew he would be hungry when he got back. Sure as hell aren't any Burger Kings or McDonalds on the way home. He laughed at the thought. He wanted to fix something special.

Jim got the spear, machete and camera case. It was time to do some gathering. When he got back, he'd do his fishing for the evening meal.

By mid-afternoon, he returned from his outing. The case was filled with all sorts of strange things. The edible water plants, he put in the stream. With a few rocks, he made a holding place for them. This would permit them to grow and multiply near the camp. When the pond was finished, it would be a perfect spot to propagate several of the water plants he'd found. But the dam had to be completed first.

After getting the fishing gear and setting it all up, he decided to strip down to his underwear. The sun was warm. Over the last two weeks, he'd worked on a rather good tan. All his hair had slight streaks of blond. He laughed. "All I need now is a surfboard and I'll be ready for the beach."

After a while, there were a few fish on the line. He was just about to cast again, when he heard a sound in the distant woods to the west. It sounded like his name. He sat straight up, listening intently. Then it came again.

It was faint, but it was clear. "Yooo Jim!"

He jumped up smiling. Warren was home.

He ran to the top of the rock, cupped his hands around his mouth, and took a deep breath. "Yooo Warren!" He yelled as loud as he could. "Yooo Warren!" He stood silent for a moment, listening.

In the distance, the sound came again. "Yooo Jim!"

Jim quickly put on his pants and shoes, crossed the bridge,

then started in the direction of Warren's voice. Periodically, he'd stop and yell again. Warren was getting closer. After about ten minutes, he could hear movement in the bushes ahead. "I'm right here!" He yelled.

He smiled and laughed when he saw Warren. He ran up and they hugged each other. "God, it's so good to see you."

"It's good to see you, too." Warren smiled.

Jim stood back, looking at Warren. "Looks like we need to work on that. Looks kind of scruffy."

"How about a hand in getting this stuff back to camp."

Jim grabbed one leg of the litter. "How was the trip? Was the storm a problem? God! You should have seen the creek. And I heard this noise! Real strange, too. Are you hungry? Thought we'd have fish tonight." He'd not let Warren get a word in edge wise. But finally he slowed enough for Warren to respond.

"Well, I've got some interesting things, too, to tell about the trip. Some real interesting things. But let's get back to camp first."

When they walked into camp, Warren quickly perused the site. He noticed the tent was missing. He saw the garden was growing like crazy. The oven was a surprise, especially with the smoke coming out the chimney. "Well, all seems to be okay here." He grinned with the knowledge Jim had maintained the site and survived the storm.

"I moved everything to the hut. And thank God I did. Some logs and dirt caused the creek to back up. You should have seen the lake here. It was all under water." Jim pointed around.

As they brought the things to the hut, Warren wanted to know how the roof held up in the rain. He also wanted to take a trip around the area to see what was going on.

"And at the apple trees is where I heard the noise."

"What kind of noise?" Warren was curious. "Apple trees?"

"I don't know. But it was loud. Something tells me I'm glad I didn't see what made it. Yeah. There are apple trees growing there."

Warren thought of what he'd seen. "Well, wait until I tell you what I saw. You won't believe it. But I'll tell about that later. How's the meat holding out?"

"Well." Jim tried to be apologetic. "You have to go hunting. Sorry about that. That's why we're going to have fish tonight."

Warren knew Jim would probably never get over his disdain for killing and cleaning animals. But he wasn't too concerned. As long as he was around, Jim wouldn't have to worry about such things. He would be doing most of it, if not all the hunting. "What did you say we were having to eat?"

"Well, if I'd known you were coming, I'd have baked a cake. Just kidding. Actually, I'll fix one of my special salads, some steamed greens, fish, and some sassafras tea. How does that sound?"

"With what I've had the last couple of weeks, it sounds like a banquet at the Ritz. It's going to be great. But best of all, I'm not going to be alone." He reached over, giving Jim a light jab to his left shoulder.

There it was. He said it without hesitation. In his heart, he was glad to be 'home' and back to Jim again. He would never again question his thinking on the subject.

Jim smiled. "It's so good to have you back. I really missed you." He stood for a moment, then gave Warren a big hug.

Jim went to get everything ready. Warren took the fish down stream and cleaned them. By the time Warren returned with the fillets, Jim had the salad ready, and the greens were in the pot and on the grill in the fire chamber of the oven, above the hot coals.

Putting the salad makings into the metal bowls, Jim went to the hut. From one of the 'boxes' Warren had brought home, he pulled out the jar of vinegar. Mixing it with some of the honey, he had a sweet-sour type dressing. He had meant to bring the vinegar with them on the first trip, but forgot to take it out.

Warren sat next to the oven on his folded blanket after he removed all his clothes. "Listen. Before you put the fish on, I'm going to take a dip in the creek to clean up a bit."

"Think I'll join you." Jim replied. He went to the hut and got the towel. Passing the fire, he pulled the pot of greens back from the direct heat before leaving the rock.

Warren was already in the water. As he rose to the surface, his hair was hanging down over his eyes. He pushed it aside with his hand.

"I see you need a bit of a haircut." Jim laughed as he jumped in.

"You're not much better. Maybe we can do it after dinner, if there's enough light."

They dried themselves off before returning to the top of the rock. Warren ran the towel over his head a few times then threw it back to Jim, who did the same. Jim wrapped it around his waist and started the cooking. Warren sat on the blanket, naked.

Just before all was ready, Warren went to the hut, getting the other blanket. He folded it and put it next to his.

They sat quietly, eating their food. Warren had no idea he was so hungry. When they finished, it was all gone. Jim was pleased. There would be no need to store leftovers.

Sipping the tea, Jim spoke impatiently. "Okay! I want to hear about it right now!"

Warren laughed inside. He'd been waiting for the comment all evening, and was rather surprised Jim took so long to ask. "Well.

While I was at the river, you'll never guess what I saw." He paused.

"Okay! Okay! I've waited long enough. What the hell did you see?"

Warren fixed his eyes on Jim's face. He wanted to see the expression when he told. "Well, I saw a group of mastodons." He waited to see the reaction.

There was a moment of silence before Jim responded. "What!?"

"I saw a group of mastodons."

"You have to be kidding. Mastodons? The hairy elephants?"

"You've got it."

Jim's face indicated the whirling in his mind. "Maybe that's what I heard in the bamboo and at the apple trees." He paused for a few seconds. "Guess it confirms our situation. We now know we're back a few years."

"Just a few." Warren laughed out loud.

"God. Can you believe it? Mastodons. I think that's so neat. Do you think we could see them from the top of the mountain?"

"We might."

"I've been wanting to go back up there to take a few photos. I think they could prove to be valuable to someone some day. I know it sounds stupid, but who knows?"

"I've thought about this whole thing." Warren continued. "When we were there, back in our own time, there was no indication of our stay here. There had been no discovery to let someone know we were ever here. Does that tell you something?"

"Maybe they never looked hard enough. Wouldn't it be something if we could put something out here that would last? Then when we got back, we could send someone out here to discover it. No one would ever believe we were here though."

"You would do something like that, wouldn't you? But I have to admit, it would be a real trick."

"What ever we did would have to be quite substantial. I mean, look at the wall and what was left of it in our time. I can't think of anything more substantial than that wall. Damn! That's too bad. Oh well. It was a clever idea. Moving right along." Jim said nothing for a moment. "What about the mastodons? I want to hear more about them."

"There's nothing to tell. They're on the west bank of the Chattahoochee and that's probably where they'll stay."

"Do you think I could have heard mastodons?"

"Maybe. But I don't think so. If there was a herd of elephants around, I'd have seen evidence. It's a bit hard to miss a herd of elephants." Warren laughed at the thought.

"Maybe it is the *Beast of Hollow Mountain*?" Jim yelled out. "We're doomed! We don't have a quicksand pit to lure it into like Guy Madison did in the movie."

"For Christ's sake! It's not the *Beast of Hollow Mountain*. It's something very logical. Something that makes perfect sense for this place and time."

"*Caltiki, the Immortal Monster*!" Jim yelled again. "*Godzilla! Rodan! Mothra!*" He was already giggling as he spoke. "*The Thing! Them! The Creature from the Black Lagoon!*" He was laughing out loud.

Warren grabbed him, putting his right arm around his neck, and gave him a few raps to the top of the head with his knuckle.

"Ouch! Oh! Oh! That hurts!"

"You finished?"

"Yeah. Yeah. You win."

Warren released Jim and they sat quietly for a moment. Then Jim whispered in a low voice. *"The Giant Crab Monster."*

Warren immediately pounced on him, grabbing him around the neck, forcing him flat on the rock surface. His body held Jim totally immobile.

Jim was laughing all the while. Warren began to laugh. In a moment, he released Jim, rolling over on his back, laughing out loud. "I don't believe it. I don't believe it. You can't take him anywhere."

Jim lay face down. He, too, was laughing, but began to calm. "How about some more tea?"

"Sounds good to me."

Jim jumped up, standing next to Warren. He extended his hand to help Warren get up. He grabbed hold.

Jim went to fill the pot, then set it on the grill. Warren went to the hut, getting his guitar and Jim's recorder. "I really need to tune this thing." He handed the recorder to Jim.

Putting it to his mouth, a 'C' note sounded. "How's that?"

Warren turned the key to the string. Within a minor twist and a few plucks, the guitar was set to tune the rest of the strings.

Soon, he was strumming away. Jim joined in on the recorder. They played together until the tea was ready. The honey came in nicely as the sweetener.

"How about we go to the top of the mountain tomorrow?" Warren asked. "What do you think?"

"Terrific!"

"We'll make a day of it. Maybe there's something to be learned up there, if we really look."

Sipping the rest of the tea, the light of day turned to the darkness of night. It was getting close to the time to call it. Jim knew Warren was tired. They pulled the sleeping bags out and put them on the rock in the out doors. The night air was cool. The air mattresses would insulate them from the warm rock beneath them.

Jim was not concerned about sleeping outside since Warren was there. His presence gave him the confidence, as well as a feeling of wellbeing.

As they lay there, they had some minor chitchat. Slowly, the comments subsided.

After a long silence, Jim spoke softly. "It's good to have you home, Warren."

"It's good to be back."

Jim was lying on his stomach. He reached over with his right arm, setting it on Warren's chest. Warren placed his hand on top of Jim's arm.

The night sounds filled the warm summer's air. Although all was quiet, Warren had the machete to his left.

And so, another day ended. The two were together again. With occasional surprises, they were becoming more and more familiar with their new world.

Jim was glad Warren returned safe and sound with the rest of his things. It eased his mind to know they were not sitting out by the Chattahoochee any longer.

Warren, being tired, was quickly asleep. Jim was not far behind. His inner clock took over. It was night. And when it was night, one was suppose to be asleep. His eyes closed.

The night sounds sang a monotone nocturne to the starry sky.

CHAPTER XXVII

As the daylight broke, they were up and getting ready for their trip to the top of the mountain. As Jim put the one hundred and fourth notch on his stick, Warren pulled the coals out of the oven and started a new fire in a ring of rocks. He pulled the grill out of the oven chamber and placed it on the ring of rocks.

Jim went to the hut to get the comb and scissors. It was hair-cutting time. "We're going to look decent for the photos I'm taking today."

"The pot's on for tea. I'm ready for my trim." Warren positioned himself for the cutting. "I'll take a quick dip afterwards to get off the loose hair. By then, the tea should be ready."

Within an hour, both had completed each other's cutting. They tried not to be too critical about the finished products. Jim indicated that any long ends could be dealt with later. He picked up the towel from the hut and they were off and into the creek.

"You know, I can remember when Blackwater Swamp would flood." He watched several clumps of hair floating away on the surface of the water. "We use to put notes in bottles and jars and throw them in. Then we'd sit and watch them float down stream, pretending they might even reach the ocean."

"We use to do the same thing at the ocean." Warren added. "It was great fun trying to get the bottles as far out as we could throw them. We thought the further we threw them out, the farther they would drift. Like to China or England or some other far away place." He gave a push in the water, creating a wave that caused the tufts of hair to float further down stream.

Diving and splashing, they finally got all the hair off their skin. "I sure do miss the soap." Warren commented.

"Yes. I know. I do, too, and I hate to say it, but I have no idea how to make soap. Guess we'll just have to do without it. Another slice of civilization, gone."

Finishing their swim, they climbed back to the rock to dry off. Warren did not want to wear long pants. It was too warm. He knew he didn't dare cut off his pants to make shorts. Then he'd limit what would be available for the winter. "I'm wearing just my underwear. It's too hot for long pants."

"*C'est bien! C'est bien!* Think I'll do the same thing." He put on his pair of brief underwear then grabbed his camera. "We might even improve our tan this way." He took his spear and camera case, too.

Warren put on his pair of brief underwear and picked up the machete and binoculars. He was ready to go.

On their way up the west face of Stone Mountain, they came upon a large outcropping of stone. Jim told Warren to stand some twenty feet from the formation. He adjusted the camera, set it on a rock, made some minor adjustments, and it was ready. "Okay!" He yelled and pushed the button. 'ZZZZZZZ'. The time release was in action. He grabbed his spear then ran to stand next to Warren. "Quick! Smile!" 'ZZZZZZZZ'. 'Click'.

"We'll probably look like the last of the Mohicans." Jim laughed.

"Yeah. Especially with us standing here holding a machete, binoculars, spear, wearing just our underwear. We should look terrific." Warren tried to visualize the picture in his mind.

"That's alright. We can say we were the Stanley and Livingston of Stone Mountain. And what a fashion statement. You in your underwear and boots and me in underwear and shoes. Yeah. We'll be on the cover of GQ, trust me!"

When they reached the top, Jim took the binoculars and quickly climbed the central tower. His continuous scan of the countryside proved fruitless. "Okay! I give up! Where the hell are they? *Je ne c'est pas. Je suis* confused."

Warren was below, giving close scrutiny to the marks on the surface of the stone. He could hear Jim's moaning, but knew he was referring either to the people or the mastodons. It made no difference. He wanted to see if he could make anything from the glyphs. Kneeling down, he traced one of the inch deep markings with his fingers. The answer is here. I know it. All I have to do is see it.

Jim looked down. "What are you doing?"

"The answer. It's right here. If only I could make out something with the glyphs."

All the marks and glyphs were tied to the lines curving down to the surrounding wall. Soon it became evident that each and every mark was cut in the rock in such a way that a channel, on the lowest side of the sloping surface of each mark, was connected to one of the long sloping lines. "Now that's brilliance!" He exclaimed out loud. "Everything on the surface is cut to drain away water that might collect in them. This would prevent it from freezing in the wintertime and cracking the glyphs and lines. No wonder it's all so well preserved. The weather's not a major factor here. With no leaves or limbs from trees to clog up the drain ways, not one drop of water would stand in the marks."

"You think so? Maybe we should have brought some water to test it."

"Well." Warren gave a huge grin and flexed his eyebrows. "We sort of did." His face was a bit sinister, as if getting ready to pull a prank. He pulled down his underwear and began to pee on the surface.

Jim, watching the spectacle, yelled out. "That's disgusting!

Absolutely disgusting! Pissing on an ancient artifact." He could not restrain himself and started to laugh loudly.

The fluid flowed into the marks and glyphs, ran through the channels to the lines, then down the lines toward the wall. Warren, finally finishing his display, watched the run off. It went directly to the wall and under it, through holes cut in the wall. The point was proved.

He climbed the central tower to observe the entire thing as a whole. After a while, he ran his hand through his beard. "It really is a puzzle. If only I could find the key."

Jim looked over the edge of the tower, down to the surface. "We may not have the key, but there are a few wet marks down there."

All the lines, arcs, and circular shapes had glyphs next to them. It was obvious they were indications as to what each marking was. And it all had to do with the sky, somehow or another.

Warren continued to examine everything very closely. Suddenly, he shouted. "Look at that!" He pointed toward the surface, then quickly turned, running down the stairs.

Jim almost had heart failure he was so startled. He expected to see some horrible snake or creature, from the tone of his voice and it's urgency. Gathering his wits again, he was right behind Warren.

Warren ran to an area in the northeast section of the space. "Look at all these markings." He pointed to the many in the area. "Now look at these." He pointed to ones along an arced line that started at the wall of stone, then curving in toward the tower. One inch glyphs were adjacent to diamond shaped marks on the arced line, spaced approximately two inches apart. "Look at these glyphs close to the tower." He pointed at the one at the end of the arced line. "Also note the diamond shapes." He walked along the line, outward toward the wall, passing some sixty to eighty marks. "Now! Do you see any difference in these from the ones near the tower?"

"Sure. These are more worn from the weather than the ones near the tower. They look a lot older than the ones over there. The edges are not as sharp and well defined."

They continued to walk further until they reached the wall. In the mean time, they'd passed well over several hundred glyphs and diamond shapes. The ones near the wall were even older still.

Jim went back toward the tower again. "These first ten to twenty marks look pretty fresh, if that's the right word to use." He got down on his hands and knees, feeling the marks with his hands. He compared each and every one until he'd felt the first fourteen glyphs. Each was similar, but there was a minor modification or addition from the one before it. "There's a difference though." He rubbed the first, then the twelfth. "The twelfth one is just a tad more worn than the first." He moved along until he was at the twenty-third mark. "This one's more worn than the twelfth. Not by much." He crawled further, feeling the thirty-eighth mark. "And this one's more worn than the twenty-third."

Warren came slowly back toward the tower, looking at the markings very closely. Soon he realized he could put them into groups of ten, because of their similarity. Every tenth one of the group was significantly different than the eleventh glyph. The eleventh one was similar to each in the next group of nine. The next one was greatly different again. "I've got it! I've got it! They have to be time designations, probably year designations of some sort. Just think about it. All the years are in groups of ten."

"But what if their years are not in groups of ten?"

"Of course they would be. It's logical. Any intelligent culture would develop a ten digit numerical system, from zero to nine. It's quite logical. It's happened in all the past cultures of history. Even with ones having no relation to another."

"Maybe it's because we have ten fingers or ten toes." He laughed. "So you think it's significant?"

"You bet! And this mark and line is the key. If we can find out what this line means, we'll have the meaning to the whole thing here." Warren was exuberant in his revelation. "And the glyphs are year intervals. Maybe ten year intervals."

"Do I hear one hundred? A thousand?" Jim couldn't help but joke. "But why not five years or twenty?"

"Because of the marking changes, dummy." Warren said sarcastically. "Use your head. If the marks were every five years, there would be a significant change every twenty glyphs, instead of ten. If they were twenty, the glyphs would occur after every five. Therefore, for every ten glyphs, we're talking either ten years or one hundred years. I doubt seriously, from the lack of wear in the first ten, that each glyph was a hundred year interval. That would make the tenth glyph a thousand years older. And it doesn't look that old to me."

"From the engravings I've seen on tombstones, I tend to agree. Stone would wear more than that over a thousand years." Jim turned to Warren. "Well! Congratulations on your conclusion. But we still don't know what the lines represent."

"One step at a time. Have a little patience. As you would say, 'Rome wasn't built in a day'." Warren crossed his arms, pleased in his revelation.

"Well if they come here every year, they've only got around nine months to get back. We've been here, what, one hundred and four days? That's just over three months and haven't seen anyone yet."

"But maybe they're gone, like in never coming back. Maybe they've finished using the mountain. If so, there'd be no reason to come back." Warren interjected. "But we should be more optimistic. Maybe they will be back."

Suddenly, it dawned on Jim of the possibility of 'them' returning. "Warren! We'll be found. When they come back. Maybe they can help us get back! He began to jump up and down.

Warren had been so engrossed in his thoughts, he had not even thought about the return. Jim was right. "You're right! All we have to do is hold it together till they get back." But then he thought more about them. What if they are violent? What if they get killed by them? These things would ponder in his head, but he didn't want to tell Jim, as the negative thoughts might depress him. He changed the subject. "Say. How about we get back to camp and fix something to eat? The tea from this morning is gone."

"I should say it is." Jim looked down at the still damp groves. "And when they come back, they'll get you for pissing on their rock." Jim made an ugly face.

"One of these days, your face…" Warren began.

"I know! I know! My face is going to freeze and I'll look like that for the rest of my life. Yeah. Yeah. Mom use to say it all the time." Jim commented. "I can hear her saying it right now. But before we leave, I'd like to get a few more shots. They're going to love the one I took from the top of the tower. The one of you pissing on the glyphs."

"You mean you took one when I wasn't looking?"

"Yeah. Another great 'Piss Shot'. Now stand over there by the tower." Jim ran completely across the surface to the wall then turned. His camera gave a 'click'. "Now stand over there!" He pointed to an interesting sculptural feature on the wall.

"Let me take one of you." Warren headed toward Jim to get the camera.

"Okay. I'll stand over here." He handed the camera to Warren, running to another section of the wall. Jim got by one of the carvings of a figure on the wall, then stood in an Egyptian stance poses, like in one of those old silly cartoons.

'Click'.

"Idiot!" Warren yelled out.

Soon the photo session was over and they started back to camp. It was late afternoon when they arrived.

"Guess we'll have fish again." Jim commented. "Hope you don't mind."

"We can't really complain." Warren shrugged his shoulders. "We'll just have to wait until they finish that new Publix Grocery Store around the corner." He laughed and got his fishing rod.

Jim gathered two of the nearly ripe tomatoes from the garden, a few onions, then went to the creek, getting some of the wild watercress plants. These would be added to the wild mushrooms he'd picked on their trip, earlier. It would make a nice salad.

Warren caught two fish and cleaned them. This provided four fillets for cooking. The salad was ready to go in no time. Shortly, they were eating and discussing the events of the day, especially about the possibilities of being found and maybe getting back. Warren was still gloating over his major revelation. Jim thought it all a bit too easy, but he had to admit, once Warren made a puzzle piece fit, it always looked easy, especially after his explanation. So maybe he was right. But it didn't matter. The attitude of both was on a high. It would make things go well for the next days to come.

They decided to continue to sleep outside the hut, since the weather was good and there wasn't a major infestation of insects. The moon that night gave a great brightness and the sound of the crickets, frogs and other night creatures filled the cool air.

They'd been lying quietly when Jim made a comment. "Frog Legs! Frog Legs! We should have frog legs! And there might be crawfish, too."

"We need a gig and the flashlight." Warren added.

"Yeah. And they would make a nice change from the fish and the meat. And they taste like chicken!!" He laughed.

"Tomorrow. Tomorrow." Warren pleaded. "We'll talk tomorrow. Now go to sleep. Yeah. Chicken."

"Aye, aye, Captain. Tomorrow." There was a momentary pause. "Just think! We might go home."

Warren lay there on his back, looking up at the moonlit sky. His mind continued to contemplate the top of the mountain. He wanted to pin down those glyphs a little better. If they were on year intervals, the spiraling line would signify just over five hundred years. If they were ten year marks, it would mean a time of over five thousand years. Now that's a long time. Jim could probably explain the significance of art, music and architecture over the five thousand years, from the Egyptians to the Twentieth Century. He would put it in terms to make you realize just how long five thousand years really is. Most people see zeros but have no tangible feel for them.

It was like the time Jim explained about the amount of money the government spends. He would first explain to you what a million dollars was. Most people can't even grasp that until it's explained. Using one thousand dollar bills, a million dollars is a stack of thousand dollar bills around four inches high. A billion, with a 'B', is a stack of thousand dollar bills almost the height of a thirty-four story building. Now a hundred billion is a stack of thousand dollar bills some six miles high. This is something someone can grasp and can imagine. Jim liked to put the intangible into a perspective that almost anyone could visualize. He could make zeros have volume and meaning.

Warren lay there with a smile on his face. He turned his head, looking at Jim who had fallen asleep. He reached over and lightly patted Jim.

Soon the monotone sounds of the night crept into his thoughts. Shortly, he was also asleep.

CHAPTER XXVIII

"Ladies and gentlemen. Please stand and take a break. Stretch a bit." The holographic figure stands, stretching his arms into the air. "I think we've really had enough for today. I don't know about you, but I need some sleep. When you reach my age, you just aren't as spry as you use to be, even though you don't feel older in your mind." He turns and rearranges the red cushions in the chair. Then he turns back again, looking slowly across the room.

I'd swear the old man is looking right at me when his eyes meet mine. It's rather disconcerting to think a projection can have that effect, especially one that must be several thousand years old.

The old man smiles. "Twelve hours! I'll be back in twelve hours. Maybe twelve and a half." He chuckles. "I'll probably be late to my own funeral." He laughs again. "Get some rest and don't forget to bring something to drink and munch on. I still have a lot to tell you. *Bonsoir*." He gives a little wave with his left hand, steps toward the edge of the podium and disappears.

After a few moments, the deep red cushions and the chair fade away. The light has also begun to decrease. Everyone clamors for their hand lights, fearing they might be left in total darkness. But finally the light in the room stabilizes at a low glow. The conversations start up.

Turning, I see the same guy I had chatted with slightly and made humorous comments with on the way in here. I realized he was from the Smithsonian group. Interestingly enough, he is heading my way. Wonder what he wants?

"Aren't you Phillip Martin?"

He's about my age, dark hair with touches of gray, especially around the temples, mustache, and he smiles, extending his right hand. "Tim Coffin, Smithsonian."

I smile, offering my right hand. "Yes. Phillip Martin. How are you, Tim?" Wonder how he knew who I was?

"Sorry I didn't really get to speak and introduce myself before now, but you know how hectic it's been until now. It was impossible to let a ton of folks in here, the way in being so damn small, as you well know. Have to say, I loved your comments on the way in. I thought it might have been you then, but wasn't quite sure. I'm familiar with your work and told them that you had to be one of the few reporters chosen for this venture. You obviously are a guy who has balls to tell it like it is in a story, regardless of how strange it sounds. We wanted to make sure we had competent, honest journalists for this. I told them that you were the right man for the job. You shoot from the hip."

"I wondered what it was. But you're right. That entry tunnel IS too small for a mob to get through, with their cameras and stuff."

"Yeah. When I called your office and spoke to your secretary, I was glad you were going to be with us."

"Well, to be honest, I'm glad I got to be on this one. I had no idea it would be like this."

"I know what you mean. We weren't quite sure what to expect either, when we were first called by the Department of Archaeology." Tim looks around. "It is quite something."

"How would you like to get something to eat? I know a few good spots."

"Love to. Let me tell the rest of the crew where I'm off to. If they need me, they can call my cell phone. I'm looking forward to talking with you. Heard a lot of good things, and I've read some of the things you've done. You're a damn good reporter. I have to admit that some of the stories you've covered are really in left field. But somehow you make people take notice and really think about the subject, regardless of how far fetched it is." Tim turns to an associate. "See you here tomorrow. In twelve hours." He turns back to Phillip. "Would you mind dropping me at the hotel after dinner?"

"No problem." I answered.

We quickly make our way through the seemingly endless tunnel and flights of stairs. Our conversations began immediately, starting with basic introductions about ourselves. Emerging into the early evening air, we both reach for our cigarettes. We laugh, reflecting on what had been said earlier.

We get in my car. "Tim. I need to stop by the office for just a few minutes to check on some info I wanted Maggie to look up for me. She's the one you talked to. Do you mind?"

"Go for it."

I can tell immediately that I like Tim. He is real and down to earth. A gut feeling tells me I can really talk with him. "You know the folks the old man was talking about? The names sounded familiar for some damn reason. During our first break, I asked Maggie to see if there was anything on them. Thought you might like to come along and get in on some of the stuff that I'm sure no one else will know about."

"This is great! Thanks Phillip. It'll really give some meaning to the people I'm hearing about. And it'll save me a great deal of leg work down the road."

"If you should have any questions about anything, let me know. I might be able to help you out. I'll show you a map of the Atlanta area, so you'll get a hold on the whole scene. It'll give you some relationships as to distance and locations mentioned."

"Sure is warm down here." Tim comments.

"It's not too bad for mid-September." I laugh. "You should have been here at the end of July and early August. You could have baked bread in the damn car."

We finally pull into the underground parking lot. The air-conditioned building is a pleasant change from the outside. The elevator takes us up to the floor where my office is. As I open the door to the office, I see Maggie across the room. "Maggie. What are you still doing here?"

"When you called, it sounded too important and I wanted to make sure you got it all. Want a cup of coffee?" Maggie turns to Tim. "How about you?"

"Oh Maggie. This is Tim Coffin from the Smithsonian Institute."

"Maggie Morrison. Smithsonian Institute? Wow! Yes. We talked on the phone several days ago. Well welcome to Atlanta, Mr. Coffin. Hope you enjoy your stay." She shakes his hand. "If you're a friend of Phillip's, you're a friend of mine. If you need anything, don't hesitate to call and let me know."

"Thanks Maggie. And yes, I'd like mine black." Tim smiles.

"Where's my old map of Atlanta?" I fumble through the drawers of the desk.

"Bottom drawer, right hand side." Maggie heads for the coffee.

Tim pulls up a nearby chair to the desk and sits down. He pulls his pack of cigarettes from his pocket, extending it toward Phillip. "I noticed earlier that we smoke the same brand."

"Thanks." I take one from the pack. Tim has his lighter out already. Spreading the large map out flat on the desk, I start pointing to the different spots referred to earlier. "This is downtown, where we are right now." My fingers are in the central portion of the map. I move my finger to the upper eastern corner of the map.

"This is where they started, at Buford Dam. As you can see, it's located some thirty miles northeast of the city." I begin moving my finger along, tracing the river, in the southwesterly direction. "Now this is Morgan Falls Dam." My finger stops. "It's about fifteen miles, directly north of downtown." I move my finger a little further south. "This is where Johnson Ferry Road crosses the river." Moving it further, I stop at a point between Johnson Ferry Road and where the perimeter highway, I-285, crosses the river. "Somewhere here." I wiggle my finger back and forth a few inches, following the river. "Somewhere here is where they went through to the other time." Then I move my hand across to the eastern side of the map. "Here, about fifteen miles from downtown, is Stone Mountain. One of the largest masses of granite in the world."

Tim closely examines the map, as Phillip indicates the locations. "Now I'm beginning to get a feel for what we're being told. And that's one hell of a trek from the river to Stone Mountain. Don't think I'd like to walk it, even on a good day."

"Do you remember the reference to Buckhead?" I put my finger just north of downtown. "This is a rather affluent area, about six to seven miles from downtown. A lot of people living here have lots of 'bucks'. But that's not how it got its name. There's some story about a man who owned a country store, a long time ago, and was a hunter. He killed a rather large deer with an impressive set of antlers. To display his prize, he put the head on a pike outside his store and it stayed there a very long time. Everyone who wanted to go see it would say they wanted to go see the 'buck head'. And so its name."

"Nice piece of memorabilia. Might use it sometime." Tim chuckles. "What about Marietta?"

"That's up here." I reposition my hand. "It's about sixteen miles northwest of downtown."

Maggie returns with the coffee. She hands one to Tim and the other to Phillip. "There are a few things you might like to read."

She hands Phillip several sheets of paper, but retained two. "It was a minor story, as you can see."

I begin to peruse the photocopies of the news story. "It's about their disappearance, Tim. An interview with Warren's wife, Linda." I read further. "Says they went on a camping trip but never arrived at the pick up point, at Charlie Brown Airport." I pointed to a spot on the map some eight miles directly west of Atlanta. "At first she thought it a situation where they hadn't judged the distance properly and were still up stream. But when they didn't call or show up in the next couple of days, she called the police." I hand the top sheet to Tim, then look at the second. "This story's dated about a month later. An update. Says the police searched nearly three weeks, but found nothing. Not even a piece of their gear."

"Now read these. It is a police report with information on the matter." Maggie hands Phillip the two pieces she held back.

Looking at the pages, I am quite surprised. "I don't believe this." I hand the first page to Tim and start on the second.

"You have to admit, there's something strange there." Maggie comments.

I finish the second page, handing it to Tim. "Wait until you read the rest."

"And that's it." Maggie comments. "There's nothing more on the story. I called the police department and they said there was an extensive interview done by a detective, Mike Johnson, but somehow he slipped away and disappeared from the face of the earth. They never found him."

"I'm sure we'll hear more about this tomorrow." I shake my head in disbelief.

"At least, I hope we do." Tim jokes. "I'll tell you. I got a bit concerned today when the old man didn't show up on time. I'd have been real disappointed to get the beginning of this story, then not know how it turned out. Now, after reading this, I'm sure we may know more than the others, regarding what will be told tomorrow." Tim pauses, puffing his cigarette.

I take a drag on my cigarette, thinking about the story. "We shall see. We shall see."

A moment of almost reverent silence occurs, as we stand there, finishing our cigarettes. Finally, I break it. "Let's go get something to eat. Want to go, Maggie?"

She smiles. "Now I don't want to mess up a boys 'night on the town'. Maybe next time."

I want to take Tim to a really nice local restaurant in Mid-town, so we go to Einstein's for dinner, to discuss further the events of the day. The food and service there has always been superb. We can only make conjecture on what we would hear the next day, especially in relation to the police report. Before we walk in, Tim wanted to make a phone call. I couldn't hear the conversation, but I could tell he was asking for something and trying to get something done before tomorrow morning.

It's around twelve thirty when I drop Tim at his hotel. I tell him I'll pick him up in the morning since it is on the way.

As I open my front door, I hear the clock in the living room. Only one chime. Christ, only four hours. And that's if I fall asleep instantly.

I set the clock by the bed for five. We had to be there by seven.

After a quick shower, I lie in bed, trying not to think of the whole thing. I have to get some sleep. Maybe one more cigarette.

I sit up in bed, turn on the lamp and light a cigarette from the nearly empty pack. A few puffs later, I crush the butt out in the ashtray, turn out the light and lie down. I smile and softly speak. "Tomorrow's going to be very interesting. Very interesting indeed."

CHAPTER XXIX

'RAZZZZZZ'. The rasping noise belches from the alarm clock by the bed. I have no idea how long I've slept, but it feels like I just closed my eyes. No matter, I have to get up. The event of the year, if not the century, is taking place, and I want to see it through.

As I take another shower, mainly to wake my ass up, shave, and dress, I begin to think about Tim. Our talk last night had been quite informative, letting each of us to slowly penetrate the world of the other.

When I get to the front desk at the hotel, there's not even enough time to ask for him. I hear his voice.

"Phillip! Over here!" Tim yells out from the other side of the lobby.

I turn and see him waving; four large thermos containers and six ice chests are by his side. I walk over and we shake hands. "Looks like you're ready for the siege." I laugh.

Tim chuckles. "Yeah. Last night, when we were going into the restaurant, I called and told them I would like all this and ready by five thirty to take with me today. And so we have this. They're extremely accommodating here. Great service. So we're not going to starve today. Told them I wanted enough for twenty people. Think that'll hold them for a while?"

I smile. This guy is incredible. I didn't think any one would be so considerate. "I think it'll be just fine. I think it's real thoughtful, you doing this for everybody. Things sure have changed." I pull out my cigarettes, offering one to Tim. "Here. Have one of mine."

"Thanks."

Everything finally in the car, they are off by six. They joke about not getting enough sleep. They agree it's a hazard of the business. They arrive at six thirty-five. Phillip had rather 'lead-footed' it to make sure they wouldn't be late.

The park service security has been guarding the whole scene since the beginning. Their passes are a necessity to gain entrance. A few of Tim's cohorts, already there, help with the ice chests and the four thermoses, taking them to the room.

The room is just as we left it. The level of light has been improved, as the park electricians installed portable electric lights during the night. A slew of folding chairs have also been set around the area near the dais. Looks like we're not going to have to sit on the floor today. Seems someone has his shit together. That's nice to know. At least we all won't look like bumpkins. I hate nothing more than the world seeing the south as a bunch of inept rednecks. And this event making the focus of all civilization on Atlanta, I'm very pleased. What can I say?

Everything is a beehive of activity.

"Phillip." Tim motions for me. "Would you mind helping me set this stuff up? I might be a big shot in the organization, but when it comes to the recording of events, such as this, the camera men, recorders, and lighting crew are like gods." He laughs. "When they say something, I'm the one who jumps."

How interesting. He really is 'real'. "Be glad to."

Two eight foot tables had been set up behind the chairs on a large tarpaulin. It would protect the floors if something spilled. Tim and I spread out the items from the ice chests. The thermos urns went on the far end of one table. Surprisingly, there are many other items brought by several members of the group. Finishing the layout, it is amazing how many yummies are there. Styrofoam cups, plastic spoons and forks, small plastic plates and paper napkins complete the set up.

Several of Tim's party come over for introductions, as do members of the National Geographic team. I'm pleasantly surprised at the camaraderie among everyone. I need to get out more or something. Things seem to have really changed since days gone by. Maybe I need to get over my bitterness. Grudges never do anyone any good. But try going through it. Maybe this event will do me more good than I thought. So far, it seems to be working. He reflected on a time where he was to report on an event and got dismissed due to members of an archaeological organization not wanting him there, fearing he would turn the event into a circus when he wrote about it, knowing he wrote about the unusual and strange. It left a very bad taste in his mouth about similar organizations.

I noticed a number of cameras set up outside the entrance, when we came in. The news media of the world are covering the whole thing from there. The two cameras set up in the room are the only ones inside, but they are sending their images to the media vans parked out beyond the entrance. Only two still cameras are on the scene. These do not use flash. There is no desire to distort the holographic figure. We are allowed just our camcorders and tape recorders.

So far, the entire spectacle is being witnessed by the greatest number of people in the history of media events. Only one local independent station is carrying the entire event, without commercial interruption. Of course, Turner Broadcasting is noted for being courageous enough to do such a thing. I think the other stations will regret not carrying this whole thing live. Too many people are interested in what's going on. Many will be watching the Turner Channel, as it's being broadcast around the world.

As the seven o'clock hour rolls around, the chatter is a bit electrified with the anticipation of the continuing event. We all gather to take our seats. Tim is sitting next to me. The camera crew and recording personnel softly utter commands and numbers into their mouthpieces, as they coordinate with the truck and van technicians outside. To assure the sound, relay boxes had to be put up in the corridors to carry the signals of the headsets, to overcome the block that prevents the use of cell transmission. The portable lights have been put out.

Shortly, the voices begin to diminish. Tim and I check our watches. It's two minutes after seven. I chuckle, leaning toward Tim. "He's late again." Tim snickers at my comment.

Suddenly, I hear someone else say the same thing. Slowly, a low laughter begins to hum through the room, in response to the comment and it's relationship to the previous day. I take one last sip of my coffee, then place the cup down by my chair, on the tarp covering the entire area.

Finally, at a quarter after seven, the room begins to light, as it did the previous day. As it gets brighter, I hear one of the camera crew say something, but I can't make it out. It is the only sound audible. I'm sure it has to do with some light setting for the technicians. Within five minutes, the room is aglow, like before.

The chair with red cushions appears on the platform. In an instant, there he is again, standing in elegant splendor. His robe is just as elaborate as the one he'd worn the day before. The style is the same, too, but the color is incredible. A multitude of interconnecting hues of bright yellow. A large number of faceted, dark green stones are set among the elaborate, undulating, and intertwining gold embroidery.

He looks out across the room with a radiant smile. He is as a gleaming jewel on its pedestal. The glinting light off the faceted stones and gold thread must be a problem for the camera crew. I hear another whispered command. I lean over to Tim, jabbing him with my left elbow. "Oh my God. Liberace would be proud! Should have brought my sun glasses." I joke, quietly laughing.

"I hear that." Tim snickers.

"Hello. Hello again. *Bonjour.*" He sits and arranges the pillows.

He looks out over the room. "Sorry, I am late again." He shakes his head.

The whole room erupts with laughter for several seconds, responding to the tardiness, again.

The old man chuckles. I'm sure you got a laugh out of that. I'll bet you did." He smiles. "I do hope you all got some rest. HEY! I have no idea what time it is and I don't know when you first came in here. I was hoping that before you came through the last door, you would have waited till the next day to begin again." He laughs in his pause. "Did you go look to see if Jim and Warren were real? Were you successful in finding anything? Well, maybe it happened too long ago. Maybe they have been totally forgotten." His eyes have a jolly gleam, as if wondering if anyone had discovered anything regarding the story, putting it together. His smile broadens; his perfect white teeth shine between his lips. He laughs again. "You might have found something, but did you really figure the whole thing out yet?"

Tim and I look at one another, remembering the articles and reports we read the previous evening. We smile in our secret knowledge. True, we don't know the whole story, but we do have that slight edge on the others.

"Well. Is everybody ready? I hope so, because here goes." He pauses. "Now, I finished yesterday, at the day they'd gone to the top of Stone Mountain. Well, over the next few weeks, they tried to get things back to normal. Warren did some hunting to increase their supply of meat. They worked on the dam, getting it to the point it would be finished in another two to three weeks. Jim's garden thrived."

The figure stops and looks up to his right. Shortly, he looks back out across the group and begins again.

"Then came the day. The day of the dreaded unexpected. It came totally out of the blue. Deep in their minds, they knew something could happen, but they just tried not to think about it. It was on their one hundred and thirty-first day. Yes. That's right. That's the day it happened."

CHAPTER XXX

Day one hundred thirty-one started like the rest. Jim notched his counting stick, as he always did, before doing anything else. He put on his pair of underwear. For the last few weeks, if they'd worn anything, it was their underwear briefs.

Warren was taking his morning dip, as Jim climbed down to the creek. He brought the powdered rock they were now using as a teeth cleaner and the toothbrushes. A morning bath had become a ritual. Afterwards, Jim would start something for breakfast while Warren began whatever project he was working on that day.

Today, Warren planned to check his traps and do some hunting. Jim would work more on the dam.

Going to the hut, Warren put on his shirt and long pants. They helped protect his body against the underbrush as well as the claws of some of the small animals he would catch. Next, he put on his socks and boots. With his machete, hunting knife, bow and arrows, he was ready.

"Jim. I'll be back in a few hours." He headed to the east.

"Okay. See you then." Jim went to wash up the cooking pan.

All morning and into the early afternoon, Jim worked at moving more rock to the dam. He added more reeds, mud and small stones to plug the holes between the larger rocks. It was his desire to make the dam as strong as he possibly could. For his breaks, he took quick dips in the creek to cool off. The dam was now holding water and increasing the size of the pond it was forming. Hopefully, with the finish of the dam, the water would be backed up enough to stretch from the south bank to the stone wall of the mountain.

As the hours passed, Jim became a bit concerned that Warren had not returned. He looked up into the sky to check the position of the sun. He faced directly south, looking at his shadow. It pointed a little southwest. It must be around one thirty or two.

Then, suddenly, he heard a sound to the east. It was Warren's voice. But there was something alarmingly wrong. Its tone was that of urgency and pain.

"Jim! Jim! Jim!"

Jim's head turned quickly in the direction of the voice. He jumped over the top of the dam where he was working and started running toward it. His concern overrode the pain of the stones and sticks beneath his bare feet. He ran into the underbrush, then stopped short, hoping to hear the sound again. All was quite. He yelled out. "Warren! Warren!" There was no answer. He continued further east.

Within moments, ahead of him on the ground, he saw Warren lying face down, not moving. Terror shot through his entire body. He screamed. "Warren!" He ran over and knelt down.

There was a wet spot on Warren's left pant leg. It was wet with blood. He pulled up the pants and saw cuts on the calf, a few inches above the top of his boot. He wiped the blood away. Below the cut, he noticed two small holes. It was immediately obvious. Warren had been bitten by a snake. Warren had made the cuts trying to prevent the poison from getting further into his system. The position of the bite made it impossible for him to suck out the poison with his own mouth. He'd also wrapped a vine around his leg, just below the knee, as a tourniquet, trying to stop the flow of poison.

Jim put his mouth over the bleeding cuts, sucked hard, then spit out the bloody fluid. God, please let him be alright. The short prayer repeated itself in his mind. He sucked the cuts again and spit. His brain flooded with the horror. What if this was not enough? There was only one other thing he could do. He would have to make another cut, higher on Warren's calf. But could he do it? The thought of cutting Warren recoiled in every fiber. His whole body shuddered. He could not stand the thought he would cause pain. But then, Warren was not conscience and would not feel the pain. Regardless, the thought of what he had to do became increasingly upsetting.

He took Warren's knife, wiping it on Warren's shirt to get it as clean as possible. The steel blade glinted in the sunlight when he placed the point against Warren's calf just below the tourniquet vine. He began to tremble. "Oh God. Help me." He held the knife tightly with his right hand. He could feel his entire being writhe with agony at the thought. He began to cry out loud. "I can't! I can't do it! But I must! If I don't, he'll die." He wiped the tears from his eyes and face.

He braced himself and his body shook, trying to gather the courage to use the knife. He used his left fingers to hold the blade so it would allow about three quarters of an inch of the blade to penetrate. He drew a deep breath. "Ahhhhhhh!" The sound of his scream pierced the forest. The blade pushed into Warren's leg and up to his fingers. Blood poured from the wound. He quickly removed the blade, turned it ninety degrees, and pushed it again. "Ahhhhhhh!" It was like an electric shock that raced through him, as he imagined the pain.

He was going to be sick. His muscles wretched and shook. The thought of having cut someone, not to mention his friend, twisted his stomach. His metabolism revolted. He turned and heaved. Not having eaten in some time, the heaves were dry. Suddenly, he stopped and he gathered his senses. He had to complete the process.

He quickly bent down, putting his mouth over the bloody gash. He sucked and spit. This was repeated six times. He stopped, as his head began to spin. God, don't let me pass out. He took several deep breaths.

"Please let him be alright." He looked down at the cuts, still bleeding. "I have to stop the bleeding." He removed his underwear, cutting it into pieces with the knife. The cloth, he placed over the cuts. The elastic, he used to hold the cloth against the leg. He rolled Warren over onto his back.

He looked into Warren's seemingly lifeless face. "Warren. I'm taking off the vine. Tell me it's alright to do it." A tear rolled down Jim's cheek, disappearing in the dark hair of his beard. "Warren, good buddy, please don't die."

The only movement was the shallow rise and fall of Warren's chest. Jim bent down, putting his ear over Warren's heart. He could hear it beating erratically. He rose, looking back at Warren's face. Not one muscle moved.

Jim used his right hand to remove a leaf from Warren's beard. He touched his forehead, moving it down over the edge of his face. Jim's heart pounded like a pump running rampant. "Please don't die." He whispered. "Please don't die."

He had to get Warren back to camp. He picked him up under his arms and pulled. Slowly, but surely, he moved Warren along the ground. He pulled until he reached the creek. Crossing the creek to the south side was not as difficult, since work on the dam had restricted some of the flow of the water. The south bank at that point was only about two feet high. He removed Warren's boots first before dragging him through the water. It wasn't until much later that he thought how surprised he was to have moved Warren's weight. He attributed it to the physical work he'd been doing the last few months. He was in better shape than he'd ever been in his life.

Getting Warren to the south side of the creek was enough. He realized he could not get him all the way back to the hut area. He would set everything up right there, near the creek. He lay Warren down then ran to the hut, getting one of the bottles of scotch and one of his linen napkins. Returning to Warren's side, he removed the underwear covering and took off the vine. Opening the bottle, he poured some of the scotch on the napkin, then to the cuts. He wiped the cuts with the napkin. They continued to bleed. He wasn't sure if he was glad or not about this, but he did know the scotch would act as a disinfectant.

His concern now was the poison. Had he sucked enough out? What would happen if he hadn't? Would Warren eventually die? Would he end up a vegetable?

Jim ran to the rock again to get the air mattress and the bedding items. He got the towel to dry Warren after he removed his wet clothes from dragging him through the creek. He lifted him onto one of the mattresses to make him comfortable. Wetting the napkin with more scotch, he folded it and placed it against the cuts. The elastic from the cut underwear, he used to hold the napkin on the leg.

He looked down into Warren's still face. He ran his left hand over his forehead, pushing back Warren's still damp hair. Finally, his anxiety and terror broke loose. He leaned forward, his head rested on Warren's chest, and his arms clutched around him. He whispered. "Warren. Please be alright. Good buddy, please don't die. Please don't leave me."

Jim was scared to death, but he had to gather his wits. There was no time to cry. He had to do what ever he could to keep Warren comfortable.

Suddenly, Warren's whole body shook violently with convulsions. His breath came in pants and his voice let out a loud moan as if in pain.

Jim was startled. He didn't know what to do. He looked skyward. His voice was deliberate and stern as he screamed. "NO! PLEASE DON'T TAKE HIM! PLEASE DON'T TAKE HIM! NO!"

Warren shook for several seconds, moaning loudly. Then he went completely limp.

"NO!" Jim screamed. His eyes grew large with distress. He took a deep breath.

Momentarily, he noticed the slight rise and fall of Warren's chest. He was still breathing. He was still alive. "Oh God. You're still alive." Jim started to choke on his tears and anxiety. He had to regain his senses. He closed his eyes, taking a few more deep breaths.

He placed the second air mattress next to the one Warren was on. He gently rolled Warren off the first one. He unzipped one of the sleeping bags and laid it on top of both mattresses. He then placed the linen tablecloth on top of the bedding. He lifted Warren on to the bedding.

His next move was to set the tent up to protect Warren from the elements. There was no way he could get him to the hut. He would surely drop him off the bridge. He got the folded tent from the hut and carefully erected it over Warren so he would not have to be moved again.

By late afternoon, the tent was up. To keep Warren cool, he took one of the towels, dipped and wrung out at the creek, and laid it across Warren's chest. He used the other linen napkin to wipe the sweat from his skin.

Kneeling by Warren's side, the time began to pass and he began to contemplate all the dangers out in the woods. Since there had never been a major confrontation, he'd grown somewhat immune to the thought there were real dangers out there. The 'it will never happen to me' syndrome prevailed without him ever realizing it. What he had to be careful of now was over reaction. He could not jump at every sound, but he would have to be more aware.

At that moment, he thought of the machete, knife, bow and arrows. He jumped up quickly, then ran back to the spot where he'd found Warren, and retrieved the hunting gear. He hurried back to Warren's side.

As evening approached, he realized his hunger, and had to fix something. He knew the only thing he might be able to get Warren to eat would be soup and hot tea.

He gathered a few stones and constructed a fire right outside the tent. Shortly, he had a pot heating on the grill. A few pieces of dry meat from the hut, along with some of the veggies from the garden, were the ingredients. These would make a nice broth. Tea with the honey would be good for him, too.

It was dark when the soup was ready. He knew he had to have light to try and feed Warren. He got one of the lanterns. "I think this is emergency enough to light the lantern." He dished the broth into a tin bowl and let it cool slightly. He propped Warren's head up on a folded blanket, then placing a napkin under Warren's chin, Jim spooned some of the warm fluid to Warren's lips. With his left hand, he pried Warren's teeth apart and poured the spoon full into his mouth, then released his teeth. The broth seeped from his lips.

"Come on now. You've got to eat something." He said softly. He tried several times to get Warren to swallow the soup, with no results. He feared Warren might choke if he tried too hard. Later would be soon enough. It was obvious nothing would be accomplished at that moment.

Jim rinsed the napkin and towel in the creek. Although dark outside, his eyes quickly became accustomed to it. He placed a few more sticks on the coals and moved the soup pot to the edge of the grill so it would stay warm. He placed the lid over the top.

Returning to the tent, he knelt down next to Warren to wipe his body. It finally hit him at how tired he was. The strain of the last several hours of the day had been exhausting. Never in his life had he encountered the decisions made that day.

He gently rubbed the wet napkin over Warren's chest, arms and legs. Then he spread out the towel over his body. The folded napkin, he put on his forehead.

Checking the napkin on his leg, he saw the bleeding seemed to have stopped. He did not remove the napkin for fear it might start again. Since Warren appeared to be stable for the time being, he didn't want to cause any further disturbance.

Jim was ready for sleep. He turned out the lantern, then

crawled onto the bedding and laid down beside Warren.

He was just about to doze off when he heard the sound of a light drizzle outside, the drops pattering on the tent. Quickly, he got up and checked the outside. There was nothing more he could do. Everything was protected as well as it could be. If it wasn't in the tent, it was in the hut on the rock. There wasn't too much concern over the fire, as there were hot coals in the oven fire chamber. He could use them to start a new fire if needed. He had a lid on the soup to keep it warm and protected.

He looked up into the sky. The small drops fell cool upon his face and naked body. He stood there for a few moments. "Please God. Help me do the right thing. Help me take care of him. Please don't let him die." He quietly spoke his prayer.

Jim walked back into the tent and lay on his side of the bedding. The drops of rain on his skin were refreshing. He placed his hand on Warren's chest. It moved with his slow breathing.

The sound of the rain on the roof of the tent was soothing and hypnotic. The horrors of the day and the possible consequences faded from his mind. He was too tired to think about it all, right then. Within minutes, Jim was asleep.

CHAPTER XXXI

It was the gentle, increasing and decreasing rumblings of thunder that woke Jim up. A light rain fell. Because it was still dark, Jim could not see so he reached over and felt Warren's chest. Very slowly, it moved with his shallow breathing. He placed his hand on Warren's forehead. Finding it hot and sweaty, he took the napkin and wiped his face. He put his hand on several points on Warren's body. It was burning and wet with perspiration. Since Warren hadn't eaten or drank anything, Jim feared he might dehydrate. Keeping him cool was paramount to prevent other possible complications.

Jim grabbed the towel and napkin to rinse off in the creek. Why didn't I fill a pot up last night, before it got dark? He began to think of snakes at the creek, causing his whole body to shake. He couldn't see well since it was dark, but he had to go.

He put on his shoes and socks, picked up the machete then stepped out of the tent. The cool drops hit his naked body. It actually had a soothing effect, but his phobia took hold again. Everything in view was mentally turned into a snake. A rock took on the form of a coiled viper, ready to strike. A stick looked like one slithering on the ground. "Stop it!" He became angry with himself. "Get over it!"

Fighting his mental torture, he cautiously proceeded to the creek. Maybe the rain will keep them from coming out tonight. It seemed like forever to get to the low spot in the bank where he brought Warren across, but he attributed it to his anxiety. Quickly, he rinsed out the linens and filled the pot he'd brought with water.

Turning to return to the tent, he scanned the ground with squinted eyes, thinking it would help see into the night. A surge of energy raced through his body making him want to leap back to the tent.

The feeling reminded him of a time he had to go to bed after seeing a horror movie, when he was a child. He stood at the door of the dark room, waiting for just the right moment. Then, suddenly, he sprang for the bed and got quickly under the covers, head and all. Once there, he was safe. Covers were magic. Monsters could not get you if you were under the covers or a sheet. It took a while for the tingle of the moment to subside.

So there he was, wanting to leap for the tent. The tent was the covers. If he could get there he'd be safe. The surge increased in his whole being and his heart pounded. "This is ridiculous! I'm not ten years old any more." He gathered his wits and slowly made his way back to the tent.

Darkness in the tent was blacker than outside. He used his hands to see. With the folded cool towel, he wiped Warren's whole body. He folded the napkin; dabbed Warren's face then placed it on his forehead. The towel, he laid on his chest.

He sat there in the dark, the rainwater dripping from his hair and beard, staring down at Warren, lying in front of him. He couldn't see him, but that was alright. He knew he was there. His mind began to dwell on the thoughts of what he would do if Warren died. He tried to dismiss it, but it kept nagging him.

He picked up Warren's right arm, held it in his lap and stroked it with his right hand. "You'll be okay. Don't worry. I'll make you better, somehow." He spoke as if to a sleeping child.

The camp was now in his hands. He had to do all he could to keep Warren comfortable. But what could he do to increase Warren's chance for recovery? His capabilities to cope were not enough without Warren. There hadn't been enough time to learn everything he needed to know. The fact was perfectly clear that if Warren died, his chances for survival in this wilderness were zero to none.

Jim needed Warren for more than physical survival. Without him, loneliness and the lack of companionship would be the final cause for his demise.

He reached over and wiped Warren's face once more with the napkin then replaced it on his forehead. After a moment, he lay down on his bedding and closed his eyes. Sleep was essential.

Suddenly, Warren gave a loud groan. Jim sat straight up with a start. He reached over, touching Warren, who was dripping with sweat. He touched his forehead. Warren was burning up. The only thing he knew to do was to cool him off as quickly as possible.

He wasn't sure how long he'd slept, but the mid-morning light filtered into the tent. The sound of the rain had stopped.

He jumped up and ran from the tent. His eyes squinted, as he looked around. It seemed to be about ten o'clock. He quickly ran to the hut and grabbed the life jackets and set them on the ground outside the tent.

Back inside the tent, he reached under Warren's arms and slowly dragged his naked body out and put one on Warren and the other on himself. Quickly, he maneuvered Warren down to the creek and into the water.

The water was cool and would help pull the temperature down. The life jacket made it easier to keep his head above the surface. The only concern now was sunburn. He thought for a minute. Pulling Warren to shallow water, he went running back up to the tent for the towel. Once it was spread over Warren's head and shoulders, the sun was no longer a problem. He pulled him back into deeper water.

Jim kept Warren in the water for some time. He wanted to make sure the temperature stayed down. This was a great opportunity to give him a bath, too.

Finally, he got him into shallow water again and went to the tent for the tablecloth, being used for the top layer of bedding for Warren. He rinsed it out in the creek, down stream from where they were in the water, to remove the sweat and the results of Warren's uncontrollable body functions. Laying it on a near rock, it would dry quickly in the sun.

He pulled Warren from the water and dragged him back to the tent. To keep him comfortable while the cloth dried, he placed him on the sleeping bag, then he left the tent.

Now his concern shifted to getting Warren to eat and drink. If he didn't, he would surely dehydrate and lose weight. Somehow he had to force him to do this.

The broth prepared the night before was still on the grill. He smelled and tasted it to make sure it hadn't soured. All was fine. He started a pot to make tea.

With some dry kindling from the shelter by the hut, he restarted the fire and heated the broth. It took almost an hour to warm.

By this time, the tablecloth was dry. He put it back on Warren's bed, then moved Warren on top of it. He checked his forehead. The heat was gone for the moment and Warren was quiet.

Although bland, the broth would be good for Warren, if he could get him to eat it. He took a bowl into the tent and tried to spoon the broth into Warren's mouth. After several tries, Warren finally swallowed. Jim was ecstatic. Even in his comatose state, something within his being must have realized his need to eat. Jim kept spooning in the broth until the entire bowl was empty. Quickly refilling the bowl and testing it to make sure it wasn't too hot, he tried giving him more. This was not successful. The liquid dribbled down his cheek.

"You can't be full yet! Eat more!" Jim yelled. He placed another spoon full into Warren's mouth. It was useless. Again and again Jim tried with no success. Well at least he ate something. A little is better than nothing at all. Maybe later. He put a root into the pot heating on the grill. He would have tea soon.

He wanted to go pick a few things from the woods that afternoon, but this would mean leaving Warren alone for a couple of hours. This caused some anxiety, but there was nothing else to do. He couldn't just get on the phone and call for assistance.

Warren seemed comfortable. Jim wet the towel again and put it across his chest. This would keep Warren cool for a while. He made some tea with the honey and saw if Warren would drink any. To his surprise, he did. He drank almost a whole cup full. He would try more of this later. He had use the last of the honey so he wanted to get more.

After putting on his clothes, shoes and socks, he wrapped two of the skins Warren cured around the lower legs of his pants. He thought it might be some additional protection against snakebite. He picked up the machete, the hunting knife, the camera case and the silver coffeepot and was off. The main goal for the day was to get to the honey tree. This wouldn't take long.

Warren had cut several holes weeks earlier with his hatchet along with several triangular shaped sections higher on the tree, then placed the pieces back over the holes. Warren had done this very carefully so as not to create a major disturbance of the bees. These holes made it possible to get into the inner chamber where the honeycomb was located. This would also, to a great extent, prevent disturbing the hive. The original hole Jim had cut with the machete still made it easy to obtain honey and comb from the tree.

Both he and Warren had agreed to remove only small pieces of the comb since this would shorten the time it would take for the bees to rebuild the missing sections. There was no need to be greedy. They had no desire for the bees to leave.

Jim recalled Warren saying he wanted to build a hive or two near camp. Bamboo and reeds would be the materials used. This project would keep him busy during the coming winter. Then he'd set the hives out the next spring. When the new queen bees hatched in the honey tree, he'd move a few of them to the hives.

Using the hunting knife, he carefully removed one of the triangular sections, pushed the bees aside and cut on the huge comb that filled the interior hollow of the trunk. He cut two sections of the older comb and placed them in the silver pot. Carefully, the wood sections were put back in place.

The silver coffeepot was a rather elaborate vessel to store the honey, but it could be poured easily and was better than one of the old used vegetable cans. Since the spout could be covered, invasion by possible insects was prevented.

Next, he went to check the blackberry bushes. Now this was a perfect place for snakes. He was very cautious while he looked to see if there was anything ripe. A few were in the early stages, but none were ready for picking. Maybe in a few more weeks they'll be ready.

On the way back to camp, he found some interesting morsels. They would make nice additions to the diet. He also hoped they might add something to the source of nourishment for Warren.

When he arrived back at the tent, he moved the pot of tea back on the fire to get it hot again. Maybe Warren would drink some more. Another pot was filled and put on the grill. It was practice to boil any water they would drink. This started in the very beginning, even at the beginning of the original camping trip, at Warren's insistence. Jim thought it strange they would swim in it, sometimes getting it in their mouths, but Warren demanded they boil it. One thing was certain. It couldn't hurt.

With the pots on the grill, he entered the tent and took off his clothes. When he touched Warren's head, he knew it was time for another trip to the creek. He reflected on the fact that Warren was not in the hut. He was glad of that. Getting him off the rock would have been a major ordeal. He was also glad for the life jackets.

While in the water, Warren's body made an erratic jerk and he gave an unintelligible grumble. His eyes opened, but it was obvious he was unaware. He quickly slipped back into his previous state and his blue eyes closed.

"Warren! Warren!" Jim yelled out loud. He shook his shoulders hoping for a response, but Warren was motionless. Jim gently pulled Warren's head against his chest, his arms around his neck. "You're going to be just fine. Don't you worry." He patted the top of Warren's head with his right hand. "Jim's going to take good care of you."

His emotional state began to fray. Tears started down his cheeks. He quietly whispered. "Don't worry. Jim's going to take good care of you."

He kept Warren in the creek for just over an hour. There was no time to feel sorry for himself or the situation. It was the touch and go action that was important.

He wanted to make absolutely sure Warren's temperature stayed as close to normal as possible. A high fever could damage the brain. It would be necessary to keep a closer check of Warren's temperature.

Taking care of Warren was keeping his mind off the dangers out and around the area. This was probably a good thing as it prevented him from dwelling on things over which he had no control.

Throughout the rest of the day and evening, he tried feeding Warren. Jim was pleased that some of these attempts were successful, even with the tea. He felt it was a good sign. There were no guideposts to follow with Warren in this coma like state. He could only do what he thought was right. There was no indication how long this situation would last or if Warren would even recover. This was something he did not want to think about, but he did have to accept it as a possibility. All he could do was wait and roll with the punches.

Jim finally got Warren back on the bedding, positioning him on his back. Night made the air much cooler. He placed the wet towel and napkin like before. The pot of water was placed beside the bedding, in close reach. A trip to the creek in the dark would not be necessary.

The day was gone when he lay down. Warren was to his left, lying motionless. Jim could hear the slow breathing next to him.

His mind started reviewing the situation. The terror came in the thought Warren would not recover. His heart increased its beat thinking of all the scenarios. He shook his head back and forth. "God, I can't do this. But I've got to. I've got to keep my head about this and do what I can. He'll recover. He has to recover." He squeezed his eyes shut. "I've got to stop this. Go to sleep."

Would he be put through a living hell of being alone for the rest of his life? Would he be the keeper of a living vegetable? Would everything end making it impossible to survive?

Jim shook his head again. "Help me." His voice was a soft whisper. He reached over, grabbing Warren's hand. "God, help us both."

The sounds of the night grew louder outside the tent. Another day was at an end.

CHAPTER XXXII

Day one hundred and forty-two started as usual. Jim notched his stick calendar. He was tired, even though he just woke up. There was nothing he could do except to keep going.

Over the last days, Warren had been slipping in and out of his comatose state, never knowing his actions. Jim was doing his best to get Warren to eat and drink tea and water. The fever would come and go, so Jim brought him to the creek for a bath and to keep him cool several times a day, even though the moves were exhausting. The summer heat combined with Warren's unbalanced metabolism, made the problem significant.

Several afternoon rain showers were a blessing, reducing the temperature. Some would last a few minutes and some would last several hours, extending into the night. These had kept the vegetable plants from needing manual watering.

Two days prior, Jim had checked the cuts on Warren's leg to find they were irritated and infected. He went to the fire, sticking the blade of the hunting knife into the hot coals. He held it there for a while so it would get hot. Returning to the tent, the knife was used to lance the swelling. He squeezed the infected areas to push out the pus and fluid. The scotch was used to wash the wound. Jim cleaned the napkin by boiling it. Soaking it with scotch, he folded it and placed it on the cuts. The elastic from the old pair of cut up underwear held it in place. This cleaning was done after every bath in the creek to try and keep infection to a minimum.

Today he checked the wound. It seemed to be doing quite well. He smiled, feeling he was doing something right. He sat next to Warren and patted him on the head. "Your leg seems to be getting better. Later, I'll take you down to the creek for your bath. I've got to clean these napkins and things first so you'll have a nice clean bed to get back into. Let me get that started and I'll be back in a while." He looked into Warren's quiet, still face. "We're going to be fine."

He maneuvered Warren to remove the tablecloth. He took it and the napkins to clean them.

The morning air was warm. The sun had been up for about an hour. Restarting the fire, he went to the creek to fill the pot so he could boil the linens. Shortly, the grill was set up and the pot began to heat.

He pulled Warren from the tent to get him out into the sunlight. He put him in the life jacket and prepped him for bath time. He took the sleeping bag and laid it over a bush to air out. He moved the air mattress outside, near the tent entrance.

While the water heated, Jim got Warren into the creek to cool him down, before the heat of the day set in. All the while, Jim talked to him, mainly to keep up his own spirits, but also for Warren, in case he sensed anything.

"Okay. Time to get out of the pool." He pulled Warren up to the tent and dried him off with the towel, before laying him on the air mattress. "I'm going to have to give you a haircut and trim your beard and mustache before this afternoon's swim. Now let's get these things clean."

He picked up the towel and the linens and went to dip them into the boiling water. Just before dipping one of the napkins, he held it up, looking at it. The once white, ornately monogrammed, linen was now a dingy beige. Brown stains were the result of elements in the water and the bloody fluids from Warren's wounds. The same was true for the tablecloth. Darkened spots, caused from sweat and uncontrolled bodily functions, marred the fine material. They would never come out and would always be a reminder of this trying period.

Jim was not concerned. If it were another place and time, it might have been different. But this was another matter. They were serving a much more important function, a function of survival.

He used a fork to push the pieces of material through the hot water. After a few minutes, he pulled each piece out with the fork as steam billowed up. They were spread on the rocks to dry.

It was time to eat something. He looked at Warren. "What would you like to have today? Lobster Thermidor? Fillet Mignon? How about some of Jim's Wonder Soup?" He laughed, patting Warren on the shoulder.

Going up to the garden, he picked a few tomatoes. He dug into the ground around one of the potato plants, mainly for curiosity. "By God! I don't believe it." He could feel a fairly large tuber beneath the surface. He dug further, coming across another. "God is being good to us." He yelled out so Warren could hear, knowing full well he didn't. He gently removed the two potatoes then smoothed the dirt back in place so not to upset the rest of the plant. A few onions were next.

He stood up and looked down to Warren lying near the tent. "Potato Tomato Soup! You're going to love it!"

By mid-day, the soup was ready. A few strips of dry meat had been added for flavor.

Warren consumed almost two bowls full. Of course, some dribbled down his cheek and into his beard, but this was no concern. Jim was glad he was eating. Maybe it was a sign he was getting better. He drank some tea, too.

Mealtime finished, Jim wiped Warren's face off with the dry napkin. Warren had lost weight, but Jim could do nothing about that. If Warren would only come out of his stupor, it would make feeding him a lot simpler.

After a while, he turned Warren over on his stomach to keep him from getting too much sun on one side. He also cleaned the wounds again with some scotch.

"Well, how do you feel now?" He rubbed his hand up and down Warren's back, occasionally giving him a pat. "I think you're doing just fine." Although Warren probably couldn't hear what he was saying, the conversation was doing himself good.

Later that afternoon, he got the scissors and comb and trimmed Warren's hair, beard and mustache. "Looks pretty good. Now I think it's time to cool off a bit." He took Warren to the creek for one last dip for the day.

As night came, Jim had everything under control. Warren was back in the tent on fresh clean bedding. The wound was clean. And the wet towel across his chest was keeping him cool. It was time to shut it all down for the day.

Jim sat beside Warren with the guitar. He strummed while tuning. Shortly, the guitar was in tune and the chords to *Puff the Magic Dragon* lilted on the air. Several other melodies came as a medley. Just before stopping, Jim looked down at Warren and softly sang *Gypsy Boy*, a Donovan song he remembered from his days at school. The words of the song seemed so appropriate at that moment. The words left their impression and a tear ran down his face. After the last chord, he paused a moment then wiped his face with his left hand. "Good night, Warren. I love you, man." His voice was a whisper. He was slightly embarrassed at the words, even though there wasn't a soul to hear them. He moved his right hand slowly over Warren's face. "I'm doing my best. I think you'd be real proud of me."

He sat silent for some time. Finally, he set the guitar aside and lay down on his own bedding.

Warren lay there, breathing slowly. His fever was gone.

Jim closed his eyes and began to slip into a state of alert slumber.

His whole body ached from the hardships of the last days.

Suddenly, Warren's body bolted with convulsions and he began to make strange sounds.

Jim reacted instantly, sitting up and looking down. It was impossible to see Warren in the dark. But before he could do anything, Warren's condition changed. He seemed to return to his normal placid state.

Jim placed his right hand on Warren's chest. That's when he noticed Warren was shivering. He was cold. But I don't understand. The air is warm. How can he be cold? He moved his hand over Warren's body. It felt like he'd been thrown into a freezer.

He jumped up. He went outside the tent and waited for his eyes to become accustomed to the dark. He headed to the hut to get the other sleeping bag and the blankets. Finally he was back in the tent and laid the open sleeping bag over Warren and then the two blankets. He continued to feel of Warren's body. It shook for some twenty minutes. "What the fuck can I do? There's nothing more to cover him with." Then he thought of himself. Of course. I'd be a perfect blanket. And I radiate heat, too.

Quickly, he got under the sleeping bag and went into a crawl position over Warren. Slowly, he lowered his body down until his chest was touching Warren's. None of his weight rested on Warren. He supported himself with his arms and legs. He did not want to impede Warren's breathing.

This has to work. I don't know what else to do. He laid his head on Warren's left shoulder.

Warren began to convulse again, but it stopped almost as it started. Jim remained in this position over three hours. It seemed forever. But it worked. Warren almost ceased his shivering. After a few more hours, he began to get warm again. The shivering stopped completely.

Jim was very tired. Even in this crouched position resting was not easy. He shut his eyes and slowly drifted into a half sleep. Before he knew it, his eyes opened. There was the sound of birds outside. Night was over and another day was beginning.

Getting up, he replaced the covers on Warren. He went outside to find it was already mid-morning. He shook his head. "God help me. I'm still tired." He scratched his head then went to take a leak.

Back in the tent, he notched the stick. Then he noticed Warren was shivering again. He got back into the bed with Warren to keep him warm. The entire day was spent this way to keep Warren's temperature from falling.

The strain of the days was taking its toll. Jim finally dozed off.

Sometime in the mid-afternoon, Warren jolted again. This time, Warren's right arm swung over, hitting Jim in the left eye. Jim was startled. The pain covered his face.

He sat up on Warren's mid-section, placing Warren's arm back against his side. He looked down. "Son-of-a-bitch!" He caught himself. Warren obviously had no idea what he was doing. Jim smiled in his pain. "Well. At least you're still alive. And you're feisty, too. That's a good thing." He put his left hand on his eye. "Bet this one's going to be a winner." He began to laugh at the whole thing.

"Since my sleep has been so rudely interrupted…" He got up and went outside. He rekindled the fire. A quick taste proved the soup to be alright. He moved it to heat on the grill. He got the old coffeepot, filling it in the creek. It would take it a little time to heat.

He rinsed the towel and other linens in the creek. When it got hot, he dipped the napkin in the pot and carried it to the tent. With the warm water, he bathed Warren.

After trying to feed Warren, to no avail, and doing a few things around the camp, he returned to the tent. Warren was shivering again. He tried to figure it out. It made no sense. The days were quite hot. Why was Warren shivering? He got next to Warren again. He would try to feed him something later.

Half sleep came back. Somehow the day was gone. Day one hundred and forty-three was of no consequence except for the fact they were still alive.

CHAPTER XXXIII

Jim woke early, but still tired. The whole night he'd kept Warren warm. It felt like Warren was beginning to retain heat, but he didn't want to take any chances. Getting up, he made sure Warren was well covered.

He notched the stick and went to get the fire started. The soup broth was beginning to turn. He was hungry and was sure Warren was too. He looked around. Suddenly, he had a flash of self-pity. He bit his lower lip. "How long will this go on? I can't do this forever."

He took hold of himself. There's too much to do to get all upset about.

Soon the fire was burning and the water was heating. He ran to the creek for a quick dip.

After his short swim, he went to the garden for a few things to make some fresh broth. In about an hour, he had things in hand at the grill. He was stirring the broth when out of the corner of his eye he became aware of a subtle movement near the tent.

Before he had time to turn, his brain thought of some wild thing creeping up to attack. But when he actually did get his head around he knew what it was. There was Warren, standing with the towel in his hand.

"WARREN!" Jim jumped up, almost falling in surprise. "WARREN!" He ran to the slightly staggering figure.

Warren stood, as if in a daze, trying to figure out what was going on and where he was.

Warren! Are you alright? Warren! Do you know who I am?" Jim grabbed his arms and looked up into his eyes.

Warren looked down with a strange expression. No sound came from his mouth.

Jim's joy suddenly shattered, thinking his brain was gone and Warren was now a vegetable. He stared deep into Warren's blue eyes.

Warren's eyes shifted back and forth. A questioned look was there, a look of being lost. But in a moment, Warren's mouth began to form a smile. "What the fuck happened to your eye?" His voice was soft and his eyes glinted.

Jim hugged him. "Warren. Oh Warren." He began to laugh and cry at the same time. Pulling away, he looked up to Warren's face. He continued to laugh and cry.

Warren moved his arms slowly. He placed his hands on either side of Jim's head. "What happened to you?"

"Oh. It's nothing. I ran into a door. I'll tell you about it one day."

He looked real hard at Warren. "God. It's good to have you back." He hugged him tight.

"I smell something cooking. Boy, am I starved. By the way, how long have I been gone? And damn, my leg really hurts."

"Just a couple of days. But don't worry about it now. Let me fix you something to eat." He ran to the fire and stirred the broth. "Here. Sit here. I'll be right back." Jim ran to the garden, picking several tomatoes and things to make a quick salad. He gathered some of the water plants to go in it. Coming back, he stopped by the hut to get a few strips of the dry meat to put in the soup. This would give Warren something solid for his stomach.

Coming back to the tent, he didn't see Warren anywhere in sight.

"Hey! Where are you?"

Warren stepped from the tent. "Thought I might go take a dip in the creek. I feel a bit grungy."

"NO! You can't do that!" Jim was adamant.

"Why not?" Warren was puzzled.

"Because you might get chills or drown, or something." He was emphatic.

"All I want to do is take a quick dip."

"You're not well enough. And I don't need another hit in the eye."

"Did I do that?"

"We'll talk about that later. First I want you to eat something. Later, I'll put the life jacket on you and then we can get in the water."

"I thought you said I was only out a few days. From this, it looks like it's been more than a few days." Warren tried to grab 'love handles' at his waist, but there wasn't much there. "Hey! I can't even 'pinch and inch'!" He started to chuckle.

"I'll tell you later. But for right now, you're not going into the creek."

Warren thought for a minute. Jim was right. He didn't need to do anything else that might jeopardize his health. He sat by the fire while Jim cooked.

Jim began talking about the past days, all the way up to the shiner, while Warren listened intently. He was quite surprised how much time did go by. He was very sorry for hitting him in the eye. Then he thought of the snake that bit him. "Carelessness! Just damn carelessness. If I'd been watching where I was walking, it never would have happened." He looked down at his leg. "But you know. If you didn't do what you did, I probably would have died. I'm real proud of you. I'd have never thought you would have had the balls to cut me." He gave Jim a big grin to express his thanks. "Yeah. It hurts like hell, but I'm glad you did what you did."

"Well if you must know, it wasn't easy. Just thinking about it right now makes me sick. I don't ever want to have to do that again."

"If it makes you feel any better, I don't remember anything." Warren paused for a long moment, looking at the ground. His whole tone of voice quieted. "Jim. I saw your linens in the tent. They're ruined aren't they?" He paused for another minute. "If we ever get out of this, I promise I'm going to buy you the best set of linens available."

"Fuck them! They served a much better purpose than decorating a table or wiping gravy off someone's mouth. What good is having something if you can't put it to a really good use? And I feel they have been put to the most important use there could ever be. The saving of your life. So don't sweat it. It's no big deal."

"I owe you, buddy."

"You owe me nothing. If it had been me you'd have done the same thing. And anyway, I had ulterior motives." Jim said nothing more.

"Ulterior motives?"

There were a few minutes before Jim answered. "Yeah. I knew I couldn't make it alone. I don't know enough yet. See. It might be good that you didn't teach me too much. I might have just said fuck it, if you had." He quickly glanced at Warren. "You asshole! What the fuck are friends for anyway? Holy shit!"

Warren grinned and they began to chuckle. For a split second they had both been vulnerable in their honesty. Jim handed one of the salads to Warren, then stirred the stew.

Night began to arrive and Jim placed a pot of water on the grill to heat. He was going to heat up the towel and napkins. "I'll wipe your back for you when the water heats up. It'll be a lot easier since you can sit up."

"I'll bet it was a bitch to move me." Warren laughed.

"You sure as hell have that right. But it wasn't too bad once I got the hang of it."

"I'm sure those dunkings were good for me. They probably gave me some of the exercise I needed and it did keep me clean."

"I hope you don't mind that I didn't put clothes on you. It would have been too much of a hassle to put them on and take them off every time."

Warren looked down at his nakedness. "Well. You know modesty was never one of my strong suits. And who the hell cares anyway?" He looked over at Jim. "I see you weren't too concerned about what you wore." He began to snicker.

Jim looked down at his own naked body. "It's summer and I was hot." He, too, began to laugh. "Listen. I want you to take it easy for a while. I think you really should take time to recuperate."

When the water heated, Jim dipped and wrung out the napkin. He wiped it across Warren's back. He then handed it to him so he could wipe his own arms, legs and chest. In the mean time, he ran to the creek for a short bath.

It was evening when they went to the tent. Warren went inside and lay on his bedding. Jim stood outside, looking up to the starry sky. He smiled and closed his eyes. "Thank you, God." His short prayer was quiet and soft. He turned and went inside.

They were silent for some time. Only the night sounds could be heard.

"I owe you, buddy." Warren reached over with his left hand and patted Jim's chest.

"Was nothing." Jim placed his hands on top of Warren's and patted. "I'm glad you're alright. I missed you."

Warren stared up into the darkness. He thought about it all. Thank God Jim was there. Thank God for such a friend. He paused in his thinking. "I'm really sorry about the eye."

Jim gave a little chuckle. "Forget it."

All was quiet. Jim's exhaustion and sense of wellbeing, now that Warren was alright, let him sink into a sleep of no concern. It would be the first real sleep he'd had since the beginning of the snakebite.

Warren drifted off, too. Even though he was back, he still needed recovery.

An unseen smile was on both of their faces. Each was glad of the other and their friendship.

CHAPTER XXXIV

Over the next few weeks, Warren regained his strength, but not much of the weight. He would remain without it for the rest of his life. His hunting and other routines eventually returned to normal. The experience taught them both a very valuable lesson and they became more cautious.

By late autumn, they accomplished several things. One that pleased Jim was the small underground fruit and vegetable cellar they built right down from the end of the bridge to the rock. It was only a hole in the ground, covered with bamboo supports, and dirt piled on top, but it would do until they could build a larger one. They pitched the dirt in such a way as not to let rain water stay over the cellar to keep it from flooding. They even put down a layer of the thick dense mud from the creek bottom to form a barrier between the bamboo and the dirt above.

While on their outings, they collected many things to go into the cellar. There were potatoes from the garden, apples, dried grapes and several other things. Only time would tell if the things they'd collected would store well. Jim collected seeds, drying and storing them in the hut for next season.

Yes. All in all, Warren was very pleased with everything they'd done over the summer. The hut was completed and the spaces sealed with mud. The interior was about eight feet square and had a four foot high, two foot wide opening near the southwest corner. A flap made from animal skins covered this and a door made of bamboo, tied together with braided grass and vines. It had no hinges. It just fit over the opening. The fireplace was virtually in the middle of the north wall of the hut. A narrow shelf, made of bamboo poles, was on the south wall, to the door opening. The south wall was the highest at about six feet. The roof sloped from the top of this wall to the five foot high north wall. There were no windows. There was no desire to have places where the heat could escape during the cold months.

The holes in the rock surface, supported wooden logs, some four inches in diameter and five feet tall. There were eleven in all. They ran parallel to the south and east walls. They formed the uprights for the open shed structure whose roof was made of bamboo and reeds. The uprights were held with horizontal bamboo members and tied to the main structure on the ends. The grass ties were used to hold all the members together. It turned out to be a rather stable construction.

The total structure covered an area about fifteen by fifteen square feet, and took up most of the northern area on the rock. It seemed well built to Warren and its design would prevent the wind and snow drifting against the doorway, as the west end of the shed area was completely covered with bamboo. The firewood was stacked under the shed area and would act as an additional windbreak.

Warren was sure the whole thing would last a very long time. Jim's architectural expertise and his care in selecting the construction materials would be its credit.

The log bridge from the rock to the south bank of the creek would remain the only entry to the top of the rock and the hut, after they removed the steps on the north side between the rock and the mountain. They were no longer needed. The area below was now submerged by the pond created by the dam. This would be finished by the end of the next summer.

Other minor accidents needed fixing. One was the time Jim poked a hole in his air mattress. Warren made the necessary repairs and it never leaked again.

The leaves passed their peek of color and finally fell to the ground. The trees were now stark and bare. This scene made it perfectly clear the warm weather was over.

They took every advantage of bathing in the creek for as long as possible, before the water became so cold they couldn't tolerate it any more. Jim was not too concerned since he would start heating water again in the large pot so they could clean themselves. The napkins would be their washcloths. He knew this would get real tiresome and spring would be a welcome sight. They would be looking forward to their first full bath of the next season.

The nights continued to get colder and heavy clothes were in fashion again. The hut was now their residence. The fire in the fireplace kept the room heated fairly well. The coming winter would be the real test. Would it fair during a severe storm?

Warren was optimistic and his constant praise, kept Jim the same way. They had both grown physically and mentally during the past summer. Warren was very proud of Jim and his changing attitudes. Jim was more able to cope with the environment and their situation. Warren smiled to himself at how far both of them had come. Together, they would survive, of that he was sure. Now it was his job to convince Jim of the fact.

It was day two hundred and sixty-two. Gray clouds moved slowly from the southeast, hanging low in the sky. It reminded Jim of the day they got lost. By late afternoon, the first few flakes fell. This was the hallmark Jim needed.

Jim looked up into the grayness and the increasing fall of snow. "Winter just arrived." He said nothing else.

Warren was out hunting when the snow started. His first thoughts were of Jim. He knew the sight of snow might trigger a vivid reminder of the hardships they would probably encounter ahead. He'd already caught and cleaned two small animals, but it would take another two hours to check the rest of the traps. He paused for a moment. "God, don't let him panic." He looked up into the sky. The white flakes stood pronounced on his hair, dark beard and mustache. His blue eyes reflected his concern for Jim. "Please take care of us. Help us make it through." He was on his way again.

By early evening, Warren was nearly back. An inch of snow was already on the ground. When he approached the camp from the south, he saw Jim standing on the rock, just south of the hut structure. He was looking up at the sky and his face had a curious expression. The flakes were collecting on his dark hair and facial hair.

Warren stood there observing the scene. It was quite interesting. There was virtually no color. The stone was gray, the snow white, and the light gray smoke curled up from the chimney. Jim's hands were in the pockets of the red coat he wore. This and the skin tones of his face were the only color. It looked like an old photograph he'd seen in a history book regarding the early settlers of the old West. Jim would be pleased at how observant he'd become because of his influence.

"First snow!" Warren yelled, breaking Jim's trance. He tried to sound pleasant and optimistic.

Jim turned his head and watched Warren cross the log bridge to the rock. He joked. "Maybe tomorrow there will be enough snow to build a snowman."

"If there is, I can tell you it'll be the best one around for several hundred miles." He laughed.

"You mean it'll be the ONLY one for several THOUSAND miles." Jim could not resist the additional ploy. He looked back at the sky. "Sure is funny though to see it snowing in the middle of summer."

It took Warren a minute to grasp what he was saying, but he was right. By the count of the days, it was actually early July.

Jim continued. "The way I figure it, in just under four months, it'll be late October. Spring will be on its way again." He began to laugh. "Remember?" He turned to Warren.

"Yeah, you're right." He quickly changed the subject. "Enough about that. Now come see my catch." He held the cleaned animals into the air. "Thought we'd roast one for dinner."

"Sounds good to me."

They went into the hut and closed the flap. The air inside was significantly warmer and the flakes that had collected on their hair and clothes began to melt.

"Give me your coat." Jim took both coats and hung them on two of the bamboo shelf supports that were stuck between the horizontal logs and chinked with mud.

The only light was that from the small fire in the fireplace. Jim had great plans to make candles with the left over wax from the honey. He would use the candles he had brought with them in the beginning as the base and put the bees wax around them to increase the diameter of each original candle. But even after he did make several of them, they were rarely used. Fire outside the fireplace was much too risky. The light of the fire seemed to be enough for their needs.

Warren lay on his sleeping bag and turned to Jim, on his own bedding next to him. "You know. If it snows real good, it'll act like additional insulation. It might even get warmer in here."

"I just hope the roof doesn't collapse from the weight." Jim was on his back, looking at the roof. He wanted to know if there was the slightest deflection in the structural members.

"I think it'll be alright." Warren looked at the roof.

"Too bad we don't have any milk." Jim completely pulled another thought from out of the air.

"What?" Warren was confused.

"Too bad we don't have any milk. We could make snow cream." He laughed when he thought of the concoction he used to make as a child.

Warren laughed, too. "That reminds me though." His voice became more serious. "Remember not to eat the snow or ice when you're out. Eating it will reduce your body temperature. You could develop hypothermia and die. If you get thirsty, just wait until you get back here to have something to drink."

"Aye! Aye! Captain!" Jim wanted to make sure Warren knew he'd been listening. "How about angels?"

"Angels?"

"Yeah. When you lie down in the snow and move your arms and legs. You make angels."

"Oh! Oh! Yeah! They're okay." Warren chuckled, thinking of his kids making a whole slew of them in their front yard, a few years earlier. They looked like a choir group.

Not much else was said while they prepared to go to bed. It was quiet outside without wind. Warren was glad, since it would prevent the snow from drifting. It also eliminated the chill factor. He knew their main objective for the next few months would be to keep warm and alive. Most projects would be put on the back burner until then. He would work on his hives, only if time permitted. They would periodically go out and chop wood for the fire and place it under the shed area of the hut to keep dry.

When they fell asleep, little did they realize that the silent falling blanket would build to just over two feet by morning. Their trial by ice was beginning.

CHAPTER XXXV

It was the beginning of day three hundred. The wind howled outside the hut. Warren woke to the sound. He could see his breath in the atmosphere, with the dim light from the smoldering fire. It had been snowing for the last ten days and the drifts were piling up like mountains. Even with the wind, some three to four feet had built up on the roof. He and Jim were pleased there wasn't the slightest sag in the roof members. The snow not only provided the additional insulation, but it would reduce the possibility of setting the roof on fire from a burning ember. But they still remained diligent. There was no use in pushing their luck.

Snow also covered the ice on the creek. It was essential they take care not to step onto hidden thin ice and fall through. Even if they survived the drowning, the freezing temperature would be deadly.

Warren knew he had to go hunting. His last trip was unsuccessful. Meals had been rather sparse, but there were no complaints. They had been lucky just to have something in their stomachs.

Quietly, he got up and gently put two logs on the fire. There was no need to stir up the sparks and take chances of tempting Fate. The coals ignited the dry wood and it crackled and popped as it burned. He checked the pot of water Jim had boiled for them to drink. It sat on the shelf in the east corner. The water had a layer of thin ice on it. He knew it was cold in the hut, but he didn't know it was that cold. He became alarmed.

"Jim." He spoke softly, but sharply, then leaned down to the sleeping bag. The curled up lump inside did not move. He reached over with his right hand and shook. "Jim."

Slowly, the shape began to change. Jim was waking up. Suddenly, a muffled sound came from inside. "I'm freezing to death."

Warren smiled to know Jim was alright. He went over to the fire. "Yeah. I know. Come get warm."

Jim stuck his head from the bedding. He was very hungry, but said nothing. There was no use to discuss something he couldn't do a thing about. He thought of the cellar. Many of the things they'd stored there were now frozen. He thought of the mess they would have to clean up when they thawed.

He was so glad he'd moved the potatoes to the hut and put them on the top shelf, close to the roof. This was probably the warmest and driest place in the hut. They would not freeze there. His laziness had, for once, paid off. If he hadn't, there would have been no potatoes to plant in the spring.

It was so cold outside, Warren hung the meat on a pole under the shed area. It was a refrigerator out there.

But today, no meat hung out on the pole. They had eaten it over the last few days. Jim had to go to the cellar for something.

"I've got to go hunting." Warren was adamant.

"Not today. You'll be blown away in the wind. And besides, you might get lost."

"Well we've got to have something to eat."

Jim sat inside his sleeping bag, his head just sticking out, his teeth chattering. Puffs of white vapor issued from his mouth when he breathed. "We will. We'll worry about that tomorrow. So don't worry now. I'm not even hungry."

Warren looked directly into Jim's eyes. He could see the untruth, knowing full well he was hungry. He turned and stared into the fire. "Jim. Sometimes I feel so helpless."

"Listen. We're still hanging in there, and that's what counts." Jim laughed. "My problem at the moment is I can't get warm. I am fucking cold!"

Warren placed another log on the fire. "Maybe this will help. If it doesn't, let me know." He headed to the doorway, lifted the skin flap and pulled the bamboo door covering into the room. "I've got to get some more wood." He quickly closed everything behind him. Within ten minutes, he'd moved a fair size pile of wood into the hut. The snow blown onto them by the wind began to melt.

"Looks like the North Pole out there. Even though the sun's behind the clouds, it's pretty bright." He held his hands over the flames.

Jim had his stick, making another notch. "I can hardly believe it, but today makes our three hundredth day here."

"Three hundred and we're doing just fine. But you've got to get warm." Warren insisted he get out of the bedding and get next to the fire. He quickly rearranged the bedding so Jim would be between him and the fire. He unzipped both bags and laid them over the two air mattresses that were now side by side. One they would use to sleep on and the other would be the cover. Then he placed the two blankets and deerskins he'd tanned that summer, on top of everything. "Now get back under the covers."

Jim crawled in and Warren got in beside him. They both lay facing the fire, on their left sides. Warren pulled Jim's body next to his, wrapping his right arm over him.

After several minutes, Jim could feel the heat from Warren's body penetrating the layers of clothes they both wore.

"How's that? Comfortable?"

"I think I just might survive." Jim laughed. His body began to warm. "Much better."

For some reason Warren wondered what time it was, but it really didn't matter. There were only two things of import right now. One was keeping Jim warm. The other was food.

He was doing something about the first. There was nothing he could do about the other at that moment or even that day. To go hunting today would be suicide. With the wind and blowing snow, it would be too easy to get disoriented and lost. He pulled Jim close to him.

After a while, Jim was asleep. Warren moved his hand over Jim's body to feel temperature. He seemed to be fine. Slowly and quietly, he got up, putting two more logs on the fire. He knew they had to eat something and they could not eat the potatoes on the shelf. He wrapped one of the skins from the bed around himself then started for the doorway.

The light outside had diminished significantly. The wind had increased. The snow was blowing so thick, he could hardly see five feet ahead. He crouched under the shelter of the structure, looking out and up. Several flakes hit his bare face causing stinging sensations. How is it that something so beautiful could be so painful?

He headed for the cellar. He was sure he could find it in his sleep. But he couldn't make a mistake. If he got lost, he was doomed. Then he recalled the hungry look on Jim's face and his own oath to take care of him. He continued forward.

Within a few seconds, he was at the edge of the rock. He carefully crossed the log bridge. If he fell, he would end up in the creek below. And God forbid he fall through the ice. When he reached the other side, he turned in the direction of the hut. He could barely see it. Drifts were piled high against and surrounding the structure. He turned, heading for the cellar.

The wind raged. He was glad Jim didn't attempt the trip. He would have been blown away.

The bamboo door to the cellar was open and the doorway was beginning to fill with snow. He quickly entered the cellar and stuffed a few apples, dried grapes and some dried mushrooms into his pockets. He also picked up the last of the cans of food they'd saved. He pulled the skin tighter around himself. His hands were so cold, he could hardly feel them. Leaving the cellar, he tightly closed the door, making sure it would not blow open again.

Turning north, he headed back toward the hut. He could see nothing but a million small white particles, whirling furiously through the air. He looked down to the ground. The footprints he'd made earlier were quickly filling with snow. They were the only link he had to the hut.

He moved as quickly as he could against the turbulent wind. The tracks were becoming more and more indistinct. The ice hitting his face stung like needles. His beard and mustache were getting packed with ice and snow.

He finally reached the bridge and started across. In his anxiety, the severe wind caught him off guard and he lost his balance. "AHHHH!" He made every effort to keep himself from falling, but it was no use. As he went down, the cans of food slipped from his arms and disappeared into the swirling white below. The skin from around him also blew away.

"SHIT! NO!" But there was nothing he could do. They were gone. "Fucking son-of-a-bitch!" He began to sob as he pulled himself up and slowly finished crossing the bridge. He could not believe he was so clumsy. He'd lost that good food. They were both hungry and he just lost the last of the canned food. Their emergency supply was gone. Had he made a fatal error for them both? The frustration made him cry even harder. The tears began to freeze as they ran down his face.

Momentarily, he entered the hut and closed the bamboo covering over the opening. The flap was then secured.

"Where the hell have you been?" Jim's voice came from the darkness. But then he heard Warren's sobs and he spoke with great concern. "Warren, what's wrong? Are you alright? What happened?"

Shortly, Warren's eyes became accustomed to the dimness. He turned in Jim's direction. He just stood there, saying nothing. His eyes were glazed.

To Jim, he looked like some snow creature from a very bad horror movie. Then he saw the distress on Warren's face. Pain was in his eyes and his body began to shake. Tears were streaming down his cheeks.

"Jim, I…I lost the food…I lost the food." Warren's distress was now uncontained as he openly cried. "I lost the food." He stood like a statue with a stuck record. "I lost the food. Jim. I'm sorry. I lost the food." Ice melted and dropped to the floor from his hair and beard.

Jim jumped up knowing he had to act fast. He pulled Warren to the fire, speaking to him softly and quietly, but with determination. "Don't worry. Don't worry. Everything's fine. We'll find it tomorrow. Now sit down and let's get warm." He grabbed Warren's hands and began to rub them.

Jim went to the shelf on the southeast wall where several of their worldly possessions were stored. The rest, not subject to the temperatures, were still in boxes and stacked under the tarpaulin on the south side of the creek. He grabbed the open bottle of scotch. The rest were under the tarpaulin. The scotch would never freeze, even at these temperatures. In one of the tin cups, he poured some for Warren. He held the cup to Warren's lips. "Here. Drink this." He placed Warren's left hand around the cup.

Warren began to sip the drink. His right hand moved around his left, clasping the cup.

Jim used his hands to pull the ice and snow off Warren's hair. He dried him with the towel. "Let's get you out of these damn wet clothes." He started removing pieces of Warren's apparel, hanging them on the shelf to dry.

In a while, they were sitting in front of the fire. Warren finally regained his composure and explained what happened.

"Fuck the food! Just be glad you didn't fall off the damn bridge. You'd have frozen to death and I'd have never been able to find you. Now, THAT would have really sucked the big one."

"But I knew you were hungry."

"And it was damn thoughtful to think of me. But fuck it! I'd rather be starving to death than for you to take a chance like that. There were no promises from the Waldorf Astoria there'd be a smorgasbord every day when all this started. We both knew it wasn't going to be a picnic. So don't go taking chances, just to make it a little cushy for me. Thanks, but no thanks."

Warren smiled, hardly believing what he was hearing. Jim was accepting the whole thing and taking it rather well. No rose-colored glasses were softening his sight. He was telling it just the way it was, with all the harsh realities. He leaned over and gave Jim a big hug.

They hugged each other, slowly moving back and forth. From that day on, the only chances taken would be ones well calculated in their favor.

They shared the apples and things Warren had retrieved from the cellar then discussed things and projects they wanted to do when spring arrived. This conversation uplifted their spirits. Warren put four logs on the fire before they turned in for the night. He held Jim close, keeping him between himself and the fire. He would never let Jim be cold again.

This sleeping position became so natural, it would continue for the rest of their lives. Each would find it difficult to sleep without the other. They both found some sort of indefinable security in being next to one another.

Shortly, the low whistling of the wind put them to sleep. As night progressed, the wind would cease and the world would be turned into a white and crystal fantasyland.

Warren's hunting over the next three days was good. There was enough meat to last them for some time. They even tried their hand at ice fishing. Actually, Jim did this sport while Warren was out hunting. Jim liked this because he didn't have to go far to do it.

Only one thing was a real problem, going to the bathroom. On tolerable days it could be done outside and away from the hut. But on severe days, they couldn't avoid staying in the hut. This is where the shovel and one of the empty vegetable cans came in handy. A piece of the towel became important. After it was used, Jim would rinse the cloth in a pot of hot water, then hang it on the shelf to dry. When it came to this problem, neither could wait for warmer weather.

A few times it was necessary to go and cut additional wood for the fire. This was not easy in the snow. The litters became virtually useless because the snow would pile up under them.

Jim tried to keep a pot of soup on at all times. It was a quick way to warm themselves after coming in from outside.

They knew this winter was not typical of the Atlanta area. It was much harsher. There was a lot more snow and it stayed on the ground much longer.

Jim took several pictures during the snow time. The scenes were so beautiful. He wasn't sure why he did, but he just did. It was the doing that was important. Deep inside, he hoped someone might see them one day.

As the days passed slowly by, Warren had his work cut out for himself. Not only did he have to hunt, but he had to make sure he didn't lose Jim to mental suicide.

On one day, he dragged Jim out and they built a giant snowman and a giant snow woman. Of course, they ended up turning out rather obscene. Jim used a stick to support an erect snow penis, while Warren built humongous boobs. They actually enjoyed their snow outings, but they had to be short lived, to prevent getting too cold.

They took extra precautions when they had to go far from the hut. There was no safety away from the hut and the fire. The skins from animals he'd killed, Warren put under his clothes, with the fur toward his body. This helped retain body heat better, allowing him to stay outside longer. It was his hands and feet that he had to be extremely aware of to make sure they didn't get frostbite.

On a few occasions, he brought Jim along to see how the traps worked as well as how to get the animals out without getting bit or scratched. These companion outings were done on the warmer days when the wind wasn't a problem. They also got him out of the hut and into the sun and air.

Although it upset him, Jim knew he had to see the way Warren killed the animals. It was necessary should he ever have to do it.

Warren discussed a project of hanging skins on the interior of the hut to cut down on any drafts and increase the insulation. Jim thought it a great idea, but knew they'd have to take care of the skins so crawly creatures wouldn't invade their home. A thought of the beautiful tapestries used for the same purpose at Versailles crossed his mind. The only difference was they didn't have to worry about small crawlies in the tapestries.

Every once in a while, they would get out the guitar and the recorder. This helped keep them amused. Warren was always concerned over what he would do if he broke a string. Fortunately, this problem never arose. The strings would last long enough.

CHAPTER XXXVI

Jim continued to keep track of their days. Each notch brought them closer and closer to spring and warmer weather.

Finally, there were three hundred and sixty-five. They had survived one whole year. Most of the snow was gone, eight days prior. Only a few patches remained in shadowed areas. The last snow flurry was twenty days earlier.

"Warren. We've been here a year." Jim shouted with glee.

Warren looked up and smiled. They actually made it through the first winter. He knew it would be the worse one, not knowing what to expect. But now he did and they could prepare for the next one. The best thing of all is he knew they would survive. Barring some unusual disaster, they would make it. Now they would have to concern themselves with the onset of age. They would have to prepare for their old age, over the coming years, to make it easier when they got there.

They had had several discussions of the 'Stone Mountain People', as they started to refer to those who built the wall on top of the mountain. But since they had not shown up, they could not depend on an encounter with them to help their survival, much less in trying to return to their own time.

Warren sipped his cup of sassafras tea. The honey had run out long ago. He knew they would be better prepared the next winter by storing up more of it in the cooler "It's hard to think it's been a year."

"I know. Seems more like a life time." Jim laughed. "But you said we'd do it. And, by God, you were right!"

Warren just gave a little chuckle. It was his way of showing humble victory. They had won, at least for now. His eyes glinted. He was not only proud of himself, but he was really proud of Jim. Jim had been a good soldier in the battle. Thank you for a partner like him. We will be just fine.

"I think we should have some sort of celebration to usher in the spring." He held his fist in the air. "And to the first dip in the creek. The sooner the better. I'm getting tired of the 'bath from a pot' routine."

Warren laughed. He did agree. It would be nice to take a full bath again.

"Remember the morning you slipped on the rock, and I thought you were drowning? That was the first time we took a dunk in the river."

"Yes. But that was a mistake. And the water's too damn cold to get in it right now, or any time real soon, for that fact. Not unless you want to freeze your ass off."

Although the sky was a bit gray and overcast, they were still planning their spring and summer projects. The dam was first on the agenda. And since he hadn't been able to get to it during the winter, Warren wanted to get the hives built quickly and in place before the hatching of the new queens. The cellar would have to be rebuilt. They had to prevent stored items from freezing, but cold enough to slow deterioration.

On this day, they decided to take another trip to the top of the mountain. They needed to do something with activity.

The ground was covered with the brown litter of the previously colorful autumn. The naked trees stretched their fingers into the air. Jim knew it wouldn't be long before they would show their coats of green.

When they crossed the creek, Jim looked down from the bridge, scanning the area below. Ever since the snow began to melt, he looked for the cans of food Warren dropped that memorable night. Somehow they must have reached the water and floated down stream. Maybe they made it to the ocean. He laughed at his thoughts. They were never to see the cans again.

Jim carried his spear and Warren his bow, arrows and machete. Walking up the west side of the mountain, they recalled the first day they set eyes on the area and the trip to the top. During the trip up, the sky became clear.

A drift of snow was still in the ring. It was along the south wall in the shadow. Another patch set on the north side of the central pedestal.

A crisp breeze swept through their hair when they climbed to the top of the central tower. Warren thought it rather funny that they automatically looked to the west. But it was normal since that's the way you would look to view the skyline of Atlanta. Although the position was automatic, their thoughts were not of the city. They were seeing the very early spring of their world and they thought of their future existence. No more did they have any expectations of getting back, even with the help of the 'Stone Mountain People'.

Their minds were becoming more in tune with the new time and place. Jim slowly stopped relating everything to the time they had left behind. Although this day was mid-October in their original time, Jim was not concerned. He now accepted the fact it was early spring, and that's exactly how he was seeing it.

The months were losing their names. It was the seasons that were important. In a few weeks, he would start his seeds and make the mounds for the potatoes. He was becoming aware of the signs. It was necessary to know when the last frost would come. Warren wanted to know when the migrating animals would return. When could they hunt frogs again? How much would they get done before the next winter?

Their inner clocks were almost ticking in time with the earth clock of this new world. Only their memories would prevent total coordination.

Their interests were of other things. Would they ever figure out who constructed the monument here on the mountain? Would they ever know what it was for? Would they ever see another human? How long would they survive before they were too old? Would their existence ever have any bearing on the future? Would anyone ever know what happened to them?

Each day would be dealt with as it came. For today, they just accepted the fact they were alive and together. Maybe they were a little worse for wear, but they were still kicking.

Simultaneously, Warren placed his right arm on Jim's shoulders as Jim put his left arm around Warren's waist. They stood silently, surveying their domain.

After a moment, Warren spoke softly. "Happy New Year, Jim."

Another moment passed, then Jim quietly responded. "Happy New Year, Warren."

They stood silent, smiling, each happy with the knowledge they were alive. Tomorrow would be the first day of year two for them. They hoped it truly would be a 'happy new year'.

CHAPTER XXXVII

The seasons had come and gone. It was late fall again. They had accomplished many things in the years that had passed.

The dam, now completed, held back the water, forming a nice pond around the rock. Jim liked it because the slow moving water heated more quickly, allowing them to start their bathing earlier in the spring. Before the winter's thaw, they would remove chunks of ice and put them in the rebuilt cold cellar. Food items they stored there were keeping very well.

Jim was planting more and storing more. Warren had cleared additional land on the south bank.

More of the year was spent out of the hut structure. Just the winter seasons made it a necessity to take refuge there. It was used more and more for the cool dry storage of meats.

Jim's oven became the center of cooking. It also protected the coals during the rains. The fire never went out. Warren's lighter and matches became memory pieces, never used again.

There had been two frosts already. Jim requested they move into the hut. The cold still bothered him, but he came to complain less about it. He just accepted the inevitable. Winter did not frighten him as it had in the beginning. He trusted Warren and knew deep inside he would take care of him.

It was early the next morning when they were awakened by the sound. It made them both sit straight up in the bed.

"What the hell was that?" Jim looked around in the darkness of the hut, trying to figure what he'd heard or if it was a dream.

"There's something in the lake." Warren was listening intently. "At the west end."

The noise became clearer to Jim. It was the sound of splashing water mixed with what sounded like animal noises.

They both rose quickly and exited the hut and looked west. Jim was amazed, speechless. His eyes were round as saucers. Finally, he spoke in surprise of it all. "Warren. There are elephants in the pond!"

Warren was not surprised at all, having seen them years earlier, on the Chattahoochee. What did surprise him was they were this far to the east. He'd not seen evidence of them before this, east of the river. Had their territory changed? If so, why?

Jim wasn't sure what to think. He thought them rather cute, all hairy and all, but he also could imagine what they could do to the hut or the cold cellar if they got near them.

The group of eight did not look too intimidating, since he and Warren were on the rock looking down. Jim wasn't sure how he'd handle it seeing them up close and at ground level. "What if they come over here and wreck the hut?" He whispered.

"I don't think we'll have to worry about that. They're just taking their morning dip."

"Well I hope this doesn't become a daily habit. I don't think I could handle it."

Warren and Jim crouched there watching for some time. Becoming more courageous, they slowly moved to the western edge of the rock, sitting on the edge.

The mastodons were soon aware of their presence. They all stopped and turned toward the two small creatures sitting at the rock's edge. The curiosity of one made it come a bit closer. It raised its trunk in the direction of the rock and seemed to take a few sniffs. After a moment, it turned back and joined the group again. It made some loud bellow and trumpeted, then continued to play in the water.

"I don't think they're afraid of us." Warren spoke in a normal tone of voice. They don't see us as a threat.

They watched for some time, but there was much to do. They couldn't wait on a herd of elephants. Being careful in their chores, they remained aware of the creatures so as not to create a problem with them.

Periodically, the mastodons would raise their trunks, sniffing the air to see where the two small creatures had gone. Once they seemed to know where they were, they went about their business as if nothing was wrong. Several hours passed before the herd moved slowly into the woods to the northwest.

This was not the last of them. They would return in the spring, staying the entire summer in the area. Warren was right. For some reason their territory had changed. They would be constant visitors to the area in their migration.

In the future times, it would get to the point where Warren and Jim would take the mastodons for granted, basically ignoring them. Of course, the mastodons would do what ever they wanted to do and Jim and Warren would just have to get over it. The hairy elephants would become their large woolly neighbors with whom they would have to co-exist.

A bamboo barrier as well as the high bank of the south side of the creek, now the pond, prevented them from getting into the garden area. If that was not sufficient and they seemed to be getting too close, an occasional yell of: "Get the hell out of the garden!" would do.

Jim quickly got use to the periodic morning ritual of the bath at the west end of the pond. The creatures virtually took claim to that end.

Warren had to laugh. He could not believe how fast they both became accustomed to the herd being around. By the end of the next summer, Jim had given them all names. He constantly had to remind Jim that they were wild beasts and not pets. They had to be careful around them.

There would never be an incident. They would always live in harmony with the furry animals. Future reminiscences of the mastodons would be pleasant and humorous. Jim would forever remember them with great fondness.

Over time, Warren was very pleased with his and Jim's relationship. They had settled into being comfortable with each other. They had very few disagreements, mainly because there wasn't time to argue about things. They were both of the philosophy that life was too short and there was no time to throw away in stupidity and discontent. Each understood the other, letting each be individuals.

Although Warren taught Jim to hunt and clean animals, he was the one who always did it. Refresher courses for Jim remained just that. Jim continued the cooking as his part of the partnership.

Their conversations continued as normal and covered a multitude of subjects. Neither got tired of things brought from the other's mind.

Jim kept them civilized as far as their looks were concerned, insisting on the trimming of their hair, beards and mustaches. Occasionally, they would get out the china and silver just to say they did. Warren did it mainly to humor Jim and because it seemed important. They had learned to live with a 'give and take' attitude.

If it helped their wellbeing, they felt it was good to do it. Warren's scotch was kept for medicinal purposes, but occasionally, Jim would pour Warren a glass, just because he deserved it. He wanted it to last as long as possible before another piece of the civilized world went extinct.

CHAPTER XXXVIII

It was coming autumn again. Warren sensed the weather chilling sooner than normal. Jim had done exceptionally well with his gardening. The experiences of previous summers made the garden spot a sight to behold. One benefit, the neighboring mastodons helped in the fertilizer department.

This spring and summer had been different from the previous five years. There had been very little rain. The creeks had stopped running in early summer. Jim was glad of the pond. It was how he'd kept the garden watered. But the pond was getting lower. Even the mastodons had moved on from the area, looking for food and more water. Most of the wild game had done the same thing.

Warren was concerned about their supply of smoked and dried meat getting low. He had to make sure it was adequate for the up and coming winter. He knew he was going to have to hunt farther away. "Well, I've got to head northwest tomorrow. I think all the game is heading for the river."

"Yeah. Without rain I'm sure everything's running for the last drops of water. Have you seen the trees? The leaves look real bad. There won't be any coloring this year." Jim looked to the west, as he stood on the edge of the rock. "And look at my poor pond. If any more water evaporates it'll turn into a mud hole."

"I know. Guess that's why our furry friends moved on two months ago. Maybe they knew something." Warren stood beside Jim. "Did you get everything in the cellar?"

"Sure did. Last of the potatoes went in the other day." Jim paused for a moment before changing the subject, as usual. "Did you know, just last week we hit day two thousand and thirty? Can you believe it? We've been here over five and a half years? I think we've done real well." He patted Warren on the back with his right hand. "How long do you think you'll be gone?"

"Oh, maybe two weeks. Three at the most." He paused for a moment. "I hope. But if I get a deer or a wild boar, I'll have to bring it back on a litter. Keep your fingers crossed. Yeah. I hope I'll be back before it starts to get really cold."

"While you're gone, I think I'll do a little touch up work around here. I've been meaning to put a few more rocks on the barrier walls over there."

He referred to the five foot walls constructed on either side of the opening where the bridge came to the rock from the south bank. This project was a never-ending one that started several years earlier. A bamboo gate blocked the opening in the wall making it almost impossible to get onto the rock without going through the gate. "As a matter of fact, I think I'll do some of that this morning."

Warren headed for the hut. "I'm going to rest up for my trek. If you need anything, give me a holler."

Jim worked on the walls for several hours, shifting the stones around on the eastern wall. Although the day was cool, he was getting warm. He took off his coat, shirt and long pants. He laughed, thinking about the pants situation. They both had brought only two pair on the outing. For some time now, every time he'd gone to wash Warren's, there was a new rip or a place where the threads were coming undone. His sewing kit, one of the items in the notorious five boxes, had been of significance.

But it was inevitable. In another year or two, he was going to have to start making their significant wardrobe from skins. This was not a foreign thing to him. Already, he'd made a fur skin belt for them both.

He'd also made Warren a special hat and gave it to him as a Christmas present over a year ago. It was made of fur with feather stuffing. On the top was a set of small antlers, ornamented with large bird feathers at the base. It was his way of showing Warren how proud he was of his hunting and being such a good provider. He knew Warren liked the hat, too, because he refused to go hunting without it. He was glad since he'd taken a lot of time in making it.

Another present was a deerskin jacket. This really wasn't a jacket but a vest. There were no sleeves. He put the fur to the inside to keep in the warmth. A few pieces of skin strips were used to tie up the front.

Jim loved to see Warren all dressed to go hunting, wearing the hat and all. There was something kind of cute yet caveman about the whole outfit. It was the sight of the deer vest over his flannel shirt, tattered jeans, the hat, the bow, arrows, knife and machete. He looked like a character out of some strange barbarian tale. The sienna and white fur and black feathers of the cap contrasted with Warren's dark hair, beard and mustache. His blue eyes were like bright beacons. When he smiled, his teeth gleamed. Jim had taken several photos of Warren dressed in his regalia. Warren conceded to the photos because he knew no one would ever see them.

Jim was standing at the edge of the rock, near the bridge, still trying to repair the east wall. The mental image of Warren dressed in his getup made him start laughing out loud. This was a major error, as he lost his balance. In trying to catch himself, he reached for the wall. This was of no consequence and he fell.

Jim let out a loud scream. It was almost ten feet to the shallow pond below. When he hit the bottom, his head hit a rock in the mud.

Warren was aroused from his light sleep, alarmed by the yell, and he came running from the hut. He was squinting, trying to get his eyes accustomed to the bright light of the mid-day. Standing in the center of the open area of the rock, he turned in all directions, looking for Jim.

"Where the fuck is he?" He mumbled as he ran to the middle of the bridge. He stopped again to look around. Still there was nothing. Just as he began to head for the garden area, he noticed something out of the corner of his eye. Turning and looking down, he saw Jim's seemingly lifeless body lying below. There was a patch of blood in the shallow water around his head.

"OH GOD! OH GOD!" Warren yelled out and his heart began to pound. He knelt down on the bridge, swung over the side and dropped. He landed not far from Jim. Jim was not moving. All his mind would register is that he was dead. His breath began to quicken in his panic. "Oh God! Please don't let him be dead."

He immediately knelt down, putting his right hand under Jim's head. Removing it, he saw it was covered with blood. "Jim! Jim! Oh God! He's dead! Oh God! No! No!" Tears began to blur his vision. He pulled him tight against him. He grabbed Jim's right wrist. Suddenly, he felt a pulse. He immediately regained his composure.

"Don't worry, good buddy. You'll be alright." Warren had Jim in his arms within a second and was heading for the dam. Crossing over the top of the dam, he climbed the south bank, racing him over the bridge and to the shade in the shed part of the hut. From the hut, he got the two napkins and one of the sleeping bags. He also had the bottle of scotch.

After placing Jim on the bedding, he began to treat the wound on the back of his head. He rolled Jim over to see the extent of the cut. Blood poured from the opening. He had to stop the bleeding. He wet a napkin with the scotch and wiped the wound. There was only one thing he could think to do.

Getting Jim's sewing kit, he threaded the largest needle. Carefully, even lovingly, trying not to cause pain, he put a few stitches to hold the skin together. After applying a little pressure for a few moments, the bleeding slowed. He placed one folded napkin on the cut and the other wrapped around his head to hold it in place. Why is it that cuts on the head seem to bleed like nowhere else on the body?

By evening, he had Jim in the hut by the fire. He'd put all his clothes back on so he would stay warm.

It was late, when Jim began to come around. Finally, he moved, moaning in pain. "Ohhhh! I hurt! I hurt! Warren! Help me!"

Warren grabbed him up in his arms. "It's alright! It's alright! I'm here."

Jim slowly became aware, but his head pounded like a kettledrum. "Oh Warren. I hurt real bad." He chuckled in pain trying to make it go away. "How stupid of me. How clumsy. Let's hear it for grace. Oh Warren." He slowly opened his eyes and blinked. "Holy shit! I think I'm going to have one hell of a headache. And I think the rest of my body is going to disown me. Feels like I've been beat with a club." He tried to laugh.

"I think you're going to make it." Warren held him tight.

Jim blinked a few more times then closed his eyes. "I can't believe how stupid I was. That's what I get for not keeping my mind on what I was doing." He moved his left hand to his forehead. "My head feels like it got run over by a truck." He opened his eyes. He was looking in the direction of the fire. He looked up at Warren and around the hut. He blinked then closed his eyes again.

Warren continued to hold him tight in his arms. Nothing was said for a while.

Jim opened his eyes, blinked and looked right at Warren. "Warren? I think I've got a little problem." He bit his lower lip between his teeth. He grabbed Warren's arm with his left hand. "Warren." He spoke quietly and slowly. "Warren. I can't see a thing. Is it dark in here?"

Warren moved his left hand back and forth in front of Jim's eyes. There was no response to the movement.

"Of course it's not dark in here. I can feel the heat of the fire and hear it burning. Warren." He grabbed tighter on his arm. "Warren. Oh God. I can't see. Warren, I can't see."

Warren's heart began to sink. He waved his hand again. There was no response. He grit his teeth and bent his head back, shaking it. He pulled Jim close and whispered. "Oh God. Hasn't he suffered enough?" He began to sob and tears ran down his face. "Please God. It's not fair." He could not control his feelings.

Jim hung on to Warren, realizing the horrible truth. He felt sad, but his sadness wasn't for himself. It was for Warren. "Warren." He spoke softly. "Oh Warren. Don't cry. Don't worry. It's my stupid fault for not paying attention." He clinched his right fist and hit the ground several times. "Oh Warren. Don't cry. Everything will be okay."

They sat holding one another for a long time. Neither said a word. They were resolve in the fact that they had each other.

Finally, Warren broke the silence. "Jim, I've got to put more wood on the fire, but I'll be right back." Warren got up and put two logs on the fire, but was quickly back holding Jim again.

Jim could feel the renewed heat of the flames. He could feel the heat from Warren's body. He was not cold.

Turning in, Jim lay in his normal position, his back against Warren's chest. Warren's right arm pulled him close. The throbbing of the bumps and bruises began to overwhelm him. He closed his eyes, trying not to think about them. Somehow he forced away the pain and he fell into a restless sleep.

Warren held Jim close. The reality he'd almost lost his friend was gnawing in his guts. His mind played quick scenarios of what his existence would be like without Jim. The terror of being alone was crushing. He knew now, more than ever, how important Jim was to him. Jim was more than just another voice. He also knew he loved him more than he could have ever imagined. He kissed Jim's head. "I love you, Jim." He whispered. "Please God, don't ever take him from me." After his anxiety calmed down, he finally went into an uneasy sleep.

Outside the temperature was falling. The air was crisp and quiet. There was no wind, nor the sound of night creatures. It was silent. Fine feathers of ice began to form on the edges of the shallow waters of the pond. There would be frost by morning. Warren was surprised that the weather was chilling so early. The first frost of the season was normally weeks away. There was no explanation.

CHAPTER XXXIX

Warren was climbing the eastern slope of the high ridge. It was some time around noon and the sky was turning dark and gray. Shortly, gray-black clouds began to move in from the east. All morning there had been rumblings, indicating a possible storm. The temperature was very cold, just as it had been since he left camp. He did not relish the thought of rain or snow with it being so cold. It would not only make hunting more difficult, but it would make traveling more difficult, too.

He thought of Jim, back at the hut. They had hoped Jim's loss of sight would be only temporary and would return after a few days of recuperation, but it was not the case. This had postponed his leaving. But he'd have never left if he hadn't felt confident Jim could take care of himself for the two to three weeks he would be gone.

Jim knew where everything was and promised not to leave the rock. Warren set the bamboo gate up at the bridge to prevent any wild animal from getting to the rock. Jim's loss of sight would be a hinder only in the respect it would take him longer to do something. Jim would be just fine.

Warren had no desire to leave Jim alone, but there was no way to prevent the hunting trip. It was essential and they both knew it.

Suddenly, his thoughts were shattered by an enormous crack. The sky was filled with a blinding flash. The cold wind began to pick up until it was almost at gale force. Warren knew a major electrical storm was in the making. He thought it seemed unusual for such a storm in cold weather.

Thunder roared in the east, the direction from where the storm was coming. Little did he know that some eight miles away, a disaster was brewing.

Two hours later, he was nearing the crest of the ridge. It was virtually the same place where over five and a half years earlier, he'd discovered their predicament after climbing a tall tree. Not one drop of rain or snow had fallen, but he became aware of something terrible. He could smell it in the air. The odor was that of burning wood and leaves. He knew instantly, the forest was on fire. With the direction the wind was blowing, he was in extreme danger. The fire was coming right his way. The lack of rain all summer made the forest a tinderbox. The wind was a giant bellows, fanning the flames into a enormous conflagration.

Warren quickly moved to the west and the top of the ridge. From there, the raging fire to the east became evident. He could hear the crackling roar of the blaze. The sky was filled with the thick, choking smoke. It was essential he hurry as fast as possible, as the fire would be on him in no time. Flames raced up the slope and over the crest. The heat started to build and it was difficult to breathe. Warren knew that reaching the river was paramount. It was the only place where he might be able to survive the fire. Staying in the forest meant certain cremation.

It was early evening when he got to the river. The electrical storm was over, but the forest continued to blaze. The clouds in the sky to the east were aglow in orange as the fire raged westward.

Staying ahead of the fire was his only chance. He noticed a significant drop in the temperature. Even with his running to escape the fire, the decrease in temperature was extremely noticeable.

He began to run upstream on the east bank. For a moment, he had to stop to catch his breath. It was then; he realized where he was. Not ten feet away from him was the pile of stones he and Jim had constructed years earlier. His mind flashed back to that time. His body was engulfed with a cold chill that brought him back to his senses. He had to keep moving. He continued northward. In the diminishing light of day, he could see a thick fog ahead. Within seconds, he found himself in the heavy cold mist. It was difficult to see, but he continued forward. The temperature plummeted further and the air filled with fine crystals of ice. He kept running northward through the mist. After a while, the mist dissipated, disappearing behind him.

He had to stay ahead of the fire until he could reach a place to cross the river. That's when he remembered the waterfall somewhere up stream. That would be a good place to try and cross. His heart pounded. He had to rest. Standing there panting, he suddenly became aware of it. It was a sound he knew from another time.

'Thump'. 'Thump'.

He stood erect and listened intently. The sound came again.

'Thump'. 'Thump'.

He knew that sound. But was it possible?

'Thump'. 'Thump'.'Thump'. 'Thump'.

Warren looked up in front of him. There it was. But how? His mind whirled, trying to put the pieces together.

'Thump'. 'Thump'.

He slowly climbed the embankment and out onto the concrete structure. He stood there in the darkening of evening, looking at a highway, stretching out in front of him. His mind was racing. The pieces of the puzzle were coming together.

"It's not the time. Time is of no consequence. It's the cold!" He yelled out. "The cold is the answer. It's the cold. Why didn't I get it sooner? It's the cold."

Momentarily, he saw sets of lights approaching. Within seconds, the lights passed him by. 'Thump'. 'Thump'. 'Thump'. 'Thump'. It was the sound of vehicle tires on the expansion joints of the bridge. Warren turned to watch red taillights move down the road. Several vehicles passed by from both directions.

Suddenly, one vehicle passed by then slowed as it put on the brakes. The two policemen in the car could not believe their eyes. The car came to a screeching halt. They looked at one another.

"Did you see what I saw?" He spoke to his partner.

"I think so. Better check this one out."

The police car made a 'U' turn and the blue lights flashed. Slowly, the car headed toward the lone figure standing at the edge of the road.

The bright headlights only reinforced what the policemen thought they saw in the fading daylight. They were not dreaming.

There stood Warren, wearing his full regalia, with his bow, arrows, knife and machete. One of the fifty foot lengths of rope was looped around his neck and under his arm. He had brought it to construct a litter, if he needed one to carry game back to camp. The car stopped some twenty feet from him.

Warren did not move. He just kept chanting quietly, as if in a trance. "It's the cold. Why didn't I get it before? And we could have come back long ago. It's the cold."

Both men got out of the car. They stopped, their hands on their hips, staring at Warren.

After a minute, one of the policemen spoke. "Bob. Keep the traffic moving. I'll try to see what's up here." He turned to Warren. "Okay buddy." He pulled his gun to assure their safety. "Who are you and what party are you going to? And what are you doing out here?"

Bob waved the oncoming traffic to keep moving, but kept and

eye on the situation. He wanted to make sure his partner was not in any trouble.

Warren was still in a state of profound shock and amazement. He was dumbstruck. He could hardly believe it. There were people talking to him. He lost control, starting to laugh and cry hysterically, at the same time. He looked up into the air. "People! Jim, there are people!" Warren yelled and began to lose control in the mixture of his crying and laughter. "But I know the answer now! It's the cold! It's the cold!"

"Okay buddy! Stop right there!" He turned to his partner. "God. We've got a crazy on our hands. Bob. Get on the radio! Quick!"

His partner went to the car radio.

"Say, buddy. What's your name?" He yelled to Warren.

"My name?" Warren was still trying to gather his wits. "My name. My name is Warren. Warren Glass. My name is Warren Glass." Then he started laughing again, hysterically. "It's the cold! It's the cold!"

"Headquarters. We have a white male standing in Johnson Ferry Road, on the bridge over the Chattahoochee. And you should see the getup he's wearing. Says his name's Warren Glass. And he's jabbering something about the cold. Over."

The radio popped and a voice returned, echoing in the still cold air. "What name again? Over."

"Warren Glass. Over."

There was a minute of silence. Finally the radio popped again. "Did you say Warren Glass? Over"

"That's what he said his name is. Over"

"Bring him in for questioning. Seems we have an open file on this guy. Over."

"Is he dangerous? You should see this outfit he has on. And he's carrying a bow and arrows and a machete. Over."

"Shouldn't be. Just bring him in. Over." The radio popped and was silent.

"Okay buddy. Okay Warren. Put down the machete. Everything's gonna be alright. Lay down the machete. And the bow. You can take the rope off, too." He spoke with authority.

Warren crouched down, placing everything on the pavement. He stood up again, looked at them, and in a pleading voice spoke again. "It's the cold. It's the cold."

Bob calmly walked over and put a set of handcuffs on Warren's wrists, then directed him to the rear seat of the car. As he did, he read him his rights. Before he got in, Bob carefully removed the antler hat. "You'll get all this back when we get this straightened out." He placed everything in the trunk.

On the way to the department, Bob called the dispatcher again. "We're on our way in. And he keeps talking about the cold. Over."

"Okay. I'm sure it will get straight when you get in here. Over."

Within an hour, they were at headquarters and Warren was going through the procedures. Soon finished, Warren was placed in a room and asked to wait.

The room contained a table and three chairs. A clear glass ashtray sat in the middle of the table. The walls were stark. One wall contained a one-way mirror-window.

In about twenty minutes, a tall stocky black man, short hair, no facial hair, dressed in a dark suit, entered the room. He carried two file folders, a pad of paper, several pencils, a portable tape recorder and Warren's antler hat. These were all placed on the table. He stood across from Warren, looked down at the antler hat, then back at Warren. His mind began to chuckle. He had seen many things in his fifteen year career, but noting like this. He turned on the recorder then extended his right hand. "Mike. Mike Johnson."

Warren was already standing. He did so when Mike Johnson walked into the room. He shook his hand. "Warren Glass. But I have the answer. It's the cold. It's the cold." He looked directly into Mike's eyes. "And we could have come back a long time ago. If I had only figured it out. It's the cold."

"It's the cold? Okay. We'll get to that in a minute. You can tell me all about it." Mike paused and looked down at the table. "Like the hat." A big grin went from ear to ear.

Warren looked down at his hat. "Oh. Yes. Jim. My friend, Jim, made it for me. I wear it all the time when I go hunting."

"Please sit down, if you don't mind, Mr. Glass." He reached into his jacket pocket and pulled out a lighter and pack of cigarettes. He extended the pack toward Warren and smiled.

Warren looked at the cigarettes. He snapped back to reality again, leaving his strange trance state and giggled. "No. Gave them up a long time ago. But please feel free, if you'd like. And please. Call me Warren." He looked at the cigarette pack. "I thought they banned smoking in public buildings?"

"They have. But this room was set up to allow it. Only room anyone can smoke in." Mike took one and lighted it, taking a draw. "Did they read you your rights?"

"Rights? Oh. Yes. When they picked me up."

"Is there any reason why you might need legal council?"

"No. I don't think so."

"Do you mind if I record the session of questions?"

"No. No problem at all."

"Now, you say your name is Warren Glass."

"Correct. But I have a lot of questions. And it's the cold. That's the answer to the puzzle. It's the cold." Warren tried to remain calm for fear they might lock him up, thinking him a wacko. But then he thought again. He had probably already passed that mark from his attire and actions.

Mike looked directly at him for a minute before continuing. "We, too, have a lot of questions. And, yes. We'll get to the cold. But first, where have you been for the last five and a half months and where is James Stone?"

Warren was shocked with surprise. "Five and a half months? But that can't be."

Mike watched to see his reactions and his sincerity. "What do you mean?"

"Why, it's been over five and a half years we've been gone. Not five and a half months. And we could have come back any time. Any time it was cold. If we had only known. If only I had thought of that." He looked directly at Mike. Then he realized he was not making any sense.

"I'm sorry to disagree with you Warren, but you and your friend…" Mike looked down on the table and opened a folder. "You and Mr. James Stone, left the middle of last October on an outing down the Chattahoochee. It is now the last few days in March. By my calculations, that's five and a half months. Half of October. November. December. January. February. March. Five and a half months."

A very disturbed and confused expression came to Warren's face. "But that can't be." He shook his head in disbelief.

"Listen. Would you like a cup of coffee? It might make it easier to gather our wits about us."

Warren's face changed. A smile replaced the anxiety. "Coffee? I'd love a cup. Black."

"Now, about your friend."

Warren cut him short. "Yes. Jim. We've got to get Jim back. If only I had known it sooner. Five and a half years sooner. It's so simple. How stupid of me for not figuring it out before." He pounded his fist on the table. "Mike. I'm so sorry, but I have finally figured the whole thing out. Now we can go get Jim. But we have to hurry."

Suddenly the door opened and an officer brought in two cups of coffee. This reinforced the presence of the one-way mirror and someone else listening on the other side.

Mike took one of the cups, handing it to Warren.

"Thanks, Mike." He took a sip. "I'd forgotten how good it is."

Mike wanted him to explain his theory regarding the cold.

Warren's mental wheels became verbal. "It's the cold. And the mist. When we left last October, it was cold that morning. It was not only cold here, but it was cold there. The same as tonight. It is cold there and it is cold here. The mist is the doorway between, but it has to be cold in both places at the same time. The door won't work if the criteria aren't met. And you have to pass through in the mist." Warren began to laugh and to cry. "We can get back. We both can get back. But we could have come back a long time ago. Why didn't I figure it out before? The reason we couldn't get back immediately is because there was no cold there. It was the beginning of spring there and there was no more cold weather. But when it got cold again there, we could have tried to come back again because it was still cold here. We could have come home a long time ago." He looked up; his face was wet with tears. "And he's blind. Jim's blind! I've got to go get him. We can get back. We can get back. We can." He set his head on the table and cried.

Mike was somewhat apprehensive over the rambling, but he had watched carefully. He had listened to every word trying to understand. From the files, he knew Warren was an educated man, not prone to violence or flights of fantasy. But what was he talking about? To what door was he referring? Maybe the coffee would help. He reached over and patted his back. "Drink your coffee and we'll have some more." He made some motion at the mirror on the wall. Within five minutes an officer brought in a whole tray full of cups of coffee.

Warren slowly pulled himself together. He picked up the cup and smelled the aroma. He took another sip. His eyes closed and he smiled.

"Warren? I've got to get this story straight. Can you tell me what happened? I mean from the top. Maybe it'll help me understand what's going on."

Warren set the cup down. "Mike? What time is it?"

Mike turned his left wrist. "It's twenty after nine."

"We've got to hurry. There's not much time to get Jim back." Warren pleaded.

"Look. We'll get to him later. But we're not going anywhere until I get some answers. First I have to find out if you are who you say you are. We'd bring in your wife, but she's gone."

"Linda's gone? Yeah. She probably took the kids and went back to Texas." Warren looked blankly into space.

"The kids?" Mike opened one of the file folders.

"I've got two boys." He glanced at the files then at Mike. "There are things I can tell you about myself that only I would know. And I'll tell you things about Jim Stone only he or his best friends would know. That should convince you who I am."

"True. Your wife gave us a lot of information on you when she filed the missing person's report. Mr. Stone's relatives gave us information on him."

"And why don't you know anything from the finger prints they took when I got here? Because I've never been printed before. Guess they'll be on file now." He laughed.

"Okay. Any time. The floor's all yours."

"You might want to get a few tapes. It's a long story."

Mike looked at Warren. "Don't worry. I'll get them when I need them." He glanced over to the mirror.

First, Warren pointed out specific information on himself and Jim. Mike finally conceded the fact he really was Warren Glass. "Okay. I know you're telling the truth about who you are. Now I want to know where you've been the last months."

Warren chuckled then sipped his coffee. He stared right into Mike's eyes. "It's been over five and a half years. Five and a half fucking hard as hell years. And I've got to get back there and get Jim. We sit here jabbering while time ticks away. Hours are passing here, but days are passing there."

"Well, we're not going anywhere until I have a complete explanation. Is that clear?" Mike was emphatic. "Now. I will sit here and listen. If I have any questions, I'll ask. So let's have it."

"But I don't think you're going to believe me."

"I'll be the judge of that." He leaned back in his chair, lighting a cigarette. He pushed the pack and lighter toward Warren. He gave Warren a quick smile. "Just in case you change your mind."

It took Warren some time to cover the whole story from the beginning of their trip down the river to him coming back through the portal. Finally, Warren sat in silence, his story finished.

The table was littered with wrappers from several hamburgers and fries. Many styrofoam cups sat empty.

Mike took the last draw on his cigarette and put it out in the overflowing ashtray. He looked over to check the recorder. It was still running. "I like the touch about the mastodons."

"I told you, you weren't going to believe me." He shook his head.

Mike reached over and turned off the recorder. "I'll be back in a minute." He got up and left the room for a few minutes. Although the tale was preposterous, but with all his training in psychology and human nature, he knew the story he had just heard was the truth. When he returned, he quietly closed the door and looked at the mirror. "Seems they've gone home for the night. I think they just thought this was a tall tale and knew it would be on the tapes. Guess they didn't think they needed to stay any longer"

He looked right at Warren. "I didn't say I don't believe you. As a matter of fact, it's so incredible; it has to be true. No one has that good of an imagination." He lit another cigarette. "That's why I turned the damn recorder off. If they thought I believed some cockamamie story like that, they'd have me back in a car again." He paused for a moment then chuckled. "Have to admit. That's one hell of a way to stop smoking."

Warren joined the laughter. He became relaxed knowing Mike believed him.

Mike picked up his pad where he'd made some notes. "The way I figure it, there are twelve days there for every day here. And Jim's back there, blind." He shook his head. "You know the press is going to eat your lunch when all this comes out."

"But we'll be able to prove it. We just have to be at the door when all the conditions are right. Just think how scientists are going to love the opportunity. They'll be able to go back and study the past."

Mike pushed away his wrapper, with a few remaining fries on it. "Want anything else?"

Warren reached over to the wrapper. He moved the fries to a napkin in front of himself. "No. But I sure wish Jim could have some of this."

"Are you sure? It would be no problem to send out for more."

"No. I'm fine."

Mike stood up and headed for the door, after picking up the files and used tape cassettes. "Back in a minute."

On the way down the hall, he ran into another officer who asked how it was going with Warren. Mike put his right hand to his temple and rotated it counterclockwise. "The guy's ready for Milledgeville. Not violent, but he's really out of it. A few more questions and it will be off to psychiatric."

"We were going to notify his wife in Texas, but wanted your okay first."

"I'll let you know. I've still got a few more questions. Will probably finish up tomorrow. I don't want him going anywhere or having contact with anyone until I'm finished." He placed the files and cassettes on the desk. "Put this stuff in an envelope and keep it together. File it under 'Warren Glass'. Make another file. Label it James Stone. Put a note in it to see the Warren Glass file." He happened to look up and saw the clock on the wall. He checked his watch. "Holy shit! I can't believe it's already morning." He returned to the room where they were keeping Warren.

He looked at Warren. "Listen. It's already early morning and I've got to get some sleep. I'm going to take you down stairs and put you in a cell. You can get some rest, too. We'll pick this up again in a few hours." His eyes were intense while peering at Warren. "Trust me. Everything is going to be just fine."

He led Warren to another floor of the building where they went to the isolation block. "I'll be back in a few hours." He closed the door of the cell.

Mike was so tired when he walked into his apartment. He'd not slept in almost thirty-six hours. He'd been working on a murder case when Warren Glass walked onto the scene.

He took a shower, trying to unwind. He set the alarm on the clock before getting into bed. Six hours of rest would be significant.

Lying there, looking at the ceiling, he quickly pondered Warren's story. He knew he was sincere. His face told him that. Fifteen years on the force taught him to read people well. Warren's story, though strange as hell, was real. It was not bullshit. He'd find out more tomorrow.

He closed his eyes. Needed sleep overwhelmed his mind.

CHAPTER XL

A little after noon, Mike headed back to the station. As he pulled into the parking lot, a news broadcast was on the car radio. He half listened. When he started up the walk, he looked down at the bright yellow tulips, blooming in a clump by the walk. Stopping short, his mind clicked back to the report he'd just heard on the radio.

Quickly, he went to his office and turned on the radio. He found a station broadcasting the news and weather. It was the weather report he wanted to hear. Momentarily, it began.

"Tonight the temperature will drop into the low thirties in the city and high twenties in the suburbs. Should be the last of the cold weather until the fall. I think spring has finally arrived."

Mike flipped the radio off and headed for the isolation cellblock. On the way, he told one of the officers to call the weather bureau. "I want verification of the weather for the next twenty-four hours. And find out when they expect the last frost of the season."

Within a few minutes, he opened the door to the cell. Warren was awake, but lying on the bed. "Warren. We need to talk. Let's go back to my office."

Warren sat in one of the chairs next to Mike's desk. Mike sat down behind the desk and looked right across at Warren. "I want you to explain again what you were saying last night about the thing about the cold."

Warren carefully explained his premise of the cold and its importance to the passing between the two time periods. It was clear to him that without the cold being on both sides of the portal, at the same time, passage was not possible. It was the reason why they couldn't get through when they tried that first time. It wasn't cold enough in the other time period.

Mike thought about it for some time. He knew spring had arrived and the report indicated that most likely, the last frost of the season would occur that night. It would be the last possible time the portal would be open until autumn. According to all the calculations, this would mean six years or more would pass on the other side. He explained the situation to Warren.

"I have to get back!" Warren was adamant. "He'll die if I don't go back. I can't let him die! And I'm part of that time now, not this one."

Mike stared at him. "What about your wife and kids?"

Warren peered at Mike. "Don't you think I've thought of that? No one should be forced into such a decision." He pounded his fist on the desk.

"Do you have any guarantee you'll make it back to the same time period?"

"There are no guarantees, but I must try. I love that man and I can't let him die. He needs me."

"Look!" Mike paused for a moment. "I want to ask you about something else." He paused again, trying to think how he was going to phrase his next comment and question. "There's a thread here that leads me to something I want to know." He was silent for a few seconds. "Are you gay?"

Warren didn't speak for some time, staring into Mike's eyes. Finally, with a bit of temper, he spoke. "What's this all about? God!" Warren shook his head. "A man doesn't have to be homosexual to care for or love another man." He bent his head down, looking at the top of the desk. After a few moments of silence, he lifted his eyes, staring off into nowhere, then back at

Mike. "Weren't you listening? I wouldn't be here if it weren't for that man. I would have died from the snake bite if it weren't for Jim, and now he needs me." He didn't speak for some time. "He needs me more than Linda does. She's got the kids and her family. Jim's got nobody. Regardless how long it's been here, I'm virtually six years older than I was when I left, and I've changed. Significantly. My life is still back there. And until Jim and I are both back here, I can't think differently. I can't leave him there. I can't sentence him to certain death. Not like that. Blind. And I promised him. Even at the very beginning. I promised him I would NEVER leave him behind."

Mike interrupted with a shout. "But! As we sit here. Jim's been dead for some fifteen to twenty thousand years!"

Warren flared with anger. He rose in his chair, leaning forward over the desk toward Mike. "To you he may be dead! But he's not to me! I belong there, with him! I will not give him up."

An interrupting knock came to the door. An officer entered, handing a piece of paper to Mike. He looked at Mike, as if asking if everything was alright.

"Everything's fine. And thanks for getting me this." The officer left, closing the door behind him, while Mike perused the information. "Son-of-a-bitch!" He shook his head, crumpling the paper in his hand. He looked at Warren. "Sorry. I had to ask about all that. It was necessary. Made a bearing on my decision."

"Decision?" Warren was puzzled.

"Yeah. I had to find out where your head was, and how your real feelings were toward Stone." He looked down, then back at Warren. "You really care for the guy, don't you?"

Warren said nothing.

"And it's not because you feel sorry for him, being blind and all. I think you'd go back even if he could see. But there's something else."

Warren spoke softly. "Do you know what loneliness is? I mean real loneliness?" He was silent for a moment. "Do you know what it's like to be somewhere, and there's no one else? I'm talking NO ONE. Loneliness is probably the worse thing that could ever happen to someone. I like my solitude, as most people do, but I need people, too. Well, let me tell you. I've experienced loneliness back there, especially when I've had to go away on extended hunting trips. It was all I could do, wanting to get back to camp. Solitude's fine for me in small doses. But Jim's a different animal. He'd never admit it, but he needs someone around almost all the time. People are the basis for his life. Without someone, he'd cease to exist. His reason for being would be gone. I don't say this in a conceded way, but I know he'd have given up by now, if I hadn't been there. He's alive because he wants to prove to me he can cut it. When I'm there to pat him on the back, you should see what he can do. But it's not a one-way street. I also found myself going that extra mile, because of him. He's given me a reason to do things and be the best I can be. I need him as much as he needs me. If it weren't for him, I'd have gone out of my mind long ago. He's kept me human. He's given me friendship, companionship. And yes. Love." His eyes were riveted to Mike's showing his determination and sincerity. He wanted Mike to know there was no shame or guilt in his mind. "I could never let him die. All alone. Without love."

Not a sound was spoken for some time. Finally, Mike quietly commented. "I've got bad news." He tossed the wad of paper to the desk. "It's from the weather bureau. The report on the radio was right." He looked at Warren. "If you don't go back tonight, you most likely would not be able to try again until fall." He paused. "Damn! If only there'd been more time. You could have gone back, got Stone, and come back here again. But there's no time. You'll be stuck there for around six years before you can try to come back."

Warren smiled in the knowledge that Mike truly understood it all. "It's alright. We'll have something to look forward to. We'll be back, don't worry, now that I know what's going on. By the way?" He stopped for a second. "What was the decision you were making?"

Mike was uneasy by the question, speaking softly. "I wasn't going to let you go. I was going to lock you up, call your wife, and hold you until she got here." He looked at Warren. "But I can't keep you from trying to reach your buddy. I want you to know that I do know what you mean. When you work with someone, like we do here in the department, you have to trust your partner, a lot of times with your life. A man learns to love and care for his partner. The guys here spend more time with one another than they do with their own wives. And no one thinks a thing about it." He chuckled. "I have to hand it to you. You've got guts to take such a long shot chance on going back. I hope he realizes how lucky he is to have a friend like you. Not many have a friend who'd lay their life on the line for them." Mike shook his head. "But you know, what you want to do is scary as hell. If you don't get back to the right time, Stone's going to die, and you're going to be up shit's creek. I don't know if I'd want to take that chance, to leave all this behind, to go back to nothing. Glass, I wish you all the luck in the world." He reached across the desk. They shook hands.

"Thanks, Mike. I'll need it."

"Listen. There's a lot to do before you get on your way. I'll make everyone think I'm taking you down to Psycho. That'll give us a chance to pick up a bunch of stuff for your trip. We have to hurry though. There's not much time."

"Psycho?"

Mike chuckled. "Well. Where the hell would YOU be taking someone who was found dressed like you were and told a story like the one you told?"

Warren laughed and shrugged his shoulders. "You know, you're right. But what…"

"Don't worry about a thing. I've got it all worked out. No one will ever know I'm helping you."

"Will it be possible to have the things I brought with me? I'll need them back there real bad, especially the knife, machete and bow. And I need the rope so I can build a litter."

"No problem." Mike got up and went outside the door and went over to one of the officers. "Would you mind putting all the things that belong to Glass in the trunk of my car. The guys down at Psycho might want to see them. Put the things he was wearing in a duffel bag. I don't want that dirt and fur all over my trunk. I'll be down shortly."

Mike returned to the room and closed the door. "Well. The ball is rolling. Now, we have to make this look convincing. I'll be right back." He left the room for about fifteen minutes. When he returned, he had a set of handcuffs. "We're going to make this look real good."

Warren held his wrists together in front of him. "Front or back?"

"Back. Don't want anyone to get suspicious."

When they left the room, they walked into the open office area. All business as usual stopped and every eye was focused on the two men, as they walked through. Nothing was said, but Warren knew what everyone was thinking. They all knew who he was and how he'd come to be there. Their eyes said 'Milledgeville', location of the major mental institution in Georgia.

They stopped at one of the desks and Mike spoke to the officer sitting there. "Going to Psychiatric. After that I'm going home. Was up late last night. See you tomorrow."

"Want me to call them and let them know you're coming?" The

officer responded.

"No. I've already done that. Thanks." Mike took Warren's arm and they headed for the door leading to the parking lot. He knew this lie would buy them time. No one from psychiatric would be calling to find out where he was when they didn't show up in a few hours. Since Psycho was not even aware of the situation, it was unlikely they would ever call wondering where Warren was. Mike was sure days would pass before there would be any inquiry. Hopefully by then he would have some believable story to tell as to why he never showed up.

There were a couple of policemen standing just outside. When Mike and Warren passed, their conversation hushed and they watched Mike help Warren into the back seat of the patrol car.

They were out of the parking lot and almost a quarter mile down the street before they said anything. It began as a low laughter by both of them, slowly building to a roar.

"I thought we did real well." Mike laughed.

"I thought so, too."

"When we get to the sporting goods store, I'll take those cuffs off and you can sit up here. We'll need the back seat for the stuff we need to get. And I'll get you something to wear and get you out of those jail clothes you're wearing."

At the sporting goods store, Mike bought a small raft, many boxes of ammo for Warren's guns back at the camp, gun cleaning gear, six new hunting bows, as many bunches of hunting arrows as they could round up, a few hunting knives, a stone to sharpen the knives, and several other items they thought would be helpful in the future. The clerk was suspicious about the buy until Mike showed his credentials. Then they went to a local hardware store to get a few more essential items.

Mike looked at Warren as they saw everything piled in the back seat of the car. "I hope it all fits in the raft." He started to chuckle.

"I think it will. I just hope I can drag it all back to camp without any problems." Warren began to laugh, too.

They got in the car and headed north. Their destination would eventually be the same bridge on Johnson Ferry Road, over the Chattahoochee. They would make a few more stops on the way before nightfall. During this time, Warren asked Mike about his life and found out many things that made Mike tick. He laughed when Mike told him that on his vacations, he loved to totally get away to places where there were no phones, TV, and other such distracting things. He wanted to only be with nature and his fishing. He told Warren about the great vacation he had planned later on in the year, hopefully in mid-September. He was really looking forward to it. As for marriage, he had seen too many of them break up because of the job. He had finally reconciled himself to the fact that his wife was his job. And he really didn't mind it. He had basically been one of those solitary guys virtually all his life.

"Mike, when Jim and I get back, I promise I'll pay you back." Warren was sincere and optimistic.

Mike laughed. "Just get back. That'll be pay enough. And it'll get me out of the doghouse." He paused for a moment then laughed out loud. "And when you write the book and they make the movie, remember me then."

Warren laughed. "I'll bet that's right. But how ARE you going to explain how I got away? They're going to have your ass."

"I'll think of something, but I sure hope you both get back here in the fall. It'll make everything go a lot better in the long run."

Stops at the grocery and drug stores were made before Warren made one last request. When Mike walked from the music store, he had three sets of guitar strings. Handing them to Warren, he smiled. "These should last you for a while."

Mike was going to take Warren to a restaurant, but Warren couldn't let him do it. A fast food drive through would be good enough. "You've done enough for me already. How about we go when we get back? And Jim and I are going to buy you the biggest and best steak in Atlanta."

"It's a deal."

As the sun was setting, Mike pulled the car into an area north of Johnson Ferry Road and on the east bank of the river. This area was off the main road so no one would question the parked car being there. They unloaded the car, carrying everything down to the river. In no time, Warren had the raft inflated, using the small air pump Mike picked up at the hardware store. He arranged all the supplies carefully in the raft for the trip.

With everything ready, they got back in the car and waited. The temperature began to drop. It would be warmer in the car than waiting on the bank near the raft.

Mike pulled out his cigarettes. "You sure you don't want one for the road?" He held the pack toward Warren.

"Oh hell! Why not." Warren pulled one from the pack and put it in his mouth.

Mike opened the car window before he took out the lighter.

When Warren puffed, he began to choke and cough. He became light headed and dizzy. With a laugh, he looked at the cigarette and then at Mike. "Sorry, Mike. It's been too long." He crushed it out in the ashtray.

Mike laughed, too. "That's okay. Maybe I'll try to quit. How about by the time you get back?"

"I'll hold you to it." Warren snickered.

While waiting, they discussed more about the other world. Warren explained that he was sure the port only joined the two places and no others. It was logical. If it joined more than the two periods, it was likely he would never have come back to this place. The odds were on his side. Mike tended to agree with the explanation. It did seem logical.

In no time, night closed in and the temperature continued to fall. The sky began to glow with the reflected light of the city.

It was just after midnight when it happened. The air became misty and cool. A fog began to rise from the water. It was the event they waited for.

Their conversation became sporadic; both realizing their parting was at hand. Warren would soon be making his attempt to cross the barrier. They got out of the car.

Warren looked up in the sky. "This looks like it." He headed for the raft, Mike right behind. He turned and shook Mike's hand. "I don't know how to thank you, Mike. And I promise, I'll pay you back." His face expressed his sincerity. "See you in six months." He placed his left hand on top of their still clinched right hands.

Mike put his left hand on top of Warren's and he smiled. "See you in six years. Take care and God speed."

Warren looked into Mike's eyes. "God bless you for believing." He pulled Mike toward him in a hug, then pulled away. He smiled.

"Just take care of yourselves and get back here safe and sound."

Warren zipped up the new coat Mike had purchased. It was quite warm. Then he pushed at a few things in the raft to make sure they were secure then stepped in. He positioned himself in the rear and pushed off. "Thanks again for everything, Mike. Especially for believing. I won't forget it."

Mike began to laugh. "Don't forget to write!"

"Yeah. I'll send you an email."

They both were laughing as Warren slipped into the misty darkness. In a moment, he disappeared into the vaporous cloud.

"Bye Mike!" Warren's voice pierced from the fog.

Mike cupped his hands around his mouth. "Bye Warren! God be with you!"

Mike smoked another cigarette while he stood watching the fog rise and the mist thicken. He rubbed his hands. They were cold. He thought of the two heavy wool blankets and the two police overcoats he'd put in the duffel bag. "I know they'll get some good use."

He took the last draw and threw the butt out into the fog. He heard it sizzle when it hit the cold water of the river. For a few more minutes, he peered into the darkness. "God be with you. God be with you both." His voice was soft.

Mike turned and climbed the bank up to the car. "Now! What the fuck am I going to tell them about what happened to Glass?" He turned the ignition key and drove off, chuckling. "What ever it is, it will have to be good."

CHAPTER XLI

Tim and I give each other the elbow and look at one another, smiling. We recall the story from the information Maggie had gathered, the previous evening.

"We'll have to check with Mike Johnson. Maybe he's still got the tapes." I whisper to Tim.

"Good point. Another voice from the past." Tim comments. "You know? I'm really glad I came on this assignment. Who'd have ever guessed all this?"

Tim was right. All this is happening because of some strange fluke. My mind begins to recall the incident that started the whole thing.

Back in early summer, a bulldozer, clearing an area around the base of the north side of Stone Mountain, scraped against the rock face. This jarred a stone, so perfectly cut and placed into the face, no one had ever seen it before. Only the very top of the stone was visible above the dirt and rubble against the face of the mountain.

Once the park officials dug down and uncovered the stone and had it moved, they found the entrance to a tunnel. It was not a large tunnel, just eight feet wide and ten feet high. The walls and ceiling were smooth as glass. The gray granite of the mountain glistened like highly polished mirrors, reflecting the glow of their hand held lights. The level tunnel extended some two hundred feet to the base of a long stairway. At the top of the stair, the tunnel went on for sixty more feet, leading them to a room. The room was about twenty feet square, but the ceiling remained at ten feet. On the wall, opposite from where the tunnel entered, there was a recess of about eight feet deep. At the end was a carved stone. It was obvious the stone was a door to what ever lay beyond.

It was decorated with vines and flowers, carved in relief, around a short musical score. Set in the door was a great gold seal, with a single letter in the middle. The 'P' was in a simple Roman block style.

There was no indication who made the tunnel or its age. Because of the sophisticated method used in its making, no one knew how to assess it to a time period. And to confuse the issue, there was the rope.

Draped across the door, tied into gold rings set in the walls on either side, was a heavy rope of woven natural fiber. They questioned its authenticity to the find. But why would someone deliberately set out to make the whole thing so difficult? Why was the rope there? The only thing they could come up with was it was a signal to call in the best authorities in the field. The rope was there for a reason. Since it was natural fiber it could be used to date the find.

The rope was immediately removed and an analysis was made of its fibers. The test was conducted several times because they thought there was some error. But again and again, the tests indicated it was almost sixteen thousand years old. All were in agreement the rope was an actual part of the discovery. Because nothing else, so far, could be dated through scientific means, the rope had obviously been placed there for this purpose. But this flabbergasted everyone because the letter 'P', in Roman block style, did not exist sixteen thousand years ago, not to mention the manner in which the tunnel was constructed.

At this point, the state historians and archaeologists wanted representatives from National Geographic and the Smithsonian Institute on the scene. This required some time to get all the proper individuals together, but once there, all the proper steps were taken to preserve and record the event. A local independent TV station was asked if they would consider covering the event from start to finish, without commercial interruption. There would be only one station to have cameras directly on the scene. All other cameras would have to remain on the outside. The only others allowed would be those of the invited historic and archaeological groups.

Between the time the entrance was discovered and the gathering of all the officials, a string of lights was set up in the tunnel. Provisions were made for additional lighting because no one knew what to expect behind the door. They wanted to make sure there would be no problem to continue, regardless of what was beyond. Several generators were placed outside the tunnel entrance to supply the electricity for the lighting.

Many photos were made of the door. These pictures were put on promotional clips on TV for weeks to entice the public to watch the event when it finally would unfold. By the time it would all begin, the whole world seemed captured by the possibilities of what was beyond the door. It was being toted as the great mystery of the century.

The final consensus was, since there were no handles or other opening devices, it seemed that the musical passage on the door was most likely its key. Here again, there was no knowledge of music that old. The musical notations and the style of key signature did not come into use until relatively modern times, compared to sixteen thousand years ago.

The single note melody turned out to be rather simplistic, except for the last three note chord. Because of this element, it was decided to use an electronic keyboard to play the score. The instrument would be in a van outside, connected electronically to a portable speaker, located in the tunnel. A camera would focus on the music score so the notes could be seen clearly on a screen in the van.

Finally, the day arrived and all was ready to commence the event. The eyes of the world were looking to Atlanta, Georgia and the tunnel in the side of Stone Mountain. We were all gathered at the door waiting for the moment. Everyone was doing so many tasks, introductions were impossible except for superficial social gestures and greetings. It was early September and mid-morning when the opening of the portal was planned.

A strange inner feeling had been gnawing at my psyche since I set foot in the tunnel. It persisted as we waited in anticipation of the opening of the portal. My mind imagined the booby traps like those one sees in movies about archaeological discoveries. "Sure hope that door opening doesn't set off some trigger to have the ceiling come down on us all!" I speak without thinking and cringe, looking up around the ceiling. "Maybe some poisonous arrows out of the walls or some bottomless pit!"

My words evoke concern from others in the group. They are not pleased that I spoke aloud what was in their heads. One guy in particular started to chuckle and hid his amusement with his right hand, covering his mouth.

The pianist in the van looked at the notes on his screen and played the keyboard. As the last chord faded from the speaker, not a thing happened. He played the notes again. Still, nothing happened. What was wrong? The pianist looked closer at the door, displayed on his screen, to make sure he was playing it properly. Suddenly, his voice shouted from the speaker. "Of course! I didn't see it before. There's two numeric markings, hidden in the upper left section of the door, in the vines and leaves. It's a metronome marking for tempo and the other is for the 'A' note. It indicates 'A' four forty. And for those of you who are not familiar, it is the basic standard for the tone of the 'A' note." After a minor pause, we heard the notes played again, only slower than before.

With the sound of the last chord, the stone monolith moved slowly, without the slightest whisper, into a pocket in the left wall. Much to my contentment and pleasure, none of my mental horrors came to fruition.

Everyone clapped their approval of the pianist's expertise and astuteness for accomplishing the desired effect.

With the door open, it was immediately obvious the tunnel continued further into the mountain. We were surprised at the freshness of the air. This would be the case for the rest of the discovery.

The tunnel went about two hundred feet into the mountain and up two flights of stairs, rising in a counterclockwise direction. A pair of electricians hurriedly strung lights along the floor of the corridor. At the top of the stairs, the tunnel extended another forty feet, then opened into another room, some twenty feet square. Across the room was another recess and another door, heavily carved and set with another gold seal. The seal was designed around the letter 'E', in the same style as the previous letter. This had everyone whispering questions and making theories.

There was another musical composition carved in the stone surface. It was somewhat more difficult than the first. The pianist had to search a little harder for the tempo marking, too. None of us was sure what was going on, but we knew there was some reason for the increased difficulty in getting through the door.

After a few minutes, the pianist played the score and the door began to move. Everyone, again, expressed appreciation. The electricians carried many looped strands of lights on their shoulders to keep the tunnel illuminated.

This door opened into another tunnel. We went one hundred and fifty feet and came into another room. There, again, in a recess was another portal. A large 'A' adorned the great seal. We also noticed the decorations were more elaborate and intricate.

The musical composition was not on this door but on the wall adjacent to the door and was the most difficult yet. It took the pianist a few minutes to decipher. He ran through a few of the passages on the keys to make sure of the proper fingering.

Shortly, he started, but struck a wrong note in a chord, but continued to play to the end. When he finished, the door remained in place. He knew then it was not only important to play the score at the right tempo, but every note had to be correct, too. He played it again, more carefully.

Within moments of the last chord, the door slid away into the left wall. Approving applause and whistles complimented his efforts.

We entered another hall, still with the same dimensions as the previous. The tunnel remained level for seventy-five feet then there was a spiral stair leading to another level section. This went one hundred feet into another room of previous dimensions. Another door in a recess was across on the opposite wall. A 'C' appeared on the great gold seal.

I remember looking at one of the members of the group and whispering. "There's going to be one more door after this." It was the same guy who concealed his snickering earlier.

His expression at the time was one of question, but after a few seconds, he'd put it all together. "Damn! You're right! I get it!" His voice had been more than a whisper and everyone had looked at him wondering what was going on with him. We looked at each other and smiled. We knew we had both figured it out. I would find out later, this man was Tim. But at this moment, I wondered who this guy was. I knew he was important since he was here and seemed to have some control over some of what was going on. I noticed he had a great smile and ugly did not know his name.

It took a little while for the lights to get into place. One electrician ran out to the main truck to obtain several more strands of lights. When asked, he said they had enough lights to run from Atlanta to Macon and back if needed. They wanted to be prepared for anything.

The light shining on the wall beside the door made it clear that to play what was carved on this stone required some real musical prowess. We all groaned when we saw the vast number of notes, chords and other musical notations. Finding the metronome marking was a feat unto itself. The numbers were noted by the ends of curling tendrils, on one of the vines.

The pianist had to work very hard on several passages to get the fingering and notations correct. Surprisingly, within a short while, he ran through the piece, replaying difficult sections, to get them correct and make sure there would be no problem in the final playing.

You could have heard a pin drop when we realized he was to start. The melodic notes and chords of the composition echoed down through the hall. The music was warm, almost tugging at the heart. It truly was an incredible composition.

As the top note of the last rolled chord faded, a smile came to everyone's face. We not only applauded the efforts of the pianist, but the talents of the unknown composer. We were the first to hear the beauty of his work. The giant stone slab quietly and slowly slid away into the right wall.

When this door opened, it revealed a large chamber, thirty feet wide and eighty feet long. The ceiling vaulted to twenty feet. The entire walls and ceiling were covered with a smooth, plaster-like surface. The walls were painted to look like you were in an elegant garden. The curved ceiling was painted to depict a mid-summer's sky, complete with many puffy clouds. The intricate marquetry and parquetry patterns in the floor were of many colored marbles and stone.

No one could believe his or her eyes. Here was a mural, presumably several thousand years old, containing all the principles of atmospheric perspective and depth perception. The colors were so crisp and brilliant, it seemed the artists had finished just prior to us walking into the space.

The realism was astonishing. An explanation could not be given. It challenged the entire history of art. If all this turned out to be authentic, it would change every art book and art history class, forever. It was always considered that extreme realism and especially perspective did not occur in painting until the Renaissance. The art world was about to be set on its ear.

At the end of this room was another door, unlike all the others and not in a recess. This eight foot wide and ten foot high portal had a set of double doors. The two, four foot panels of solid gold, were elaborately designed with sculpted gold vines, flowers and architectural ornaments. Around the doorway was a magnificent architectural structure of colored marbles. It was classic in style, with a full pediment architrave. Golden della robbia decorated the pilasters, flanking the portal. In the middle, half on one door and half on the other, was another seal. The letter 'E' was in the center, designed with deep green, faceted stones. Other faceted, colored stones accented the ornamentation.

The guy and I had looked at one another with a big smile and we both did a thumbs up. "This is it." He whispered softly. "This is the last door." We had both put it together. "What ever is the secret of this discovery, it is behind this door."

Just like the previous doors, there was another musical composition. But this time, it was painted not carved on the wall adjacent to the doorway. The score was extremely long, extremely involved and complicated and covered a large portion of the wall. When the pianist looked at the score, he hung his head. An audible groan could be heard over the speaker. This was the most difficult of all. His musical talents would come into play since he could find no metronome marking. He would have to choose one appropriate for the composition. His voice could be heard again over the speaker. "It's going to take me a while to practice this one and get it right. Can we call it until tomorrow?"

Everyone took a consensus that since it was now early evening, it would be beneficial to begin again in the morning. This would give the park time to get better lighting in place and it would give the pianist time to work on the very difficult musical composition.

We all agreed this had to be the last door. No one could think of anything that could surpass it in decoration and extravagance. The seal also contained the last letter of 'the word'. This is what I realized earlier. "And in English. Interesting." I whisper to myself.

There was light and hushed conversation as everyone began heading out of the tunnels. It was agreed that this find was beyond belief and was probably the most spectacular of the century. We were all anxious to know what lay beyond the golden doors. I could hear theories starting to develop as to what might be there. I had never witnessed such enthusiasm and expectation. It would be interesting to see what theories would be correct, if any, the next day.

I made my way out of the tunnels and drove home, not taking time to formally meet any of the members of the group. I was exhausted and needed some rest. I knew it was going to be difficult to turn off my head with all I had seen, but since it was decided to re-group around nine in the morning, I had to try to sleep.

Everyone had gathered at nine in the morning. Making sure all were accounted for, we slowly and carefully entered the tunnel, finally reaching the large painted room. Waiting for the pianist to perform, many began to examine the murals.

In the van, the pianist was diligently working through the music on the keyboard. He was amazed at the melody line and chording. He had commented that the music seemed to have similarities to the music composed by Debussy and Rachmaninoff, but totally original in its innovations. The tempo did not seem to be a challenge. It was the score that was incredibly difficult. Playing it required a true and accomplished musician. Some of the chords were huge and would require a broad reach to play them.

Eventually we all heard a voice on the speaker. "Okay, ladies and gentlemen. Here goes. Keep your fingers crossed. I have to admit. I'm sure glad I have pretty big hands. Some of these chords have a rather broad span." At that, and after a momentary pause, the pianist began. With every note and chord in place, the melody flooded the vaulted room. All were moved by its complexity and beauty. A feeling of outpouring love came from the music, affecting everyone's attitude. An expression of contentment and peace filled every face. All hearts were touched. It was a most spectacular composition. The melody line would be one that would be hummed and whistled often, it was so memorable. The question in everyone's head was who was the composer?

The final notes played and a quiet came upon the entire scene. It was like a magic spell had been placed on everyone there. No one moved, so as not to disturb the feeling. It was the movement of the doors swinging into the tunnel beyond and resting in pockets in the walls on either side. This brought us back to the task at hand.

A great adulation rose from the group in appreciation of a job well done. Joy filled the air.

The open doors revealed a short tunnel about ten feet long and a vast darkness beyond. Every eye strained to focus on anything within. I found it difficult to restrain myself. My first impulse was to push everyone out of the way and rush in to be the first to see. But suddenly a quiet calm came over me, just as it did everyone there. We all managed to contain our excitement, and calmly passed through the portal and through the tunnel.

The illumination from the strings of lights reflected from the surfaces within, filling our eyes with wonder and disbelief. I could not help myself. My mouth opened and I unconsciously spoke out loud. "Holy shit!" As the words reverberated through the space, I became aware of my crassness, but quickly became unconcerned. I had only expressed the sentiments of everyone there. Smiles and a low chuckle from the entire group confirmed the fact, as they looked in my direction. Soon, whispers of amazement were heard from the members of the party.

"I don't believe it! Are the cameras getting all this? Is there enough light for the cameras?" It was spoken by the same guy from the previous day.

"This is incredible!" Another commented.

"It's unreal!"

"My God! How?"

"How magnificent!"

What I wanted to know was the 'who, what, when, why and how' of it all. I knew there had to be an answer, and I was bound and determined to find it out. I pulled out my camcorder and started doing my own video, speaking softly.

"We have just passed through a door in the…" I stopped for a moment to find out direction from one of the archaeologists. This accomplished, I started again. "In the center of the east wall. We are in a vast chamber." I would find out later it was one hundred and thirty feet long and one hundred feet wide. The incredible, coffered ceiling was sixty feet from the highly polished floor.

"I can see by the beams of light there are columns forming a colonnade on either side, running east and west. They are fluted white marble, eight feet in diameter at the bottom, with deep green marble bases and gold Corinthian styled caps." The centers of the eastern most set were located twenty feet from the walls. All columns were thirty feet on center. The fourth set was also twenty feet from the walls. "There are half column pilasters on all the walls and of the same construction materials, mocking the eight columns out in the room. Half column pilasters are situated in the corners, one on each wall and butting one another in the corners."

"The columns and pilasters support an elaborate, looks like ten foot frieze that divides the ceiling into fifteen rectangular coffer sections. It's of the high Corinthian style and made of gold and multicolored marbles. The five foot wide lower section is adorned with marble della robbia motifs, trailing from the centers toward the corners. The multileveled upper section contains an extensive display of dental key and acanthus leaf designs."

"All the walls are of highly polished gold and set with raised panels between the pilasters and portals. Yes. There is a door in the middle of the north and south walls. It should be interesting to see what is behind them. The panels are decorated with gold, colored marbles and multicolored, faceted stones depicting ornate florals. The only difference is the large panel on the west wall. Its surface is a smooth, glassy white material. The framing around the panels is sculpted in the ornate Louis Fifteenth French style."

"A four foot wide, classically sculpted base molding of deep green marble goes around the entire room. It reflects the lines of the four foot high column and pilaster bases."

"The portals are ornamented with classical architectural treatments. Multicolored marbles and gold decorate them. Trailing della robbia designs, done in marbles to resemble the actual fruit and flowers, compliment the pilasters. Above the architectural work of each door are swags and garlands of fruit and flowers, made of colored marbles and gold."

"Great cartouches, with ten foot tall, slightly bulging oval centers are in the middle of the designs over the doors. They are of deep green marble. Intricate monograms of gold enhance the center sections of each cartouche. I cannot decipher the letters."

"The floor contains wide bands of deep green marble, connecting the bases of the columns and pilasters, dividing the floor into fifteen sections, reflecting the coffered frieze in the ceiling. The rectangular sections between the bands are decorated with elaborate marquetry patterns in light colored marbles. In the very center of the room is a slab set in the floor, and flush with it, of black onyx-like material, eight feet by six feet."

"The flat sections of the ceiling look like the sky on a bright summer's day. The surface texture is not a painting. It's smooth as glass similar to the panel on the west wall."

"In the very center section of the ceiling is an enormous della robbia arabesque. From its center, on an eight foot long golden colored chain, hangs a most magnificent crystal chandelier." We found out later it was just over thirty feet from top to bottom and twenty feet in diameter at its widest part. The prisms were of actual rock quartz crystal, the way the original chandeliers were done, and so derived the name. "It reminds me of the one that hangs in the 'Peace Room' at the south end of the 'Hall of Mirrors' at Versailles. The framework of the fixture appears to be of gold, set with faceted clear stones. The prisms, and there must be several thousand, are cut in the elaborate French manner."

"There are four tiers of candles." These were three inches in diameter and twenty-four inches tall, ecru in color. Each was topped with a six inch long light bulb, shaped like a flame. "Must be over a hundred of them."

"A cut crystal ball hangs from the bottom and is about sixteen feet off the floor." This, too, was made of rock quartz and was two feet in diameter. "I have only one question. How much does the damn thing weigh? Sure would be nice to see it lit. It might be noted that the chandelier hangs directly over the center of the onyx-like rectangle in the floor."

"A three tiered platform is located in the center and three feet from the west wall. Each rise is about six inches and is of a different colored marble. The bottom tier is ten feet in diameter and deep green. The second is eight feet in diameter and peach in color. The top tier is six feet in diameter and white."

We were in the room only twenty minutes when we heard a voice fill the space and the room began to illuminate. This really rattled everyone, wondering where the voice was coming from and what was happening. The lighted ceiling sections glowed, looking like huge picture panels of the sky, beaming with the light of day and slowly moving clouds. The chandelier also began to light. The two foot candle shafts radiated a soft inner light and the crystal tops began to gleam. It was truly a sight to behold. I felt like I was standing in the courtyard of some huge elegant villa. The colors of the marbles, faceted stones and gold became rich and clear. Everything was visible, as if by the subtle light of day. It was difficult to think we were deep inside the granite monolith of Stone Mountain.

Yes. This was just the beginning of the whole ordeal. It was the beginning of the story for us.

Suddenly, my reminiscent mind, recalling previous events, is jarred, as Tim elbows me.

"Hey. Don't fall asleep on us." He whispers with a chuckle.

The old man stands. "Now. How many of you already know that part of the story? Was it still on file with the police department or was it too long ago?" His eyes glint as he looks out, scanning the group. "Now come on. Someone out there must have been ingenious enough to look into the subject." He looks out seemingly to wait for a response.

Tim and I raise our hands, forgetting the object commanding our attention is only a holograph. This causes some commotion in the room. Low murmurs and whispers rise and everyone looks in our direction.

Why had we raised our hands? The thought pops into my mind and I quickly pull my hand down. Tim does the same. I look at him. "Sorry. I did it automatically."

"So did I." Tim chuckles.

"Oh well." The old man moves to the edge of the top tier. "I'm going to zip for a moment. Nature calls. I'll be back in thirty minutes." He steps forward and disappears.

Everyone stands and stretches. Low conversations begin. Several approach Tim and me. They are looking to find out more about what we know.

After some short discussion, Tim nudges me. "I've got to take a leak. Be back in a minute."

"Wait up! I have to do the same."

In no time at all we are down the halls and stairways and out the entrance. Walking to the portable toilets, we both light a cigarette.

"I thought I was going to have a nicotine fit every time he mentioned a cigarette." I snicker.

"So did I." Tim joins the laugh.

I step inside and unzip my pants. I always hated these damn things and the way they smell. But I guess it's better than exposing myself in front of everybody so I could piss on a tree.

There is no time to call Maggie to have her check on Mike Johnson. We will just have to wait on that.

Tim and I return as quickly as possible and fix ourselves a snack from the tables. I didn't realize how hungry I really was.

Shortly, everyone is checking their watches and preparing to take their seats. The old man reappears and sits in his chair. He shifts the pillows and his garments. Everyone is silent.

"Did you all have a little something to eat?" He snickers. "I'm sure you had a cigarette." He breaks into full laughter. In a moment, he settles down. "Now. Moving right along. Yes. Warren pushed off into the mist. Before long, he was out in the river, moving south. The fog thickened and the mist filled with crystals of ice. He shivered as the air chilled his body. He was so glad of the coat Mike had bought him."

CHAPTER XLII

Warren reached for the duffel bag. He knew his skin vest and old coat was there. He smiled when he opened the bag and saw the two blankets and the dark blue, wool overcoats. "As God is my witness, somehow I'll pay him back." He wrapped one of the blankets around himself.

Ever since his original talk with Mike, he had calculated that for each day passing here, there were around twelve to thirteen days passing in the other time. The two days he had been here, plus the few days from camp to the river, was about a month in the other time. He knew it was going to take at least eight to ten days to get back to camp, with dragging the new supplies. This was over a month. Would Jim be alright? Would he make it back to that time again? "God only knows." He spoke softly.

He hadn't been drifting very long, when the thick fog became even colder. He could feel small particles of ice in the air. He realized it was the key. "Please let it be cold there, too." He spoke a quiet prayer. After a while, the thick dense fog disappeared behind him into the darkness. It was cold and so dark, he could hardly see. His mind flashed. Had he made it or was he stranded somewhere else? What if he hadn't left the original time?

There was no way he would know until he deciphered his location, when there was daylight and he could see. He looked up. The sky was clear, spotted with millions of stars. The bare tree limbs stretched into the blue-blackness. There was no sign of the city light he had seen earlier in the evening. It was time to go ashore.

Suddenly there was a shooting star. "I wish I make it back to

Jim." He shook his head at his superstitious action and laughed.

When the raft landed, Warren jumped out. Although anxious to start eastward, it was not possible until morning. He pulled the raft onto the bank then stepped back in. This would be his bed for the night. He wrapped himself with the blankets and tried to sleep.

When dawn arrived, the sky was filled with heavy gray clouds. He hadn't slept a wink. But this was of no concern. He got up as soon as he could see and went to cut some small trees to make a litter to carry the supplies. This project took nearly three hours.

The litter packed, covered with the deflated raft and secured with the new rope, it was almost time to go. He rummaged through the duffel bags and found his antler hat. He tied it tight on his head. It was lucky. He got in the litter and headed east. His mind kept asking the same question, but the answer would not be known until he could see something he recognized.

The gray clouds remained low in the sky and the air was still, but crisp. The breath from his mouth formed white billows when he exhaled.

An hour and a half later, he came to an area of the forest where the trees were marred and heat damaged. What he saw next made his heart leap. Maybe he had made it back to the right place in time.

In front of him was a gigantic desolate burned area. Black logs and tree stumps, sticking as high as ten feet in the air, stretched to the top of the up coming ridgeline. Warren continued onward, as quickly as possible.

By early afternoon, he crested the highest ridge. Looking to the east, an immense area laid waste for miles down in front of him. The entire area was in shades of black and gray. Mounds of ash and char existed where huge trees once stood. Blackened outcroppings of rock made it look like the surface of the moon. Not a living thing was in sight.

The extent of the burnout went from the northeast, far south and to the east. The fire had been devastating, but he could see the undamaged forest, miles to the east. Beyond that was the monolith of Stone Mountain. There was no indication why or how the fire stopped.

His heart pounded. Something deep in his guts told him he was back. "Please God. Let Jim be okay." He looked up, speaking softly. He cupped his hands around his mouth and yelled as loud as he could in the direction of the mountain. "JIM! I'M HOME!" He knew his voice could not go that far, but it made him feel good.

Warren started down the ridge, choosing the least difficult path. With nothing in his line of sight, this was simple.

The gray ash made him think about the future. With no vegetation and protection of the forest, animals would be scarce. He would have to hunt to the north, east and south. Floods would be a certainty when there came a heavy rain. Without vegetation to hold the soil, run off would be significant. There were going to be some really hard times ahead.

*   *   *   *   *

It took eight more days to reach the eastern edge of the burnout. He was glad Mike took him to the grocery store since there was nothing to catch or eat in the devastation zone. But he was very frugal with what he ate. He wanted the food for both Jim and himself. Pictures of the aftermath of the Mount Saint Helen's explosion constantly popped into his mind, as he walked through the area. The only color during the daylight was the blue sky above, when it would peek through the grayness. It would take years for the area to grow back again. He wondered if he would live long enough to see it. But hopefully he and Jim would be back in the future time again by then.

Two days later, he was near the camp. It was late afternoon and a light snow was coming down. He strained to hurry. His heart beat with expectation. He came to a dry creek. Crossing to the southern bank, he was sure it was the one that fed the pond around the rock. He followed it to the east.

An hour later, he could see the rock through the naked trees and falling snow. Everything had a light coat of white, making him remember the first snow of their first winter. The image was virtually the same as it was then. The only exception, Jim was not standing on the rock, outside the hut, as he was years before. Warren choked in his thankfulness at his return. A tear trickled from his eyes. He laughed through the cries, knowing his efforts had not been in vain.

Pulling the litter up to the southern end of the bridge, he became aware of something, which caused great concern. No smoke rose from the chimney of the hut. Nor was there smoke from the oven. This didn't make sense. Why would the fires be out? Jim hated the cold. The gate that he had shut to protect the entrance to the rock was open. His heart pounded. His previous joy had suddenly turned to fear. He began to think the worse. His blood ran cold and a shiver shot through his body. His mind pictured Jim lying dead. "Oh God. Don't do this to me. Please God. Please."

He climbed out of the litter and ran onto the bridge. Stopping half way, he looked down into the almost dry pond and around the rock base. Jim was not there. He hurried to the hut. The interior was cold and dark. Not even a smolder existed in the fireplace. When his eyes adjusted to the light, it was evident Jim was not there.

He knelt down to check the ashes. There was no heat. Even the stones were cold. No fire had burned there for some time.

Where could he be? A sinking feeling filled his stomach. Why wasn't he in the hut? What happened? What went wrong? His eyes closed and he shook his head. His fists clinched. "I told him not to leave the hut." He whispered.

There was no sign of violence, negating an animal attack. But maybe he wandered off. Why would he have done that? His mind imagined Jim's body lying out in the woods. His heart pounded faster.

Warren exited the hut, running out onto the rock. He looked in all directions. Where would he start his search? How far could a blind person go? Starting across the bridge, he stopped, cupped his hands around his mouth and took a deep breath. "JIIIMMMM!" He waited a moment to see if there was a response. Nothing. He turned, repeating his call. "JIIIMMMM!"

Almost ethereal, soft, faint and muffled, there came the sound. "Warren, you're home!"

Warren, slightly stunned, smiled, tears welling in his eyes. His whole body shook with glee, as he cried out loud through his tears. He ran toward the cold cellar.

Just as he arrived, the door pushed open and Jim climbed out. "Warren! You're back!" Jim's voice was glad, but lacked the urgency that ran through Warren. He turned in the direction of the hut. A big grin filled his face.

Warren ran up and clinched his arms around Jim, squeezing him tight and lifting him off the ground. He gave Jim a glad kiss on the mouth, then started laughing and crying at the same time. "You're alright! You crazy thing! You're alright! I thought something happened. God, you're alright." He hugged Jim tighter and kissed him again.

"Wow! You're going to have to go away more often." Jim joked with laughter. "You go away for a couple of days and you find you just can't live without me." He laughed, patting Warren on the back. He really was glad he'd returned from the hunting trip.

"Jim! Jim! You're not going to believe it. There's so much to tell you. Come on. Let's go get the fire started again and get you warm." He picked Jim up in his arms, carrying him to the hut.

Jim had no idea what was going on. He could only attribute it to a good hunt. "Well, was your hunt that successful? You must have bagged a major big game."

"More than you could believe. Sit down here and I'll start the fire. But first, let me get the stuff in here. I'll be right back." He exited the hut, running to the litter, which he pulled to the door of the hut, negotiating the bridge very carefully so as not to have everything go over the edge. Warren had everything in the hut in no time. He heaped it all in the corner. He would sort it later for storage. He did pull out the coat that Mike had bought for Jim and set it down for use later. He grabbed an orange. "Let me give you one of the things I caught." He handed it to Jim.

Jim felt its shape and a puzzled expression came to his face. He put it to his nose and sniffed. "An orange! This smells like an orange!" He frantically started peeling it. Every moment, he'd smell it to reassure his senses. "How can this be? I know you didn't go to Florida!"

Warren knelt down in front of Jim, putting his hands on Jim's shoulders, giving him a shake. "Better. Better than going to

Florida. We can get back! I was there! I went back!"

"You mean back home? For real?"

"Yeah. We can do it."

"But how? When can we leave? Is there time to get everything ready? Tell me about it while we get everything ready to go."

Warren looked down, hating to disappoint Jim with what he had to say. "Well. We have to wait a while." His voice was soft.

Jim could not see Warren's expression. "That's alright. Just as long as there's enough time to pack."

"Jim. We can't go back right now. We have to wait…about six years." He saw a puzzled expression come to Jim's face.

There was a long silence before Jim spoke. "But I don't understand. Why so long?"

"I'll explain it in a minute, but first we need to get this place warm."

Jim chuckled and yelled out. "Who cares! So it takes six years! Who cares! We'll stick it out until then. Now, we've really got something to look forward to."

Warren stopped putting the logs in the fireplace and gave Jim a hug. "And we'll make it, too." He placed some twigs under the logs and set them aflame using the new cigarette lighter Mike gave him. "What happened to the fire? Why did it go out?"

"Stupid me let the damn thing go out a few days ago, at least I think it was a few days ago. But I think there's still hot coals in the oven outside. Warren. I've lost count of the days. It's screwed up the notching on my sticks. How many has it been? Has it been two or three weeks?"

"Jim! It's been over a month. From what I can calculate with the time that has past back there, yeah, it's been over a month."

"You have to be kidding. That long? I guess the days just melted together. Well. Maybe there aren't any hot coals in the oven. Oh well." He paused for a moment to continue the peeling of his orange. "Okay. I'm ready. I want to hear all about it." He paused for a minute. "But if you got back, why didn't you stay? I don't get it. What made you so sure you'd get back here? What if you'd got lost somewhere else in time? That was real stupid. DUMB! DUMB! And to top it all, you have to wait another six years to get back!" He shook his head. "That was REAL DUMB!"

"WELL! You stupid shit! I couldn't leave you here, could I? You'd have frozen to death. SEE!" He pointed to the fireplace. "You couldn't even keep the damn fire going." He began to laugh to ease his angry frustration.

"But Linda. You could have stayed with her and the kids."

"Linda wasn't there. She'd gone back to Texas already. I never saw her. I was only there a little over twenty four hours." He poked at the fire. "It's been only five and a half months there." He grabbed the coat. "Here." He threw it into Jim's lap. "Mike bought this for you. Wait until you see what else I brought back."

"Feels like a coat. Cool! A new coat. Five and a half months? Only five and a half months?"

"Yep. By the way, the blankets and coats, and there are two heavy wool ones in the duffel bag, as well as everything else, are compliments of a Mr. Mike Johnson. Or should I say, Detective Mike Johnson."

"Mike Johnson?"

"Yeah. We owe him, big time. But let me start at the beginning so it'll all make sense." He stopped for a second and took the orange from Jim. "Here! Let me peel it for you. And enjoy it. There are no more. I only had room for so much, but wanted something special to give to you when I got back here." He began his story. "It started because of the fire."

Jim interrupted. "I was pretty sure there was a fire. Not long after you left. I could smell the burning. Was it a bad fire?"

"Think Mount Saint Helen, but I'll get to that in a minute."

"That bad? Not good. We're going to have the floods of Ranchipur." Jim interjected again.

"If we're lucky." He was sarcastic.

Warren organized the bedding with the new blankets and helped Jim into the new coat. It was large for him, but it didn't matter. The fire began to warm the hut. "Here. Get in the blankets until I can get some water heated and some food started. We're going to take a bath before we eat." He picked out one of the six bars of soap from the supplies and gave it to Jim. "And we have new toothbrushes and several tubes of toothpaste."

"God. I'd forgot what soap smelled like. I can hardly wait. And I know I could really use a bath. And our teeth are saved. That rock powder we were using was going to destroy our teeth in time."

"I was going to bring some toilet paper, but it took up too much space. Sorry about that."

Warren started the telling of the entire ordeal while he got the food started. When the water heated, he got Jim undressed and helped him with his bath. That done, he washed himself.

Jim would periodically interrupt to ask a question. He wanted to make sure he understood it all.

The conversation continued through the meal. Jim was ecstatic with the salt and pepper. Warren apologized that it would soon be gone, but Jim was grateful for having it at all.

"I also brought back some seeds. I thought we'd try to grow them this spring."

"What kind?"

"You name it. I even brought a few packs of flower seeds. Thought you might like that."

Jim smiled. "But where did you get them? Seeds aren't on sale until spring."

"But remember? It IS spring there."

"Oh, that's right. Five and a half months. October, November, 'na na na na'…it's the end of March."

"I thought it was better to bring the seeds because the payoff might be better in the long run."

Jim chuckled. "We're going to have an incredible garden next year. I can hardly wait. And flowers, too. Thanks, Warren."

"That's okay. And anyway, they didn't take up that much space."

The snow was falling harder outside the hut, but they were warm inside.

Jim laughed when Warren told about Mike and the cigarette. That was one habit he was glad they didn't have anymore.

Finally, Warren completed the story. "And what, may I ask were you doing in the cold cellar? It scared the shit out of me when I couldn't find you."

"Since I was so dumb as to let the fire go out, and I can't believe I did that, I went over there to get something to munch on. I really wasn't concerned. You were going to be home, sooner or later, and you'd get it started again."

There was a silence for a few seconds before Warren spoke. "What would you have done if I hadn't come back?" His voice was serious. "What if I'd not been able to make it back?"

"Well." There was a long pause in Jim's comment. "Well. I'd have…I'd have done…something." He knew full well there was nothing he could have done. When the food ran out he would have to go out and try to find something. With winter coming, the prospects would be slim to none. The chances of being discovered by some animal were significantly greater. His demise would have been a matter of time.

Then he thought of the decision Warren had to make. It would have been so easy for him to have stayed. He could have rationalized it through, if he wanted to. After all, from where Warren was, he had long since been dead. And there was no guarantee, even if he'd tried; he was going to get back to the right time period. "Warren? If you had ended up in some other time, you would have been lost, too."

"The chances weren't that bad. I was telling Mike, I figure the portal joins only these two time periods. That's why I got back to the time from where we left. There was no logical reason for me to end up anywhere else. Now, when we get back, it's going to be late fall there. One whole year will have gone by, but we'll be twelve years older. Think of the consequences of the whole thing."

"I know. Scientists can come here and study the past. I'm sure they'll get a kick out of what's on the mountain. Maybe people could move here." Jim quickly stood up, extending his arms out and slowly turned. "I claim all the land for a thousand miles in all directions, in the name of Warren Glass and James Stone." He began to laugh out loud. "We're going to be rich! I knew something good was going to come of all this! We're the first landowners."

All Warren could do was join the laughter.

"There's something else I wanted to fix." He opened the bag and the aroma filled the air.

"Coffee!" Jim yelled. "I smell coffee!"

"Hold your horses. It'll be ready in a little while."

"It's like Christmas." Jim's jubilance and hope permeated the atmosphere. He was ecstatic about the future. There was much to look forward to.

The day was coming to an end. They were both excited, but needed sleep.

Jim lay on the bedding, on his side, between the fire and Warren's body. It felt good to have him there again. He felt safe and knew everything was going to be alright. It had been silent for some time when he spoke. "Warren? I don't know how many days. For my notches."

"Don't worry. We'll figure it out." Warren pulled Jim close and checked to make sure they were both under the covers. Shortly, Jim was asleep.

Warren thought about it all. He was glad to be back and knowing Jim was safe. He was determined they would be just fine for the next six years. He smiled in the contemplation of their future projects. He gently held Jim closer and he quietly whispered. "Thank you, God, for letting me get back and finding him okay." He was quiet for a few minutes. "I love you, Jim."

A breeze was blowing outside. The snowfall increased and the flakes began to pile and drift. It was the first major snowfall of the season. Winter was early this year. By morning, it would be almost a foot deep.

CHAPTER XLIII

The snow stopped before sunrise and the day was clear and bright. Nice weather continued for the next three days allowing Warren to hunt. He did a lot of thinking during his outings. He was sure the next year would be a lot better. Maybe the pond would fill up again from the melting snow. Maybe the mastodons would return. He hoped they would, for Jim's sake. He knew Jim would like it, even if he couldn't see them. And maybe Jim would somehow get his sight back.

Over the next two weeks, there was more snow. Their discussions centered on getting back. The probability brought new developments to their thinking. Jim wanted to start a campaign to 'Save the Mastodons'. He wanted the herd rounded up and brought back to the Atlanta Zoo. What an attraction it would be. It would be the only zoo in the world with live mastodons. But then he hated to take them out, losing their freedom. Maybe it would be better to have expeditions come here to see them in their natural habitat. It was something he was going to have to think about.

Night arrived and they were getting ready to turn in. Warren went out to bring in additional wood for the fire. The air was still and it was quiet. He took advantage of the situation to observe the beauty of the snowy landscape. A Christmas card should look so good, he thought. Everything was a cool blue color in the starlight. All the hard edges were softened by the collection of snow on and around them.

Suddenly, his eyes became aware of an unusual flickering, reflecting off the snow. He walked further out on the rock. The light was coming from overhead. He looked up seeing it was being reflected off the few clouds in the sky. It reminded him of a candle in a light breeze, at first, but then it dawned on him it was more like the time he watched an electric arc welder working.

He watched for a few minutes, seeing the flickering come and go. The source of the phenomenon was not the sky. It was instantly obvious. It originated from the top of the mountain.

His adrenaline rushed. "JIM! JIM! Get dressed and come out here. Quick! Hurry!" He walked to the southern edge of the rock and then across the bridge, looking to see if he could spot anything on the mountain.

"Holy shit!" He moaned, running back to the hut. "Why the hell am I calling Jim? He can't see. Saints preserve idiots and fools."

Entering the hut, he saw Jim trying to dress himself and put on his shoes.

Jim struggled to hurry. "I'm trying to hurry, Warren. It's just a little difficult when…"

Warren hugged Jim. "God! Jim, I'm sorry. I wasn't thinking. Guess I don't think about you as being blind."

"Don't sweat it. But what's going on?"

Warren helped Jim get dressed. "There's something real funny going on and I think we need to check it out. Make sure you're warm because we're going to take a little hike. Put on that new coat Mike bought."

"Where are we going?"

"The top of the mountain." He paused for a second. "I think the

'Stone Mountain People' are back!"

"Really? You're kidding? But how do you know? You are kidding? Tell me you're kidding."

"No I'm not kidding. It's important for us to check this out and see what's going on up there. I can just feel it. And I don't want to leave you here. I want you with me." Warren dressed in warmer clothing then put on his skin vest over his new coat.

"But you can make better time without me. I might get in the way. What if they are violent?"

"I don't care. This is too strange and I'm not leaving you alone. I will never leave you alone again." Warren snapped the fasteners on the coat Jim was wearing to make sure he would keep warm. He tied on his antler hat good and tight so it would not fall off, as he considered it lucky, then grabbed the machete. They headed out of the hut.

Long spans of time would elapse between the flickers. Warren remained aware of this fact. Not one sound could be heard.

The snow was about three feet deep and made it a bit difficult for Jim, but he held his own. There was one advantage to the snow. It reflected the available natural light, making it fairly easy to see where they were going. They needed no torch or flashlight.

It was easy to cross the creek to the north side with the creek basically being dry from the drought. They headed to the northeast toward the location of the west side of the mountain where they would go to the top.

"Well what the hell is going on?" Jim had received no information.

"It's the flickering. It has to be them."

"You mean the 'Stone Mountain People'?"

"I'm sure of it, but we'll find out when we get up there."

A little more than two hours later, they reached the location of the path on the western slope. Warren bolted. "My God!" He whispered.

"What?" Jim yelled.

"SSSSSSHHHHH!" Warren sounded. "They're here!"

"Can you see them?" Jim yelled again.

"Not so loud, damn it! I don't know, I can't see them. But there's a lot of them."

The snow was packed down from the weight of many boots walking on the wide path. This made the rest of the going rather easy, but Warren felt they would have to be careful. What if they were hostile, as they had considered? He headed up the path, pulling Jim close behind.

The closer they got to the top, the flickering was accompanied by the sound of loud popping.

"I swear, it sounds like an arc welder to me." He whispered. He also noticed the clouds were dispersing. The flickering and popping continued as they got closer to the top. When they were within a hundred feet of the opening in the wall, he thought he heard the sound of voices.

Jim confirmed the fact. "I can hear them, but I don't know what they're saying."

Just at that moment, a great beam of white light shot straight into the sky, accompanied by a low humming noise. The beam seemed to stretch into infinity. A roar of applause and whistles resounded from within the wall.

"What's going on?" Jim whispered.

"Come on. We'll go see." Warren pulled Jim behind him. "I want to see what's happening in there, too."

Cautiously, they came to within thirty feet of the portal. Warren craned his neck trying to see.

Suddenly, he became aware of something approaching from behind. A group was coming up the mountain. He frantically sought a place for them to hide. It was futile. Any exit from the path would be evident in the snow on either side. There was no choice but to stand their ground.

Warren led Jim to the middle of the path. If we have to fight, we might as well show we are not trying to hide. He turned, facing whatever was coming from below. Jim stood close behind. "Whatever happens, don't move! And stay close to me." Warren ordered.

The sounds of voices and many feet crunching on the packed snow grew louder. The group was getting closer.

First, bright globes of light became visible. They were floating ten feet above the dozen or so men who finally were in sight.

Warren stood firm, the machete raised in his right hand. His left hand reached back to hold Jim close. He looked straight ahead at the advancing troop.

The many glowing globes lighted the entire scene, like day. Then one of them raced to right directly over the spot where Warren and Jim stood. There was no way to hide now.

Within seconds, the group was aware of the two. They immediately halted, some forty feet from Warren and Jim, and their conversations ceased. They looked at one another then back at Warren and Jim. Shortly, there were low mumblings in an unfamiliar language. After a moment, all was silent.

A handsome, but formidable looking man stepped forward. He looked to be the leader. Three others followed behind. All the others remained where they were.

He was just over six feet tall and was wearing something similar to a sweat suit, like the others in the group. His boots came to just below the knee. Wavy black hair, beard and mustache were visible through the opening in his hood. A gold band, set with a large faceted, deep red stone, encircled his forehead, disappearing beneath the hood.

The other three, dressed in the same manner, were right there, too. One walked up and stood at the right side of the leader. He was taller, still. The other two flanked them, but stood slightly back.

The man's dark inquisitive eyes stared at Warren. He reached to his belt, pulling off a small device. It flashed with a multitude of tiny colored lights.

"We're not afraid!" Warren yelled very loud; his adrenalin was pumping at full blast. "We're not afraid! And you better know! I'm pretty good with this thing!" He defiantly waved the machete in the air above his antler hat.

There was no movement or sound from the group, but the commotion brought another group through the opening in the wall. Warren maneuvered quickly around Jim to face the new adversaries, then immediately jumped back to his original position.

Warren waved the machete in the air. "If you want to take on someone, I'm first! You leave Jim alone! I'm not afraid!" His heart pounded in his lie.

The man looked down at the device in his right hand and pressed a sequence of buttons. The words Warren had spoken were loudly repeated from the device. As they repeated again, they changed. By the sixth time, the words were unintelligible to Warren and Jim, but a low chuckle rose from the groups. The man only grinned, his white teeth shining and his dark eyes glinted. He looked to his tall handsome companion to the right, who was smiling, too. He looked back at Warren.

"What the fuck's so funny? Just because you have us surrounded, doesn't mean you've got us licked! FUCK! You'll never take us!"

The man played the device again. With the sixth garbled run of Warren's words, there was another touch of laughter from the groups. He just stood his ground, shaking his head. His grin grew wider. He uttered several syllables. His voice was mellow, with deep resounding tones. His companions responded with additional laughter. They turned back to Warren and Jim.

Warren immediately realized what was happening. How could he have been so stupid? His fear waned slightly, but he kept his guard. He lowered the machete.

It was obvious the device was some kind of interpreter. He felt rather foolish and immediately tried to amend his hostile blunder. "Hello! Damn! I'm so sorry! I'm so sorry I sounded so hostile." He saw the device twinkle. "My name is Warren." He turned grabbing Jim. "This is Jim. Alphabet! Our language has twenty-six letters. A. B. C. D. E. F. G. H. I. J. K. L. M. N. O. P. Q. R. S. T. U. V. W. X. Y. Z." He held up his hands. "Our mathematical system is based on ten, zero through nine. The numbers are zero, one, two, three…" He flipped a finger up each time. "Four, five, six, seven, eight, nine", and with the last finger up, "ten." Warren stood quietly, staring directly into the man's eyes.

The interpreter played the program again. After the sixth play, everyone in the groups smiled, shaking their heads affirmatively, and a mellow laughter came to their garbled conversation.

A warm expression came to the face of the man. He placed the still blinking device back on his belt and cleared his throat several times. Everyone became silent. His mouth opened and he spoke deliberately, and with distinction. "Hello. Hello, Warren. Hello, Jim. Do you? Do you understand me?"

Warren grabbed Jim and they started to laugh. "Yes! Yes we do!" Warren responded, vigorously shaking his head up and down in the affirmative.

The man took one step forward. "We mean you no harm. We do not understand." He paused with a questioning look on his face. "Why you are here? Where did you come from? This whole area is uninhabited. How did you get here? And you are obviously with intelligence." He stopped for a moment. "First." He held up the index finger of his right hand. "First, we must get you to a warm place. You are not adequately protected against the cold." He turned to one of the men in the group behind him, and handed him the device from his belt. "Please take this below for the others. We will be down shortly. From now on, we speak in their tongue. Alert all of my request. Also ask them to prepare food and drink."

"Yes, Sire." The man responded with a quick bow, then was off down the path.

He turned to Warren and Jim again. "Come. Let us go below and talk. And by the way…I like the hat." A huge grin covered his face. A warm laughter came from the group.

"Oh. Yeah. Jim made it for me. It's my lucky hat." Warren chuckled.

The man stretched out his right hand as if wanting Warren to shake it. "My name is Alton."

Warren slowly took fifteen steps forward, pulling Jim along. He put his right hand in Alton's and shook. The greeting was strong, firm and sincere.

"This is Jim. My friend." He turned toward Jim.

Alton extended his hand and smiled down at Jim.

Jim automatically smiled at the warmth of the voice and stuck out his hand. Not knowing exactly where to direct it, it fell eight inches below Alton's. "Hello. I'm Jim."

Alton gave a curious look and turned to Warren.

"Oh. I'm sorry. Jim's blind. He can't see. He fell." Warren gestured, pointing to his eyes.

"Your friend." Alton looked back at Jim and reached with both of his hands to take Jim's. He shook gently. "We will have to see what we can do about that."

"You mean you might be able to fix it?" Warren was excited.

"We might. We will know later, after examination." Pausing slightly, he turned to the three men standing with him. "This is my friend Dereck." He extended his left hand in the direction of the man to his left. "My friend Hadon." He stretched his right hand to the man on the far right. "And last but not least, my friend Tog." He grabbed the left shoulder of the very tall man on his immediate right. All shook hands. "Give me a little time to see the progress up here and I will be right back. He headed through the portal to the area within the wall. Almost as quickly as he left, he was back. He turned to his friends. "They will keep us appraised of the progress."

Alton turned to Jim. "Here. It will be quicker if I carry you." He turned to Warren. "Warren. Walk next to me so we may talk on the way down the mountain."

"But Sire. I'll be glad to carry Jim." Tog spoke. "It will make it easier for you to talk with Warren."

"Thank you, Tog. That would be nice."

"Okay, little friend. Climb on." Tog crouched down and pulled Jim high on to his shoulders. They started below.

"There are a million questions." Warren was excited. "But I hardly know where to begin. But let me take my hat off before one of the antlers pokes someone's eye out." Warren pulls off his antler hat, carrying it in his left hand.

"Your first question will be where we are from." Alton interjected.

"There is a large island out in the great sea. In that direction." He pointed to the east.

"I don't believe it, Jim. He's pointing to the east."

"East? Atlantis! You're from Atlantis?" Jim uttered his disbelief.

"Atlantis?" Alton was puzzled. "We call the island Pelaton."

Warren bubbled. "You may call it Pelaton, but it will be known throughout all history as Atlantis. Everyone thinks it's a myth. Just wait until we get back. This is too incredible."

"Get back? Myth?" Another questioning expression came to Alton's face.

"It's kind of a strange story. You see, we're actually from the Twentieth Century."

"What's the Twentieth Century?" Tog inquired.

"God! How do I explain?" Warren tried to think how to start at a point of significance. "Stop! Let me try to explain." Warren crouched down on the ground and patted the snowy surface. "The earth." He pointed to the ground. "We are standing on the earth. It moves around the sun." He moved his right fist around his left, holding the antler hat. "It takes three hundred and sixty-five days for the earth to accomplish one revolution." He stood up again.

"It actually takes three hundred sixty-five and one quarter days." Jim interrupted.

"Let's not confuse the issue." Warren continued. "One revolution, we call a year. One hundred years..." He put the hat under his armpit then flashed his hands ten times. "One hundred years is equal to one century. We are twenty centuries from..." He stopped for a moment. "This is harder to explain than I thought. A lot harder." He shook his head and they all started walking again. "I will try to explain it later."

Jim started. "We mark the time from the life of one of the greatest men in our history. His name was Jesus."

"Yes." Warren continued. "Everything after Jesus is called 'AD'. It refers to when Christ died. He's also called Christ. Jesus Christ! We are from the time, twenty centuries after the death of this Man." He hit the side of his head with his left hand. "Now! Is everyone totally confused?" He began to laugh in the dilemma.

Jim picked it up. "To those of us who believe it so, Jesus is the Son of God."

"OH! The Great One to Come!" Dereck seemed to understand. "But He is not to come for a very long time."

"You know of Jesus?" Warren was surprised.

"If He is the One to whom you refer, we call Him 'The Great One to Come'. He will be born pure and of a pure woman. He will be the Son of the Great Seer of All." Dereck added. "But there will be other great ones, also. There will be several Great Knowers who will lead those to understand the significance of the Great Seer of All."

Jim laughed. "Who'd have ever guessed? I'll bet he is referring to Mohammad, Buddha, Moses and all the other great religious leaders and founders of history."

"This seems to be a vast avenue for future discussions." Alton commented. "Dereck has a great love of religious teachings and attitudes. I know he will enjoy these talks. But I still do not understand your time in relation to us."

Warren was frustrated trying to explain. But he continued, hoping there would be some common thread to use as a focal point to work from. All he could do was hope to hit it by talking. "Let's see. Conjecture has it that the Atlantians lived some ten to twenty thousand years before the time from where we came. This is one hundred to two hundred centuries."

Alton chuckled. And shook his head "That's a very long time between us. Did you get here by time travel? We have not discovered how to do that."

"No. We got here by some crazy mistake. There's a portal joining this time to our time, but it's only open when it's cold on both sides. I promise to discuss it with you later when there's more time to get into it."

"A door to the future. Interesting. I would like to know and see the future."

"And so you shall." Warren laughed. "But we have to wait about six years to do it. That will be part of the explanation. Now. To change the subject, I'm curious to know what you are doing here, so far from home?"

"It is the rock." Hadon stated.

"Rock?" Jim was lost.

"Yes. Our astronomers and scientists have been watching it for millennia." Hadon explained. "Every ten years we have come here to measure how far it has moved toward the earth. When it was discovered, they were afraid it was going to someday hit. By watching it, they would know what to do to protect the population as well as warn any peoples that might be in the destruction areas. We were also hoping there would be enough time to move to another world, but it has not been the case. Our advances have been significant, but we have not found a way to move the entire population to another world as yet. The nearest habitable one is too many lifetimes away. We come here and stay from fourteen to twenty days since it takes that long to collect the information and do the calculations."

"But why here?" Warren questioned.

"This is the closest location to Pelaton where there are no distortions in the magnetic or electrical fields of the earth." Alton added.

"Yes." Hadon continued. "We must have a free field to conduct our monitoring. We are not sure why this place is so perfect. It just is and has been since the time of the building of the observatory on top of the mountain, back in the beginning. The movement of the rock has been recorded since that time. It is in the floor of the observatory. The light beam is how we gather information on the rock. We know the mass, composition, speed of travel, and many other things about it. Several visits in the past, we discovered it was highly fragmented. Once it hits the outer atmosphere, it will become a meteor and shatter into many pieces. This will be advantageous because the smaller ones will burn up before they strike the surface of the earth. Only a few large pieces will actually hit. But they will be of significance. This monitor will let us know the size and weight of every fragment as well as allow us to pin point the exact location each piece will fall."

"That's amazing." Warren was intrigued by the information. "But why every ten years?"

"The rock is moving so slowly through space, a ten year period was the optimum time interval." Tog indicated.

"So. When you return to Atlantis, ah, Pelaton, you won't be back for another ten years?" Jim wondered.

"No." Tog spoke again. "This is our last visit. Our last calculation. We are expecting it to strike just over a year from now. Four hundred and seventy-three days to be a bit closer to the mark. When we are done we will know the exact time of each hit, to the precise millisecond."

"One thing that disturbed us greatly was the survival of everything on earth, but finding you two, and knowing you are from the future, has made us extremely joyful. When we give this knowledge to the high council, there will be celebration over the fact that all will not be destroyed."

"When we found you two, we were on our way up to try and assist." Dereck laughed. "There had been some sort of problem in getting the beam going tonight."

"It is so strange how you happen to be there." Alton hinted. "I think if it hadn't happened, we may never have known about you."

"True. I saw the flickering. If the beam had been working properly, I may never have seen the light and wondered what was happening up here on the mountain."

"Everything happens for a reason." Jim preached. "I've always believed it and always will."

Tog chuckled. "Sorry for changing the subject, but I have to know this. We cannot put our finger on one word you used when we were on top of the mountain. 'Fuck'. It seems to have a vulgar connotation."

Warren was rather embarrassed in his laughter. "Well. It's an ugly word, a vulgarity. An expression of, well, I'll have to go into detail sometime about it. Remind me and I'll explain a number of words we use that have not so nice meanings."

"Great!" Tog was ecstatic. "And I'll tell you our ugly words."

Alton laughed. "Yes. I call Tog my friend with the foul mouth. If there is a bad word, he knows it and can explain in great detail its meaning."

"Fuck!" Tog enunciated it correctly and with verve. "Fuck! I think I like that word. It sounds so absolutely and wonderfully filthy."

Everyone laughed out loud.

"Yes. He and Jim will get along famously. Jim has a mouth on him, too." Warren continued to laugh.

"Great!" Tog gave a big grin, his eyes looking up at Jim atop his shoulders. "Jim, we need to get together and compare notes!"

"Oh, what have we done?" Alton chuckled and shook his head.

Everyone laughed even louder.

They were soon entering the camp. It was situated just north of the mountain. Warren, even in the dark, remembered it was the same place he and Jim first looked for the carving on the mountain, years earlier.

The camp structures were fabricated of some plastic-like substance. They were large, rectangular in shape, two and three stories high, arranged in groups with narrow avenues between them. Alton indicated the modules were extremely lightweight and required only a day to set up. Since they arrived two days earlier, today was the first day in getting the equipment to the top of the mountain and starting their work.

"After some food and drink we will rest. Tomorrow we will show you all around." Alton was the perfect host.

The dining room was large. The tables and chairs were very modern in design, very lightweight and of soft colors.

There were only a few people in the room when they arrived. Warren's thoughts of Alton's influence and position were reinforced by the actions of others. Everyone treated him with respect as if he were someone of high authority, as they would slightly bow when they saw him.

By the time they were all seated, food was being brought to the table. Warren placed his antler hat on a side chair. The large gold and silver trays contained sliced meats, breads, fruits and other culinary delights. Warren was surprised at the care taken to present the food. "Jim. You should see how beautiful the food is arranged. And it looks so good. You would really appreciate it. You'd kill for one of these trays, too. Just your style. Outrageously ornate, verging on gaudy." He turned to Alton. "Jim is a caterer and is a great cook.

"Here. Let me fix him something." Tog picked up one of the gold plates, putting several selections from the trays into it. The plate looked unusually small in his large hand. But he was a large man, standing taller than Alton. "We have some rather unusual foods. Some you may have never tried. They come from all over the earth." His dark brown eyes sparkled with enthusiasm and a warm smile was visible through the closely trimmed dark brown hair of his beard and mustache. It was the same color as the slightly wavy hair on his head. Tog placed the plate in front of Jim, then took Jim's hand and put it on the edge of the plate so he would know where it was. "The fork and knife are to the left of the plate, Jim."

Jim recognized the voices already. "Thanks, Tog. I appreciate your consideration." He started eating.

"Jim loves to try new things." Warren patted Jim on the back. "Back home, he used to fix some of the most exotic dishes."

"They will bring us one of our favorite hot drinks in a few moments." Hadon's crystal blue eyes seemed to glow. He was a handsome, blond, curly headed Viking of a man, whose blond mustache curled up on the ends. "I think you will find it quite nice. They do not start making it until they see Alton coming. They know he likes it fresh. We have been drinking it for generations. I think it has been around forever. It is rather exotic, since it comes from a very long way from here. I hope you like it as much as we do." The large tray arrived with a large silver pot and enough golden cups for the group. "I do not know what it is about it, but we just cannot seem to live without it."

Alton handed out the cups and Hadon prepared to pour.

"Our guests first." Alton gestured.

As the dark hot fluid poured into Warren's cup, the aroma permeated through the air.

"COFFEE!" Jim and Warren yelled simultaneously.

"You know this?" Dereck was surprised.

Warren laughed. "And where we come from, we can't seem to live without it either. Especially in the morning."

Everyone at the table laughed out loud. They truly had something in common.

"Smells like Colombian." Jim sniffed the air.

"Colombian?" Dereck was curious. He ran his hand over the light brown mustache and beard of his angular face. A lock of his light brown hair slipped over his forehead. His eyes looked like a mosaic of blues and greens.

"Do you have something that I can draw on and a marker?" Warren looked at Dereck. "I'll show you Colombia."

"I'll get something." Hadon got up from the table and went to a cabinet across the room. When he came back, he handed several large pieces of paper and marking pens to Warren.

Warren laid one of the sheets in front of him and started sketching a rough global map, showing the Americas. He moved the marker to the right, leaving a large space, then sketched a semblance of the British Isles and the coasts of Europe and Africa and the Middle East. While sketching, he described everything he was trying to draw, naming the areas.

Completing the sketch, he put the marker just inland from the east coast of North America. "We are about here." He moved the marker to the northern section of South America. "This is where Colombia is located and where the coffee beans come from."

Hadon, Tog, Dereck and Alton broke out laughing.

Dereck spoke. "We get them from far in this direction." He pointed to a place far off the map to the east. "We'll have to see about planting some of them where you indicate, as it would be a lot easier to get them there than from where we do now. We call them Moila beans. They grow on trees."

While they sat eating, Tog left the room. Within several minutes, he returned, carrying a large roll of paper. He unrolled it and held it up. It was a large map. It looked very much like the maps Warren was familiar with. There were some variations, but basically it was the same. The major difference was the existence of a very large island out in the Atlantic Ocean. Its north shore was some two thousand miles south of Iceland. The island was about the size of Alaska. Tog smiled and pointed to the island. "This is Pelaton." He was proud to be the one to introduce his homeland. The dark brown hair on his face accentuated his perfect white teeth.

All were pleased with Tog's presentation, applauding the announcement of the location of their homeland. Alton raised his coffee cup. All raised their cups. Even Warren did in the exuberance of the moment. "To Pelaton!" Alton saluted.

"To Pelaton!" The group responded.

There was a moment of silence when Jim raised his cup. "To Atlantis!" He began to laugh. All laughed and raised their cups and in unison, cheered. "To Atlantis!" They all continued to laugh.

After another hour of discussion, Alton indicated it was time to retire. "I know we could sit here all night, but we must get some sleep. It's been a tiring two days for us." He turned to Warren and Jim. "A place has been prepared for you."

"I was wondering if I could make one request." Jim seemed slightly embarrassed. "I'd really like to take a shower, if possible. I mean, we took a wash bath earlier tonight, but it sure would be nice to stand under a shower, if you have that kind of thing."

Tog laughed. "No problem. Everything is in the room, adjacent to where you will be sleeping." He turned to Alton. "Sire. May I take them to their room?"

"Thank you, Tog."

Tog led Warren and Jim to a third story room. The accommodations were Spartan, but very nice. Warren attributed it to the situation. If he was going to spend only twenty days in one place, and that place was over a thousand miles from home, he would only bring the light essentials.

Hanging in a small closet were two jump suit outfits and two pair of boots. The machete lay on the floor in front of the boots.

There were toothbrushes, of sorts, on a narrow shelf below a mirror, along with a paste. Warren put a line of paste on one brush and placed it in his mouth and started the normal process of brushing. He was amazed at the fact there was no foam. He never felt like he had to spit. The brush was acting like a vacuum, pulling everything from his mouth. In less than a minute, he pulled out the brush. His mouth was clean. He grinned into the mirror. Every stain was gone and his whole mouth felt fresh as new. "Here. You have to try out this toothbrush system. And don't worry. You don't need a sink."

Jim put the other brush in his mouth ad started to brush. After about a minute, he took the brush out. "Damn! That was great! David, my dentist, needs to see this thing. He will love it."

Next, they were ready for the shower. Warren got into the shower stall with Jim. He wanted to make sure the water was adjusted properly. But when he turned on the faucet, nothing came from the nozzle above them. Nothing they could see, but they could feel it.

"The water feels so good." Jim turned his face up into the invisible spray.

Warren was slightly puzzled. "There is no water."

"No water? But I can feel it. And my skin feels wet."

"I know. I feel it, too, but believe me, there's not one drop coming out of the sprayer. It's invisible."

"Well, I don't care. It feels good to me. I love it." Jim turned around and around. He was like a child in a yard sprinkler for the first time. The warm nothingness pulsated his skin. They so enjoyed it, they stayed for a long time under the invisible spray. There was no need for soap. Something in the spray acted as a cleaning agent, removing the dirt and oil from their skin.

When they stepped out of the stall, Jim could not believe how clean he felt. Warren handed him a towel, even though there was nothing to dry, then walked into the sleeping area. "I guess they use the towels to just wrap around themselves after they get out before they get dressed.

There were two large beds in the room, but Warren turned down only one of them. He rubbed the towel through his hair, to make sure it really was dry. He set the towel aside and got in the bed. Jim was still standing under the heat element in the bathroom and wiping himself with his towel. Warren looked in. "Okay. Don't wear out the system. Get in here and get in bed." He joked.

Getting in next to Warren, the clean sheets felt good against Jim's naked body.

"Jim?" Warren spoke softly.

"Yes?" He turned to face Warren.

"There are two beds. If you want, I will sleep in the other one so you'll have more room."

Jim chuckled. "I know. I bumped into it when I first came into the room. To be honest, I'm too used to having you beside me. I'd like you to stay with me. I don't know if I could sleep without you next to me. But if you want to sleep in the other bed, it's alright."

Warren grabbed Jim and rolled him over and pulled Jim's back against his chest. He was glad. He had no desire to sleep alone.

They talked for a while about the events of the last several hours, laughing and chuckling about some of the incidents. Shortly, they quieted down.

"Warren." Jim whispered. "I want you to know. I'm glad you're here, and, I love you. Thank you for all you've done for me." He pulled Warren's arm and hand tight against his chest.

"I love you, too, Jim." He moved his hand slightly, patting Jim's chest.

Even with all the excitement, they were very tired and could hardly hold their eyes open. They were asleep, almost instantly.

CHAPTER XLIV

Warren was not sure when he woke up. No one disturbed them. The night before seemed like a dream, but he could not deny the fact he was lying in a nice bed, on clean sheets. Maybe the whole thing had been a dream. He looked around the room. He looked at Jim lying next to him. No. This was not his bedroom at home and that was not Linda beside him. This was real.

There seemed to be no rush in getting out of bed. Their old clothes were on the adjacent bed, but Warren wanted to see the suits in the closet. Opening the closet door, he pulled out the larger jump suit and boots. Looking at the machete, he snickered. He tried to imagine how he and Jim must have looked, standing together the night before, dressed the way they were and wielding the blade in the air. He picked up the weapon and put it on top of the old clothes.

Jim was beginning to move and stretch as he woke up.

"Get your ass out of bed. We have to see what's going on." Warren went to the closet, getting the other suit and boots. He was surprised how light the clothes were and how soft it was against the skin. It almost felt like a soft flannel, nothing at all. The boots were similar. "How the hell does something this light keep them warm?"

"I can't believe how soft the clothes are." Jim started putting on the suit. "Am I getting this right?"

"Yeah, but let me help you."

They started discussing and speculating about the Atlantians. There were a million questions and probably a million they hadn't thought of yet.

Warren guided Jim down the corridors toward the dining room on the first level, retracing their direction from the night before when Tog escorted them to the room. No one was in the halls, but when they entered the dining room, a multitude was seated at the tables. All eyes turned to them when they walked in. The many faces were warm and kind, all smiling. Most were men, but about a third were women.

Warren had to laugh inside. Everyone was dressed in robes and looked like a bunch of extras from a Steve Reeves movie, or some Greek or Roman epic. He almost expected the ancient Roman arena to be right outside the doors. Most of the men looked to be in their mid-thirties, tall, well built, and most were sporting beards and mustaches. The women were stunning, with clear soft skin. Most of them had long hair, styled in various manners you would associate with a movie about ancient Rome or the Minoans. Many wore headbands of gold, in various designs, and accented by a colored stone.

Everyone who was seated, immediately stood and the entire group applauded and whistled a roar of welcome. Those close by, patted them on the back as they walked through.

Out of the group, Tog appeared. He ushered them to the table where he was sitting. It was the same table as the night before. Several of his friends were there, but shifted around to make room for them to sit down. Hands stretched out to shake and greet. All knew of Jim's blindness, so they took his hand first.

Tog smiled. "We hope you slept well. Would you like a cup of moi…coffee?"

"Sounds great!" Warren answered.

The minute they walked into the room, food was started for them. After Tog got the coffee, he started introducing Warren and Jim to the entire group. There was a genuine warmth and exuberance from everyone.

Suddenly, a hush came over the room. Everyone stood, facing the door, smiles on their faces and their left arms held out in salute. Alton was there with Dereck and Hadon. Alton raised his left arm and smiled. "Good day everyone."

"Good day, Alton. Good day, Hadon and Dereck." The group greeted the three as they walked to the table. All returned to normal again.

Warren couldn't get over everyone's genuine sincerity. They were truly glad to greet everyone. He also noticed that no one seemed to have animosity or jealousy regarding Alton's position. It was almost unsettling to be among people so content with everything.

"Good day, Tog, my friend." Alton gave Tog a hug and kissed him on the cheek.

"And you, Alton, my brother." Tog returned the gesture. "Good day, Dereck. And to you, Hadon." Again, Tog repeated the hug and kiss. Soon, all were seated and the conversation returned to normal.

Warren was flabbergasted. "Jim. You're not going to believe this."

"Oh, but I can. I can feel it in the air. Don't ask me how I know, but I can feel a warmth of love and friendship." Jim stared off into space. "It is so powerful and sincere."

Alton responded to the surprised look on Warren's face. "We are not familiar with your customs, but we hope ours do not seem too strange or different."

"Well, ah. It's just that. Well." Warren stumbled for words to explain his reaction.

Jim interrupted. "I could not see, but I know you hugged Tog and kissed him. I could tell by the sounds. What Warren's trying to say is that where we come from, a man does not usually express physical affection towards another man. At least not like that. Two men hugging, much less kissing, is presently not considered 'the norm'."

"But why?" Alton turned to Jim. "I don't understand why there is such needless concern over a show of friendship."

"Well." Jim continued. "Men just don't do it. It is considered, well, strange, unmasculine, homosexual."

"Homosexual?" Dereck broke in. "What is that?"

"A man who desires and loves another man or a woman who desires or loves another woman."

It is really too bad." Alton shook his head. "We believe there is nothing wrong with expressing genuine affection and love toward another, especially a friend, whether it be man or woman. We have men and women in our society who are 'homosexual', as you call it, but this is of no consequence. We believe that it is the will of the Great Seer of All who made them that way. It is all part of the great design of man. We find nothing wrong with the way we greet another. Friendship and love are necessary to the human soul. Without them, it withers and dies. What better way to show someone you care than to hug and kiss them? Do you permit this toward your brothers and fathers?"

Jim laughed. "Oh. That's okay."

"So, strangeness and homosexuality is alright among relatives?" Alton was putting Jim on the spot, indicating how foolish the whole thing was.

Jim laughed again. "No! No! I know it doesn't make sense. It's just the way it is."

Hadon laughed. "Maybe someday your people will wake up,

grow up and stop this silliness. I would hope they would come out of their shell of ignorance and bigotry and see the light. They may someday realize that people are people and it is not wrong to express affection, regardless the gender."

"Men of your society and time must be incredibly insecure with their masculinity." Tog commented. "What is their problem?"

"No one's been able to answer that one." Warren shook his head. "We do have a lot of growing up to do." His conversation with Mike Johnson flashed through his mind.

More food was brought to the table along with a fresh pot of coffee for Alton.

"Warren?" Alton sipped the cup. "Today I wanted to take you around so you can see the labs, computers and other things here." He grabbed both of Jim's hands. "As for you, Doctor Mennot wants to see you. I spoke with him before coming here."

"You mean Jim really might be able to see again? You weren't kidding?" Warren was surprised.

"There are no guarantees. Only Doctor Mennot will be able to answer that question. He is one of the greatest medical specialists we have."

Warren hugged Jim. "Oh, Jim. I hope it's true."

Alton watched Warren's actions and smiled. It was obvious he was thinking what was said in the earlier conversation.

"He's my friend. And I love him." His face blushed.

Alton just grinned. "You are so defensive. Remember, we see nothing wrong with your actions. If you genuinely care, you should let him know." He leaned over hugging Jim. "I wish you all the chances possible, Jim." He kisses him on the cheek. "We must check into this matter immediately."

After they finished eating, Alton turned to Tog. "Would you mind taking Jim to Doctor Mennot while I show Warren around?"

"Certainly, Sire." Tog patted Jim on the shoulders. "Come, little friend, let's go see the doc."

Dereck and Hadon hugged and kissed Jim. "We wish you all chances, too." Dereck squeezed Jim's shoulder.

All went their ways. Tog guided Jim to Doctor Mennot's office.

Doctor Mennot smiled when they walked into the infirmary. "So this is our young man? Come with me. We'll see what we can do for you."

Tog hugged and kissed Jim and placed Jim's hand in Doctor Mennot's. "I'll be here when you come out. All chances, little friend."

"Thanks, Tog."

Doctor Mennot led Jim to another room, having him lay on a narrow table. "This will be over in no time." There was the 'click' sound of a switch, starting some apparatus.

Meanwhile, Warren's tour was extremely informative, but raised a lot more questions. Alton wanted to know more about the Twentieth Century. Their conversations jumped to so many subjects. Warren superficially covered how Jim and he arrived and how they had been surviving. They also discussed the prospects for the future, the passing between the two time periods, and the sharing of information, culture, and customs.

Alton was rather distressed over how man had this great penchant for war. He considered it wasteful and a tragedy to mankind. He could not understand the lack of human harmony or the waste of so many resources on war. Maybe his people's philosophy would be of significance. Maybe they would be able to influence the thinking of Twentieth Century man.

Warren agreed. He knew the impact of the Atlantian society and science would be overwhelming to modern man. Maybe there would be an end to senseless warring. They could offer so much. Warren was concerned that modern man had nothing to offer the Atlantians. Modern man was too greedy, selfish, and conceded to give anything without thinking there was something in it for him.

This subject would be the center of many future discussions. Warren, being a perfect 'devil's advocate', would make it very difficult to make Twentieth Century man seem worthy of the wonderful gifts that could be bestowed on them. But the Atlantians would be constantly optimistic. Maybe there was hope.

Completing their tour, they returned to the dining room. Dereck wanted to know more about the future and what caused the deterioration of civilization. "What happened to OUR culture? Why didn't our standards endure? What happened to civilization?"

Warren didn't know how to answer without being brutal. "Your entire civilization disappeared from the face of the earth before our recorded history. Atlantis lives in the minds of the future as legend and myth. It is thought a great cataclysm occurred. Absolutely nothing survived as evidence your society even existed. Even the island went. There is no record of it throughout the history of man. Never has it shown up on any map, not even the oldest of maps. Only ocean exists where you show your island to be. Some archaeologists believe there were survivors from the catastrophe and they migrated to other areas of the world. There are ancient stories of men coming from the seas who were teachers to their societies."

"But what happened?" Hadon was emphatic. "What could cause an entire civilization to be obliterated, and when did it happen? This is very disturbing to me."

"One theory is..." Warren's expression was that of distress.

Alton saw the alarm. "What's wrong?"

"I just remembered some of the legends." He paused in his anguish.

"Well? What's wrong?" Alton inquired.

"One of the theories is that Atlantis was struck by a great comet or meteor. It could have been the Carolinian Meteor. Many of the pieces fell in the Carolinas. That's how it got its name."

"The Carolinas?" Dereck didn't understand.

"Yeah. Let's see Tog's map again. I'll show you where."

Hadon jumped up and returned shortly with the map. He spread it out on the table, holding the corners down with a few saucers.

Warren used his index finger to make a circular motion on the map. "This is the area I'm talking about. This is where North and South Carolina are located. Aerial photos have shown what's left of ancient craters. It's thought the main section of the meteor landed far to the east." He moved his hand over the spot where the island was situated. "And when it did, it could have destroyed the Continent of Atlantis. That's why nothing was left to substantiate its existence."

They all looked at one another. "We better make sure we check and double check our calculations on this one." Alton was firm. "It could mean life or death for us all."

Silence prevailed a few minutes before Alton spoke again. "What are some of the other theories?"

"Well." Warren cleared his throat. "Another is a gigantic subterranean chamber collapsed beneath the continent, taking everything with it. Another is volcanic action. It shifted the earth's crust, pushing the land below the surface of the ocean. Quakes and tidal waves did the rest."

There was another period of silence, then Hadon shook his head. "We can't seem to win on this. It doesn't look good, regardless."

"Maybe the portal is the answer!" Warren was excited. "Everyone can locate to a safe area off and away from the island, then after the meteor comes, we can all go back through the portal in six years."

"Maybe he has something." Dereck perked up. "Maybe that was the great plan after all. Maybe that's how it is suppose to be. If we survive the meteor."

"Let's not count the ploys before they hatch." Hadon added. "But it does seem to be a way to prevent the extinction of our people."

"Not to mention the wonderful things you believe in and know." Warren was glad there might be a solution.

"Time will tell." Alton picked up his cup and sipped the coffee. "I hate the thought that everything we hold dear will be wiped out without a trace. If the portal is an option, so may the prospects of going to other worlds. Maybe that is where we will end up. But let's talk of other things."

Warren told how amazed he was over the construction of the observatory. The interlocking design of the construction materials in the observatory made adhesives or mortar unnecessary.

Hadon indicated it was the equipment. One of the machines worked using a very fine beam. It could cut and disintegrate anything. Stone was like hot butter. The instrument was so accurate, it could be set to cut as shallow as one millionth of an inch. It was also used in their surgical processes, as well.

The machine was so accurate, a plan or model could be placed in the machine and used as a pattern and the beam would cut the exact three-dimensional item again in any material, regardless of how intricate or detailed it was. This made it possible to make many copies of the same item, sculpture or architectural feature. The whole thing could be set up on an assembly line and left to do its work, requiring no waste of human time in watching or waiting.

Anti-gravity devices made it possible to move virtually any object. It was used in the set up of the village. Even their transportation equipment worked on its principle. Unfortunately, it was not developed to the extent that it could be used in space travel. But this was a project in progress that might allow space travel in the future. They were even investigating the possible travel through wormholes in space to go to distant locations of the universe quickly.

When Hadon indicated they had harnessed the process of cold fusion, Warren laughed inside thinking what that would mean to the electric companies back home.

The ocean floor and sea water were the sources of many raw materials to benefit their society. One of the by-products of several of the processes was the production of gold. The fact it didn't tarnish or corrode made it a significant material in their electrical systems. They also found it a beautiful material to use for ornamentation, both as jewelry and architectural. The enormous supply made it possible for everyone to use it however they wanted.

The manufacture of precious stones was no great task. They were produced synthetically and mechanically, in almost any size desired. The only difference in the real ones and those made artificially was the molecular structure. There were no flaws in the synthetic stones. Warren laughed when he heard all this. He wondered how this would affect the world money markets, not to mention the value of precious jewels. Tiffany and Cartier would go wild. Stock in De Beers might even plummet. But then, it might become the status to have a flawed, real stone rather than a perfect, artificially made gem. But who would know it except a jeweler. Oh, the trials and tribulations of the wealthy, he thought.

Great strides had been made in the medical area, as well. Their medical science developed cures for major diseases, eons ago. An insignificant fact to them, but what astounded Warren was their longevity. These wonderful people, who appeared to be in their thirties, were actually somewhere around two hundred years old.

The average life span was way over four hundred years. He was sure these things would definitely be of interest to the Twentieth Century.

Their governmental structure was of great interest to Warren, having studied Political Science. He wanted to know what problems existed in their society with regards to government. Had they influenced any other cultures that might exist at the time? Where had they come from? Did they develop here on earth? How long had their civilization been in existence? Warren knew these and more would be answered in time.

They sat talking and eating for several hours. Their discussions of many topics were at first superficial, but these would be addressed in greater detail at future times. The outside world was far from Warren's mind. The warmth and friendship within the village complex obscured the fact it was lightly snowing outside. This was of no consequence to him.

Dereck looked up toward the doorway. "Tog! Jim! How did it go?"

Tog was leading Jim to the table. Jim's head was completely surrounded by a black globe, like a space helmet, but no one could see through it.

Warren winced with concern.

"Doctor Mennot says he had to keep it on for six hours. Then, he'll take it off and check things out." Tog assured.

"What did he do?" Warren was still anxious.

"Seems the fall caused some little problem in the vision center of the brain. Everything Jim saw was getting there, but that's as far as it went. Since the brain had no idea it was receiving the message, everything was dark and Jim couldn't see. Doctor Mennot indicated it was a minor operation. Everything should be just fine."

"You mean Jim's going to be able to see again? He's going to be alright?" Warren was excited.

Tog smiled. "We'll know in six hours."

"But why the space helmet?"

"Something about light. No light can enter until the healing finishes. The helmet is totally light proof."

"But it's not soundproof." Jim's muffled voice issued from the orb. "So you better be nice in what you say. I can hear every word. And speaking of saying ugly things, I sure as hell didn't understand what Doctor Mennot meant when he said I looked pretty good for someone around one hundred and seventy years old. Do I look that bad? Maybe I need massive doses of Oil of Olay."

The group laughed then explained the aging process to Jim.

"Now, it makes some sense." Jim laughed. "But will Warren and I continue to age normally, or will we have increased life spans if we stay here?"

"Only time will tell." Alton stated. "But with what we've been discussing, it may all become academic. The meteor may be the end of a whole way of life."

"Sounds like the 'Recent Unpleasantness'." Jim was sarcastic. "Those damn Yankees took everything and burned the plantation. Sure was the end of a whole way of life for us in Virginia."

Warren watched strange expressions come to all the faces. "Jim's referring to the Civil War. It took place well over a hundred and twenty years ago, back there, in the other time." He chuckles. "I'll tell you all about it some time. It's quite involved."

"Another war?" Alton spoke softly but with a touch of anger. "And you make jest of it. What happened to mankind? Much seems to be equated with war. I just don't understand. It does not make sense to continue something that causes destruction, death and suffering. It saddens me. All I can think of are all those lives ending before their time, and what they may have contributed to humanity. Some may have become great and important people. But instead, they died before they could contribute." He shook his head again. "Warren, you must explain the procedure of war and the reason for its existence. I just don't understand."

"Someday, we'll sit down and I'll try." Warren was a little embarrassed. "And you're right. It's not a laughing matter. But it's extremely involved."

Hadon stood up, heading toward the door. "I'm going to check on things on the mountain. It's about time for me to do my shift up there."

"Wait for me." Dereck called out. "I'll go with you. It's about my time to help out, too." He turned to Alton and bowed slightly. "Later, Sire."

Dereck and Hadon would be gone for several hours. Tog took his time eating. Alton finally took some time to give further explanation about their culture.

He was the first son of the Great Zadee, leader of the Pelatonian Civilization. The Great Zadee was basically a figurehead and was subject to society. Alton wanted to become an astronomer and directed his studies in this area. It was one reason why he was on this expedition. Being the son of the Great Zadee did not exempt him from contributing and carrying his own weight.

Because of their longevity, it was not unusual to get involved with several occupations throughout a single person's lifetime. If you chose an area that turned out to be unacceptable to you, you could choose another. It was important to do something you enjoyed.

Discontentment was non-existent. "And what you call envy and jealousy, do not exist either. There is no basis. Greed is of no consequence since everyone has what they desire."

"When we become older, we continue in our fields of endeavor, if we so desire. Our elders are considered great treasures. They are our teachers. We regard life and human worth with extreme value and reverence. I guess that's why your wars concern me."

"I promise. We will discuss it." Warren answered.

Soon the hour arrived for Jim to return to Doctor Mennot. He could hardly wait to get the headpiece off, because he was getting hungry again. Before Tog guided him from the dining room, all hugged him, wishing him well.

Not long after Jim and Tog left, Dereck and Hadon returned.

"It's quite cold outside." Hadon poured a cup of coffee and made a small sandwich. "Everything is going well. The beam is functioning perfectly. The readings are being relayed to the computers and we just might be finished a few days early. We will be double checking the figures to make absolutely sure of the readings. They are too important."

"Yes." Alton agreed. "It is imperative we know all we can about that thing, and where it's going to hit."

"By the time we are finished, we will not only know where each piece is going to land, but where and how far up in the atmosphere the smaller pieces will burn up." Dereck laughed then sipped his coffee.

"Now, that's what we like to hear." Warren interjected. "I call that super efficiency."

Almost an hour passed before Tog and Jim appeared at the door of the dining room. Everyone stood up in anticipation. Warren stood up and his mouth opened slightly in anxiety. He said nothing but stared into Jim's eyes.

Jim stared back, then slowly began to grin.

"You can see!" Warren popped his palms together and ran to Jim.

Alton, Dereck, Hadon and Tog expressed joy with their applause.

Warren hugged him and lifted him off the floor. "I'm so happy for you. Oh, thank You, God." He set Jim back down. "Come on. You have to see everybody."

Jim looked toward the table at the standing men. "Don't say anything!" He quickly exclaimed. "I want to see if I can pick out who is who, without hearing their voices." Tog, Warren and Jim walked to the table. He stopped, looking up into the smiling faces of the three men. He turned to Warren and grinned. "Nothing small about these guys. And they're around two hundred years old? I should look so good." He joked, then turned pointing to each as he named them. "You're Alton. You're Dereck. And you're Hadon."

"How could he know?" Hadon questioned Jim's totally correct connection of name to man.

"Well. There's a cheat factor." Jim laughed.

"A cheat factor?" Tog sat down, as everyone took a seat.

"You see. When I was at school, my friends and I ate all our meals together. In no time at all, we invariably ended up sitting in the same spot. I don't see why this would not hold true with other good friends. Think about it. Alton always sits at the head of the table, doesn't he? And then there is Hadon and Dereck. Dereck and Hadon to his left. This space, where Warren and I are sitting is where Tog would be. To Alton's right. He'd be here if we weren't. Hadon and Dereck are like brothers, but they are most important to Alton. That's why they are together and to Alton's left. Tog is like Alton's brother and his 'right hand man'. That's why he sits to Alton's right. In a group, they are like the Four Musketeers. I have to admit. Knowing exactly which one was Hadon and which one was Dereck was touch and go. Both are devoted to one another from the way I have sensed they interact. And I think Hadon treats Dereck as a slightly older brother, therefore letting him sit closer to Alton. Not that his position would diminish Alton's friendship with either one. It is just the respect he has for Dereck."

Alton's eyes sparkled and a huge grin filled his face. "Jim sees beyond sight. He sees with his heart." He was pleasantly surprised at Jim's inner perception.

A special culinary treat was brought to the table to celebrate Jim's good fortune. All enjoyed a morsel before time to retire.

As the group broke, good nights were exchanged all around. Additional joy was expressed over Jim's restoration.

Warren and Jim entered their quarters, showered and were quickly in bed.

"I'm so damn happy for you, Jim." Warren hugged him.

There were a few minutes of silence when Jim whispered. "You know? It's disgusting. They all look like they went to the Tom Selleck 'school of good looks'. And to think, they're around two hundred years old. I think I'm going to fucking puke."

"Jim, you're disgusting."

"I know it."

They both began to chuckle.

"No envy in his family." Warren laughed. "He's got it all."

They laughed and talked a little more. They were so glad of their fortunate meeting of the people of Pelaton. Their lives would be easier and without care from that day forward.

Warren pulled Jim close to him knowing all was well. Shortly, they were asleep.

CHAPTER XLV

"Now comes the fun." The old man stands. "I sure hope this thing works." He turns, looking at the huge framed white area on the wall behind him. Momentarily, he turns back around. "If it does, you're going to see the rest of the story up there. Keep your fingers crossed."

I nudge Tim. "Welcome to the new Fox Theater." But then I realize he's probably unfamiliar with the great Fox Theater, the historical landmark in downtown Atlanta. I will take him to see it before he leaves town. Then he'll understand the comment.

The light of the room begins to diminish and the white area on the wall begins to glow. Suddenly, the area is filled with the moving image of a blue-green ocean on a bright day. The just audible sounds of the waves and seabirds begin to reach our ears. It does not seem to be a projection but a window into another space. It looks like you could get up and go right into the image there was so much spacial dimensionality.

The old man sits and continues his commentary. "The entire party remained at Stone Mountain for two weeks. In the mean time, Warren and Jim showed off their camp. The covering of snow made it a little difficult to explain projects they'd been working on. But it didn't matter. Alton and his friends were generally enthusiastic about what Warren and Jim had been doing."

"The results of the calculations did not lie. The meteor was going to break up. Most of the pieces would be landing in the ocean, just off the east coast of the United States. It also became evident that Warren and Jim could not stay at Stone Mountain, not that they would be left there in the first place. Several smaller pieces would be hitting the area. Calculations indicated that one small piece, unfortunately, would hit directly on top of the mountain. Warren and Jim understood why the observatory would be destroyed beyond recognition, and why no one ever knew the 'who' or 'why' of the ancient wall."

"The strange thing is that the island of Pelaton would not be struck. Tidal action would be expected, but plans were in the works to deal with that situation."

The old man paused for a moment. "Everything Warren and Jim owned was packed and they readied to move to Pelaton. They would stay the six years, then would be brought back. They could return to their own time through the portal, at that time."

I look close at the screen. In the center of the screen, several distant objects become apparent. The closer they come toward us, the clearer they become. They remind me of a group of Nautilus subs, from the Walt Disney movie. But these are huge in comparison.

"It's *Twenty Thousand Leagues Under the Sea*, 'Revisited'." Tim whispers with a chuckle.

"My thoughts, too." I whisper back.

Finally the large subs come to dock. Many figures are seen leaving the lead sub through a door in the top section of the vessel. The size is now evident with the human scale. The ships are truly enormous.

The old man gestures with his hand and speaks again. "Now, follow the story. Just watch and you will see. I'll be back at the end." The figure of the old man fades. The volume increases, and all eyes are glued to the moving image on the wall. It was like a 3-D movie, without the glasses.

CHAPTER XLVI

A large group gathered to greet the returning expedition. All heard of the two, through the communications, and were anxious to meet these visitors from the future.

Jim and Warren were with Alton, Dereck, Hadon and Tog when they walked down to the dock and the cheering crowd. Yells of 'welcome home' could be heard in the roar of voices, both in English and their own language.

Alton indicated he must inform his father and the high council of their findings, immediately. They were waiting at the Great Hall. Since the Hall was not that far away, they decided to walk. It was a beautiful day and the few extra minutes would not be a problem.

Proceeding through the city, Jim and Warren noticed how clean everything was. The houses were elegant. All were designed, using classic facades. Gardens tiered between and around the houses. The colors of the building materials were subtle pastels, with ornaments of gold. Jim thought of it as Rome in the tropics. And tropical it was. The warm moist air repressed all thoughts of the winter they'd left behind.

"Alton. The city is stunning and so elegant." Jim was soaking up the beauty. "I can't get over how neat and clean everything is. And the gardens are absolutely gorgeous. Warren! Look at that lovely bougainvillea over there. At least it looks like bougainvillea." He pointed to a red variety, trained up the side of a house and across the top of the frieze of its long columned porch. The brilliant display cascaded in great bunches. The vibrant red bracts and deep green foliage contrasted exquisitely with the pale yellows and pinks of the ornate columns and frieze. The small ornaments of gold gleamed in the sunlight. "Now! THAT should be in Architectural Digest! It's magnificent! Such class! Such beauty! Such taste!"

Everyone laughed and Tog commented. "Wait until he sees the Great Hall. We'll never shut him up."

"I know that's right." Warren added. "If it's got columns, watch out. I'll never get him to leave."

The streets brought them closer to the Great Hall, sitting on the high hill, near the center of the city. It took them almost an hour to get there, mainly because they were stopped by so many people who wanted to meet the strangers.

Finally, they came to an enormous plaza, paved with large blocks of pale blue marble. Around the plaza were large gardens. Flowering shrubs, cascading to the surface of the plaza, surrounded groups of tall yew trees, trimmed into slender conical shapes. Classical balustrades of white marble cordoned the plaza and the gardens. Square end posts were mounted with della robbia urns, the fruit and flowers carved in colored stone and marbles.

In the central area of the plaza stood the Great Hall. Jim was overwhelmed. It was a vision like the Hanging Gardens of Babylon, but in high Classic Style. Each of the five levels contained rows of thirty foot, fluted Corinthian styled columns, supporting an elaborate six foot frieze, and topped with a four foot classical balustrade. At first sight, the whole structure looked to be made of white marble, but there was a subtle mixture of multiple pastel shades, softening the overall effect. The columned porches and terraces supported beautiful cascading gardens, statuary and fountains. Numerous, wide, graceful staircases joined each level. Although titanic in size, it's proportions made it very light and airy.

Jim stood dumbfounded. His mouth hung open, speechless.

"I don't believe it! He's actually quiet." Tog laughed.

"Watch out!" Warren warned. "Once he's absorbed it all, we'll have to cut out his vocal chords to shut him up."

They watched Jim's face. Suddenly, he spoke. "Holy Shit! I don't believe it! I've never seen anything so…so fucking…there aren't words to describe this." He pointed to the structure. "Look at the shadow of the cloud on the marble. The marble has a pale white-blue-lavender color. Now! See! As the shadow moves, the same area in the sunlight has touches of pale yellows, pinks, and peach. It's incredible! And look at the use of the trees, shrubs and flowers. It's like something out of a dream. I have to paint this, if I can. Those colors are so illusive."

"Let's get him moving or we'll never hear the end of it." Alton led the group across the plaza, between the rows of columns, and through a set of large doors, clad in panels of gold. The interior was sectioned into courtyards, piercing up through the many levels and covered with huge clear roofs. Sculptures, flowers and fountains enhanced the architecture. Proceeding through several areas, each seemed more beautiful than the one before.

"And you live here?" Jim just gawked.

"Yes. It is the home of the Great Zadee and his family. It is also the seat of the government. Official meetings and governmental meetings are held here. The library, cultural center and the educational complex are located here, too. My family lives in a section of the top level. We'll be going there after we meet with the officials in the government hall."

They came to another set of huge double doors. Automatically, they opened slowly, inwards.

The assembly hall was a huge oval room with a domed ceiling of spectacular stained glass. The room, itself, was lavishly ornamented. There were tiers of seats filled with men and women dressed in fine Grecian styled robes.

All stood, applauding, when they entered. At the far end of the room, in a raised chair, sat an older man. He looked to be in his late fifties or early sixties. His hair was snow white, glistening in the light. His warm, clean-shaven face had a big smile and his brown eyes sparkled. Standing, he held out his arms. "Welcome home, Alton, my son. And Dereck. Hadon. And Tog."

Alton walked up to hug and kiss his father. His companions followed. Jim and Warren waited

Finishing his greetings with Alton and his friends, he held out his arms to the two. "And who do we have here?" He stepped down and started across the floor. "Welcome to Pelaton." He embraced and kissed them both. "Alton tells me you are from the distant future. I'm sure you have many stories to tell us." His face seemed to glow with an inner radiance. "I anxiously await our talks. But first we must know of the expedition. Please come sit with me while our learned colleagues discuss their findings." He led Jim and Warren to chairs near his.

The proceedings began with Dereck and Hadon leading the discussion and the appearance of a huge holographic globe of the earth. Technical data also displayed, hanging in the air, like magic. After several points were discussed, the area of impact became larger so more detailed places could be shown. The proceedings continued for about two hours. This completed, the assembly was recessed. All were pleased the island would not be hit by any part of the meteor. The data would now be turned over to the scientists to aid in the protection of the island. Protective measures against the tidal surge was already in progress.

The apartments of the Great Zadee were extremely lavish. Food was prepared and set out just prior to their arrival. Alton's father led Warren and Jim out on to the terrace. They could see down over the city, out to the ocean and the far western horizon. The view was spectacular. Walking around to the eastern terrace, they could see the distant hills and volcanic peaks. The land was lush and green. Great houses and gardens were everywhere.

When they reentered the apartment, they prepared plates from the buffet. When all were seated around in the sitting area, Jim was the first to speak out, commanding everyone's attention. "Well. I must admit. The next six years are going to be a real bitch! I just don't know if I can handle all this poverty."

"You are unhappy? Poverty? I don't understand." Alton's father was concerned. He looked at Alton with distress on his face.

"No, father." A smile and laugh came to Alton's face. "When you get to know this character, you will come to understand him. Jim uses sarcasm for numerous purposes. In this case, his meaning is one hundred and eighty degrees from what he said. You may accept his caustic comment as a compliment of the highest form. He's actually saying that he is very pleased to be here."

"You can say that again." Dereck joked. "We've all learned his pranks."

"And with all these columns, I'll never get him home again." Warren chuckled. "It's the architecture of his heart. A return to the Old South. 'Windsor Plantation' and all."

"The next few years will be quite interesting to see what the fates have in store." Hadon raised his goblet. "A toast. May the next years be happy and prosperous. And may the fates be kind."

They all raised their goblets. "Here! Here!"

And so it was. Hadon's toast came true. Warren and Jim introduced the people to the future history of the world. It spanned from the known prehistoric, through the early Egyptians and Babylonians, all the way to the late Twentieth Century. Warren told of the governments and the philosophies of the different cultures. He also described, in great detail, the reasons and ramifications of war. Jim covered art, architecture, and music.

Through Jim's descriptions and drawings, several pianos and harpsichords were built. After many conversations with Dereck and Hadon, their engineering knowledge allowed construction of a great pipe organ for the Shrine. He became their first piano teacher. Many of Jim's students became extremely accomplished with their musical talents, writing their own exceptional compositions and songs, but none as much as Tog. He began playing and writing like no other. Tog's huge hands allowed him to reach an eleventh on the keyboard with little effort, an unheard of stretch of the hands. He became a master at the piano, harpsichord and the organ.

Warren made an in-depth study of their government and how it operated. He was surprised that every single person had the chance to participate. All, who were of rational thinking age, had their names placed in a selection pool. When it came time to re-elect the governing body, the specific names were drawn from the pool, at random, and those chosen would serve the term. It was possible that the same individual could serve more than once since all names were placed in the pool for every draw. Warren recalled how everyone he remembered tried to get out of jury duty. When chosen, they hated to serve, thinking it a huge waste of time with virtually nothing in compensation. But the people of Pelaton looked forward to serving in their government. They felt it helped in making major and important decisions for everyone. And since there was no greed or struggle for power, money or self-ingratiation, there was no reason for anyone to be biased in his or her decisions. All decisions were made to benefit everyone and all were unbigoted and undiscriminating. He realized that such a government in the other time would not work. Too many in the governing bodies were selfish, greedy, self-centered and made decisions based only on their own benefit and how it would increase their power and wealth, regardless of how it helped the general public.

The only position that did not change was the position of the Great Zadee. This was a family dynasty that had been in existence for eons. This man was basically a figurehead for the land, much like the monarchy in England.

Warren would often go out on expeditions with the group that studied the growing cultures of the world. The interpreter mechanism came in very handy to understand their languages. These studies were done without letting the other cultures know they were observing. There was no desire to influence the natural growth of any culture. This gave Warren a 'hands on' view of pre-history. When he got back, he knew it would help him write a very factual book about pre-history peoples.

In time, a house was constructed for them. Several architectural styles were incorporated on the interior. The exterior was in keeping with the rest of the surrounding architecture. Warren laughed in his thought, while the house was in construction. Jim finally got his columns.

The house became a show place. Many were interested in the different styles, especially the light, elegance of the Gothic chapel Jim designed into the house.

Jim indicated the Gothic style was used in the great cathedrals of Europe because the design of the Gothic arch made it possible for the building to reach higher towards the heavens.

After telling of the Christian teachings, as well as those of Moses, Mohammad, Buddha, Confucius and others, there was a great desire to construct a great shrine. It would be the center of the new, enlightened religious thought that meshed perfectly with the existing religious teachings of Pelaton, because all were so similar in their philosophies and beliefs.

It would be located on the large plain, ten miles from the eastern edge of the city. Many acres were prepared around the site. These would eventually be developed into enormous gardens and vistas from which to view the structure, when it was completed.

Within the first year, the drawings and foundations were completed. The ability to elevate stone with anti-gravity devices and the laser machines that could cut stone like hot butter made it possible to obtaining materials from around the globe, cut them to precise dimensions and gather them quickly.

The building would not be in the typical design of the cathedrals of Gothic Europe. It would have two naves, each one hundred feet wide and six hundred feet long, crossing in the middle: one nave in the north-south direction and the other in the east-west direction. There would be an entrance at the end of each one, making four great portals to the building. And above each portal, a huge rose window would be installed. The peak of the naves would rise to three hundred feet.

Four long chapels would be built in each inner corner where the naves met. They would be forty-eight feet wide and peak to one hundred and twenty feet. They would extend one hundred and fifty feet to a rounded apse at the end, at a forty-five degree angle to the naves.

The tower at the crossing would be one hundred feet square and built to five hundred feet high with a two hundred and fifty foot spire on top of it. Even with all the technology available, it would take some nine years to complete. In the center of the crossing would be the main alter. This would make any ceremony visible from all of the naves.

Towers flanked all four portals at the ends of each nave, each with a spire to five hundred and fifty feet high. The eight towers contained great sets of bells arranged to be as one huge carillon, played with pneumatic plungers and hammers. The north portal was designed as the Winter Portal, the east, the Spring Portal, the south, the Summer Portal and the west, the Autumn Portal.

Although not true to authentic Gothic construction, a metal

framework supported and was covered by the stonework, allowing the building to reach such great heights, higher than a building made solely of stone could be. Even earthquake was taken into account in the engineering design.

The entire exterior and interior of a white marble was covered with intricately carved ornaments, gargoyles, and statuary. Enormous, long stained glass windows, worthy of a great Gothic styled building, filled the walls. The tracery work in the windows, arches and flying buttresses would look like fine lace. A final clear seal coating would be applied to the entire surface to prevent the white marble from ever being damaged by the weather or any other elements. The ribbed vaulted ceiling was covered with a roof of metal framing and a metal roof covering, glazed in a pale blue color. No wood would be used to prevent the possibility of fire anywhere in the structure.

With its immense size and height, the delicate carvings over its surfaces made it seem light and airy. Even before it was completed, it would lovingly become known as the 'Shrine of Lace'. Thousands would visit it every year to see its beauty and pray and contemplate within its walls.

Dereck and Hadon, being the two most superior engineers and technicians of the time, were amazed at the final product. Both were greatly pleased with how it looked and knew it would be a structure that would last for the ages.

In the tenth year, the opening ceremonies would be held. It would be a celebration never forgotten. All the music would be performed on the great organ. And of course, the compositions would be written and played by Tog.

Warren and Jim told of many of the holidays celebrated in the their time. One of the holidays embraced with great liking was the celebration of Christmas and the decorating of the Christmas tree. The religious meaning of Christmas was slightly altered since Christ had not been born yet. It leaned more toward the traditions of Hanukkah with influences of the belief concepts of Pelaton.

As time passed, the day of the meteor drew near. Preparations were long underway for the event. Many power stations were constructed and moved to all along the western coastline. At the proper time, they would be activated, creating a line of deflector shields to repel the expected tide.

Numerous cameras and microphones were set up on the mainland, in the areas of impact. They were located, not only on the ground, but floated at various elevations in the sky. The highest ones were some fifty miles up. They would give a sound and visual display of the event, from a multitude of vantage points, without endangering a single human life.

It was mid-morning, the day of the historic fireworks display. Countdown for the meteor entry continued. Everyone was calm, yet a spark of anxiety was evident, in anticipation of the visual display. Huge screens were set up on terraces and balconies all over the city. All citizens would be able to see the event. Many had traveled from distant eastern areas to be witness to the happening of the day. All ocean going vessels were moved to the eastern ports days earlier to protect them against the expected surges.

Warren and Jim stood with Alton, his father and friends on the high western terrace of the Great Hall. Tables were set up, covered with sumptuous foods and drink. It was going to be a day to remember.

Looking to the horizon, miles out to sea, Jim stood with Warren next to the marble balustrade. Both were dressed in the style of their newly adopted land. Jim's philosophy was that of, 'when in Rome, do as the Romans do'. He recalled the many discussions regarding the expected display. It was rather terrifying to think it would all begin very shortly. He held a goblet of wine in his left hand. The fingers of his right, thumped on the top of the balustrade.

"Here she comes!" Alton pointed to the southeastern sky.

There was a pinpoint of light, brighter than the day. It moved slowly, yet closer, growing larger and brighter. Its path would take it just south of Pelaton and to the west. All equipment was in action. The cards were on the table. Now, it was in the hands of fate.

Warren looked at Jim. "Sure hope those calculations are right."

All eyes looked to the sky. Momentarily, it was evident the main meteor was breaking into hundreds of pieces. The larger chunks seemed to move ahead of the smaller ones, leaving brilliant trails of incinerating debris.

As the white-hot light blazed to impact, the many cameras and microphones relayed the entire event of sights and sounds. The screens made it like they were there in person at the late afternoon happening in the Carolinas and Georgia.

The systems suspended high above the earth showed the sizzling masses rushing by, plunging toward the surface. Finally, the impacts began with tremendous explosions. Huge craters were blown into the earth's crust, one after the other. Vast forests were leveled. Large pieces, landing in the ocean, off the coast of the Carolinas, caused titanic displacements of water and great eruptions of exploding steam. It was an amazing sight and sound show. Although the streaking lights disappeared below the western horizon, the event continued on the screens.

Then there was a view of Stone Mountain. The camera was located some three thousand feet in the air and two miles southwest of the monolith. A small bright orb came into view, smashing into the summit. An enormous fountain of glowing sparks accompanied the roaring explosion.

"Good thing we're not sitting in the hut right now." Jim cringed. "I think we can kiss the hut goodbye." He paused with a sad face. "I hope the oudies made it." It was Jim's penchant for referring to special animals, especially lovable, furry ones.

"I think they're alright." Warren assured, realizing he was referring to the great furry mastodons. "Animals have a tendency to know about such things. I'm sure they left the area." He had nothing else to say trying to ease Jim's mind.

Hearing Jim's concern, Tog walked up. "Don't worry. Nothing is in the area. We put large sounding devices throughout all areas to be affected. The sounds and vibrations chased out all creatures, great and small, weeks ago. Even on the coasts where tidal surges would take place." He was glad Jim showed concern for the creatures. He, too, considered everything alive a gift from the Great Seer of All, and should be protected as much as possible.

Jim smiled in the knowledge that everything had been considered. "I feel much better knowing they're not in danger." After a few moments he spoke again in a very loud voice. "I now know how the dinosaurs felt." Great laughter from everyone was a reaction to his comment.

Finally, nature's light show concluded. Not a single fragment went off course. All went exactly as calculated. A roar of jubilation rose from the rooftops and terraces below.

So much for the meteor theory regarding the destruction of Atlantis, Warren thought.

"Now we wait." Alton spoke out. "The first wave will be here in a few hours."

The screens continued to show the aftermath and devastation, as the sun began to set over the eastern mainland of the Americas. Enormous fires, clouds of dust and smoke and steam filled the sky. Warren could not believe it. In his wildest imagination, he could not have seen such an event. It was something that had to be experienced. In time, the dust and smoke would rise into the atmosphere and shroud the whole earth. It would cause some temperature fluctuations. Action was already underway to significantly reduce the dust and debris from the atmosphere with huge flying air filtering machines. Within a week, the sky would be virtually as clear as it had been before the event.

Mid-afternoon came to the western coast of Pelaton. Conversations, eating and drinking continued as the afternoon progressed. Replays of the cataclysmic events were shown on the screens.

Suddenly, there was a low rumbling that grew louder as the earth shook. Although the tremor was significant, it was not enough to damage anything. All structures were built to withstand major quakes, since the island was volcanic. These tremors were the result of the impacts of the meteor fragments. The tidal waves would start shortly.

The hour arrived. All stood at the edge of the terrace, looking to the west. The power stations feeding the shield generators were at full impulse. The generators were creating an invisible barrier that went from one hundred feet in the ground to several thousand feet in the air. Hadon had explained the workings were electrical and associated with the magnetic field of the earth. Jim could see nothing indicating the shields were operating. In his mind was the thought that if one of the shields failed, the result would be disastrous.

The first thing noticed was the water receding from the shoreline. The water just continued to withdraw further and further out. Then there was a slight deflection of the western horizon line. The sea began to pile up on itself, mounting higher and higher.

Even though it was miles away, it was obvious. A rolling massive mountain of water was getting closer. It grew to a height of over thirteen hundred feet, and kept coming. It dwarfed everything.

Jim grabbed Warren's wrist and squeezed. Warren knew Jim was petrified. It was his tidal wave dreams coming true. Jim let out a piercing death scream, but stood fast.

Jim was not alone. Fear and panic loomed up in everyone. A roar of terror resounded from below, in the city. No one had ever seen such a frightening sight.

At the same instant, millions of gallons slammed into the invisible deflector shields. The thundering force of the collision threw tons of water several thousand feet into the air. The rumbling sound of the crashing water was almost deafening and absolutely terrifying.

Alton's mind thought of one of the theories about the demise of Atlantis. Maybe this is what wiped it all away. His heart pounded at the prospects of a shield failure. Failure would not be possible. He knew Dereck and Hadon were the ones who designed the shields and they were not only his friends but the most knowledgeable engineers of the land.

The terrifying wall seemed to stand high in the air forever, before it started to fall back against itself. Slowly, the wall began to recede. Deflection of the main wave back into the others, advancing from the west, would help dissipate their power. By the time the ricocheting water reached other shores, it would have minimal destructive influence. The northern and southern most shields forced most of the wave action away from the eastern side of the island. Little damage was sustained.

Alton turned to Dereck and Hadon. "My brothers! An excellent job! Well done. We all owe you our lives. You have saved Pelaton. I am fortunate to know men such as you and call you friends." He hugged and kissed them both. Everyone on the terrace applauded their achievement and responded with hugs and kisses.

There was revelry in the city that night, celebrating the survival. No one ever wanted to see such an event again. Every year from then on this date would be celebrated with great joy and was named in honor of Hadon and Dereck.

Over the next years, Jim and Warren became a part of the culture and life on Pelaton. They even began calling it by that name instead of Atlantis.

The vegetable seeds Warren brought back were propagated and developed into giant hybrids of wonderful flavor. The flower seeds became common throughout the island.

Jim had all generations dancing in the streets, doing everything from the Minuet to Rock and Roll. With his memory of music, there were selections from Pre-Baroque to the Twentieth Century Contemporary. A competition was established every year for accomplished musicians to compose and perform, then judged by the people. It came as no surprise that Tog took home the first prize every year with his incredibly interesting and wonderful and moving pieces. Alton was so proud of him as the prizes were well deserved. Never was there any animosity over his wins. Everyone realized how superior his works were. The main reason others entered was to keep Tog on his toes and do his best. Jim, too, was extremely pleased, as Tog was a true natural when it came to musical composition and playing. He knew he had taught Tog well.

During their stay, it became known that they did not have the longevity of the others. Their aging diminished only slightly.

* * * * *

Time passed quickly and before they realized, it was time for them to go back. Their great joy was in knowing they would return. Fine and wonderful friends had been made.

Alton, Dereck, Hadon and Tog escorted the return trip to the mainland. The monstrous submarine took them to the eastern coast. From there, the airlift carried them inland.

Even though some four years had passed since the meteor, the destruction was still quite evident. They were approaching the area of Stone Mountain at around two thousand feet off the ground. The air was cold. This is one thing Jim had repressed, having lived so long in the paradise of Pelaton.

Looking through the ports of the craft, they could see the devastated landscape below, in the late afternoon light. There was evidence of the first light snows of the season.

One of the pilots entered the cabin. "Sire. There's a change in the readings for the area. Nothing major, but you might want to be aware. It might affect the instruments."

"Thank you, Aaron." Alton took notice of the comment, his eyes still surveying the unbelievable damage passing slowly beneath them.

Within twenty minutes, they passed over the burned out area where the forest fire had been six years earlier, then to the high ridgeline and down to the river. It took a few minutes to locate a place to land.

Once on the ground, they headed upstream along the east bank of the river. In a very short time, they reached the stone marker Warren and Jim built, years before. It had changed little, except for a covering of leafless vines and a light layer of snow.

To Jim, the area was the same as it was when he first saw it, almost twelve years earlier. His heart was filled with mixed emotions. There was the expectation of going home, but there was the sadness of leaving the wonderful friends he'd made. He smiled though, knowing he'd return again very soon. He wondered what changes had occurred in the time he'd been gone, but then stopped and realized it was only one year there, not twelve.

They built a small fire and waited. Although it was quite cool, they knew that the coming night would bring the necessary cold. Alton gave Warren a communicator. "We'll stay here while you and Jim go through. We'll stay until we don't hear you any more or you give us the all clear."

As the sun set, the air got colder. The mist rose and a thick fog rolled off the water.

Strangely, they all stood up. It was like they simultaneously knew it was time. It was hard to express their feelings. Each was happy of the returning but they didn't want to leave their friends. Over the years they had all become closer than brothers.

Alton stepped toward Warren, looking into his eyes. He pulled Warren into a hug. His voice was soft and a tear ran down his face. "Take care and be safe, until we meet again." He kissed Warren on the cheek. "I will miss you."

"And I will miss you, Alton. How do I thank you for all you have done? Go with God, until we see each other again." He kissed Alton.

Alton turned to Jim. "And you, little brother." He picked Jim up into a big hug. "Your craziness will be remembered like none before you. Take care and be safe." He kissed him on the cheek.

Jim hugged Alton and kissed him. "I will never forget, but I will return soon." He tried to have some sense of happiness, even though something in his mind said there was a chance something might prevent them from getting back to Pelaton again. "I will never forget any of you. God has been kind to let me know such fine and considerate friends."

Jim hugged and kissed Dereck and Hadon. "You have been wonderful and helpful friends. I owe you both a great deal."

Then he turned to Tog. He ran to him with a big hug and kiss. "I guess I will miss you the most, not that I don't love the rest, but you have been rather special to me. The things we've done over the years. And you were the one who carried me down from the mountain that first cold night we all met, then you brought me to Doctor Mennot's office so I could see. I love you all so much." He began to cry. "And you keep writing and playing the piano. You truly are a great composer and musician. You have a talent far beyond all others. It is a rare gift. Remember that."

"Don't cry, little friend." Tog patted him on the back. "We will see each other again. If not soon, we will meet in the great beyond. I will remember you always. And I promise. I will keep at the keyboard." He gave a big grin.

Warren hugged and kissed the others. Each expressed their hearts, and then it was time to depart.

Jim and Warren headed into the mist while they walked along the bank. Warren kept the communicator open.

After about fifteen minutes, Warren realized something was wrong. "Alton. This is Warren. Nothing yet. We'll keep going."

"Read you loud and clear." Alton's voice sounded through the communicator.

After a while, they became aware of pouring water. Even in the darkness, the old waterfall was visible. Warren's mind whirled. Had they missed the portal? Was it the wrong time? Was it cold enough? He looked around into the mist. Everything was as it should be. "Warren to Alton. We must have missed it. We're heading back that way again."

"Okay. We'll wait to hear from you again."

Jim followed closely. He had no desire to get lost in the fog. He could sense Warren's concern. He said nothing.

They walked back and forth several times along the bank. Nothing happened. It was cold enough as the ice crystals were in the fog. Warren racked his brain, trying to figure out what was wrong. Eventually, they returned to the little fire.

"I just don't understand." Warren shook his head. "Everything is as it should be. Our calculations show it should be cold on both sides of the portal. What could be wrong?"

"Here." Alton handed them each a cup of coffee. "While you were gone, Hadon went back to the craft and brought the coffee pot. At least it'll warm you a little while we do some quick thinking."

They sat for almost an hour, discussing the problem. They knew their calculations were correct, but there was a slight possibility of an error.

"Maybe tonight's not the night." Hadon tried to be optimistic. "We can stay until it is the right time. I'll check the computer again to make sure our numbers are right. Maybe there's a warm spell on the other side."

"We'll try again in a while." Warren sipped his coffee. His mind kept trying to figure out a possible catch.

The mist and fog were thick and cold. The air was filled with flickers of light, as the glowing campfire reflected off the tiny crystals, floating in the white-gray mass.

"All is as you described." Alton looked about in the mist.

"Come on, Jim. We'll try again." Warren took the last gulp of coffee and set the cup down.

"Well. We say goodbye again." Jim stood up.

They disappeared into the mist to the north. Alton listened on the communicator. After fifteen minutes, he pressed a button and spoke. "Alton to Warren. Anything yet?"

"Not a damn thing. Something is wrong." Warren's voice was relayed through the device.

"I'm going to double check the calculations again." Hadon headed for the craft.

By the time Hadon returned, Warren and Jim were on their way back, too. Hadon brought another pot of coffee for the group. "Well. All results from the computer are that there should be cold in both time zones. There is no rhyme or reason why you're not going through."

"Could there be something I forgot?" Warren stroked his beard with his right hand. "There can't be. I know everything has been taken into account."

"We'll just stay here a few days. It will give us time to explore the area and check out, first hand, the damage done. We'll be able to check the rate of recovery the area's taking." Dereck stood. "We'll stay in the craft. There are plenty of supplies for us to stay here over a week or more."

"Not a bad idea." Alton continued the enthusiasm. "It will give us some time to really look at things close up."

They all decided it was the thing to do. No further tries would be attempted that night. They returned to the craft.

For the next four days, they examined the area around Stone Mountain. At night, they made their attempts to get through the portal, with no results. All conditions were right for the move back through, but nothing was happening.

On the fifth day, Hadon sent a message back to Pelaton to check all points related to the area. He wanted all information, regardless of its significance, concerning the area. He wanted to know if there was something they had overlooked.

By late morning, the computer messages were coming through. The screens indicated the many discrepancies. All had been considered. But then, something displayed they hadn't considered. It was something the pilot mentioned when they first arrived in the area. The meteor strike completely changed the magnetic and electrical fields. The previously undistorted fields were now erratic and varying in energy intensity. The free field was now a hodgepodge of fluctuating energy waves. From the computer information, the entire area, for several hundred miles around, was affected.

Hadon perused the information. He worked at the console several hours, punching in numbers and questions. A huge list of numerical information appeared on the computer screen. Each time a new list appeared, Hadon checked each and every figure. These seemed to generate more and more input. Finally, he reviewed the last set of numbers. The answer was clear. He rose from his seat and walked into the cabin, where the others were eating a light meal.

A sad expression was on his face. "The worse has occurred." He paused and looked up. "It seems the meteor did more damage than we thought. I put several scenarios into the computer concerning the relationship of the electrical and magnetic fields to the portal. It seems they were significantly related. One could not exist without the other."

"Destruction of the free field in this time eliminated the portal?" Dereck gave a surprised gaze.

"Correct." Hadon's face looked down again. "And there's nothing we can do about it. Even though the meteor event was already ancient history in the future time period, it took it happening here in this time period to completely seal the door closed and destroy the free field here."

There was a long silence before Hadon spoke again. "I tried all the means of bypassing, even artificially inducing a localized reestablishment of the previous free field. But it was not satisfactory. Once the disturbance took place, the port closed and it cannot be reopened. It seems the door to the future is gone forever. For all of us."

"Thank you, Hadon." Alton patted him on the shoulder. "I know you did all you could." He looked at Warren and Jim's disappointed faces. "I don't know what to say."

"Thank you, Hadon." Warren stood and shook his hand. "Thanks for trying. But it's no one's fault. No one had any idea the meteor would destroy the portal."

"I guess that's the way it's meant to be." Jim tried to sound philosophically positive. "As Thomas Wolfe said, 'you can't go home again'."

Tog spoke softly. "I am sorry you can't return to your own time, but, but, to be honest, I'm glad you're not leaving. I would have missed you both. Now, you can come home and stay with us. Everyone will be glad you're not going. Everyone told me they hated to see you leave."

Warren took Jim's hand. "We tried. We did our best. I guess it just wasn't meant to be."

Jim looked at Warren. "I feel most sorry for you. You could have stayed when you were there. If it hadn't been for me, you could have stayed."

"That was six years ago, and I have no regrets. I couldn't have left you." Warren hugged him. "Maybe we'll find another way to get back. Who knows?" He turned to Alton. "Do you really think you'll be able to put up with us?"

Alton hugged them both. "I agree with Tog. To be honest, I'm glad you're not going, either. I would have missed you greatly."

All hugged the two, sorry they couldn't return to their own time, but joyous they were not leaving them.

Alton spoke. "Shall we go home?"

Warren and Jim looked at one another and they smiled. "Let's go home."

Alton went forward, directing the pilot to head back to the submarine.

The airlift rose to two thousand feet and slowly started east. The late afternoon sun shown on the eastern slope of the monolith of Stone Mountain. Warren and Jim stood, peering through the large ports on the south side of the craft. The mountain slowly passed to the west and faded from sight. Warren's right arm was over Jim's shoulder. Jim's left arm was around Warren's waist. They both knew in their hearts they would never return to their own time. The rest of their lives would be spent with their new friends, on the island, in the middle of the Atlantic.

CHAPTER XLVII

The huge screen is still the focus of attention. Everyone is watching and they see Warren and Jim return to their daily lives in the capital city of Pelaton. The time sequences skip rapidly forward, showing their many accomplishments. Warren and Jim continually grow older, their dark hair turning grayer, and the lines of time leaving their marks on their faces.

Warren came to realize, virtually immediately, that he could not attach himself and form a major relationship with someone who was of Pelaton. They didn't age at the same rate as well as his tie to his wife, Linda. In his mind, he was still married to her. So his companion for the rest of his life would be his friend, Jim. He didn't mind. He was comfortable with Jim and Jim knew him probably better than anyone alive. It was a relationship that worked. "And if it ain't broke…don't fix it!" He would always say with a joking tone in his voice.

Finally, standing alone at the entrance to the Great Hall is Jim. It is now evident; he is the old man telling the story. The projection focuses in and draws closer and closer. "'All right, Mr. DeMille, I'm ready for my close up.'" As it draws closer and closer, his eyes get bigger and bigger as does his grin, and his face takes on a crazed insane look. Finally, the screen is filled with his happy, hugely grinning face then slowly fades as the light in the room increases in intensity.

Laughter erupts in the room and heads shake at the last view of the old man's face. The final strokes are being applied to the whole picture. All is beginning to make sense.

The holograph quickly appears, standing in the center of the raised platform. He is wearing the most spectacular robe of all. Reflections off the brilliant stones send out sparks of rainbow colors. He is smiling but not quite the huge grin that just faded on the screen. He starts to chuckle. "Okay. Okay. I know you are laughing. I couldn't help it. I just had to do it. And my apologies to Gloria Swanson and Cecil B. DeMille. But as Paul Harvey use to say: 'and now you know…the rest of the story'." He walks over and makes himself comfortable in the chair. Soon, he looks up and across the group. "You see. I have to first explain all this." He stretches his arms in an arc, displaying the room. "Well? What do you think? *C'est magnifique! Tres* gaudy?" He laughs. "But what did you expect?" His eyes sparkle in his joy. "You have to admit. It sure as hell beats some dinky, fucking little hole in the ground. This is so incredible, it's beyond belief. Isn't it? Now, come on. Admit it. You ARE impressed!" He appears to be full of himself. "We knew we'd have to do something absolutely and outrageously fantastic and extraordinary so you'd believe the whole thing. And you know? It wasn't difficult at all to complete. Of course, getting some of those pieces of marble through the halls was real interesting. But I think it was worth it. I love it." He continues to look around, smiling the whole time, super pleased with the way the project turned out. "I just hope it still looks like it does now. You see. We have no idea when you are going to find this, if ever. But we know it will be sometime after Warren and I disappear. And that's a long time from now. We estimate some sixteen thousand years." He pauses momentarily. "This whole thing started out as a tribute from the people of Pelaton, or Atlantis, as you will call it, to Warren and me. But we all agreed it would also be a wonderful gift for mankind. Alton, Dereck, Hadon and Tog want the greatness of their lovely civilization to survive. We could think of no better way than to preserve it all here with us, hoping someday, someone would discover it."

He looks to the right, then to the left. "Through the north and south doors lie the wonders of Pelaton. Those vaults contain the history and accomplishments of this great and wonderful people.

There, you will find many things. They are for the benefit of mankind. With them will come an end to hunger, suffering and pain."

He begins to laugh. "We decided not to include the process to make gold and precious stones. With the information provided in the archives and a little ingenuity, you'll be able to accomplish doing that soon enough. To give it to you too easily, might cause the collapse of the world monetary standards. The time it takes for you to figure it out will hopefully give you enough time for reevaluation of everything. But maybe you have already discovered how to do these things. In that case, it's of no consequence."

A serious expression comes to his face. "We hope you will learn the lessons Pelaton has to offer, instead of continuing in your stupid ignorance, and petty jealousies. With these gifts, you can do much good, or, you can use them to destroy the entire world. The choice is yours. For once, why don't you use those damn thick skulls for something other than fucking hat racks? Will it be prosperity, or will you perish? You will determine the ending. You will write the script to the rest of the story."

He sits silent, as if contemplating the decision that might be made. Finally, he begins again. "I also said this place is for us, Warren and me. And so it is." He points to the door on his right. It is the entrance to the southern vault. "In there, on the south wall, you will find the stairway down. It leads to a corridor under the floor. At the end, you will come to a small room, just beneath the onyx, out there." He points to the eight by six square foot rectangle of black, in the center of the room. "Yes. Out there. Under my outrageous chandelier." He looks up at the enormous fixture. "Did it light? I hope so. I hope it hasn't fallen, after all this time." He laughs. "But I doubt it. Hadon says it will be there for the rest of eternity, he and I designed the support so well." He looks remorsefully out toward the rectangle, and is silent for some time, staring at the spot. "We're there. Warren and me. We're down there in the room, waiting. We have finally come home."

Shortly, a smile comes back to his face and a glint to his eyes. "And, by the way, there's a little something for a man named Mike Johnson, if he's still around. And he better get it, too." He is dogmatic. "Now, Mr. Johnson was with the police department. So tell him this gift is from two friends in thanking him for his generosity and kindness. And because he believed enough to help. Without it, it's possible and most probable, that none of this would have happened. If he has joined us in the great beyond, our gift is to go to his heirs."

"I want to thank you all for being so patient and putting up with the shenanigans. Tell all we love them and miss them." He stands and walks to the edge of the top tier. He holds out his arms and his face gleams. "We wish you joy. We wish you happiness. We wish you peace. But most of all, we wish you friendship and love. With these two things, great things are possible." He lowers his arms, returning to his seat. "Now, I must go. My time is over. *Adieux, mais amies*." His face beams with gladness and a broad grin. The holograph slowly fades away.

The room is silent for some time. Everyone is dumbstruck.

Suddenly, the light in the room begins to diminish, triggering everyone back to reality. The lighting crew turns on their systems.

I turn to Tim. "Now! That's incredible! I have to admit. I wanted to get up and run like hell when I saw that tidal wave coming. And I'm sure someone will be working quickly to organize an expedition to search for the ruins of Atlantis…Pelaton."

Tim laughs. "I know. So did I. I almost shit. I think everybody was affected the way they all screamed out. It was hard to remember we were watching a projection. And yeah. I'll probably be getting a call very soon about a trip to the ocean floor."

It is the consensus of all to wait in the exploration of the vaults until the next day. Everyone is exhausted. We will return at ten o'clock in the morning.

"Let me take you back to the hotel, Tim." I suggest, while we pack up the coolers and other items we brought that day from the hotel.

"I appreciate it."

Nothing much is said until we get outside and light our cigarettes. Our minds are still reeling with what we have seen.

We are headed for the car when Tim finally speaks. "I still cannot fathom this whole thing. It's just too fantastic. If I hadn't seen it myself, I'd never believe it."

"We have to find Mike Johnson, too." I start the car.

When we get to Tim's hotel room, Tim calls the police department to inquire about Mike. "You're not going to believe this." He looks at me and laughs. "Just our luck. He's on vacation for two weeks. He is unreachable."

I laugh. "Yep! Just our luck. But he had his vacation planned at this time. Remember when he told Warren, before Warren left? But we'll catch him when he gets back. Listen. I'll see you tomorrow. I've got to get some sleep."

"I agree. See you tomorrow."

"I'll be by to pick you up around nine. Sound okay?"

"Sounds good to me. Thanks, Phillip."

Returning to my apartment, I quickly get ready for bed. Exhaustion has taken its toll. The instant my head hits the pillow, I'm asleep.

I swear my eyes just shut and the alarm clock is going off. There is definitely a conspiracy to keep me from getting any sleep. I know there is. "Where the hell does the time go? Okay, God! I just got to sleep." While rubbing my eyes, an added annoyance enters the scene. It's the phone ringing.

"Hello? Oh. Hi Tim. Sure. Great."

I hang up the phone. "Now that's nice. He's got a rental car and is coming to pick me up. I now know I really like this guy."

Tim and I walk into the Great Room just before ten. We sip our cups of coffee from the urns set up by the park service. Looking in the direction of the door to the southern vault, we see several members of the party getting everything ready to enter the chamber.

"It should be interesting to see what's in there." Tim pokes me with his elbow.

"No telling. But I'm sure it will affect the rest of our lives." I chuckle.

"I think you've got that right. It's kind of scary to know there are things in there that in the right hands will destroy the earth."

"The 'right' hands?"

"Bad choice of words." Tim laughs. "But Jim's right. Every time something comes along that could be used for good, it is twisted into some horrible war weapon. When will we ever learn?"

"Maybe now we will have to. As he said. If we don't, we'll annihilate ourselves."

Everyone seems to be there. We all agree we can proceed. One of the technicians turns the handle on the door. Instantly, the Great Room begins to light. The vault doors slowly swing open and the vault lights. None of the set up lights are needed.

Entering the chamber, we see there are a multitude of shelves, containing numerous golden discs. They look like compact discs. With the vast number, it is obvious a tremendous amount of information is stored here. Each shelf section is labeled. The words are written in English, on golden plaques.

Across from the shelves are display cases and pedestals containing a collection of items that must have belonged to Warren and Jim. On the walls are photographs in simple sixteen by twenty-four inch frames.

Tim examines them closer. "They're photos, but there's something about them that's different. I'm sure it has to do with the materials used. Paper would never have lasted this long. Not unless it's been treated or sealed in some way. We'll know soon enough. Of that, you can be sure." He chuckles at the one of Warren pissing from the raft into the river.

I, too, peruse the pictures. Some of them are rather humorous. The one of Warren in his skins and antler hat, holding his bow and machete, made me laugh out loud. "Tim. Come see this one."

Tim laughs. "What a character. And to think, he'll probably be on the cover of every magazine in the world, and in every news report, looking like that. He's whirling in his grave, I'm sure."

The vault is enormous with many side rooms containing many items of interest. The same would be discovered with the northern vault. But these would be dealt with at a later date. The object of this visit is to get to the room beneath the onyx slab.

Everyone congregates at the south end of the chamber and the entry to the lower room. A set of stairs gradually spirals down and to the right. At the bottom, there is a long curving corridor. The lighted section of the hall stops at a double gate. Darkness is beyond.

The gate is like one of wrought iron, elaborate in its design of swirling vines and leaves. The material is not iron, but gold. When the latch is lifted, the gates swing into the darkness. Small recessed light ports in the ceiling of the hall ahead begin to illuminate. The hall continues in a wide arc. Eventually, it is going in an easterly direction.

Tim comments on the fact. "I think we're headed east. And we're considerably lower than the floor level of the Great Room."

Fifty feet in front of us, the hall opens into a larger room, sixteen by twenty feet. The ceiling is fourteen feet from the floor. There is nothing special about the room. All the surfaces are smooth, cut from the raw granite. There is no ornamentation except around another set of gates on the east side of the room.

The framework of the portal is in the High Gothic style, made of many colored marbles. The gates are like golden lace; the tracery work is so intricate.

Momentarily, the gloom beyond the gates begins to fill with light. The soft tones of a pipe organ drift from nowhere, playing a soft, haunting, melancholy melody.

"I don't recognize the piece." I spoke quietly as my mind went through its library of music. "Have to admit. I like it. It's really pretty. But I guess I wouldn't recognize it. It was written some sixteen thousand years ago. Oh duh!"

"Yeah. But it does have a similarity to some Debussy pieces I have heard. And. That phrase sounds a little like Rachmininoff." Tim whispered. "Wonder what it is and who wrote it?"

Tim puts on a pair of latex gloves he had stashed in his pocket, then carefully pulls open the gates. We walk through. We step down into a circular room, made completely of white marble. It is thirty feet in diameter and peaks to a height of sixty feet. It is decorated in the High Gothic style.

"Reminds me of the Edward the Seventh Chapel at Westminster Abbey." I whisper to Tim.

The walls are lined with many tall narrow stained glass panels, illuminated from behind. The light reflects off the entire white marble interior, bathing the room with color.

The graceful arches stretch to the center of the ceiling. The tracery of white is extremely delicate and intricate, looking like translucent lace.

In the center of the room is a three foot high rectangular platform of white marble. It is made of several blocks and the sides are covered with intricate carvings, inlaid marbles, faceted stones and gold ornaments. The eight foot length is situated east and west. The six foot width is north and south. On the eight foot sides are carved the words 'THE LOVE OF A FRIEND ENDURES THROUGH ALL TIME AND TRANSCENDS DEATH'.

On top of the platform is a clear case, with slightly sloping sides. Lying within the case are the impeccably preserved bodies of Warren and Jim. They are dressed in fine robes. Golden bands encircle their heads, and golden sandals adorn their feet. Jim lies to the south of Warren. His right hand is on his chest. His gold class ring showing prominently on his ring finger. It had not been on his hand since he packed it away many years earlier at the Chattahoochee. Warren's left hand is on his chest. His golden wedding band gleams in the light. His right hand is at his side, clasping Jim's left hand. Their eyes are closed and there is a slight smile on their faces.

"They look like they're asleep." I hear someone quietly say. "They look so peaceful." Low hushed conversations begin discussing a variety of subjects.

I am amazed. There is a temptation to clap my hands together to see if it would awaken them. "Tim?" I whisper. "How can this possibly be? You're the expert. They are too well preserved. Is this possible?"

"If they could do all this with little effort, who knows what else they were capable of, including the preservation of their bodies."

"Jim looks exactly as he did in the holograph. Maybe he died not long after telling the tale."

"Warren must have died before him. That's why he was alone at the end." Tim walks over to the white marble altar, set in an apse in the east wall. Raised letters of gold adorn the front. They are in Roman Block style and read: 'WE ARE IMMORTAL AS LONG AS WE LIVE IN THE HEARTS AND MINDS OF OTHERS, ESPECIALLY THE HEARTS AND MINDS OF THOSE WHO LOVE US'.

There are many golden candlestick holders, set with candles like those in the enormous chandelier in the Great Room, only smaller. They glow with the same soft warm light. Over the altar is an elaborate crucifix made of gold and faceted stones. The half life size form of Christ is cast in white gold. Deep red cabochon stones are set to represent the cuts and blood.

"Phillip. Come see this." Tim gestures with his left hand, his eyes fixed on a book, on a golden bookrack, in the center of the altar. He puts on another pair of latex gloves. He opens the cover to the first page. "The pages have been laminated in some clear substance, like the photos up stairs."

I walk over and look down.

Tim starts reading out loud from the book. "'Until we meet again in the house of the Great Seer of All. I miss you both very much. Your dear and loving friend, Alton.' Look at that signature and seal. And look at the decoration around the edge of the page." Tim carefully turns a page. "Look at the calligraphic work here. Each page is a work of art. 'A part of my heart is lost with your passing. Until we meet again in the great beyond. I hope my music will be with you through your eternal sleep. Your loving friend, Tog.'" Tim looks up. "So. The piece was written by Tog. Damn. Oh Duh! Of course. It makes sense. I have to say, he was quite accomplished to write something so beautiful and memorable." He looks back down and turns another page and continues to read aloud. "'Our lives are diminished with your passing. I greatly miss you both. Love and affection, your friend, Hadon.'" He turns another. "'As you stand before the Great Seer of All, please ask Him to remember us who mourn and weep for you both. Your friend who loves you, Dereck.'" Tim pauses. "There are many pages here from others." He carefully flips through, finally reaching the last page. "Look here! It's from Jim to Warren." He reads again. "'Although you go before me, my love for you will never die. You were my friend in life. You are my friend for all eternity. I love you, my friend. Forever. Jim.'"

Tim looks at me. "Can you believe all this? The whole place seems to radiate peace, love and friendship. It's incredible." He turns, looking at the casket. "Have you ever in your life? It's like the Taj Mahal. Just more extravagant." He looks around the room. "It's uncanny. I've never been in a tomb where there was such a feeling of love and joy. I don't feel sad. I feel good. And I can't put my finger on the reason why. And look at the expressions on their faces. It's like they know we sense it all."

It's true. The presence of peace, serenity and love seems to fill the room. My arms have goose bumps. I remember being in Lenin's Tomb in Moscow. Schumann's *Traumerei* echoes there. I remember the solemn feeling I experienced, but it was nothing like this. The ornate room looks to be out of some religious fantasy dream. The delicate stonework, the beautiful colors from the stained glass, the quiet music, the lighted crucifix and altar, and the sleeping figures on the white marble make me feel I've stepped into some small religious shrine.

But finally, the analytical reporter in me comes back to take hold of reality. "Maybe the figures are made of wax or plastic." I whisper to Tim and walk closer to the casket. "I can't believe they are the actual remains. They're too fresh, too uncorrupted. They have to be made of something else." I get as close as I can to the cover so I can see. Every pore and hair of the figures is perfectly incorporated into the surface of the skin. They are too real. It is a work of art to be able to achieve such an illusion. These figures would make Madame Tussaud envious.

"There's one way we can find out." Tim whispers. "When we remove the cover and have a medical examiner check it out."

"You can't do that." The thought annoys me. "It's ghoulish."

Tim smiles. "No. This is like any ancient tomb we discover, like in Egypt. No one ever thinks it's ghoulish to go into those tombs. And this tomb is much older than recorded history. Anyway, I thought you said they couldn't be real."

"Yeah. I know I did. But what if they are? No mummy has ever looked like that." Deep inside I felt like some grave robber. To disturb them would be like doing something sacrilegious.

"Don't worry." Tim assured. "After they're examined, they'll be put back here and left in peace. But we have to find out about all this. And they are a part of it." He pats me on the back.

My thoughts turn to the future and the droves of tourists invading this quiet place. I imagine the hall and room filled with laughing, gawking people, throwing down candy wrappers and popping flash cameras, some trying to chip off something as a souvenir, and the oil from all those grimy hands staining the pristine marble. I look at the two figures lying in their eternal sleep. I shake my head in disgust.

"What's the matter?" Tim sees my expression.

"I was thinking about all those damn tourists coming in here and fucking up the place. It makes me sick."

"Don't worry. We will see that it doesn't happen. They will be alright. Trust me. Not just anyone will set foot in here. It's too private. Too personal."

For some reason, I knew what he said would be the case. And so it was. In the years to come, whenever I returned to Stone Mountain and wanted to visit, I would be one of the very few allowed into the room. The room would remain just as we found it. It's beauty never diminishing.

In the next days, Tim and I would pal around. During some of the free times we had, while the cataloguing of items in the vaults was taking place, I would show him the many sites of Atlanta. One evening when we were eating dinner, I apologized if I had, in the beginning, expected him to be standoffish and not so friendly. But I had liked him from the moment we talked together that first day in the entry halls of the discovery.

Tim only laughed. It hadn't even crossed his mind and he never noticed.

Little did either one of us realize, but this would be the beginning of a life long friendship. This episode was winding down, but the many new adventures that were install for us, would lead us down many a strange and interesting road.

The book we would co-author on this event would be filled with wonderful and interesting pictures, along with descriptive accounts to tell the whole story. It would be in high demand for many years to come. But it would be only the first book we would do. Other books would follow, telling in detail, with words and pictures, the wonderful future adventures we would explore together. Of course, the next assignment for us would be an expedition to, yes, you guessed it, the search for the ruins of Pelaton. Unfortunately, we would never discover what happened to the people of Pelaton and why they disappeared. Had they perished in some unknown catastrophe or had they found a way to leave for another world? These would remain questions for the ages. Never would there be any evidence of their existence on the ocean floor.

As for Tim and me, within the year, we would become like brothers, but more than brothers. Our friendship would continue to grow and we would spend the rest of our lives working hand in hand, becoming the best team ever of archaeologist and reporter. We would be like Mutt and Jeff. One would rarely be seen without the other.

One other interesting note. Tim and I, both, within the next year, helped each other in quitting. Quitting? Yes. Cigarettes. We quit smoking for good. Neither of us ever picked up another cigarette again.

At the end of my own life, I would look back at this event and meeting Tim. Of all the discoveries we would ever be involved in, none would be like this one. This one was one that would change the world. But for me, it was a new beginning. It was truly the dawning of a new day for me. When I would look back over it all, I would come to see that I had done some of the most incredible things ever. But most of all, I had found and shared it with a most remarkable and sterling individual. I would be one of the lucky ones. I would die a truly, totally happy man.

It soon becomes evident the compact disc library contains an incredible wealth of information. One scientist, in perusing the disc regarding the construction of the Great Room, halls, and other chambers, found the means to keep the rooms lighted without activating the holographic figure.

Several discs were found as a tribute from Tog. It was a whole set of compositions he had composed over the years. Not only were the music scores there, but also the pieces played by Tog. The entire story of how Jim taught him the piano and music composition and how this allowed him to become one of Pelaton's greatest musicians and keyboard artists. It was also discovered that the music compositions to enter the mountain were also written by Tog. In time, Tog's compositions were being learned by pianists and played in revered concert halls all over the world. Many would have to roll some of the chords, as reaching an eleventh was not capable for even the best. It was interesting, too, that several CDs were released of Tog's music, with Tog playing them, copied from the discs. His CDs went platinum virtually immediately. Everyone wanted one and to hear music written and played so many millennia in the past.

Removal of the casket lid allows the examination of the bodies. We are informed, in a few days they are real and not wax or plastic. Fingerprints are taken and checked with the records. It is hard to realize they are the two men who disappeared from the area, a year ago. Now, they are dead, looking significantly older than when they left and they are scientifically dated to be around sixteen thousand years old. This reinforced the dating of the rope that hung on the first door of the tunnel. It boggles everyone's mind.

"I have to admit. This has to be the greatest discovery of the time or the greatest hoax." Tim laughs when I tell him my thoughts. He had been thinking the same thing.

On a small table, located in the southern vault, is found a small chest. Engraved in the gold of the curved lid are the words 'FOR MIKE JOHNSON OR HIS HEIRS'.

Finally it's time for Mike to return from his vacation. Tim and I have convinced the airline to let us know the flight he is to arrive back in Atlanta. We prepare for it well in advance so we know how to handle his expected questions.

We get to the airport a little early, waiting for Mike's plane to land.

"You know it might be real difficult to get him to go." Tim comments.

"Not when we make reference to Warren Glass. That should peak his curiosity. I think he'll want to know all about it immediately."

And that is exactly what happens. Mike's plane arrives and he is escorted from the plane by local authorities and brought to us. He is confused and does not understand, but wants to get home, tired from his trip. But the mention of Warren Glass turns his interest completely around. We put his baggage into the trunk of the car and head to Stone Mountain. Tim explains it will all make sense when they get there.

Mike continues to question the reason for going out to Stone Mountain. But when we arrive and start through the halls and stairways, he gets really confused. "I never knew this stuff was here." He is truly amazed when we walk into the enormous columned Great Room. His eyes express his disbelief. Trying to give him time to adjust to the impact of the surroundings, we slowly lead him into the southern vault. His first reaction is to the items in the display cases, especially the items he gave Warren. Mike gives us a strange look. Then he sees the pictures on the wall. Recognizing Warren in a few of them, he begins to chuckle. Then he sees the photo of Warren in his antlers and fur and laughs out loud. "But what does all this have to do with me? I still don't understand."

"You know something about the photos?" I look into his eyes.

"I recognize one of the men." He points to the photo of Warren, standing in his regalia. "It's Warren Glass." He glances around the room. "I don't know what I have to do with all this."

"Are you sure?"

"You're asking a police detective if he's sure?" He looks back at the photos. "But how did these pictures get here? And what is this place?" He looks at another photo. "This must be Jim. They are two crazy guys. I sure hope they make it."

"What?" Tim is curious about Mike's statement.

"Nothing. It's a long story. A weird story. You wouldn't believe me if I told you."

"Yeah. We know. And yes we would." I agree. "And we owe all of this to you."

"What?" Mike is shocked. "What the hell do you mean?"

"If you hadn't believed in Warren Glass and his story, none of this would be here." Tim states. "Haven't you heard any news for the last two weeks?"

"When I go on vacation, there are no phones, TV, radios. I make it a point. No one knows where I am and I don't want to know what is going on out here. I like it that way."

"When was the last time you saw Warren Glass?" I interrupted.

"It was last spring." He looks at Phillip with a questioning expression.

"We wanted to make sure of that. It seems you were the last one to see him alive." I knew the statement would jar him.

Mike's expression grew sad and he shook his head. "Warren's dead? But I thought."

We said nothing.

"I was so hoping he would have made it back. But none of this is making any sense. I am totally confused and you guys know something I don't. What the fuck's going on?"

"There's something over here that is for you." Tim guides Mike to the chest.

"That's my name." Mike lifts the lid with his name on it. It is filled with gold pieces and many large faceted stones. "These look real."

"They are." Tim agrees.

"There's a fortune here." Mike picks through the box.

"There's something else. Under the box." I point.

Mike moves the box to see a note in a clear laminate. He reads aloud. "'To Mike Johnson: Warren and I were so grateful for your generosity and kindness, we wanted to pay you back. We have no idea if you or your heirs will reap these rewards, but we had to remember you and your help. Without it, none of this would have been possible. Warren was adamant about this, and that you get this chest. Thank you again. May peace and love be with you. Your friends, Warren and Jim. P.S.: Did you ever stop smoking?'" Mike looks up and laughs. He pauses a moment with mixed emotions. "He said he'd pay me back. But I really don't understand." His face looks puzzled and he quickly glances around. "How is it that I had something to do with all this? And what's the connection to Warren Glass?"

"It's a long story." Tim could only chuckle. "You'll know soon enough and eventually will see the entire account, holograph, tidal wave and all. But first, we want you to see. Then you will begin to understand."

We lead Mike down the stairs and through the corridors to the lower chamber. On the way, Tim tries to give a quick synopsis of what we knew. Mike is surprised when the part about Atlantis comes up. Tim also explains about the closing of the portal and how Warren and Jim could never return to this time. Finally, we reach the entrance to the Gothic room. No one else is present. The soft organ music is playing.

Mike is amazed when he walks in and tries to absorb the visual of the whole thing. His expression changes from amazement to puzzlement, when he looks at the two figures under the clear cover. He turns to us. "What's going on and what is this?" He points to the figures.

"Maybe you can help us with that?" Tim gestures for him to look closely at the figures. "Science has told us one thing, but we'd like to have it confirmed by someone who might know."

Mike looks intently down into the case. At first, his face is filled with question. Slowly, his mind begins to put it all together. He closely examines the smiling face of the figure lying on the north side of the case. A grin comes to his face. The long pause is broken by his whisper. "It's him. It's Warren. He's older, but it's him." His mind recalls the short chance encounter, the previous spring. His heart remembers the feelings he felt for this man and the terrible dilemma in which he was caught.

His eyes move down to the two joined hands, then back to scrutinize the two faces again. "I see you made it back to your buddy." His voice is soft. "I'm glad for you. I could tell you truly cared for him. But I was really looking forward to seeing you come through the port. Guess it just wasn't to be." He pauses a moment before speaking a little louder. "You know. He truly cared. He loved his friend."

Tim and I remain silent. We don't want to influence anything Mike has to say or do. We want it to unfold naturally.

Shortly, Mike turns toward Tim and me. A big grin fills his face.

It is evident he is holding back his emotions. "You know. When this whole story is known, people will find it to be one of the most incredible stories of courage, endurance, and companionship. It is a story of a really true friendship, a love of one human being for another. These guys went to the ends for each other. I know. I listened. What can I say? These guys were friends…forever."

Tim and I look at one another and smile then turn back looking at Mike. We both have the exact thought and in unison, we speak. "Yeah. We know."

THE END

www.ingramcontent.com/pod-product-compliance
Lightning Source LLC
Chambersburg PA
CBHW071958190726
48293CB00001B/84